Other books by Naomi Neale:

I WENT TO VASSAR FOR THIS?
CHRISTMAS CARDS FROM THE EDGE (Anthology)
CALENDAR GIRL
SHOP 'TIL YULE DROP (Anthology)

THE MILE-HIGH HAIR CLUB

NAOMI NEALE

Making it

MAKING IT®

November 2006

Published by

Dorchester Publishing Co., Inc.
200 Madison Avenue
New York, NY 10016

ISBN 0-505-52663-8

The name "Making It" and its logo are trademarks of Dorchester Publishing Co., Inc.

Printed in the United States of America.

Visit us on the web at www.dorchesterpub.com.

ACKNOWLEDGMENTS

I am so deeply indebted to my friend Patty Woodwell for all the overtime she puts into keeping me on the straight and narrow that, if I had any spare time, I would use it to do all her housework and cooking for the rest of her life. I also owe additional thanks to Mark Peikert for the amusing anecdote he told me even after being warned I might snitch one for this story.

Most of all, I'd like to thank my late mother, Penelope, in whose memory this novel is dedicated: a woman who was always strong, always determined, and who always knew when best to keep—and to reveal—her secrets.

THE MILE-HIGH HAIR CLUB

PART ONE
SOUTH TO SOUTH

Chapter One

If the CIA was ever on the lookout for an inexpensive weapon that could immobilize an army of single men, Bailey Rhodes could suggest it: the amplified sound of a empty dresser drawer being opened. When she pulled at the top knobs of the bedroom chest where she stored her socks and underwear, her boyfriend immediately froze. "What is that?" Not even his lips moved.

"It's a drawer." Bailey had expected him to be excited. Obviously, he wasn't. Until a moment ago, when he'd suddenly gone slack in the face, she'd thought she'd known every expression in Steve's repertoire. Finally, he riffled his fingers through his fringe of thin, fair hair. Then he blinked. In his pair of briefs that could have used a good bleaching, he looked like a lost little boy. "The top drawer," she said, hiding her disappointment behind pretended unconcern.

They had been preparing for bed, but for the moment, that had been forgotten. "I see." Steve's hand now covered his mouth, fingertips drumming his cheek. What were they beating? An SOS signal in Morse code? "A drawer?"

This incident might make a humorous anecdote one

day, when she and Steve eventually solidified their relationship. She could picture the monologue now: *How I Got Steve to Move In*, or hopefully, much farther down the road, *The Day I Offered Your Father a Drawer*. None of it was funny now. Every passing second was nine kinds of heinous.

Eight years ago, Bailey Rhodes had ridden through the Lincoln Tunnel in a cab loaded with little more than a suitcase of clothes, a backpack full of play collections, and a copier paper box of kitchen pots and pans, with her mother's warning still ringing in her ears: "Bailey Rhodes, there are three kinds of people in that city: gold diggers, thieves, and charlatans. Don't you dare come back a single one of them!"

Truth to tell, Bailey really made a lousy gold digger. When it came to choosing between a well-heeled moneymaker or a moneyless heel, she'd picked the pauper every time. On those rare late nights when a date had offered a twenty for her cab home, she should have tucked the bill into her purse and taken the subway. But no, out of sheer laziness, Bailey had usually ended the evening by crawling from the mandated cab and giving its driver too large a tip. She'd nearly made a good start of gold digging as a profession with Steve, though. On their second meeting, he'd presented her with a copy of *The Complete Saki*, its table of contents marked with neat ticks to indicate which stories Bailey should read first. She'd promptly erased the penciled notations and returned it to the NYU student bookstore for lunch money—and then felt so guilty that she'd bought another copy, losing more money than she'd made.

That particular episode would not make it into any future anecdotal monologues.

And after she'd given up acting and stumbled into a real job, she didn't need to gold dig. She'd transformed herself into someone she hoped guys might consider something of a catch, but Steve didn't seem to be catching so much as a clue. "An empty drawer," Bailey suggested, hoping the adjective might spark recognition.

Through his fingers, Steve repeated, "Ah. An *empty* drawer."

He wasn't going to make her explain. Surely Steve was smarter than that. His big brain was his livelihood. She waited, certain that at any minute he would break out into a smile. Or thank her. Or grunt in a way that indicated sentient thought, or at least the possibility that someone had left the pilot light burning inside. For God's sake, he was an economist! With Ivy League degrees! Steve couldn't be so dense as not to recognize the importance of this moment. He'd come through in a minute and stop that incessant finger-drumming. Right?

Oh hell. He really was going to make her explain. "For your stuff! You're here all the time. I thought you might like a little place of your own where you could leave a few . . . you know. Vitals." Had she started speaking Esperanto? His determination not to betray the slightest response made her all the more anxious to fill her bedroom with noise. "Underwear? T-shirts? Those sheer black socks you like?"

"I know what vitals are," he replied quite reasonably. "It's simply that I thought we were going to sleep. I never really expected this . . . drawer. In your . . ."

He let the sentence dangle. Steve Braithwaite never let his sentences dangle. Bailey had seen him wince when she'd let out an *um*. He actually flinched whenever someone connected together phrases with *and* or *like*. She couldn't take the suspense. "Dresser?"

At the same time, he finished with, ". . . chiffarobe."

"Chiffarobe!" She blinked, taken aback. Who besides her grandmother had ever used that word?

Steve had chosen his latest style of glasses—thick-framed, black, and rectangular—only after similar ones had appeared in *Esquire* and *Cargo* print ads for enough months that he had felt safe investing in them. He peered at her through them now, his eyes darting frantically, like tiny tadpoles swimming in a pool of terror.

"Isn't that what you call them down there where you grew up?"

"Down there, as in Virginia, you big Yankee?" She flopped down on the bed, trying to laugh. Anything to break the awkward face-off. Bailey's smart little cubbyhole of an apartment was so small that the pulled-out empty dresser drawer rested on the foot of her mattress, atop a worn old quilt that had belonged to her great-grandmother. Streamlined prefab met good old Dixie culture. Wasn't that the story of her life? "When in the world have I ever said *chiffarobe?*"

"I don't know. You know how it's been this month, when you've come back from the old Southern homestead. For a couple of days, it's Aint Bits this and Aint Bubble that and *hi y'all* and *erynge.* . . ."

"Erynge?"

Steve squinted, forecasting an attempt at humor. "As in, should I wear that erynge sweatshirt? Could I have some erynge juice with my scrambled eggs?"

"Rude! I *never* talk like that!" she howled, knowing the words were a bluff. Everyone said the same thing after one of her trips home, from her friends to random cab drivers to all the talent she signed for the network—including the heavily accented Bulgarian bodybuilder-turned-karate-film star she'd scooped from the Discovery Channel to host a miniseries on the vanishing rain forest. When you have someone inform you in Schwarzeneggerian tones, *You zound vunny!*, you knew it had to be true. Bailey swatted him with one of the pillows, kicking shut the drawer with the tip of her toe. "Now I'm not sure I *want* you moving in."

"Is that what we're talking about here?" He sat down on the bed beside where she lay, leaning on an elbow as he talked. "Me moving in? Because you know there's no room in this place for all my journals and papers, and I'm tied down to a lease that . . ."

"No, Steve." Bailey hadn't intended for this conversation to tread over such weary, familiar ground. "God-damn it." Frustration made her scalp itch. She angrily raked her nails over her head, wishing the stress away. "It's just a *drawer*. It's a cheap, stupid drawer that I put together myself when I bought this cheap, stupid, Swedish. . . ."

"Chiffarobe," Steve supplied. He was obviously try-ing to smooth things over with weak humor. "You're like that Mayella woman, luring Tom Robinson into her shanty, aren't you? Asking him to move a chiffarobe so you can take advantage of him when he's not looking?"

"Is your one cultural reference to the American South *To Kill a Mockingbird*?"

"No!" he protested, yawning widely. She stopped scratching at her scalp and let him smooth down her hair. It still itched, but she appreciated the gesture. "I watched *The Dukes of Hazzard* repeats growing up, too," he joked.

It was difficult to imagine little ten-year-old Steve watching anything other than *The McNeil-Lehrer Report*. Yet if true, the statement deserved a swat. "Don't be get-ting any fantasies of me dressing up in Daisy Dukes," she warned him. His response was unintelligible, buried as it was deep in a mouthful of her hair, this month the color of latte.

Cuddling against each other without talking was more comfortable than arguing. His hand stopped moving; his breathing grew deeper. Bailey admired the way he could drift to sleep moments after he lay down, even if it was the ultimate in avoidance techniques. Though they'd officially dated for ten months, she and Steve had known each other for so many years that they were already like an old, married couple, settled in their ways and content with their arrangements. They didn't have overblown romantic expectations of their relation-ship. After all, they were both adults, not kids.

At least, Bailey thought to herself while Steve nuzzled

in close, his arm and leg wrapping around her like a kitten clinging to the mother cat, that's what she'd been
telling herself for months. How much of it did she really
believe? They weren't old. They definitely weren't married. And these moments of repose were as romantic as it
got. Lately, and especially now, she felt as if anything
they had resembling a relationship was rapidly slipping
away, like potter's clay that had become too wet for the
wheel. With every passing moment it squeezed out between her fingers and flew away, leaving less and less to
sculpt. But no, Steve was the same he had always been.
Maybe it was the argument that made her gloomy.

Or maybe it was Saturday's trip to Virginia, and the
prospect of another week without Steve. While he slumbered, his glasses a little askew and his mouth open
while he breathed in and out, Bailey disengaged herself
from his light grasp. How often had they seen each
other in the last month? Four evenings? Five? Though
they lived less than a half-mile apart, it sometimes felt
as if they were conducting a long-distance relationship.
Under the circumstances, feeling distant and, she supposed, maybe a little overanxious to solidify things was
perfectly natural. She'd be the first to admit she wanted
to feel essential.

Steve's feet rested on her quilt. The bed covering was
a ratty old thing. Over the years some of its colorful
patches had faded and come loose. A background that
once had been white had yellowed to the shade of an
old woman's teeth. The bundle of cotton and padding
wasn't worth any money and although, when spread
out, it showed the remnants of a handsomely patterned
apple tree with fruit of red calico, it would never hang
in any folk museum. The quilt had been pieced together
a half-century before by her great-grandmother in what
little spare time she'd had when she wasn't carving a
homestead in the Georgia mountains, and since Bailey
had been twelve, it had always been on her bed. It had
followed her from New Jersey to apartment after dismal

apartment, to this place. Though she kept it on the bed during the day, she rarely slept under it; walking into the bedroom and seeing the bone-colored, shabby throw was what made her feel as if she'd come home.

Bailey softly slid the quilt from beneath his legs. She lay it on the narrow window seat crowded against the bed's far side, then left her own clothes folded neatly on top. Steve could sleep through anything. Bailey could have switched on an all–John Philip Sousa radio channel right then and he wouldn't have noticed. Still, she kept her motions close and quiet, feeling almost as if she were putting a child to sleep.

The next morning, after Steve had slipped out before she'd woken for her early meeting, it wasn't until she spread the quilt back across the bed's foot that she realized he'd never agreed to use the drawer.

Chapter Two

Ancient kings and queens had their wise men and soothsayers. The President had his cabinet of advisors. When Bailey needed counsel and direction, she could always count on her own personal Greek chorus of two. "Oh no he didn't!" they chanted in unison at the conclusion of her story.

The four words were their standard response to nearly everything Steve did—the night he'd walked out of *Hairspray* to answer a page and had forgotten to let Bailey know he'd headed in to the office, the time he'd actually asked a sushi chef whether he'd washed his hands according to city sanitary guidelines, the long parties he'd thrown where the sole attendees were economists or political theorists or people whose conversation had to do with socio . . . econo . . . demographicological . . . oh, she didn't know, but whose company was about as tedious as scrubbing an elephant with a toothbrush and a thimbleful of water. The kind of people who, as Euan had once said, "didn't know who Parker Posey was."

Across the lunch table, Euan shook his head; the pomade he'd liberally spread throughout his hair that morning made it glisten. "What?" Bailey asked, heart sinking. "Wrong move?" Sidney James pulled her face into a grimace. Her eyes sidled to Euan, who widened his eyes and pretended he hadn't heard the question. "Am I too obvious, too fast?"

"Sweetheart," Sidney said, patting Bailey's hand as if consoling her on a death in the family. "Drawer paralysis after four years of dating? Not a good sign. Oh!" she said, realizing that a slim, square-jawed waiter hovered at her side. Like all the other wait staff in the nouveau Tex-Mex grill, he wore a shirt of lemon yellow with a cactus green collar and one crimson sleeve, the vibrant colors of an American Southwest that never existed outside a marketing executive's imagination. "I'll start with the . . . let's see. The crispy squash fritters stuffed with she-crab and bleu cheese, then the twelve-herb chicken with cilantro–poppy seed sauce and sweet potato hash browns."

"Sidney, doll. I think this fine, fine fellow knows what's in the dishes," Euan said with a half-apologetic, half-flirtatious bat of his lashes in the waiter's direction. "My friend has a little bit of a menu fetish. I'll have the twelve-herb chicken as well. It's a specialty here, isn't it? Thought so. This whole place is special. Very special. Should we be ordering?" Euan asked suddenly, clutching his menu as if the waiter might make off with it. "I thought we were waiting for that infamous secretary of yours. Sandra. Zandra?"

"Are you done channeling Paul Lynde?" Bailey asked, tongue in cheek. She apologized to the attendant for both her best friends by ordering a salad with a few crisp words. Once the waiter had bowed and walked off, she added, "Her name's Chandra. She's stopping by to drop off a contract. And she's not my secretary. She's—"

"A bitch," interrupted Sidney. At Bailey's astonished glare, her girlfriend held up ten taloned fingers and raised her eyebrows. "You know my opinion on that tramp," she said, brushing back a wisp of her dark bob from her cheek. "And I do *not* have a menu fetish. It's that one time I had an appetizer that tasted like dog food. Reading stuff aloud helps me remember the ingredients, so when it comes to the table, I can make certain it's prepared properly."

"Because God forbid they leave out the poppy seeds so you wouldn't have to spend an extra five minutes in the ladies room flossing them out. And I do *not* act like Paul Lynde," said Euan, trying to act more offended than Sidney. It might have worked, had he not given his nails a quick appraisal at the sentence's end.

"Whatever, Uncle Arthur," said Sidney. "I wish I could smoke in here. Remember the days when they let us smoke in restaurants? Goddamned baby-sitter culture."

"My hair is much better than Paul Lynde's!"

"Just got it cut again, didn't you? Looks good," said Bailey.

"You like?" Pleased, Euan swiveled in his chair, posed, swiveled again, and modeled.

Sidney looked over the combed-forward do, which abruptly ended at the forehead and splayed upward, as if the front hairs had been slammed by some flat object. "Same old pelvic bone crunch, isn't it?"

"And circle takes the center square. Close your mouth or you'll catch flies," Bailey advised Euan, when he pretended to look shocked. Ever since the three of them had met six years ago in an improv class deep in the heart of Chelsea, they'd become so accustomed to each other's barbs that none of them took offense at the other. None of them had actually gone on to performance careers, instead finding niches on the fringes of the entertainment industry, as so many frustrated actors often do—Sidney had dragged Bailey kicking and screaming to the Expedition Network, while Euan O'Reilley oversaw casting for one of the CBS soaps. "If we can spare a moment for *my* problem," she suggested. Sidney looked sideways at Euan. Euan looked after the waiter and took a drink of his margarita through a sippy straw. Neither of them seemed to want to answer. "Anyone? Bueller? Anyone?"

Bailey's wait for a reply seemed as if it might go on indefinitely when finally Sidney caved. "Okay, listen," she said. "It's not merely a drawer paralysis problem. It's a four-year case of ennui, monotony, tediousness. . . ."

"Boredom," supplied Euan.

". . . boredom, flatness. . . ."

Euan, who was refolding his napkin into the shape of a peacock, added, "Bad sex."

"We haven't been *dating* for all those four years! You guys are nine shades of awful! And Steve and I don't have bad sex!" Bailey protested, feeling a nagging shame that she had to say the words aloud.

"Oh, so you didn't tell Sid that . . . hmmm, what was it?" Euan sighed and pretended to think. "That his attempts at performing oral sex reminded you of a Dippy Bird low on liquid mercury?" His peacock twice tipped its linen beak into her water glass, then fell over onto the table and lay motionless.

Half-horrified, half-diverted by Euan's all-too-accurate caricature of the few times she and Steve had attempted that particular sport, Bailey made a show of dropping her jaw. To her coworker, she said in shock, "I told you that in private!"

Sidney shrugged. "We don't hide things from each other, sweetie. You guys both were all over my case when I was dating the Scientologist, like you and I practically wanted to kill Euan when he was involved with that freakish cult."

"How many times do I have to repeat? Line dancing is *not* a cult," Euan interrupted. "I quit because you two kept making fun of my jeans."

"We didn't make fun of your jeans. Your jeans were fine. We made fun of how you had to use a shoehorn to wedge your man-parts in them," said Sidney, without dropping a beat. "And what's this thing . . . this thing about not dating all four of those years? That's exactly my point, Bail. What you guys have isn't a serious relationship. You don't date like normal people. You don't even *call* it dating."

It had been one thing for Euan to make fun of Steve's aversion to oral sex—that seemed to apply to more guys than it didn't. But Sid's criticisms verged on the personal. "There are dozens of experts who say it's better to be friends before becoming lovers," she announced. When her friends exchanged skeptical glances, she protested. "There are! You've heard them! Actual doctors!"

"Honey," said Euan with sympathy. "The pretty doctors you see on my show *aren't real*. Springfield is a *fictional city*. It's called *make-believe*."

"Hah, hah," said Bailey, without humor. "You all don't understand what kind of relationship Steve and I—what?" Her eyes darted between the pair of them as she attempted to figure out which part of her declaration had made the two cock their mouths into mirror-image smirks. "What?" When they both shook their heads, she narrowed her eyes. "Yes. I said *you all*. Linguists agree that *you all* is a perfectly acceptable way to express the second person plural, and I will thank you both—no. I'll thank *you all* not to laugh at me for it." Bailey paused to take a sip of water, then prolonged her silence by wiping the glass's condensation from her fingertips.

"Darlin', you can *y'all* me and *honeychile* me all you want, you little Southern belle, you, but I keep telling you, those linguists you see on daytime TV shows are *fic*—"

Euan's rigid pelvic bone crunch nearly met with a nasty end, right then. Sidney, however, hushed Bailey in mid-swipe. "Cheese it," she said. "Our Lady of the Brown Nose approacheth."

"Did you say 'cheese it'?" Euan asked, mildly incredulous. "You've filled up your Netflix queue with gumshoe movies from the 1930s and have been sitting at home nights with a bag of Cheetos, haven't you?"

Bailey cleared her throat and composed her face. Chandra Ellis was crossing the restaurant floor with brisk little steps and an entirely too-large smile stretched across her face. Chandra had begun work with the Expedition Network less than a year before with one of the less sympathetic male execs who shortly after announced that she "hadn't been working out." Out of principle, Bailey had stepped in and offered Chandra a position as an assistant. Chandra didn't talk to the talent or take over any of Bailey's talent producer tasks, but she was there to keep the files orderly and run interference with the legal department when needed—as it frequently was.

People always thought the talent producer had the most glamorous of jobs, constantly on the phone to Hollywood, hobnobbing with the celebs, closing deals over three-martini lunches. Maybe if she worked for some other network, some of that glamour might have rubbed off. Hell, the poor guys over at the Discovery Channel booked better talent than the D-list celebrities that the Expedition Network could barely afford. In reality, Bailey was little better than a limousine dispatcher whose primary duty was to make certain that talent made it to the sets on time with their contracts signed in all the appropriate places. In her little feminine Kay Unger suit, and with the *clip-clip-clip* of her tiny heels across the restaurant's parquet floor, Chandra reminded Bailey of herself several years ago, when she'd just started at the network and felt as if she had something to prove. Her assistant's long dark hair was neatly crimped into even waves, her mouth painted into a smile, and the slender briefcase she set on the table looked appropriately heavy.

"Oh gosh!" she said, cocking her head for approval like a retriever who'd fetched a stick and dropped it at Bailey's feet. "I hope I'm not interrupting you guys!" She promptly took the fourth chair and began to riffle through the briefcase, hauling out color-coded folders.

"Here are your calls," she said, brandishing a fistful of pink while-you-were-out slips. "Your sister phoned three times."

"It's the end of the month. She's probably scrounging for rent money," said Bailey, scrutinizing the other notes. Nothing that couldn't wait. Jeanne had left nearly a dozen messages on her voice mail at home that week alone, all of which she'd ignored. Bailey was secretly thankful she'd never given her sister her new cell number.

"I told her you'd left for Virginia. I hope that was okay? And oh, I've brought you the Jessica Munford contracts to look over. They're not signed yet, but—"

"What?" squawked Bailey, instinctively groping for the folder. She'd thought the Munford issue settled and done. She despised when someone tried to outmaneuver her. "Her legal told our legal they'd be ready this afternoon! Shooting is supposed to start Monday!"

The assistant began making cooing noises of sympathy, but Sidney interrupted. "Hi, Chandra," she said. The greeting wasn't so much out of friendliness, Bailey recognized, as of making a point about being overlooked.

"Oh, *hi*, Sidney!" said Chandra in a voice laden with syrup. "How are things at *your* end of the floor?"

Sid's reply was in the same singsong refrain. "*Fine!* I'm *so* glad you *asked!*"

Euan reached his long fingers over the table. "I'm Bailey's friend Euan. Jessica Munford, the talk-show woman? Are you guys doing a show with her?"

Chandra stared at Euan in horror, the word *oops!* written plainly over her face. "Oh jeez, I'm sorry," she said to Bailey. "These things are supposed to be confidential!"

"It's okay," she reassured the girl. To Euan, she said, "We're in talks." Munford, the ex-talk-show host turned senator's wife, had been the sharp, shooting pain in Bailey's behind for a few weeks; all the woman had to do was a week's worth of short shoots at various picturesque locations on the eastern seaboard that would be used to introduce and close out a series of shows on quaint country inns. No lines to memorize, no blocking to master. All the woman had to do was show up, read cue cards, and take home a more-than-tidy paycheck. Yet for two and a half months, her lawyers had come up with demand after demand to hold up the deal.

"Oh, I'm so so so so so so so sorry!" said Chandra, cringing like a little girl who'd let her puppy wet the floor.

"Cool it," Sidney advised, pulling out her cell phone to check its display. "I don't think the waiters are Travel Channel spies. It's not that big a deal."

"No, it's okay." Bailey couldn't help but feel sorry for the girl. After all, the days when she herself had whimpered over every error at work weren't that far behind. Since then, though, she'd learned one valuable lesson: When losing control, it was time to bluff. People respected someone essential to their well-being. She plucked several of the more important files from the pile for her Virginia trip. "You can take the rest back to the office. They'll wait a week. I'll take care of Munford myself. If her people call for me next week. . . ."

"I'll transfer them to your cell," Chandra promised.

"I'll have my laptop," Bailey reminded the girl. "I've left my flight info and my aunts' phone number. . . ."

"On your desk. I've already got them in my cell and my organizer."

"My," said Euan, his voice dangerously level. "Aren't you efficient?"

"I'm an awful airhead, really!" Chandra's dismissive laugh cut through the grill's lunchtime babble, causing more than a few of the diners to turn their heads. "Of course, Bailey's so organized that I always joke she's the one who takes care of me!"

"She does," Sidney confirmed to Euan, mouth pulled into a smile of dismay. "Often. All the time. I've heard it."

Bailey frowned at them. Her friends weren't playing nice. Chandra wasn't the straight man in one of their comedy skits, whose job it was to be blissfully unaware of the zingers flying right past. Though her assistant tried too hard, Bailey still felt, well, protective of the girl. "Chandra does a great job," she asserted with a smile. "I can't think of anyone else I'd rather have look after my desk while I'm away next week." The girl rewarded her with a tip of the head and a beam so radiant it could have lit the Chrysler Building at midnight; at the same time, she made little shooing motions with her hands.

The waiter silently reappeared at their tableside, his hands clutched humbly before him. Euan smiled broadly. "The squash fritters will be right out," he assured Sidney. "Shall I bring another menu?"

Chandra fluttered up and down in her seat as if carried by small winged creatures who couldn't quite handle her slight weight. "Oh no," she said at last. "I'm not staying." The waiter nodded and eased away.

"Ah, what a pity."

Sidney's insincerity arrived at the same time as Bailey's, "You're welcome to."

After a moment's indecision, Chandra lifted herself up. "I've probably got things to do. And this is a personal lunch, and all." When neither Euan or Sidney spoke, their faces deliberately blank and lips free of contradiction, Chandra gathered up the remaining file folders. "I'll get back to work. Oh!" she added, as if in that moment she'd realized something. "You're really going to be missed at the office next week. I'll miss you, anyway." Bailey didn't dare look at her friends for their no doubt amused reactions. With a *clip-clip-clip* of her little heels, Chandra left the table. "Have a nice vacation!" She waved from beside the station where a bored-looking cook pounded out handmade tortillas.

"It's not a vacation!" Sidney called after her. "Working leave of absence! Hell. She didn't hear. Don't let her tell people around the office you're on vacation, Bailey," she scolded. "Vacations are for wusses. They'll think you've gone soft. Say cheese." She lifted her phone to eye level, pointed it at Bailey, and squeezed a button.

"So that's what this year's Eve Harrington looks like, hmmm?" Euan said, one of his sculpted eyebrows raised. Bailey paid him no mind, instead stuffing files into her briefcase. "Oh, come on. Eve Harrington. *All About Eve*. Ann Baxter! She's a meek little mouse who goes after Bette Davis and. . . ."

"I've seen it, I've seen it," said Bailey, putting down her bag. "You and Rodrigo threw a party and had it as a double feature with *Showgirls*, remember?"

"Can you spell MGM backwards? I bet you can't," Euan automatically responded.

"Oh God. Now you've got him going with the *Showgirls* quotes," groaned Sidney.

"I'm erect," said Euan, warming to the task. "Why aren't you erect?"

"He does have a point." Sidney ostentatiously ignored Euan and his bad movie quotes. "She'll steal that job away from you first chance she gets if you give her an inch. Honestly, Bail. As competitive as you are, I'm surprised you can't see it in someone like her." She pointed the little lens on the back of her phone at Euan.

"Would you stop playing with your new camera phone? And I'm not competitive!"

Euan's jaw dropped like Kermit the Frog's upon hearing Miss Piggy assert that she wasn't at all vain. Sidney cocked her head. "Oh, come on."

"I'm not!"

"You lectured us not three weeks ago about Scrabble rules, accompanied by an extensive reading from the rules."

With a flush, Bailey felt compelled to defend the incident. "The rules state that you can't use proper nouns and . . ."

"Here she goes," said Sidney, with a roll of her eyes.

"What's the use of playing if you don't play by the rules?" Bailey said with exasperation. "That's what rules are made for. It's a simple matter of right and wrong and I was right about the rules, and I'm right about Chandra. I'm not budging a centimeter." To her own ears, she sounded stubborn. Good. Some things were worth standing up for. "Not a hair. I can control her."

"From four states away?"

"I'm just going for a week to make sure my mom's acclimating after her stroke. It's like my other trips down South, only a little longer. And instead of an airport hotel, I'll be staying—"

"At the old childhood home, yes, I know. Carry me back to ol' Virginny, and all that." Sidney spied their waiter returning from the grill's kitchen with their table as his obvious destination, a plate in his hand. She began clearing a space in front of her while she talked, sullenly adding, "Promise you'll check in, that's all. I don't like being without my best girlfriend."

"Aww!" Bailey was touched by the admission. Sidney had never been much on sentiment. Years ago in improv, her characters had all been gruff blusterers determined to bully their way through a situation. Hardly a stretch of the talents. Come to think of it, maybe none of them had strayed very far from type. Sidney had cast herself as the lonely single, the woman of a dozen cats and twice as many verbal barbs and no man to call her own. Euan had specialized in snooty gay shop boys, thin and witty gay club kids, and an outrageous creation called Glenn Closet whose sexuality was apparent to everyone save himself. And Bailey . . . well. Bailey played the fall woman, the straight guy, the center of normalcy who watched in bemusement as everyone else ran through their comic paces. She'd played the reporter who interviewed crazies, the marriage counselor trying to cope with Glenn Closet and his wife Butch, the bland waitress in a bar full of loonies. Never once had she made someone laugh. That she left to the other zanies on the stage. Someone had to keep it all together while everyone else fell apart, right? "Are you saying you don't want me to go?"

"No, on the contrary. Go!" Sidney commanded, looking at the photos she'd captured on her new phone before putting it to sleep. "I mean, I think it'll be good for you and Steve to get the hell away from each other for a while. Your mom's okay, right?"

"Oh yeah," said Bailey, forcing more cheerfulness than she felt. "The stroke was mild. The doctors told me she's recovered nearly all her mobility. They've given her exercises to do at home. I'm sure it'll be a normal visit." Bailey adopted her mother's tone of voice. *"How much are you paying for your apartment these days? Don't you know that gentrification is squeezing the lower middle class from the cities?"*

Sidney had met Bailey's mother before she'd moved back to Virginia, five years ago, and had even played a character based on her in improv. She apparently could still slip into it without any notice. "Your hair product is what's causing the ozone layer to disappear! Are you eating fruit salad picked by migrant workers *again?"*

"That hamburger's the reason there's no more rain forest!" Bailey grinned broadly, glad for the comic relief. "Do you know how many units of fuel it costs to create that silk you're wearing, when cotton can be grown and processed at so much less expense?"

Euan waggled a finger. "Don't disappear in a Crestonville trailer park and make me come down there and rip that damned Jaclyn Smith collection off your damned ass. I will stage a fashion intervention if I have to, believe you me." Ouch. Why did everyone have to associate her childhood home with trailer parks? Whenever New Yorkers discovered Bailey had spent her first twelve years in rural Virginia, they pitied her.

Sidney still had a point to make. "A week is a long stretch in New York time. Whole boroughs get built, decay, and then redeveloped by Euan's crowd in less time than that." The waiter arrived at their table and, with a swoop of a yellow sleeve, deposited the garlicky smelling fritters in front of her. "Yum."

"Not like dog food, I trust?" Bailey asked.

"Doggy Chow!" exclaimed Euan with a clap of his hands. Sidney looked up from her appetizer, lip curled with distaste. "I used to love Doggy Chow."

"I used to love Doggy Chow, too!" the waiter said, right on cue. He winked at Euan, turned on his shiny black monk-strapped shoes, and slid away.

Euan watched the waiter's butt bounce in the direction of the kitchen. When he finally turned back around, he was chewing hard on his thumb. "Those *Showgirls* quotes always bring 'em out."

Chapter Three

"Bailey, honey, are you taking care of your uterus? I'm telling you, after all the torture I've been through!" Though the air conditioning in the truck was positively glacial, Aunt Bits fanned herself rapidly with a car parts catalog she'd discovered somewhere among the back-seat's debris. "You've got to pamper it, girl, or it'll fall right out."

One hand over the speaker of her cell phone, Bailey called back, "Yeah, Aunt Bits, I'll keep that in mind." Bailey quirked her mouth with apology in the direction of Mr. Montgomery, the truck's driver and sole masculine presence. "Chandra? Are you still there? What?" Her assistant's garbled reply cut in and out.

Putting fingers over her free ear couldn't block her aunt's crowlike voice. "I detect a tone, young woman. A tone. Do you detect a tone, Bubble?"

"Well . . ." Aunt Bubble hadn't bothered to move any of the litter on the truck's rear bench. In her floral-print dress, she perched among the seed catalogues and the scratched jewel cases of country CDs with her knees together and her arms crossed at the wrist, like a plump

Dresden figurine of a prim shepherdess atop a rubbish heap. "I can't rightly say to that, but . . ."

"Chandra?" Bailey looked at her phone's display. Full battery, but only one signal bar, flickering in and out. She'd lost the connection, damn it.

As the truck lurched from the two-lane highway onto a smaller route road, Aunt Bits's four-wheel drove right over whatever her sister had been about to say. "Seems to me that everyone these days wants to pretend they don't have a uterus." A decisive sniff punctuated the declaration. "Mark my words, though, when you're walking down the street one day and it drops out, you'll notice it then."

Waving the phone around in every direction did nothing except make the single, miniscule signal bar disappear. In her exasperation, Bailey forgot for a moment her aunt's neighbor in the front seat beside her. "I know perfectly well I have a uterus!" True, she'd been more aware of it at some times than others, and while she'd avoided attending any self-awareness seminars involving hand mirrors and squats, she felt pretty certain she had a journeyman's knowledge of the organ's working functions. "I've managed to haul mine around for twenty-seven years now without folding, spindling, or mutilating it, thanks for asking. I don't see why every time I come down, all you have to talk about is the state of your innards, Bits."

Flap-a-flap-a-flap. The catalog's path through the air doubled in intensity. "Northern children are so outspoken. No respect for their elders. Isn't she outspoken, Mr. Montgomery?"

"It seems to me," Bailey dryly replied, "that they raise them pretty outspoken down here, too." What in the world was their driver thinking of this conversation? What had he thought of every inane conversation the three of them had held on their trips to and from Richmond International Airport the past month?

"Stubborn child," Bits announced from the back. "Isn't she a stubborn child, Mr. Montgomery?"

The driver rubbed his hand over his chin, rasping against a half-day's considerable growth of stubble. From under his baseball cap, the curly ends of his dark hair tumbled out. For the first time since he had nodded hello to her from the curbside pickup, Taylor Montgomery opened his mouth to speak. "Seeing as how Ms. Rhodes can hang onto her uterus for twenty-seven years without dropping it, I reckon someone did a good job of raising her somewhere along the way."

That had been the last thing Bailey expected to hear. To say her aunt's neighbor from the next farm over didn't seem the chatty type was something of an understatement; this might have been the one time she'd heard the man speak an entire sentence. Still, she'd take her support where she found it. "Thank you!" she exclaimed. The driver nodded, briefly catching her eye and grinning before turning his gaze back to the field-lined road ahead.

"Well! I don't think your sister would be so mouthy, Bailey Rhodes. You'll drive me into an early grave, I swear." There was an impossible premise! Her mother's younger sisters had been prefabricated in their late middle age and never seemed to grow any older. They'd always been simply the never-changing Aunt Bits and Aunt Bubble, one thin to the point her cheekbones could lacerate with a wayward hug, the other padded and comforting. Even in the days before they'd moved North, when Bailey and Jeanne and their mother had visited the aunts in their old Georgia home, they'd been fussy old women in faded housecoats who always smelled of bath salts and licorice.

Bailey's response to her aunt's suggestion was a laugh wedged somewhere between guilty enjoyment and outright derision; her little sister would have wasted no time telling Bits how to pick up her fallen uterus and where to reinsert it. "How is Jeanne, dear?" Aunt Bubble spoke up from her ladylike perch in the back. "Such a sweet face she always had."

Before Bailey could reply, Aunt Bits was already weighing in with an opinion. "A sweet face that can't be bothered to see her own sick mother."

"Now, now. I'm sure she's busy, dear."

"Too busy for her own mother?" Bits blew a raspberry, wet and juicy. "Don't hold a cow pat under *my* nose and tell me it's Chanel."

"How is sweet Jeanne?" asked Bubble, once again.

"Jeanne is fine, and you know her money's tight when she's between jobs." Bailey always felt uncomfortable whenever she was called upon to defend her younger sister. Why did she bother? Saying *between jobs* was stretching a euphemism to its widest—although it was certainly possible that after her one-afternoon stint selling lemonade in front of their Jersey City home thirteen years ago, Jeanne might find employment sometime before the grave. "I'm sure she'll visit eventually." Eventually, as in if someone died and if someone paid for Jeanne's plane ticket.

"Oh, it would be lovely to see her!" Without turning, Bailey could tell her older aunt was beaming from ear to ear.

"She can't use the telephone, either?" Bits asked. Bailey had sucked lemon slices that were less tart. "Oh, I forgot, they don't allow collect calls from the big city."

"I talked to her right before I left this morning. She sends her love." Fib upon fib, Bailey realized. Her family had a talent of turning her into an enormous bluffer. She hadn't talked to Jeanne that morning, or any other morning or evening for the past six weeks.

Bits, however, wasn't so easily placated. "I have worked every day of my life since I was old enough to baby-sit," she announced. "Where will she be when it's time to retire? I'm sure that boyfriend of yours could tell her she's setting herself up for ruin. Bailey's gentleman friend's an accountant," her aunt explained for Taylor's benefit.

"Economist," Bailey said, once again feeling a defensive whiplash. "And Jeanne's only twenty-three." She desperately held up her cell phone again, hoping for a signal so she could have an excuse to end the conversation.

"Accountant, economist. . . ." Bits sighed, as if they were both one and the same.

"It's an *odd* profession for a man, isn't it?" Bubble wanted to know. "Though I'm sure he's a sweet boy, dear."

"What's odd, you old crow?" Bits snapped. "Well? Accounting? My John was an accountant."

Fifty-odd years had inured Bubble to her sister's taunts, apparently. Bailey had never once heard her take offense at any of the insults thrown her way. "I know very well your husband, rest his soul, was an accountant. I meant the other profession." Bailey looked over her shoulder into the backseat, where Aunt Bubble pushed her round glasses up on her nose. The chain holding them around her neck swung back and forth, glittering in the sunlight as the truck rounded a bend. "I understand that some of the finest cooks in the world are men, of course, but it seems to me it takes a very brave man to take it up, even in this day and age."

They all fell quiet over the truck's thrumming motor, totally flummoxed. What in the world was Bubble going on about? At long last, once the short remainder of the rest of the trip seemed doomed to an uncomfortable silence, Bits swatted her sister, "You stupid bat! He isn't a *home* economist!"

While the pair squabbled in the back, Bailey cast the driver another wry and apologetic glance. His naturally dark skin and muscular arms made him better-looking than she'd remembered. Or maybe she'd been more stressed out on her previous visits? How her aunts managed to convince the poor guy to drive the thirty-odd miles in and out of the city, time after time enduring conversation that had to be idiotic to him, she had no idea. Knowing Bits, she'd probably dug up some good blackmail material. Poor schmo.

When Bailey had been a girl and lived in the house that now belonged to her aunts, her home could be seen across the cornfields from nearly a mile away, its weathered red profile stark against the horizon. The house was neither grand nor stately, but from a distance there used to be something majestic about its stubborn deadlock with its natural surroundings; the house had endured over a century of wind and rain and hot Virginia sun on its bricks and slate roof, and never bowed. Sometime since they had taken over, her aunts had let the chinaberry trees multiply in the front yard. Their veil of waxy green completely masked the house, hiding it from view. "You guys have let the trees overgrow. I miss the old view," she said aloud, as much to stop her aunt's private bickering as anything.

How many times had she taken for granted the sight of the old house, when she'd been a kid? One vision of it in particular had haunted her since a confused night trip from the old Whigfield childhood home in Carverton, Georgia. She and her sister had been pulled from their guest beds hours after they'd gone to sleep and trundled into their mother's old Dodge Dart for the long trip home. Jeanne had been stretched in the backseat for the entire trip while Bailey had curled up in front. She'd awoken at dawn by the car slowing down and by the change of road surfaces beneath the car's wheels, and had opened her eyes to see the house beneath a full moon as white and round as a floured pie pan. She'd never shaken the memory.

The truck rounded the old brick posts at the road's edge and turned into the dirt drive. "If you don't like it, you're perfectly free to re-landscape. I'd love to see you do it in those shoes."

Her aunt's implied criticism made Bailey look guiltily

down at her Kate Spade pumps. They weren't anything extraordinary; though in her short double-slit skirt and nipped Anne Klein blouse she'd been horribly aware at the Richmond airport that she'd been the one woman not wearing the Virginia state uniform—apparently mandated sometime when The Official Preppy Handbook had been written—of khaki shorts, penny loafers, and an Izod polo shirt. "What's wrong with my shoes?" she yelped. Her most casual outfits seemed horribly fussy down here.

"Why, Bailey, don't get so defensive," said Bits. "There's nothing wrong with your shoes. I'm sure they're very fashionable. I saw a pair like them in that movie with that pretty Southern girl—what's her name?—who was a big-city hooker. Mr. Montgomery, be careful along this way, now. The last rainstorm left a bump—"

Her aunt's comment was cut off as the truck lurched over a small crater, bouncing them all up into the air and back down hard onto their seats. Aunt Bubble let out the tiniest of squeals; when Bailey looked back, she caught her elder aunt smoothing down her skirt with hasty hands. "Whoops. Sorry, ladies," said their driver. Was that a wink he cast in Bailey's direction? Slants of yellow light from the setting sun had bleached her vision; he might have been simply blinking at the glare.

"Taylor, you rascal!" Aunt Bits' laughter came out as a high-pitched cackle. "I'll give you five dollars to do it again so we can all get another glimpse of Bubble's cookie."

"Elizabeth Katherine Whigfield Oates, you'll do no such thing," Bubble replied. Though her voice rose in pitch she didn't sound the least worried.

When they pulled to a stop, several other cars were already splayed at haphazard angles to each other in front of the house's verandah. Taylor shifted the truck into park, then without shutting off the ignition, hopped immediately out to open up the back door for Bubble.

"Who are all these people?" Bailey asked. Nurses, maybe? No, the pretty young women leaping up from the wooden porch and running toward the truck didn't look old enough to be any kind of nurses, save those in an old Benny Hill sketch. Had her aunts thrown together some kind of welcome home party for her mother? For her? Shouldn't they have invited people she knew?

One of the young women, barefoot and clad in cut-off jeans and a T-shirt, came flying over, dewy eyes wide open. For her relatively small size, her breasts were absolutely enormous; Bailey knew actresses who'd paid big money for boobs like those. "Miz Oates!" the girl said, so excited she nearly drooled. "Miz Oates! They've. . . ."

Bits stopped her with crossed arms and a glance so steely it could've been used to build World War II battleships. "Larkin Merino," she announced. "How many times have I said that if you are going to take the dogs out for a walk, make sure they're leashed?" Larkin's arms self-consciously flew across her chest. "We don't all want them jumping into our lap, you know."

One of the other girls, dark-haired and petite, laughed. "But Miss Whigfield, guess what?" she gabbled with excitement, taking over from Taylor the duty of escorting Aunt Bubble around the car. Like the other girls, she looked barely out of high school. "The applications are out."

"I was going to say that!" Larkin said with a pout. Then she burst into a high-pitched rush of words. "The applications are out, Miz Oates, so now you can start coaching us and. . . ."

While Larkin spoke, the four other girls bounced up and down on tippy-toe, their mouse-like squeaks of glee betraying their excitement. Bailey, on the other hand, had no idea what they were talking about. She was tired from the flight, in need of a few minutes alone in the powder room, and all the feminine squealing threatened to loosen her eyeballs from their sockets. Thankfully, Aunt Bits held up a hand and silenced the crew. "Girls," she asked in a no-nonsense tone honed from decades as a third-grade teacher, "is this any way to behave in front of a guest?"

Taylor had finished hauling out Bailey's duffle bag from the truck's bed. He wiped off his hands, nodded to the aunts, and walked around the truck. Were they really going to let him go without acknowledgment? Ignoring the fact that all eyes were upon her, Bailey touched their driver on the arm, withdrawing her fingers quickly when they accidentally brushed his bicep. "Hey, thanks for yet another lift."

He seemed much younger outside the truck than in, somehow. "Not a problem," Taylor said, touching the tip of his baseball cap. His eyes were the blue of marbles she'd collected in her childhood. When he smiled around the group, she could see his teeth were white and even. "You know where to find me. And hey," he said, his work boots scraping in the gravel as he swiveled suddenly, a mischievous grin on his face for her alone. "Hang on to that uterus, now."

"Really, Mr. Montgomery!" her aunt proclaimed to his back, as the man climbed into his truck and revved the motor.

Bailey had been secretly charmed by the irreverent remark. Over the noise, she said, "Oh, Bits, as if you weren't discussing the ins and outs of your apparatus not ten minutes ago." She hadn't a clue who all these girls were, but with every glance they took and in the few bold outright stares was a hunger she'd seen many times before. She'd witnessed it in the eyes of countless young men and women who gathered at the perimeters of location shoots, coffees in hand and seemingly nothing else to do in the world save to wait for a glimpse of a face they'd seen before on their television screens. Bailey, though, was no celebrity.

Maybe it was her clothing. It wasn't that she was the

big New Yorker and these kids were all Daisy Maes
from *Li'l Abner*. Far from it. The girls were by and large
decked out in the kind of sloppy T-shirts and shorts that
kids wore, while Bailey was dressed like a responsible,
working adult. A responsible, working adult attired in
clothing that had never appeared in the Sears and Roe-
buck Wish Book. The contrast was probably what made
them stare. "That's Prada, isn't it?" said one of the girls,
not so much gazing at the bag with admiration, as trying to sniff its composition from a distance.

"Mmm, maybe?" Bailey tried to sound as vague as
possible about the bag's origins as she lugged it up by
its strap and attempted to hide it from view. "Where's
Mom?" she asked her aunts.

"Miz Rhodes is in the backyard," said one of the
girls, the one with the enormous bosom. Larkin, Bailey
thought her name was. So at least some of the girls
knew who she was? Leave it to her aunts to talk up her
appearance. She wondered what their motive might be.

"Oh dear." Aunt Bubble shook her head and began
ambling in the direction of the house. Underneath her
faded old sundress, her enormous bottom swayed from
side to side with each step. "Perhaps I'd better make
some tea. Now, Bits, warn her."

With a bag as heavy as her own, Bailey's goal had
been to heft it to the porch as quickly as possible, as
none of the girls seemed to be offering their assistance
and she didn't want her aunts attempting to lift the
bloody thing and have more vital organs pop out. At
Bubble's words, though, she froze. "Warn me about
what?"

They were all in on something, she could tell. The
girls that weren't already facing away slowly turned,
heads down. Her cheap beige purse still swinging from
her elbow, Bits crossed her arms and complained,
"Now, why are you going to worry the girl like that?"

"It might be a shock to her system, poor thing."

"Warn me about what?"

"Bubble, all the drama you create worries people far more than anything else they'd find out on their own."

"I just think—"

"Warn me about *what?*" demanded Bailey, forgetting her mission to lug her bag to the front porch as quickly as possible. "What? What's a shock to my system? Because if it's worse a shock than seeing a mother who the day before her stroke was bragging about the tennis game she'd won suddenly lying in a hospital bed, I damn well want my warning." The girls had moved farther away by that point, but not so far that they couldn't hear every word Bailey set loose.

The aunts, though, stared at each other in the way that only sisters could—eyes locked, jaws set, chins lifted in stubborn defiance. Finally Bubble turned, loser of the unspoken battle. "I'll make tea," she announced, before turning and walking in the direction of the house.

"Warn me about what, Bits?"

"Ignore that old hag," Bits said, striding over on her spindly legs, waving her hands in an indication that they should take the family drama out of prime time and into a private showing. Bits's posture had always been ramrod straight, but she seemed more intimidating than usual. "Your mother's fine. Physically she's fine. The doctors say she'll be fine. Since she's come home, well . . . this isn't the place to discuss it."

"Fine?" Bailey supplied, growing impatient. Typical Bits, having no qualms about insulting her sister in front of strangers, but not wanting to talk about anything substantial before the same audience. "Bits. Level with me."

"What?" asked her aunt. A quick glance over her shoulder at the gaggle of spectators seemed to make her grow more self-conscious about having such a private family discussion in such a public place. "Maybe you should get some rest first. You can see your mother after you take a nap. Dear."

The last word sounded awkward and forced. Bailey wasn't buying it for a moment. "I'm not six years old. I don't need a nap. If you've got something to say about Mom, say it now."

"Your mother's simply. . . ." Bits seemed at a loss for words—a rare state of affairs that appeared to fluster her. "Well, she's been through a lot! What do you expect? With you barely visiting and your sister missing in action . . . of course she's not the same woman."

The strap of her duffel had been busily gnawing its way through the flesh of her knuckles and now seemed engaged in chewing away through bone; she shifted it to the other hand. Maybe it had been the flight, or the bumpy ride from the airport, but Bailey felt suddenly overcome by the gravity of some larger planet on which she was but an insignificant speck. Keeping her spine upright took too much effort. She didn't have the energy to play these family games. She was here, wasn't she? Wasn't that enough? "You'd better attend to your guests," she reminded her aunt.

For a moment, she enjoyed seeing Bits waffle between maintaining propriety in front of the girls, whoever they were, and wanting to spill whatever dire and no doubt overblown warnings she'd concocted for Bailey. "You really are a maddening girl," Bits at last spat out. "I blame your mother for your upbringing. If she hadn't taken you up North. . . ."

"I'd be barefoot and preg. . . ." Bailey cut herself off. The girl named Larkin was barefoot, after all. "You know, why don't I go in and see Mom now?" She turned and took a step toward the house.

"Why don't you do that?" Bits snapped back. She muttered something in an inaudible voice, stopping when Bailey swung around once again. "I didn't say a word."

"If only." Bailey pretended not to hear when the muttering began again; she let it be drowned out by the sounds of her feet crunching on the drive and of her bag bouncing against the gravel with every step. She disliked coming back to this place. She'd lived here for the first twelve years of her life, but as an adult, it never felt like home.

In the distance, the neighbor's truck vanished around the corner, bound for the next farm over. Maybe it was the long trip, or the ride from Richmond, or her crotchety old aunt, or the dread of having to see her mother in whatever state she was in, but Bailey wished she was a girl again, barefoot and fleet-legged and in cut-off shorts, running down the driveway to hop in the truck's bed and escape to somewhere bigger and better.

Chapter Four

If she had been starring in a Hallmark Hall of Fame adaptation of a tasteful literary classic, Bailey reflected as she walked up the kitchen stairs into the garden, this would be the point at which she paused at the back door and, in a misty-eyed moment, heard the ghostly voices of happy memories: her sister counting to one hundred during a game of hide-and-seek, the happy shrieks of children at play, the sound of her mother's younger self calling her to set the table. Weird as coming back to the old house felt—and it always felt plenty weird, seeing newer appliances in the kitchen where in her memory stood old fixtures from the 1950s and 1960s, still backed by wallpaper nearly as old as her younger aunt—the fact of the matter was that Bailey had more memories of New Jersey than Virginia. Up North she'd had friends from around the block and as close as next door—here "next door" meant a ten-minute walk. In New Jersey, she'd had libraries and stores and trips into the city; here they'd had a television that could pick up a mere two snowy stations.

The only sound that greeted Bailey's ears was a thud, a strangely familiar hollow sound followed by a pitter-patter of diminishing echoes across the concrete-block patio nestled in the corner where the two perpendicular halves of the house met. "Mom?" she asked a scraggly row of boxwoods that reached the bottom of her ribcage.

Thump, she heard, followed by *thunk-a-thunk-a-thunk-thunk-thunk.*

"Not bad," Bailey heard someone say—a female on the high side of the alto range. With a creak of cheap plastic, its owner rose from a low lawn chair. Bailey caught a glimpse of long dark hair with turquoise highlights swinging over the ground as the girl bent over to retrieve something. Great—another of her aunt's visitors. Were they opening a bordello? And why did that thought amuse her so much? "Try these," said the girl, turning around with her arm outstretched. For someone determined to make herself as plain as possible with hair that concealed a face devoid of makeup, she was surprisingly pretty. Yet the moment the girl saw Bailey looming over the shrubbery, her face pulled into a scowl Bailey normally saw on clients who'd discovered the dismal rates the Expedition Network was prepared to offer them. "Oh," she said finally, taking in Bailey's outfit, her glance lingering particularly in the area of the shoes. "You're one of *them*. Yeah, I don't think the weird sisters are home yet, y'know? So sorry. Hey," she added, when Bailey merely stared at her. "No offense or anything, but aren't you a little *old* for this? You're like, what, thirty-two? Thirty-four? Because if you're thinking you can pass for under twenty-two when at best you could get away with, I don't know, twenty-seven. . . ."

That was enough to prompt Bailey's amazed vocal cords into action. "I *am* twenty-seven."

"Dude!" said the girl, her brown eyes darting sideways, as if embarrassed by the very idea. "If you say so. I mean, I've got a little brother who says he's Wolverine. From *X-Men*, you know. I mean, it doesn't make him Wolverine, but if you want to . . ."

"Who are you, exactly?" Bailey demanded, dropping her duffel onto the ground. Thirty-four! Thirty-four was the age people guessed when a woman was middle-aged and they were trying to be polite! The day Bailey looked thirty-four, she'd damned well better be forty-five.

"Hey, I'm not trying to be offensive," said the girl. Whatever she was carrying in her hands, she leaned over and deposited. "I'm not your competition. I'm here with a friend, okay?" She raised her eyebrows to punctuate whatever oblique point she was trying to make, and strolled around the hedge. No wonder she'd been staring at Bailey's shoes; the girl wore a battered pair of black calf-high Doc Martens that looked as if they'd been used to hammer nails. "Beauty is only skin deep, right? That's what they say, anyway." The girl's tongue ran around her mouth as she once again sized up Bailey. "Yeah, I'm pretty sure the sisters can help you out. My friend says they're the best. *She's* the one you'd better watch out for, not me. She'd do *anything* to win this puppy." And with that last word, the girl pivoted on her rubber soles and began the long way around the house, through the dense thicket of chinaberry spindles.

Bailey's bordello theory seemed to be making more sense by the minute. "Mom?" she asked for a second time, rounding the boxwoods. As she'd half-hoped, her mother occupied one of the lawn chairs on the other side, sitting on an extra pillow with her hands in her lap. After Bits's warning, Bailey had expected the worst. And yet the scene was nearly normal; her mother was dressed in a simple and comfortable set of shorts and a tank top, exactly as she might have on any other summer's day. "Oh thank God," she said, impulsively leaning down to plant a kiss on her mom's forehead. "You've got no idea what Aunt Bits has put me through. She had me picturing you as a drooling nutcase."

Since Bailey had last seen her in the hospital, her mother's appearance had undergone a transformation for the better. The stroke had at first left her face slack, loosening muscles that Bailey hadn't known existed; half of her face had looked as if it were melting, while the other half was alert, alive, and frightened. Now, though, there was scarcely any sign of the attack, save for a slightly drooping left eyelid, and the merest hint of heaviness to the left cheek, neither of them perceptible to anyone who might not have been looking closely. Her mom's mouth parted, lips quivering as she tried to work out slow syllables: "Maybe I am."

The relief Bailey felt at hearing those few words couldn't have been measured even by a truckload of scientists wielding tape measures and slide rules. Of course it was natural to feel guilt about not having been at her mother's side every moment since the night of the stroke, but she'd been there when it counted, right? The day after it happened, she'd flown down and spent three entire days in the critical care unit; on her own dime she'd flown back the following weekend. Okay, so she hadn't been around for her mom's transfer back home, or in the two weeks since, but it wasn't as if she hadn't kept in touch. She'd checked in several times with the doctors. She'd talked, God knew, to her aunts nearly every day—so much so that she'd taken to calling from work and having Chandra interrupt after three minutes to cut short the family insanity. "Too funny!" she chuckled. Perhaps her laugh was a little loud, and a little forced, at her mother's joke. But humor was a good sign, right?

"So who was your blue-haired friend?" she asked, sitting next to her mom in the other lawn chair. Bailey had noticed almost right away that her mother's lap contained four tennis balls, all ancient, all battered, unearthed from who knew where. Her mom squeezed one of them in her left hand, over and over again. Across the patio, scattered and hidden like Easter eggs for a hunt, lay at least a dozen other tennis balls. A few peeked out from beneath the boxwoods, others from the folded deck chairs leaned against the house, and one had wedged beneath the drain spout.

Her mother didn't answer. Instead, she fixed her eyes straight ahead, as if studying something. Bailey's gaze followed. She half-expected to see a bird, or a small animal that had wandered in from the clusters of trees surrounding the house's rear, but there was nothing of interest on the weathered red brick of the house's original wing; milkweed grew between the cracks of the concrete blocks, but other than that, the only possible object drawing her mother's attention could have been a square wooden shutter, battered and probably older than Bailey herself, leaning against the brick.

Suddenly her mother jerked with a spasm that shook the entire left side of her body. Bailey's immediate reaction was to reach out and grab her mom's arm, but by the time her reflexes managed to overcome her panic, the contraction was over. A tennis ball flew across the patio blocks, hitting the ground before its low arc measured four feet. *Thunk-a-thunk-a-thunk-thunk.* With a flurry of soft sounds it thudded to a stop somewhere near the patio's corner, where other balls lay in disarray. She hadn't been convulsing at all . . . she'd been trying to throw the ball.

Leaning back in the chair, Bailey crossed her legs and tried to appear more casual than she felt. For a moment, she'd actually been frightened. Other than a hazy grasp on CPR she'd picked up from some morning talk show years before, she had no idea of what to do in a possible medical emergency. Sure, she'd read the materials her mom's doctors had recommended, and visited a few Web sites on her own from work, but if there had been another stroke, would she have had a clue how to respond? Or would she have gone running to the aunts? Not for the first time, Bailey almost wished she hadn't come. Even with the crabbing that Aunt Bits would surely have done, staying at home would have been so much easier.

"So, is that one of the exercises your therapist recommended?" Her mother's lack of response made her feel helpless. At least she could retrieve tennis balls. Yes, that would give her something to do, and give her an excuse to get out of the dirty chair. On the other side of her mother's seat lay a paper grocery bag, overturned by a breeze or an errant throw. Two balls still weighed it to the ground. Bailey grabbed one of the bag's handles and dragged it around behind her as she played fetch with nimble fingers. "That's great! Get back your coordination . . . you'll be golfing again in no time." Her mother stared, her gaze still intent on the wooden shutter. Had she been aiming at it? Her mother had been some ten or more feet off target. A twinge of guilt sprang from some unnameable source; the only balm for it was to keep talking. "I want this week to be all about you," she said, leaping to the speech she'd prepared on the plane. "Anything you need, ask." Some of these balls had to be at least twenty years old. They'd long lost their tautness. "I might have a little bit of work to do, but I'll try to . . ."

Her mother hadn't reacted to a single thing she'd said. Again, the alarm she felt was palpable; it raised the hairs on her arms. Was this odd, atypical silence the change Bits had tried to warn her about? Was it neurological? Permanent? "Are you okay?" she asked. "Do I need to call . . . ?"

"No." The word was less a protest than an outright command. Twenty-seven years of conditioning froze Bailey in place. Though her mom's face wore the same unchanging expression, in her eyes was now a flintiness that forbade Bailey from any impulsive actions. Her mom hadn't needed to speak loudly. A single syllable was all it took to communicate volumes of the stubbornness, anger, and determination of a woman who still wanted the world to follow in her footsteps. Once again, she clawed a tennis ball from her lap and flung it. Out of control, the ball spun from her mother's fingers and crashed into the boxwood to the left, whooshing through its small, dry leaves and rebounding against a rusted-out charcoal grill before bouncing to a stop underneath the shrubbery. Her mother's mouth twisted, whether upset at the ball or at her daughter, it was impossible to tell. Her eyes had never left the shutter.

Her mom was left-handed. Was it bad that she'd lost so much coordination? Or was it a good sign that she could handle a tennis ball at all? Bailey added one more question to the already-long list for the doctors. Her thighs hurt from the squatting. After a lengthy sideways glance, during which she thought she could almost feel her mother quivering with indignation, she returned to collecting tennis balls and letting them plop into the grocery bag.

"How much. . . ." she heard after a moment. "So how much did those . . . shoes . . . run you?" At least the slack muscles that had left her mom's sibilants slurred had improved. Three weeks ago, the words *those* and *shoes* would have been unintelligible, but today they merely sounded slightly drunken. *Zo. Thoze. Zhoes.*

That question itself positively perked Bailey right up. If there was anything more typical of a normal interaction with her mother, it was lying about how much she'd spent on her clothing, her appliances, or her apartment. "I don't remember," she said casually, leaning over to capture the last of the neon green balls lingering beneath the spout. "I think I picked them up in a bargain sale."

For how much? Who makes them? What did they cost originally? Don't you know that those shoes are made in the Dominican Republic by underaged workers? Do you really want to support a system of business practices that doesn't conform to an ethical social agenda? Bailey would have welcomed any one of the questions that ordinarily would have made her turn tail and run, or any of the implied criticisms she would normally have resented and nursed to herself for weeks after. She half-yearned for the demands for rationalization of a lifestyle that Bailey—and hello, most ordinary people across the country—knew didn't require justification. That's exactly what she and her mom did best, right? Her mother's role was to find ways to imply that Bailey's Fendi accessories had single-handedly brought about the triumph of the mega-conglomerate at the expense of the lower and middles classes, and that her takeout dinner on the way home from work had decimated an unspoiled tribe of Brazilian natives.

And Bailey's role was to lie her head off and feign moral outrage to get the harangue to stop. No, that hadn't been a candy bar from that company in violation with the World Health Organization for its policies in Africa. They merely had similar wrappers! No, she wasn't wearing a skirt by the designer who'd made racially insensitive comments—she never wore that guy's stuff! Of course she'd never drink that wine, eat that fish, gobble down the fruit and produce that were the target of her mother's latest boycott! She'd thought it would get easier, once her mother moved back to Virginia five years before to be with her sisters, but every visit had concentrated the woman's suspicion until it burned white-hot, like the sun's rays through a magnifying glass. Yet today, not one retort passed her mother's lips. They remained closed, too leaden to form a reply.

Funny. As much as she hated those interrogations, she would have given anything for one of them now.

"Here's most of the tennis balls," she forced herself to say, as if the couple of minutes she'd spent scrabbling around in the patio grunge had been ten different kinds of enjoyment. "It's good, seeing how good you're doing. Isn't that goo—?" It was already too late to stop the word from coming out a third time. Her mother's gaze broke away from the shutter and lifted briefly to meet

her own, full of resentment. Bailey felt a moment's
panic. She sounded patronizing, didn't she? Her mom
would hate that more than anything. "You know," she
said, trying to change tack, "maybe I should get my
bags inside. It's almost sunset, I haven't had much of a
chance to settle in, there's a lot of crazy people hanging
around out front. . . ."

"I want to go to Carverton." The words were slower
than her mother's usual fast-paced delivery, but were
distinct and emphatic.

"What?" Bailey asked, surprised. Her mother's lips
began to work again, but before she had to force out the
words once more, she intervened. "No, I heard you. I
heard you. You want to go to Carverton. Now?" No, her
head was shaking. Not now. Some grudge had kept her
mother from returning to her hometown in Georgia for
years and years—not since Bailey had been a kid, before
they'd moved North. How long a trip was it, anyway?
An eight-hour drive? She'd already taken an entire
week off for this visit! Could her mother possibly be going crazy? "We can talk about it, maybe. Just give me a
minute to get my stuff inside and—are you comfortable?" A nod. "I'll be right back out. Okay?"

Not until Bailey was close to the door did she hear her
mother's next command. "Don't you dare . . . tell your
aunts." The last word was almost unrecognizable.

Inside, the old house smelled of dry rot and lemon
Pledge. In her haste to get away from the specter of in-
firmity, Bailey had utterly forgotten the bag she'd left
on the pathway on the other side of the door. She'd have
to go back out for it. But not yet. She needed another
moment to recover her composure, to get a grip on the
anxiety that threatened to drag tears from her eyes. She
was used to wanting to escape from her family's company after a few short minutes—they had a knack for
finding her every button and jabbing at them with
roasting forks—but this time she wanted to run away
not in anger, but fear.

She hated seeing her mother so helpless, so confined. She hated that the ghostly voices she heard were not of happy memories, but of the arguments she and her mother ought to be having, but couldn't. She hated having to dab away the tiny beads of moisture budding beneath her eyelids. Most of all, though, she despised having to step back outside with a false smile that her mother, facing away, would never see, but that Bailey hoped might shine in her voice. "I'm an idiot!" she announced brightly. "Forgot my bag. Remember how Grandmamma used to say she was so forgetful she'd leave her head behind in bed in the mornings? Must be genetic!"

Thump. The bounce of a tennis ball against the concrete, like a fading heartbeat, was her reply.

Chapter Five

What had lured her into the storefront had been the aroma of dark coffee beans, roasted and brewed. Almost-visible *Looney Tunes* tentacles of scent tickled Bailey's nose and led her inside. One foggy arm congratulated her with a pat on the back. "I didn't know Crestonville had a Starbucks!" She was in heaven.

The barista, a short girl with a ponytail crowning her head, grinned at Bailey's astonishment. "Welcome to Starbucks! We opened just today!" she said, exposing even rows of white teeth that sparkled in the summer morning sun. "What can I get for you?"

"I'll have a grande mocha-frappa-latteccino," she said, then slapped a hand over her mouth. "That came out wrong. I don't like sweet coffees." She giggled, then made herself stop. When had she become such a giddy morning person? She wanted her coffee black, like her usual waking mood. "I'll have an extra-tall frappa-mocha-nillaspresso."

The barista nodded. "Coming right up!"

"No, wait." She didn't want anything fancy. Just black coffee! Bailey waved her hands to get the barista's attention, but the ponytailed girl had already returned with a cup as big as Bailey's head. "That's not what I said. I mean, that's what I said, but it's not what I meant. I wanted. . . ."

"Welcome to Starbucks!" said the girl, suddenly appearing behind the cash register again. The enormous cup had vanished. "What can I get for you?"

Black coffee, Bailey thought to herself. Her mouth betrayed her again. "I'll have a whipped mocha-fr. . . ." Only when she looked down at her hands, which seemed to have turned into a seal's flippers, did she understand. "Oh. I'm in a dream, aren't I?" she asked the barista.

"Yeah, I'm real sorry about that, honey!" said the girl, pretending to feel Bailey's pain. Then she perked up. "But would you like extra whipped cream with your order?"

"Yeah, might as well," Bailey sighed, flopping down on one of the giant frogs doubling as stools. She was naked, too, she noticed. Typical! Even in her dreams, she couldn't get away from stupid clichés!

Bailey started between the sheets. Her head felt as if someone had conked her with a pillowcase full of wet cats, plus she couldn't get rid of the tantalizing scent of coffee that had been so vivid in her dream. What time was it? How long had she slept? Prying her eyes open actually *hurt*. Overnight a crust had formed over the slits, gluing them tightly together. "Oh, crap," she moaned, once she could see the ancient electric clock perched on the nightstand. It was after nine. Had she really slept for the better part of twelve hours? "Oh, crap," she repeated. What she wouldn't give for a swig of hot, black, honest-to-God—

"Coffee?" said a voice, young and spry. With one frightened, fluid motion, Bailey lurched back in her bed, clutching the covers to her chest. She was definitely wide awake now, no longer naked but clad in La Perla pajamas. In the tiny room, everything from the musty sheets to the curtains to the paint itself had an alien, lingering odor of staleness that not even the stiffest night breezes could banish. Only her pajamas . . . and the brew . . . smelled of home. "Oh, I'm sorry, honey! Did I wake you?"

The girl stood at the foot of the bed carrying a tray set with a china coffee pot, a mismatched cup, and a creamer. She seemed impossibly young—seventeen? eighteen?—and even more impossibly blond in an effortless way Virginia girls cultivated. With her feathered hair, thirty years ago she could have been a poster girl, pinned up on some teen boy's wall beside Farrah Fawcett. "I'm CeeCee?" she announced. "And your aunt sent me up with some coffee? Oh no! Don't fuss!" she exclaimed, when Bailey let loose the covers and began to reach for the tray. "You just woke up? I'll do everything, honey?"

The girl sat right down on the bed and, once she had adjusted the tray's legs, began to pour a stream of coffee into the cup. Hot, fragrant, gloriously dark coffee. Bailey wished she'd studied for the priesthood, solely for the purpose of blessing the girl. "You're a lifesaver," she croaked. Her throat was full of morning gunk.

"Aw, it's your aunt who did all the work?" chirped the girl, serene and sweet as a Stepford wife-in-training. Her composure at this early weekend hour was a little unnerving. And why did everything she said sound like a question? "I only brought it up?" Before Bailey could protest, she had picked up the creamer and poured a little of its contents into the cup. Damn the phlegm in her throat! She couldn't seem to get rid of it! "She's the sweetest thing ever, don't you think?" *Plop!* With the spoon, the girl ladled two cubes of sugar into the cup, and stirred. "Here you go, honey?"

Bailey sighed and accepted the tainted offering. All she had wanted was a cup of coffee. Black coffee. Strong black coffee. The girl raised her eyebrows in expectation. Was Bailey supposed to drink under supervision? Apparently so. She sipped tentatively, recoiling inwardly at the unfamiliar additions to her normal morning beverage. Still, it was hot, and after the girl left, she could pour it down the bathroom sink and see if there was enough left in the pot for a purer cup. "Mmmm!" She lifted the cup into the air. "Delicious." The coffee wasn't Starbucks by a long shot, but it was a damned sight better than she could brew.

The girl merely sat there, smiling. Her blue eyes darted around the room from time to time, resting on the objects that were Bailey's—the shoes on the floor, the expensive duffel, the cell phone on her bedside table. Mostly, though, she looked at Bailey, as if expecting something. It made Bailey uncomfortable. "Well," said Bailey, after a few moments of awkward silence. She placed the coffee cup on the nightstand. "I should probably, you know. Get up."

"Oh?" A second passed before the girl realized what Bailey meant to imply. "Oh! I'm so silly? Of course?" The mattress recoiled when CeeCee sprang to her feet. She dashed to the room's other side, occupied by another twin bed made up like Bailey's own. Once firmly planted on the crocheted rag rug, the girl paused, pivoted, and then turned around shyly. "Can I show you something?" she asked.

Anything, if it would hasten an exit. "Okay," Bailey said. "But I really have to. . . ."

Without warning, CeeCee burst into song. "*Three little maids from school are we!*" she announced, holding up three fingers on her right hand to drive home the number. "*Pert as a schoolgirl well can be! Filled to the brim with girlish glee! Three little maids from school!*" Stunned, Bailey could only blink. Although CeeCee had a pretty speaking voice, her singing sounded a bit like a small kitten who'd had its tail pinched in a door. Even Sidney, with her foghorn larynx and disdain for anything

musical, could sound more tuneful at the most drunken
work karaoke bash. And still the onslaught continued,
with CeeCee accompanying her impromptu performance with more hand shtick. *"One little maid is a bride,
Yum-Yum!"* she warbled, pretending to eat from some
kind of invisible spoon, then rubbing a circle over her
tummy. She leapt backward, and pretended to be the
next little maid. *"Two little maids in attendance come!"* She
jumped back to the rug's edge, teetering slightly on her
wedged heels. *"Three little maids is the total sum!"*
CeeCee pretended to be writing something—probably
a math equation—on an imaginary pad in her hand.
"Three little maaaaaaaa-hay-ds! From school!" CeeCee
smiled broadly. Then, with a Hoover's vigor, she
sucked in a deep breath.

With dismay, Bailey realized she was going to have to
sit through the rest of the song. Was it possible that this
was another dream? If she closed her eyes and wished
real hard, could she find herself back at the coffee shop,
buck naked? No, she couldn't be so lucky. She steeled a
slight smile on her face and waited and waited and
waited for the song to come to a conclusion.

Eventually it did, with a flourish of outstretched jazz
fingers that would have done Bob Fosse proud. CeeCee
stood there, legs akimbo in a near-split, beaming broadly
for her audience of one. She seemed to expect some kind
of reaction. "That," said Bailey, choosing her words carefully, "was absolutely amazing."

CeeCee bounded back up to a normal posture, and
tried to hide her smile of delight behind a clenched fist.
"Really?"

"I love Gilbert and Sullivan." A minor lie. The closest
she'd ever come to one of their operettas was a childhood brush with *The Pirate Movie.*

"Who?"

Oh, God. What in the world had prompted this unnecessary performance? Had her aunts told the girls

she was some kind of casting director, and this was their Lucy Ricardo way of breaking into show business? Should Bailey mention she was pretty sure that Yum-Yum was one of the maid's names, and not how she tasted? Or that the three girls came from a ladies seminary, and not a ladies *cemetery?* She decided not. "I have to get dressed," she hinted.

CeeCee was still overwhelmed from both her performance and Bailey's feedback. She bounced up and down on her wedges, her hair as light and fluffy as a television conditioner ad. "I'm so glad you liked it? I'm going to be working on it some more with your aunt?" The girl must have had one of those natural inflections that made every sentence sound interrogative. "And then I'll show it to you again?"

"The hell you will," Bailey growled, swinging her legs over the bed's side.

"What?"

Served her right for being so openly snarky, to be caught. "That'll be swell?"

The girl seemed to buy it. With gratitude in her eyes, she sprang forward and grabbed the tray from the bed. "Thank you!" she whispered, then vanished from the room before Bailey could protest. All she'd wanted was the coffee in that pot, damn it!

Fine. There had to be more where that came from. With a great deal of grumpiness, Bailey shoved her feet into her suede bed slippers and, nursing the cooling creamed coffee in her hands, padded out into the hallway and down the stairs.

The old house's floors protested every step, creaking and complaining like a rheumatic old woman in winter. When she kept her feet on a worn-down runner that had felt more like cement and less like fabric when she'd been a little girl, every step on the stairs still sounded like a gunshot. She paused for a moment, looking out the window into the back garden. Her mother sat outside again, a bag of tennis balls by her side. The sight was enough to make Bailey look instantly away; if she hadn't helped her mom to her room last night, she might have sworn her aunts had left her out overnight.

The floorboards creaked, startling her back into motion. Why was she trying to creep around with such stealth? She wasn't a burglar. She could walk as loudly as she pleased.

Her aunts' kitchen lay in the basement. In the early morning summer heat, it was the coolest room in the house, an array of long white tile countertops, cabinets from the 1940s with gingerbread carving, and fat cookie jars perched on the window sills. The kitchen was Aunt Bubble's sphere, a fussy and feminine domain where ferns spread their leaves toward the high windows, and surfaces gleamed from polishing, and that smelled of . . . thank God! . . . coffee. Atop the old stove, perched on one of its electric burners, sat a tall old percolator. Steam escaped from its spout—a siren song of caffeinated promise.

Who was she to resist? Bailey floated down the last of the back stairwell's steps and across the flagstones in the stove's direction, arms outstretched as if almost sleepwalking. A few moments more, and that sluggish, stunned feeling in the back of her head would be banished. She didn't care if it was Maxwell House and not a blend of more noble pedigree, so long as the bitter brew helped her forget the performance she'd been forced to witness. A few inches more. . . .

The back door swung open. "There she is?" Bailey whipped around, clutching the collar of her pajamas. Nothing was hanging out—she simply felt naked and exposed at the sound of CeeCee's lilt. She stage-whispered to another pretty girl no older than herself, who had short black hair, enormous brown eyes, and who nibbled nervously at her thumbnail, "She's real nice? Don't be shy?" CeeCee gave the girl a shove on the shoulder, addressing Bailey at the same time. "This is my friend Austyn? She's real glad to meet you?" In a contest of apologetic expressions, between Austyn and Bailey, the winner would probably have been a toss-up. Or maybe, thought Bailey, her own expression could simply be described as *pained*. Another shove, followed by another stage whisper. "*Go on!*"

Austyn giggled slightly and then, probably mortified, immediately fixed her gaze on the flagstone floor. Her fingers suddenly dipped into her mouth, withdrawing a scarlet hard candy the size of a walnut. "I'm too shy," she said in the slightest of whispers, and then immediately popped the candy back in.

"You can't be shy up on the stage next week?" CeeCee pushed the girl forward again. "Just *do* it?"

Again, the girl reached into her mouth and withdrew the gobstopper, then cleared what sounded like a quart of phlegm. "Mem'ries," she began, then stopped. "Sorry. I'm starting over." She clutched at her throat, then cleared it again. "Mem'ries, light the corner of my mind," she sang. Or attempted to sing. From three feet away, the girl sounded as if she were whispering the lyrics from the bottom of a well. "Misty water-co . . . dang. Sorry." The girl crossed her eyes and briefly stuck out a tongue as red as her candy, then took several calming deep breaths. Maybe, thought Bailey, if she simply froze in place, she'd fade into the surroundings like a chameleon. "Mem'ries," the girl started again, wheezing out air like a dying accordion.

"CeeCee Jackson, why are you bothering Miz Oates' and Miz Whigfield's niece?" It was the pixie they called Larkin, from yesterday, bounding in through the outside door. The alligator of her Izod shirt looked as if it was mountaineering up her enormous breasts. "Now, you know they said to let the poor girl sleep!"

"Miss Whigfield told me to take coffee to her!"

CeeCee told the older girl, who tossed her long hair in reply. What was in the water down here that made the natives produce so many blondes?

"Pardon me. *Move*." Scolding CeeCee had been an excuse for barging into the kitchen. Austyn melted to the side and returned her candy to her mouth when Larkin pushed her way past. "Well hey!" she said brightly, smiling to expose a row of straight, even teeth. "Miz Whigfield's told me so much about you. Bailey Rhodes, isn't it? I'm Larkin Merino. Oh, your pants suit is beautiful! Can I?" Before Bailey could protest, Larkin had already reached out and rubbed her sleeve between two fingers. "That's real classy," she announced to the others. "Real classy. Wouldn't I look good in something like this in the interview portion?"

"They're pajamas." Bailey felt a bit as if she were telling a child that there was no Santa, but Larkin only looked her up and down with more interest. Who were these people, and why were they hanging around her aunts' house as if it were a home for bouncy blond wayward girls? It was tiring. Had her aunts told them she had show business connections? Because if they seriously entertained notions that she needed someone who could warble "The Way We Were" for the Expedition Network's earnest ecology-friendly programming, she was going to have to disabuse them of the notion. "Nice to meet you, Larkin, and I don't mean any offense, but are you going to sing at me? Because if you are, can you get it over with quickly? I really, really need a goddamned—" She looked over at CeeCee, who stared at her with big eyes as she leaned against the counter, and reworded her sentence. "I need another cup of coffee."

Larkin's lashes flew apart. "Why no, honey, I'm not going to sing! The idea!" Okay, so maybe Bailey wasn't the only sane person in the household. The exquisite expression into which Larkin curved her brows almost implied a concern for Bailey's mental health. Then she put her hands on her ample hips and pouted. "Girls, I'm ashamed of you both! Have you been bugging Miz Rhodes?" Austyn averted her gaze and sucked both on two fingers and her candy, simultaneously. CeeCee, on the other hand, feigned ignorance. "Bailey—can I call you Bailey?—you're a guest! You shouldn't be listening to all kinds of nonsense so early in the morning! You go on and get yourself some coffee, honey! Miz Oates made it fresh for you! Go on! Go on now!"

Larkin Merino, Bailey decided, was her new best friend. Sure, it was obscene how unnaturally spry she was on a weekend morning, but she alone seemed sympathetic to her morning plight. "Why, thank you!" she said, feeling warm toward the girl. "I'll do that!"

Everyone was all smiles as Bailey threw back her shoulders, turned, poured the cold contents of her cup in the sink, and took a step in the stove's direction. Then, like the keening of an Irish banshee, from behind her came a shrill cry of despair. "*Ayyyyyyyyyy!*" Up and down an octave of anguish it went, ending in a dramatic sigh. Bailey froze, microscopic hairs rising on the back of her neck. "Ay, me!" groaned Larkin in a guttural alto. "O! Romeo! Romeo! Wherefore art thou . . . Romeo?"

"Oh no." When Bailey turned, her coffee cup still sadly empty, Larkin had pulled out a lacy handkerchief from some pocket or crevice and had thrown it over her head, to evoke a virginal Veronese star-crossed lover. "Please, I . . ."

"Deny thy father!" Larkin commanded, pointing directly at Bailey, madness in her eyes. She stomped, then closed her lids tightly. "And refuse thy name! Or! If thou wilt not! Be but sworn my love, and—" Larkin struck the countertop with her hand, rattling a plate and causing her three spectators to start—"I'll no longer . . . be a Capulet!"

After a long pause, one of Larkin's eyelids snapped open. "Um," Bailey managed to muster. Was she supposed to give feedback? If a radical Manhattan off-Broadway director had completely reconceived Juliet as a bossy high school senior throwing a temper tantrum to convince her dad to take her to the mall for new school clothes, Larkin might have been perfect for the part. Fortunately, she didn't know of any directors with such a vision.

Thankfully, the kitchen door let in a small group of girls led by Bits. "Larkin Merino." She spat the name as if it were a curse. "I could hear your Juliet from halfway down the drive where, you *may* recall, we happened to be engaging in the exercise entitled Poise and Posture when you oh-so-conveniently claimed you had to excuse yourself for an emergency relating to your bladder. Unless I am gravely mistaken, this is not the little girl's room. Of course, if you *want* Shirley Jones's contestants to mop the stage with you, that's an entirely different matter." From behind her, a few more girls giggled. A few carried old volumes of the *Encyclopedia Britannica*, presumably for Posture.

Larkin heaved a sigh laden with more meaning than the ones with which she'd peppered her Shakespearean performance. "Odds bodkins, Miz Oates!"

"I'll odds bodkins your rear end, girl. I've never seen such a shameful display in my life!"

"Oh, don't be too harsh on our Larkin. I do love her Juliet!" Aunt Bubble had crowded in behind the book-carrying girls and edged her way into the kitchen. "So talented!"

"Talented at mischief!" Bailey had never seen her aunt in action during her years as an elementary school teacher, but she was getting a general idea of her classroom style. "Now, back outside, all of you! My niece is here for a nice family visit, not to listen to your assorted nonsense." Bits crossed her arms over the front of her dark blue patterned smock, which hung over a lime green pair of pants, a twin of which Bailey could have sworn she'd seen worn by Endora on a Nick at Nite *Bewitched* rerun. "Shoo! Go on!" She pushed up her glasses onto the bridge of her nose and sniffed, as if the passing girls offended her sense of smell. "Ashamed, that's what I am. Bubble, get the girl some coffee. What kind of a hostess are you, with your own poor niece standing there clutching an empty cup like a pauper from some Dickensian novel?"

"Are you actually being nice to me? Your version of nice, anyway?" Bailey wanted to know, when Larkin had slinked out through the back door and up the stone steps behind the rest of the girls. Aunt Bits's glance immediately sidled away, confirming Bailey's worst suspicions. "You're up to something."

"Nonsense."

"You," said Bailey, allowing a fluttering Bubble to pry the cup from her hand, "are not a good liar. Now, I want to know what's going on with all these girls. No, none of this we'll-tell-you-later business. I want to know now, before some teenager jumps out of my closet and sings me highlights from *Oliver!* and scares me into a stroke of my own."

"What a way to talk, with your mother . . . !" muttered Bits, clearly rattled at Bailey's candor. She choked off the thought in midsentence, when Bailey crossed her arms and cocked her head, not about to give in. "You are so much like her. It's amazing."

"I'll consider that a compliment. Spill."

"My girls—" Bits made a movement as if to escape.

"—can wait. From what I've seen, their posture is fine."

"Not good enough for. . . ." One of Bits's hands flew to her mouth. She'd let something slip, and Bailey intended to find out what it was. She raised an eyebrow. "Fine. For the pageant. For the sixty-fourth annual Miss Tidewater Butter Bean pageant. Now you know everything. Happy?"

At the stove, Aunt Bubble let the coffee pot fall with a

clatter. "We're pageant coaches, dear. We've been doing it for several years, now."

One corner of Bits's mouth had risen in a snarl that quickly vanished when Bailey turned back around. "It's nothing to you, I'm sure."

A beauty pageant made sense—the songs, the dramatics, the Poise and Posture, the house overrun with pretty girls. "Pageant coaches?" she asked. "You two?"

"Your mother might not have informed you girls, but I studied dance in my youth. Bubble was a hairdresser for five years. All three Whigfield girls got high marks in charm school." Bits's chin, held high from pride, quivered while she spoke. "We're naturals for the job. Before we came along, Shirley Jones was the only coach in town. And our girls are nearly as good as Shirley Jones's girls, I must say."

"Shirley Jones?" Bailey was utterly bewildered by the celebrity mention. "Come on, get happy?" At least Bits was looking as puzzled as she. "The *Partridge Family* mom?"

"I don't know what you're talking about, girl. Shirley Jones has been a pageant coach here for a decade. Passable, but there's no charm school training there." Bits looked smug at the thought.

"I did so love Miss Ada's School of Charm," said Bubble, moving closer. "That was in the days when your grandmother could afford such things, Bailey. I never was able to matriculate."

Her mother had attended charm school? Her *mother*, she of the frank tongue? Bailey refused to let herself get sidetracked. "If those girls think that because of my job I have any connections that might to help them get into show business. . . ."

"Don't be absurd."

"Not at all, dear," added Bubble.

Bailey scarcely noticed when her plump aunt pressed the coffee cup back into her hands. "If you've told these girls anything implying I'm helping you with your soybean festival. . . ."

"Miss Tidewater Butter Bean," corrected Bubble in a helpful tone.

"And that was the *furthest* thing from my mind, I'll have you know," said Bits, trembling with some unknown emotion. Knowing her, it was probably upset at being caught out. "In fact, if you offered your help, I'd refuse it."

"*A-ha!* Reverse psychology! It's not going to work. I'm not getting involved!"

Bits crossed her arms. "Honestly, Bailey Rhodes. Listen to yourself. Such a suspicious mind I've never known. Are we the kind of family who has to resort to deceit and trickery? Wipe that look off your face, girl. We are not." Bailey attempted to look chastened, but inside she felt convinced she was right. Why else would she be subjected to the endless talent show? Okay, the girls might have come up with the idea to perform on their own, but only because her aunts had said something to give them the impression that she mattered. "I'm not convinced that even if we needed your coaching assistance, you'd have much to contribute in the areas of carriage, deportment, or elocution." It only took one of Bits's scathing glances to prompt Bailey to straighten up from her slouching position against the counter. "So thank you very much for your offer of assistance, but I must refuse. Come, Bubble. Time is a-wasting."

Like the first Queen Elizabeth sweeping through a crowded London street, Bits grabbed the hem of her smock, turned, and with a swivel of the neck surely learned at Miss Ada's School of Charm, swept from the room. If there had been prostrate courtiers at hand, she would have walked right over them.

Miss Tidewater Butter Bean. Ridiculous. As if anyone cared. "I'm still not going to help!" Bailey called through the back door, before it closed in her face. There was no reply.

She looked down at the coffee she'd been neglecting. Aunt Bubble had creamed and sugared the brew until it was pale and syrupy.

Chapter Six

One of these days, Bailey was going to have a word with the guy who invented the cell phone—and it had to be a guy, because if a woman had invented the damned thing, the prototype would never have left the laboratory until it could hold a signal for more than fifteen seconds. Chandra's voice chirped from the other end, cutting in and out so many times that she sounded like the audio equivalent of a strobe light. ". . . frustrating to . . . I try to . . . hello? Are you th . . . ?"

"Hang on," Bailey yelled into the end of the electronic candy bar. "I'm nearly at the top of this hill, so the signal . . . Chandra?" In her ear, she heard the tripletone of doom, indicating she'd walked too far out of range: *boop-boop-boop*. "Oh no, you didn't." In all three hundred and sixty degrees she swung around with the phone held out, and for good measure, she revolved up and down on every axis to coax back one little bar on her reception.

This whole thing was ridiculous. Three little pixels were all that stood between a good working communication with her office and radio silence. Things happened on Mondays, in the business world. Bad things, usually. Deliveries of new contracts, mandates from the network executives, complaints from on-air talent through their agents. All sorts of complications that had accumulated over the weekend waited on her desk Monday mornings, most of them ticking away like time bombs on their last *Mission: Impossible* countdowns. Chandra was the operative who could snip the little green wire that would defuse the explosives, yet only with Bailey's expert—if remote—assistance.

A vine snaked out and clawed at her leg, its tendrils leaving a sharp scratch across her shin. The primary problem with Virginia, she considered, was the lush flora. In Manhattan, plants tended to grow in neat, contained spaces. In pots, for example, or tidy little parks, or courtyards, or little rows of trees up and down Madison Avenue where the earth in which they grew had been neatened and covered by grates. Even in Central Park, the vast expanses of green tended to be clipped and snipped and landscaped and controlled. Virginia was different. Hadn't the colonials considered it a tropical zone? The greenery here seemed to be in some kind of conspiracy with the man-eating plant of *Little Shop of Horrors* to take over the countryside, inch by inch. What was that blanket of green called, that had completely overtaken an old barn across Cedar Pass Road? Kudzu, wasn't it? The building looked like some kind of leafy behemoth with an open mouth, ready to gulp down unwary passers-by. "Crap," she exclaimed, jumping into the air. It hadn't been a curse. She'd nearly stepped in a pile of the stuff. Judging by the oatlike smell, probably a horse's.

Without warning, a cicada issued a steady buzz from a bush by the side of the road. She was easily a quarter of a mile from the driveway of her aunts' house by now, chasing the elusive signal, and the insect's sudden loud complaint broke her concentration on her phone's liquid crystal display. How in the world could one bug make so much damned noise? She'd heard the droning noise all the night before, during a second restless night in which the endless, tireless buzz seemed to invade her every dream, creating the illusion she was getting less sleep than she really was. She didn't need to hear it up close and pers—

Wait. One bar of signal goodness flashed, then disappeared. Then it was back again, taunting her. "Don't go," she muttered to it, half-pleading, half-demanding. As if in response, the tiny bar flickered, then returned. "It's okay." She felt as if she was murmuring encouragements to a shy groundhog on the second of February. "No, don't go!" When she stepped from the grass onto a road of dirt and gravel, she fumbled the phone. The bar flickered and disappeared as she tried not to drop the delicate bundle of electronics; it landed in her cupped palms, face up. The single bar had returned, steadily perched at the top of her display. And for a fraction of a second, a second bar, twice the height of the first, had joined it.

Bailey froze, afraid to move. She'd not had anything more than a single signal indicator for nearly forty-eight hours. Two was almost too much to hope for! She couldn't stay in this crouched-over, supplicating position forever, though. Her shoulders already ached, and moisture from her brow was running behind her ear and trickling down her neck. It was too hot for this nonsense. Her shoulder twitched; the second bar vanished at the motion, then returned. She swooped, determined to catch it.

It was a bit like chasing a butterfly. Without being able to predict in which direction the fluttering signal might fly, she took rapid steps down the road and onto the grass, back onto a lane of gravel, and finally, some fifty feet later, to a broad tree stump of some age, judging by the weather-worn smoothness of its surface. Save for making certain in her peripheral vision that she wasn't stepping in something vile that would ruin her workout shoes, she didn't dare take her eyes away from the phone. When the evasive double bar flickered into life above her head and didn't vanish, she nearly crowed with triumph. A short leap onto the stump was all she had to do to capture it for good. She pushed a button, and waited.

Had heavenly angels suddenly appeared in the clouds above, singing a celestial chorus, its sound would not have been half as sweet at that moment as the extension ringing at the line's other end. "Expedition Network, Bailey Rhodes' office, Chandra Ellis speaking, may I help you?"

"Chandra!" exclaimed Bailey. She was so happy at the sound of her assistant's voice that she jumped up and down atop the stump, only abstractedly noticing what a good view she had from the height.

"I can actually hear you!" Considering the sheer number of botched, interrupted, and plain unintelligible attempts she'd made at talking to Chandra that morning, none of which had lasted this long, no wonder the girl sounded thrilled.

"Don't talk," she said before the girl could go any further. "Just listen. On my desk there's an envelope marked *Rito* that contains all the contracts for the . . ."

"Bailey?"

"Listen." Who knew when the signal would suddenly die again? "All the documents for the Marcellus Rito celebrity chef cook-off show are in that folder, and you need to take them down to . . ."

"Bailey? I already took them down to legal." Chandra's half-apology was enough to bring Bailey up short. "And I had Franklin look at the agenda for Rito while I was at it, since I knew you'd given it the final okay. I hope you don't mind?"

"No, not at all." That had been next on her list of quick points for discussion, in fact. "I would like you to. . . ."

"And oh, and I *really* hope I didn't do the wrong thing, but I guess you were in a hurry when you left the office the other day, because you left a file on your chair with a list of potential hosts for that new series, the one about TV news bloopers and practical jokes? I saw it and because, you know, it's been so hard to get hold of you this morning, I thought to myself, 'What would Bailey do?' "

While Chandra had been talking, a tawny-colored Labrador had wandered around to the stump. Bailey eyed it, wary. She had nothing against dogs, but she preferred this one keep all four of its muddy paws firmly on the ground. "I hope you . . ."

"So I e-mailed the talent's agents and asked for preliminary salary requirements. I took the language from one of your boilerplates because they're so well-done. Was that right? If I guessed right, it was because you're *really* so good about training."

Secretly, Bailey was glad that her friend Sidney was far, far away. Chandra certainly had a talent for mingling smarm with self-promotion. "Yes," she said, looking down at the dog. "That's exactly right."

"I knew it!" The dog chose that moment to open its mouth, regard her sideways, and bark. Its tail wagged tentatively, and then it let loose with a follow-up call for attention. "I know you probably would've done it much better than me, but I kept thinking, what if this stuff *sits* here and what if Bailey *forgot* about it . . . though I know you didn't!"

By now, the Labrador had taken up barking with the vigor of an amateur who wanted to practice up, now that he'd learned his favorite pastime had been reclassified as an Olympic event. Bailey could scarcely hear her own thinking over the ruckus, much less her assistant's reassurances. She stuck the tip of a finger in her ear, turned slightly away from the barking pooch, and interrupted. "No, that's fine. That's fine. Could you—listen, Chandra." She felt like she was shouting. "About Jessica Munford. Her lawyers have *promised* me that they'd get back a signed contract before shooting starts on Wednesday. It's *very important* that . . ."

"That's what I told her lawyers when we talked an hour ago," said Chandra. Bailey felt an unpleasant sensation in the pit of her stomach at the news. Her assistant was supposed to have kept away from the Munford and her lawyers! "They wanted to talk to you directly, of course, but with the problems you've been having with reception out there I didn't want them to get all, you know, ticked off at us, so I told them what you would have said yourself if you'd been here."

Of course. Chandra would have a logical explanation for having worked around the one proscription that Bailey had left with her. It made perfect sense; it was what she herself would have done in the same situation. "Okay, fine. Tell them. . . ." Was this dog rabid, or what? Was she on the estate of the Baskervilles' American cousins? "What is your *problem?*" she yelled back at it.

"Excuse me?"

"No, not you, Chandra. Tell them that my reception problem is going to be solved very very soon, even if I have to hire my own personal satellite to . . ." Apparently the dog wasn't satisfied with howling at her from a distance; it stood up in the air on its hind legs, then landed with its front paws onto the stump's edge. "Stop that!"

Chandra's voice cut in and out. "Sorry! I . . . notes!" Bailey's instinctive jerks away from the dog's lunges caused her signal to deteriorate.

"Not you! It's this dog!" What kind of crazy fools let their dogs run around out in the open, anyway, yowling at the tops of their canine lungs like they were some kind of wild animal? Maybe she'd been exposed to mannered, well-bred city dogs for too long. "It's trying to slobber all over me!"

"You're break . . . up."

That was it. She couldn't wrench her body around like a Martha Graham dancer any longer. The display showed that she was down to a single bar of strength again, so she stood very still. "Listen, Chandra, it's very important to. . . ." Tail still wagging, the dog lunged forward, snarling. Bailey fended it off with a foot. "Go *away!*"

"You're not kicking my dog, I hope?" asked a voice behind her. Its unexpected appearance startled her far more than the dog itself ever could. She not only lost her balance, but the phone dropped from her hand and bounced off her hip. Only at the last possible millisecond did she catch it before it flew off for good.

She looked at the screen. NO SIGNAL, it said, most unhelpfully. She let loose with three choice curse words.

The man behind her chuckled. "I don't think your aunts would appreciate that kind of language, Ms. Rhodes."

"My aunts invented that language back in the Dark Ages. And no, I'm not kicking your dog, Mr. Montgomery," she said, turning around. Her aunts' neighbor stood before her, wearing a UVA T-shirt with the sleeves rolled up over his biceps and painter's pants—the latter obviously not as any fashion statement, but for painting. An actual brush rested in one of the fabric loops. She'd recognized the voice immediately—it had been the first masculine intonation she'd heard in three days. "Your crazed dog, however, has ruined the one phone call I've been able to place to my office in New York since I got here. Can you call him off, for the love of God?" she pleaded. At the man's appearance, the dog had begun wagging its tail madly, but still circled the stump and yapped out a hoarse warning, as if trying to alert its owner that he'd rounded up the goods.

"You can call me Taylor, you know." He didn't make a move, merely standing there with his arms, freckled with white paint, crossed over his chest. He worked out, obviously. Or else farmwork kept him in damned fine shape.

She averted her eyes from his physique. "Can you . . . ?"

Before she could make the request, the man had stuck two fingers in his mouth and let out a shrill whistle between them. "C'mon, Kitten. Here, girl."

"Kitten?" In utter disbelief, she watched the creamy-colored dog gambol over to her owner, where the hound threw herself at Taylor's feet and rolled around in the tall grass, snarling with content. "You named your dog Kitten? *Caligula* was too hard to pronounce, maybe? *Killer* didn't have enough panache?"

"Aw, she's no killer." Taylor squatted down to rub the dog's belly, while Kitten squirmed back and forth. "She thought you were a trespasser, is all." Oops. Bailey was on his property, wasn't she? She'd been in such a hurry to capture the signal a few minutes before that she hadn't considered where she was roaming. Before Bailey could work up any decent amount of guilt, though, Taylor said, "She'll know better next time."

"Next time?" It seemed as good a moment as any to step from the stump. Bailey felt awkward up there, anyway, as if she were the featured performer in some kind of stage play. To her surprise, Taylor sprang forward the moment she moved a muscle, and extended a hand to help her down. She didn't dare turn it down, but the moment she had both feet on the ground, she yanked back her own fingers. His skin rasped over hers like sandpaper; she could almost feel every individual ridge of his palm print.

"I don't suppose it's worth asking what you were doing on a stump in the middle of my property?"

His inquiry had been polite, but two words in particularly never boded well. They were possessive: *my property*. As in, *Get off my property*. Without intending it, she felt instantly on the defense. "I didn't mean—that is, I was trying to—okay," she said, deciding to level with him. "This is a cell phone."

"I know what a cell phone is, thank you." Was that a smirk on his face? Or had she inadvertently offended him? He crossed his arms. Even Kitten had given up rolling around like a crazy dog and sat by her master with her wet, pink tongue hanging from her mouth, staring at Bailey.

Their twin scrutiny made her more self-conscious. "Fine. Okay. I work in New York City for . . ."

"I know what you do at the Expedition Network, Ms. Rhodes." He laughed at her slack-jawed expression of surprise. "You ladies talk an awful lot on those trips to and from Richmond, you know. I might not join in, but I've got ears."

"Oh," she said, feeling deflated. What was left to say? "I guess the long and short of it is that your stump's the only place I could get a signal."

"You could get a better signal in town." Bailey's hopes swelled—she hadn't thought about venturing into Crestonville. Then they ebbed at the realization that she didn't have transportation, and that it was a long way to walk on a summer morning when the temperature had already soared into the mid-eighties. Would it be too forward to . . . ? She took a quick glance at Taylor, who stood his ground with the implacable calm of an ocean-side boulder. "It's only three miles there," he said, nodding his head as if he'd found the plan ideal. "And three miles back, of course."

"Oh," she said again. That was obviously her cue to leave. She decided to attempt as graceful an exit as possible. "It was nice meeting you, Kitten!" she said, putting her hands on her knees and talking to the dog in as near a baby-talk voice as she felt was dignified. The Labrador's tail stopped wagging. One corner of its upper lip curled in a snarl, and Kitten let out a low growl. "Okay then!" she said, abandoning the cutesy approach. "I'm sorry to have bothered you, and don't worry, I won't trespass on your . . ." Taylor's head had cocked. One of his eyebrows actually elevated an inch higher than the other. "Property?"

"Ms. Rhodes," he said, shaking his head. "I was funning you. Come on. I'll drive you into town." Taylor patted his thigh and whistled for Kitten to follow as he turned and ambled down the broad, dusty driveway.

"Seriously?" Bailey gingerly picked her way across the grass, spirits rising again. "You don't have to. I don't want to be an imposition. And please. It's Bailey."

He shrugged and said over his shoulder, "You need to do your business. I need paint and company. Seems like we could do each other some good. Meet you at the truck." And without a word more, he jogged ahead to the farmhouse that sat at the drive's end, Kitten trailing behind with the simple joy of a dog following her pack leader. With its vinyl siding, its modern, double-glazed windows, and its practical garage instead of a hulking carriage house, Taylor's home couldn't have been a further cry from the aunts' home. It even had its own updated roof adornment of a personal satellite dish, instead of an old iron weathervane. She had a vague memory of the house as a run-down old shingled cottage back when she was a kid; Taylor must have done pretty extensive work after he'd taken over. Surrounded by row upon row of neatly spaced crops, the sight of that bright, cheery siding made her feel slightly homesick after a weekend immured in the brick crypt belonging to her family. "Be right there," he called from inside the house.

"No rush," she told him. Now that she was close enough, she couldn't resist peeking through the screened window to his front room. She'd expected to find bachelor squalor, but instead his living area was neatly, if inexpensively, furnished with boxy furniture upholstered with fabric in a muted pattern, arranged around an imitation Persian carpet. A modest TV sat where she'd expected an oversized, perfect-for-ESPN monster of a set. On the room's built-in bookshelves sat some decorative mugs and a few pretty geodes, but mostly rows of books. That surprised her. She didn't think many farmers went in for reading. A hallway lay to the right of the window. She attempted to crane her head and see what might lie down it.

"Get a good look?" Startled, she whirled around to find Taylor at her side, wearing an amiable smile. He really was quite a tall man, she noticed. She'd never gotten a full sense of his height from sitting next to him in the truck.

Heart still pounding, she tried to appear more innocent than she felt. "I'd kind of forgotten what real furniture looked like," she told him. "I didn't mean to be nosy."

Luckily he didn't seem offended. "Your aunts don't have real furniture?" He moved to the truck, obviously expecting her to follow.

He swung first by the truck's passenger side and popped open the door, holding it open and waiting. Bailey was a bit surprised at the unexpected courtesy. "It's real. Real *old*." She climbed in.

"Antiques?" he called through the open window, after the door shut behind her.

"Yes, they are. So's the furniture." For a minute she thought the joke had flown right over the farmer's head, but when Taylor pulled open his own door and slid onto the seat across from her, he wore a grin. "This really is nice of you. I wish I had some way to repay . . ."

"Don't sweat it."

When Taylor backed the truck into a perfect three-point turn and headed down the driveway, Bailey couldn't help but envy his ease behind the wheel. She'd ridden in buses and cars all her life, but she couldn't contemplate actually driving one with the same confidence and effortlessness. Under his direction, the truck seemed less a three-thousand pound missile of certain death and more an extension of his body, muscled, gleaming, and seamless in its movement. And boy, was he muscled—from the thick brawn of his forearm to the

rounded steel of his biceps and to the chest they surrounded. Even his thick fingers wrapped around the
padded steering wheel as if gripping the handle of a
hammer. She cleared her throat. She'd already been
caught peeking into his living room. She didn't need to
be caught staring at his triceps. "It's very nice of you,
that's all."

"Okay," he said, pulling out onto Cedar Pass Road, "I
know how you can make it up to me." When he took his
eyes from the road for a moment to look over, mischief
played over his face.

"How?" she had to ask, though already in her head
she was making up excuses to get out of whatever he was
going to propose. If he wanted a date . . . well, she already had a boyfriend, and he would have to understand
that though Steve was several hundred miles away, she
wasn't going to allow herself to get out of control.

"Oh, you're not going to go along with it."

Lord, he actually was going to ask her for a date, or a
kiss, or something she wasn't prepared to give. His
prediction might be right. "Try me." Was her tone too
invitational?

"I've got to know something." He hesitated before
asking. "Your one aunt's name isn't really Bubble, is it?"

Oh. She'd honestly thought he was leading up to
some kind of exchange of fleshly favors. It briefly occurred to Bailey that maybe the unworthy thought said
more about her state of mind than his. She laughed at
her own stupidity. "No, not at all." Apparently that
wasn't answer enough; he looked over at her with his
dark eyebrows raised in twin arches. "It's Myrtle." She'd
had to dredge the name out of a cobweb-draped corner
of her brain. That particular moment might have been
the first time in several years she'd actually said it aloud.

"Myrtle? So why Bubble?" he asked. "Come on.
There's got to be a story. If there's one thing I know, it's
that every family's got stories."

On every trip she'd grown to accept Taylor as a silent,

almost invisible presence. Speaking to him felt a bit like a novelty. "Well, when I was a kid, I asked my mom why my grandma had named one of her girls Bubble. I thought it was kind of a cute name, like Joy or . . . I don't know. Giggle."

"No one's named Giggle. Maybe in New York, but not down here."

"Not in New York, either. But you know what I mean! It was different. I went through this phase when I was in grade school where I thought I had a stupid name." Inwardly she was surprised that the confession came tripping off her tongue. She didn't think she'd ever admitted the old shame aloud. "*Bailey*. I thought it sounded like someone scooping water out of the bottom of a boat. Or you know, someone paying to get someone out of jail. I wanted a different name entirely."

He laughed. Well, it was stupid. "What'd your mom name you after, then? *WKRP in Cincinnati?* Or is it a family name?"

"No, she named me after some anti-war crusader of the sixties." When Taylor looked at her in disbelief, Bailey nodded and rolled her eyes. "It's true. That's Mom." She cleared her throat, uncomfortable at having turned the conversation to herself. "Anyway. So I asked my mom about it when she was doing something for one of her organizations—stuffing envelopes or something—and she got very serious and sat me down and said, 'Honey, we call Myrtle that because she's spent most of her life walking around in a bubble.' There was some story about how she was jilted at the altar or something, and how she'd never been the same after, but I was too young to understand. After Mom told me that, I was all excited."

The truck was now making good speed down the route that led to town. On either side, broad expanses of low-growing greenery whizzed by, their shiny leaves gleaming as if a sickle of sun was being swept across the fields, row after row. "Excited? That sounds terrible."

Bailey couldn't help but laugh at the confession she
was about to make. "Yeah, well, it was right before one
of our trips to Georgia—where the aunts lived and
where my mom grew up, and where we used to go a lot
before my grandma died—and I was excited because,
well . . ." She sighed, knowing she was about to sound
nine kinds of idiotic. "To cut a long story short, I spent
the first two days of that vacation hiding under tables
and behind furniture, spying on my aunt. Finally my
mom caught me peeking through the bathroom door at
her."

Taylor shook his head. "Why?"

With embarrassment, Bailey covered her eyes. "I
hoped my aunt might be kind of like Glinda the Good. I
wanted to see her walk around in a magic bubble." The
truck swerved suddenly as its driver let out a hyena-like
cackle. It had been years since Bailey had made anyone
hoot so loudly and with such relish—Steve tended to express his amusement through gentle whuffs that barely
moved his nostrils. Taylor made her comfortable enough
to crack a grin. "I know. *So* stupid. But I was six or seven!"

"Oh, lord!" whooped Taylor. The truck thrummed
when he pounded his free foot on the floor. "That is the
funniest damned thing I've heard in weeks! What?" he
added, looking at her. "Something wrong? Did I make
an ass of myself?"

"No! Not at all," she hastened to say. She enjoyed his
gratification almost as much as he, and grinned in response. "I think that's the first time I've ever made
someone laugh so much!"

"You're kidding, right?" Taylor turned the truck onto
a broader avenue populated more by roadside estab-
lishments than farmland, though beyond the tiny
buildings still lay acres of growing crops. Almost all the
old gas stations and tiny stores boasted Pepsi signs that
had to be forty years old or more, and one old shack
had been abandoned with an ancient-looking ice chest

still sitting by its boarded-up entrance. The chest's doors had long been removed, and weeds grew from inside its depths. Save for the modern SUVs and trucks parked in front of the open businesses, this old stretch of road could have been straight out of some 1960s film about a sleepy pocket of the South. "I thought you were some big-time actress back in New York before you went into television."

What in the world had the aunts been telling people about her? "No!" she said, horrified. "Not in the least. I was a very small-time actor whose few parts were in occasional off-off-off-Broadway plays set against black backdrops where everyone stood very still and made long speeches in monotones. Mostly what I did, though, was take classes. That's what actors do. Take classes. Even in improv, I never made anyone laugh like that. Improv is like, when comedians get on stage and. . . ."

"I kinda know what improv is," he interrupted. "Thanks, though."

"Sorry," she said, feeling vaguely uncomfortable. The last thing she wanted to sound like was the big know-it-all who assumed anyone outside of Manhattan was little more than a country bumpkin. "Anyway."

He didn't seem to hold any grudge, though. "But no," he said. "You got a way. Hey, you get a signal yet?"

She had a way? The compliment secretly pleased her. In fact, it tickled her so much that she was happy to have an excuse not to respond immediately, for fear of gushing. She dug the cell phone from her pocket, wiped away from its face some of the residue left by her moisturizer, and checked. "Three bars!" she said, feeling pleased.

"Yeah, it should be pretty steady by the time we get into town," he told her. "I get crappy reception out at the farm, too, sometimes. It's pretty flat out here, but there's still enough ups and downs for a signal to get lost in." Though she was tempted to call her office right there and then, while she still could, instead Bailey tucked away the phone. She didn't want to seem rude. "How come you didn't use your aunts' land line?"

"The idea had occurred to me," she said, voice dry. "Except that they've put some kind of block on long-distance carriers, so that if you want to make a call, you need a calling card, and I don't have a calling card because . . ."

"You have a cell phone," he concluded with her. "Well, it won't be long. I usually come in to town in the mornings for breakfast, if you ever . . ."

He let the offer trail off. "Thanks," she told him, grateful. "I might be taking you up on that." It sure beat walking into town, anyway, and Taylor Montgomery wasn't the worst company to have, by any means. He surely had a nice smile, too.

For a moment more they were silent, until Bailey heard a huff beside her. Then another, followed by a third. Taylor's shoulders heaved into the air and he let out a bark of laughter. When he turned his head and caught her uplifted eyebrows, he drew his lips back and exposed his teeth in a broad grin. "Walking around in a bubble," he explained, breaking out into another guffaw.

At least he had the decency to look sheepish.

Chapter Seven

The town was very much the same as the last time Bailey had visited—what? Five years ago? Sometime since then, the town had cleaned up its deserted old storefronts and reinvigorated itself, like Aunt Bubble changing from one of her ancient housecoats into her Sunday best when she expected visitors. The old J.C. Penney's, deserted before Bailey's childhood, had been renovated and subdivided into a number of cute little stores and restaurants. A friendly looking bookstore occupied the spot where once had skulked a gloomy old pharmacy. Planters full of summer flowers had been interspersed between newly planted linden trees. There weren't any Starbucks in sight yet, but everywhere Bailey looked were signs of recent paint and fresh growth. Crestonville had somehow become darned cute.

Had it really been five years? After the stroke, she'd shuttled between her downtown Richmond hotel and the medical center, and before that—well, five years ago had been when her Expedition Network career had finally taken off and she'd paid a brief visit after her mother had moved back. She felt vaguely guilty about the realization. She'd always considered herself the good daughter of the family, and yet she hadn't made time to come home.

She couldn't say it felt like home, though. She felt as out of place among the century-old facades of Crestonville's main drag as she sometimes felt in Manhattan's trendier hot spots. There, she'd always seemed a pretender, an undercover hick trying to fit in among her betters. Here, however, she worried she came off as the city woman, scorned for her slickness and insincerity. Bailey sighed. She'd always be a fish out of water. The thought slipped away as she heard a click on the other end of her cell phone. "This is Marsha speaking. Thank you for your patience," said a woman's voice. After a few days home, the New York accent sounded nasal and clipped. "I'm afraid Ms. Rhodes is not available today, but I can. . . ."

"Marsha, don't hang up," Bailey commanded, impatient from having been put on hold three minutes before. "This *is* Ms. Rhodes. What happened to Chandra?"

"Ms. Rhodes?" said the receptionist with surprise. Bailey tried in vain to associate a face to the voice she vaguely recognized as one of the bland, neatly groomed people staffing the desks outside her own private office. "You sound funny." The comment made Bailey want to bare her teeth and growl like a cartoon dog. "Chandra stepped out for the morning. She's gone to an important meeting. I don't know what," she added, anticipating Bailey's next question. "But I'm sure it's important, or she wouldn't have said that it was, you know. Important."

"I see." Bailey wondered if she sounded as testy as she felt. The first thing she'd done when Taylor had gone off on his errand had been to dial in to her voice mail at home, finding only one limp request from a neighbor asking if she'd be available to cat-sit for a weekend. Steve hadn't called all weekend. He could have left a message on her cell account. He knew she picked up voice mail from home every day when she could. Okay, maybe it was stupid of her to expect a phone call from the person who'd forgotten in the middle of *Hairspray* to tell her he wasn't coming back. It wasn't as if he'd called the other weekends she'd spent in Virginia, either. Still. There weren't any of the multiple messages from her sister that Bailey almost enjoyed ignoring. "Tell Chandra I phoned. And tell her this: No contracts, no shoot. She'll know what I mean."

"No contracts, no shoot," the receptionist repeated.

That should be clear enough. Chandra had helped out in rescheduling location shoots before; this one should be no problem. "I don't suppose there are any calls for me?"

"None that Chandra didn't take care of, Ms. Rhodes," said the receptionist. "You should relax and enjoy your vacation! Is there anything else?"

"No," said Bailey, feeling glum. "Yes. Transfer me to Sidney James's office, would you?" The moment the receptionist demurred and cut the line, Bailey connected the voice with a face. Marsha. The newish one. The one who had cats instead of a boyfriend. Easy for her to suggest relaxing on a vacation. While the phone rang, Bailey slumped against the tailgate of Taylor's truck, which looked clean enough to have been washed that morning, and examined her nails, still feeling vaguely discontented. She'd only been out of the office one day, and as Sidney had predicted, everyone seemed to have forgotten her already.

It didn't help when Sidney answered the phone with an imperious, "Bailey *who?* I don't know a *Bailey.* I used to have a friend named Bailey, but she relocated to a trailer park in, I don't know, West Virginia."

"Hah! That's very funny! Only, except for the fact that it wasn't."

"Touchy, touchy!" Sidney's urbane tones, soaked in coffee and tobacco and topped off with a hint of post-meeting hoarseness, made Bailey homesick in less than a heartbeat. "I'm not the one who took vacation in the middle of sweeps planning. Larry Gilbert noticed you were gone, you know."

"Don't," said Bailey. Difficult as it might have been to feel miserable on the summer's sunniest, warmest morning, surrounded by flowers and young suburban-looking mothers pushing strollers along a street so wholesome and clean that it made Disneyland look like a red-light district in comparison, she somehow managed. "I hate this trip."

Sidney dropped the jokes. "What's the matter?" she asked with real concern. "Is your mom not okay?"

"She's fine. Really. She's not scary, like she was in the hospital. She's just—weird." Head hung down, she briefly she outlined her mother's obsession with ball-tossing, while Sidney made sympathetic noises. "She doesn't like to read, which used to be her favorite pastime. She doesn't talk. No lectures, nothing. She's not herself."

"Oh, Bail. You know how it is when people who've been independent their entire lives suddenly find themselves needing help. We've watched enough very special episodes of *ER* together."

"I know. What bugs me is that I feel useless around here. I'm not doing her any good. I'm not getting any work done. And I don't *like* feeling useless. I'm at my best when I'm. . . ."

Through the veil of hair hanging around her face, she could see that a pair of white patent leather shoes had come to a stop in front of her. They protruded from underneath a pair of white pants legs in a lightweight summer fabric, atop which sat a fat torso in a suit of the same material. The man's face had such pronounced, swinging jowls and droopy eyes that he resembled nothing more than an aging basset hound's head plopped upon a snowman's body. The man opened his mouth to speak. "Hi there, honey!" he said. A thicker, more gooey accent Bailey had not heard in some time; he managed to make the word *there* sound as if it had two syllables. "My, haven't you grown up!" He sported a matching cane that glinted in the sun's rays, and to top off the outfit, a white nautical hat. He touched its brim in greeting.

"Who's that?" Sidney said in her ear. "I hear someone there."

"Yeah, can you hang on for a minute?" asked Bailey in a bright and cheerful voice, forced as it might have been. She lowered the phone and managed to drag her eyes away from the short and rotund speaker to study his young companion. The girl hung onto the crook of his elbow with both hands and displayed a bland smile that was neither disdainful nor particularly interested. Aunt Bits would certainly have approved of her posture, though. Even dressed in the most casual of polo shirts and a pair of hip-hugging shorts, she carried herself like a princess. What was the relationship between the improbable pair? Father and daughter? Sugar daddy and hot young mama? Pimp and hooker? Captain and Tennille?

The man barely waited for Bailey to make her phone excuse before chattering away. "Honey, you have growed up so pretty! I was standing across the street when I said to Marjorie here, didn't I, Marjorie, that you have growed up so pretty. 'Who,' I said, just like that, 'Who *is* that vision in Anne Klein?'" With modesty, Bailey's hand flew to the opening of her top. She moved her mouth as if blushing, though she didn't actually feel flushed. "Didn't I, Marjorie?" The girl merely maintained the not unpleasant expression on her face. "And then I said, 'I do declare, it must be that beautiful young niece of my great and good friends Elizabeth Oates and Myrtle Whigfield, Bailey Rhodes! Doesn't she look a sight?'"

A tinny voice spoke from the phone. "Who *is* that?" Bailey moved it closer to her shoulder so that it couldn't be heard.

"And then I said to myself, 'Why don't you just go

over there and say hello and tell her how beautiful she's growed?' So I did." The man dabbed at her with one of his age-spotted hands. "And don't *ever* let anyone tell you coral is not your color."

He crossed his hands at the waist and rested them on the cane, obviously expecting some kind of answer. Was she supposed to know who he was? Had she met the man at some church function on one of her earlier visits? She couldn't recall anyone like him from her childhood years here—and you'd think it would be easy to recall meeting Truman Capote's shorter and smarmier brother. Knowing that she could clear things up with a simple, *who are you, again?* didn't make her feel any better. How in the world could she ask such a question of a man who'd complimented her with such fulsomeness? It would be rude! "You're looking so well," she hedged.

The man tipped back his head and laughed, setting his jowls swinging like pink velvet draperies in a stiff breeze. "Aren't you the sweetest thing? Isn't she the sweetest thing?" he repeated to his companion, who kept the composure maintained by foreign language speakers who didn't understand a word of English. "I thank you for that, my dear. So kind of you. And how is your mama? Is she recuperating?" Bailey nodded. "And your aunts? I wager they're busy-busy-busy now that the pageant's accepting applications?"

"Oh, busy-busy-busy describes them, all right," Bailey conceded with a polite laugh. The man was talkative, it was true, and seemed to have all the time in the world. She tried pulling her cell phone back into view, as if she intended to resume her conversation.

The little man, however, seemed to have nowhere to be anytime soon. "You will be staying for the pageant, won't you, my dear? No? Whyever not? It's in less than two weeks. You must stay for it. I insist. Your aunts always send some of the best girls on to the Miss Tidewater Butter Bean pageant. Why, some of them even make second or third runner-up, sometimes! You must be very proud. Very, very proud!"

Bailey decided to leave the issue of her pride unspoken. "I'm afraid I'm here just for the week," she told him, while he made a moue of disappointment. "Then I'm back to Manhattan."

"Oh, but it's the event of the county, this time of year! Isn't it, Marjorie? Why, not five years ago one of our very own Miss Tidewater Butter Beans went on to be in the Miss Virginia pageant! Not one of your aunt's girls, I'm sorry to say, but my goodness, weren't we all proud of our little Dawn when she was up there on the stage of the Tanglewood Mall in Roanoke, Marjorie?" When the man smiled, his teeth gleamed like mirrors on a disco ball. "It was a proud moment for Crestonville. A proud, proud moment."

"I'm sure it must have been!" By now, Bailey's voice had risen to the same cheerful pitch the man had been using. Her mouth hurt from all the grinning. "Well, I'll be sure to tell the aunts that you asked after them," she said, hoping that he'd take the hint. With his suit reflecting the blinding sun, he was a little hard on the eyes, but he was exactly the kind of local color with which she always hoped the crews on her shows would return to the studios. She wished she knew who he was, but the statute of limitations on asking had expired at the beginning of their conversation.

"No indeedy!" said the man with a long, drawn-out exclamation. "Why, don't you bother your pretty little self with something like that! No, no, no, no, no! I'm always running into your aunts. I do love them so! Not a word will I hear said against them! You enjoy your vacation, young lady!" What was he trying to do with those little fluttering motions of his hands, buffet her back against the truck with little wisps of air? "You enjoy everything Crestonville has to offer! Oh, and that hair

color? It really works for you. Suits your complexion.
Don't let anyone say otherwise, you hear?" Even as he
began to walk back across the street, Marjorie still
clutching his arm—or maybe her hand was simply
stuck in it, for all Bailey could tell—he still kept talking.
"And I *love* the shoes," he called out.

Bailey looked down at her workout shoes. She'd
never worn them off the shiny laminate floors of the Ji-
vamukti Yoga Center before that morning, and they'd
started the day as pristine and spotless white as the
man's own. Now they were streaked with dirt and
grass stains. "Oh my God," she giggled into the phone,
feeling like an embarrassed fifteen-year-old girl who'd
moments before encountered a schoolteacher who'd
dared to show his face in public. "Did you hear any of
that?"

"Did I!" exclaimed Sidney. "I could've pulled up a
chair and roasted marshmallows over that little flamer!
What did he look like?"

"The Burl Ives snowman from that Rudolph Clayma-
tion special we used to watch when we were kids,
dressed up like Colonel Sanders."

Sidney completely lost her cool and squawked, "Who
was Marjorie? His elderly, toothless mother?"

"A hot young chick!" Bailey cackled, turning away
from the sidewalk and the teenagers strolling by.

"No! What's she look like? I'm picturing *Jerry Springer*
skank crossed with goth-y *Buffy* vampire chic."

"You remember that special we did a couple of years
ago on scoliosis? And how those people walked after all
those months in a back brace? Like that, with Lindsay
Lohan boobs—post-implant—and a Chloe Sevigny
neck and that Denise Richards kind of vacant stare,
dressed all *Desperate Housewives*-y."

"I can picture it exactly!" For someone who derided
this area of the country with the regularity of Old Faith-
ful, Sidney certain seemed excited to hear everything
about it. "And what's this . . . the Land-o-Lakes thing?"

"Land-o-Lakes is Michigan, silly. Or Wisconsin. One of those. You mean the Miss Tidewater Butter Bean Pageant." The contest's title sounded very self-important in her mouth; she couldn't help but mock it. "I don't know what the hell it is, but my aunts are coaching some of the contestants. You know how these things are. Vaseline on the teeth to keep your mouth from closing, bouquets, crying, backstabbing, big hair. I'm glad I'll be the hell out of here before it happens."

"You know you wish you could see it," Sidney teased. "It's in your Virginia blood, honeychile."

Odd, but no matter how much Bailey felt entitled to tease the people she'd been born among, she disliked it when others took the liberty. "Sid, I don't think there's a Southerner alive who actually says *honeychile*. And I don't know what the hell a butter bean is, anyway."

"Isn't it like a lima bean or something?"

"I hope not. Lima beans are the hemorrhoids of Satan. They're twenty-seven kinds of heinous. Can you imagine an entire festival for them? I'd rather celebrate gonorrhea."

"Come *home*," Sidney urged. "You don't belong down there with those people."

"I don't belong with all the rednecks and hicks?" Bailey said flatly, trying to cut to the chase. She curled up a leg and rested it on the truck's tire, knowing exactly what Sidney was thinking, and resenting it. How big a leap was it from Sid or anyone else up there thinking those things about other people, to thinking it about herself? "Down here with the wife-beaters and mouth-breathers?"

"Don't get defensive. Your home is up here. That's all I'm saying." It wasn't much of an apology, but it was obvious Sidney realized she'd touched a nerve. "You know the only things I know about the South are those cartoonish stereotypes on television. And *Designing Women*. Hell, I get my whole life from television."

"And don't you confuse me with them. That's all I'm

asking." A gentle vibration, accompanied by a metallic clunk, roused Bailey from her seclusion at the truck's side. Taylor stood there, paint cans hanging from both hands at his side. One of them still clunked slightly against the bumper. "Crap," she told Sidney, feeling a burning sensation in the center of her chest. "I've got to go."

"Now?" she heard Sidney say as she pulled the phone away from her ear. "But. . . ."

Her thumb snaked out and pressed the button to end the call. How much of that conversation had Taylor heard? Running over it in her head didn't help any— everything she recalled saying within the last thirty seconds sounded negative. Not merely negative— spectacularly negative on a scale that called for sets to be flown in from the Lincoln Center, with costumes by Cirque du Soleil. "Get everything you needed?" she asked, trying to sound more cheerful than she felt.

"I did," he said. The pleasant expression on his face didn't seem at all forced, she decided, after regarding it with considerable anxiety. "How's your signal?"

"Fantastic," she said. "Great. Five bars. Absolutely incredible. Better than I get at home, most of the time, in fact." Even to herself, she sounded unnaturally bubbly.

He nodded, then lifted the paint cans up and over the gate and into the bed, where they scraped as Taylor tucked them behind a bungee. "Anything else you need while we're here?" Was he not looking at her because he thought she'd called him a hick and a wife-beater? Or maybe, just maybe, was she overanalyzing, and he was simply attending to the task of walking around the car?

Clearing her throat seemed more of a chore when it was choked with doubt. "No. No, I'm good," she told him.

The keys dangled from his hand. "You want to drive?"

"I don't. . . ." She choked down a laugh. "Sorry, I can't."

"Whole family of women who can't drive," he said,

shaking his head and grinning. "Somebody should learn!"

"Well, I get around by train and cab at home, and my mom was driving for the aunts until her stroke. . . ." Why was he talking about this particular subject? "I really hope it's not been an imposition for you. I could work out some kind of reimbursement if you'd like."

His hand snapped shut and dropped. Taylor shook his head. "Not necessary." He opened up the door with one hand and with the other, beckoned her to enter. Had she offended him in yet another way? He was still being a gentleman, at least. Wasn't that a good sign?

She waited until they'd both climbed back into the truck and he'd pulled away from the curb before talking again. "You all have cleaned up the downtown area since I was here last," she ventured, still taking in new details—the antiques stores where there used to be run-down homes for seniors, or a 7-Eleven that had curled like a chameleon into what had been a corner hardware store, barely anachronistic among the brick and stone carvings of its turn-of-the-century facade. There was even a pizza parlor tucked away in one of the old storefronts.

"Maybe it seems that way to someone who's been away for a while," Taylor commented, checking over his shoulder for oncoming traffic as he pulled into a left turn lane. "When I moved here, it was pretty much like this."

"When was that?"

"Three years ago." He nodded as if mentally checking the date in his head, and then remarked, "It sounds funny . . . a northern girl saying that." When she didn't understand, he added, "Y'all."

Again, she felt uncomfortable. This week was already difficult enough without having to be constantly reminded of being an outsider. "I grew up here, you know," she told him with more than a touch of self-defensiveness. "This town is where I lived until I was twelve. I took piano lessons in a flat over that 7-Eleven. My sister and I used to lay pennies on the train tracks over yonder," she said, pointing to the railroad crossing down the intersecting street onto which they turned, "to see if a train could flatten them. I'm not some . . . some carpetbagger from Yankee-land, come to rob you of your contractions."

"I never used the word *Yankee*," he replied, his words slow and considered. "Does anyone actually say that?"

"You haven't spent a lot of time with my mother, obviously." She sat back in her seat, arms folded over the seatbelt. Pique was a nasty feeling. She wanted nothing more than to argue out the issue, but she barely knew Taylor. She was one of that big family of women who didn't know how to drive. She'd rather not alienate someone friendly who was willing to drive her into town that week, solely so she could make a point about how she had a perfect birthright to utter the words *you all*. It was especially difficult to feel resentful when she'd said more than a few things that could have been misinterpreted, mere moments before.

Either Taylor didn't notice her silence, or he felt disinclined to talk. With a series of bumps they drove over the rails that delimited the official edge of the town and turned onto the county road. She started a bit when his hand reached in her direction, but it angled toward the radio and flipped the knob. A snippet of a familiar NPR announcer's voice escaped through the loudspeakers before Taylor's thumb stroked a button and changed to a rock station. The volume was low. They could have continued talking if they wanted. Yet Bailey decided it was a signal that she should simply remain silent.

By the time they finally turned back onto Cedar Pass Road, she thought the pair of them had fallen into some kind of verbal détente from which there might be no return. From the window, through the blurred foreground of trees whizzing by, she could see brief flashes of the aunts' house in the distance. A few minutes more, and she could shake off this unpleasant feeling with a walk back to the house, followed maybe by some television, or a simple lie-down in her bedroom, if she could stand the fusty smell made worse by the daytime heat. At the driveway to Taylor's house, he didn't slow down. "You don't have to take me home," she told him.

He didn't say anything, though he did look over and quirk the corners of his mouth in an expression that wasn't quite a smile, but wasn't exactly forbidding. A hundred yards down the road, he slowed down and pulled to the side of the road. But why? Was he going to make her walk the rest of the way? Before Bailey could frame the question, Taylor had turned off the ignition, grabbed his keys, and exited, walking around the back. The last traces of air-conditioning faded from the truck's interior while Bailey considered what to do. She'd finished unfastening her seatbelt when, without warning, her own door swung open. With a sweep of his arm, Taylor invited her to step out.

A weedy ditch lay a few feet below the road's gravel shoulder, overgrown with Queen Anne's lace and high grasses. Beyond it was a clump of cedar that, in the noon sun, cast little shadow over the edge of the field beyond. Once the truck's door had shut behind her, Taylor hopped into the gully, turned, and withdrew a battered cloth baseball cap from his back pocket. He pulled the brim low over his face, then extended his hand.

Again, why were they stopping there? Why in the world did he want to drag her into a ditch? In these shoes? If he had any funny notions. . . . "I'm seeing someone," she blurted out. He raised his eyebrows, not moving his hand. "I mean—I don't know why I said that. Where are we going?"

"You'll see," he said.

Fine. She took his hand, letting the calluses of his palm press into her own white skin. With the lightest touch possible, his other hand rested under her upper arm as he helped her step down. She could have done it herself, of course, but there was something gentlemanly, even courtly, about the gesture. Once they were both on the same level, he kept a grip on her hand and led her in the direction of the trees. She thought of wrestling away, but Bailey felt no real meaning in the handhold. It was intimate without being sexual. Friendly, but with a purpose. He dropped her fingers after a moment anyway, when they reached the tall cedars and he swept aside branches to create a path and let her pass.

Down the slopes he stepped into the fields, where row after row of green vines spiraled up and around poles spaced evenly apart, wide enough for a single person to walk through the aisles. There must have been thousands upon thousands of the plants, extending toward both their houses and toward the cluster of trees at the horizon. Their pointed leaves were large and flat, and higher on her leg than she'd expected from her glimpses of them from the road. "Come on," he told her, jerking his head. She followed, watching him turn over the leaves of some of the plants as if searching for something. At long last, he knelt down by a pole where the stalks had snaked up a few inches higher than most of the others. From his back pocket he retrieved some kind of tool—a penknife, it looked like, and sliced something open. He repeated the action a few more times, collecting something in his hand, until at last he had what he'd come for. Taylor stood and approached, closing the penknife by pressing it against his belt, and replacing it into his back pocket. When finally he stood close to Bailey, he opened his palm.

On that broad expanse of lines and valley lay several large flat, kidney-shaped objects, a few of them still in the slug-shaped pods in which they'd grown. "Carolina Sieva," he told her, pushing the legumes around with his fingertip. His nail was slightly dirty, Bailey noticed; it was flecked with white paint. "Commonly known around these parts as the butter bean."

THE MILE-HIGH HAIR CLUB 91

She froze. Her face flamed. Her feet felt as if she walked on ice, while her armpits prickled with heat. She was experiencing more variations in temperature than the Weather Channel could predict in an entire day, and it was all due to her own mortification. Bailey opened her mouth, and then shut it, afraid of what she might say. She opened it again, and then decided the better of it and turned, walking with angry strides in the direction of the road.

"Some people think lima beans and butter beans are the same thing," said Taylor, following behind. "They're interchangeable terms, from an agricultural standpoint. But we Southern folk know that butter beans are tastier." She was at the trees, now, and didn't bother to hold the branches so the farmer could follow. Was it bad to hope they hit him in the face? Or the groin? "Ever had them fresh off the vine? Much better that way than frozen. Way, way better than canned. They don't taste like the hemorrhoids of Satan when you pick 'em yourself."

She summoned words when they reached the road's side. "Okay, look."

"Need a boost?" he said with a grin, offering the hand not full of beans.

"Shut up. I mean, sorry. That was rude. *I* was rude. No, what I mean is that back in town I probably *sounded* rude. But I wasn't."

"No?" Taylor took off his cap, curled the brim, and stuffed it back into his pocket. "I never said that you . . ."

"My friend in New York said some things, all right? Ignorant things. Or she was about to say some ignorant things, and I just . . . said them before she had a chance. That's what you heard. Of course, I'm making the assumption you heard everything."

"I didn't hear a thing," he said, cocking his head and crunching together his eyebrows.

How could she suspect those big, blue peepers of insincerity? "You didn't?" she asked, hopeful.

"Cross my heart, hope to die, stick a needle in my
eye." He made a vague X over his chest. "I didn't hear a
word about rednecks, hicks, and mouth-breathers."

"Oh—you!"

He caught her as she tried to scrabble her way up the
culvert and back onto the road. "Hey, hey! Don't you
have a sense of humor?" When she didn't answer, he
provided his own. "I know you do. Hey, you made me
laugh."

"Laugh all you want," she growled, accepting his
hand and letting him ease her back up. She brushed off
the seat of her pants. "Laugh *all* you want, mister."

"I'm the injured mouth-breather here!" he protested.
With athletic grace, he vaulted up and joined her by the
truck's side. "Besides, I wasn't asking you to apologize.
Who said I assumed you were bad-mouthing me?"

"I wasn't!"

He unlocked the car and pulled open the car door for
her. "I didn't say you did!"

"And I wasn't!" she said again, climbing in.

"Then why so defensive?" he asked, rounding the
truck. "You know, my mama used to tell a story," he
continued, once he was inside and had started the motor. "It was about an old woman who used to sleep in
the same room with a bunch of hound dogs, and how
one night the old woman baked a pie and put it on the
windowsill to cool before she went to bed." Bailey
didn't know where the story was going, but she listened
over the noise of the tires crunching on the gravel, as
they pulled back onto the road. "In the middle of the
night, she woke up and heard the sound of all the
hound dogs sleeping. All except one, who was sniffing
around on his hind legs around that pie, trying to get a
bite of it. So she picked up a shoe and flung it at the dog
and heard it yip and yowl when she beaned it."

"This is very *Beverly Hillbillies*," Bailey couldn't help but comment, her feelings still hurt.

"Bear with me. So the next day she woke up, and all her dogs were in a good mood save one, who was covering his nose with his paws and howling to beat the band. She pointed at it and said, *Hit dog howls loudest!*" Taylor turned and looked at her. "So that's what my mama used to say to me, whenever I'd done something bad, and was trying to pretend that I hadn't. *Hit dog howls loudest.*"

"Are you saying I'm a dog?" she asked, trying to make sense of the story. Her aunts' house was growing larger against the horizon, flickering through the trees as they bounced farther down the road.

"No, ma'am. I'm saying that sometimes, when a person protests too much, sometimes it means they're guilty of that thing. Maybe you weren't bad-mouthing us mouth-breathers. But maybe again, somewhere inside you, you were."

"No," she said, surprised at how firm her denial was. "You don't know what it's like, having to defend where you grew up to where you live, and then to turn around and have to defend where you live now to the people where you grew up. I didn't choose to be born here. I didn't choose to move up North." Her voice wasn't raised, precisely, but she definitely wasn't at her calmest. This entire visit seemed to be turning into an inconvenience of the greatest magnitude. She would have gotten as much accomplished had she spent it holed up in her apartment, eating junk food and binging on television and books in her to-read pile. Exactly like all her other vacations. Modulating her voice, she added an apology. "I'm sorry if I sound snippy. What you heard was out of context, and I figured you'd take it the wrong way. I'm tired of having to defend where I came from. That's all. I feel like I have to do it all the damned time."

They were turning into her aunts' driveway, now. Bailey could see farther down, toward the house, Bubble's and Bits's empty rocking chairs on the grassiest part of the front yard. Around them, six or eight girls walked in calm procession. "Even to that boyfriend of yours?" he asked, not taking his eyes from the gravel road.

"Even to him." It was impossible not to think back to the last time she'd seen Steve, the night of the drawer incident.

"How long have you been seeing the guy? Where'd you meet?"

When she glanced over at Taylor, his face betrayed nothing but polite interest. The prick of mild annoyance she felt turned on its axis—why in the world was she assuming that Taylor was asking because he had some kind of wild, manly interest in her relationship status? He was simply making conversation of a general sort. Nothing more, nothing less. He offered to give them a more graceful dismount to the morning's gyrations than she'd provided herself. "It's complicated," she ventured, after waffling over whether to claim the longer friendship or the much shorter actual period of dating. "And we met at Barnes and Noble. A bookstore." She moved hastily on, in case he felt compelled to tell her he knew what Barnes and Noble was. "Sidney—my girlfriend back home—used to call Friday nights at Barnes and Noble 'second chance at love' night. Because if you went after six or seven o'clock, the place would be filled with lonely singles, was her theory. She even gave it a theme song. *Sec-ond chance at loooooove.*"

Taylor laughed a little at her goopy rendition of the brief tune. The response encouraged her. Maybe they could have that graceful dismount, after all. "So Sidney was off trying to chat up this clerk that she had the hots for—he'd been in an acting class with us—and I went to the café and got a table and waited. Only it was crowded, and the table I'd picked had a couple of books on it, because the guy sitting there had gotten up to get a refill. Then he came back and sat down, and . . . well, that was Steve."

"Romantic," Taylor commented.

"Mmmm." Bailey felt an odd discontent at the remark, worse than a few minutes before when they'd been outright arguing. Steve had pointed to the copy of Saki and the thick tome on economic cycles and asked her to move. She'd been the one to suggest sharing the table together for a few minutes, and it had been because she'd kept the conversation sparkly and lively that he'd eventually warmed up enough to talk about the books he'd liked. All because she'd been too lazy and tired to want to find another table to share. It hadn't been romantic at all.

"Everyone's got stories, I tell you." At some point while she'd been talking, he'd pulled the truck to a stop at the bottom of the drive. Over the idling engine, he added, "And people want to tell them, too."

She let out a laugh as shy denial. "That wasn't much of a story." They sat there for a moment more. "Well," she said at last, unbuckling her lap belt and opening the door. "I should let you go. Thank you for the ride and for everything."

"No problem. And now you know what a butter bean looks like," he joked.

"Couldn't have lived without that," she retorted, joking right back as she slid from the seat. Her feet hit the ground. The dismount was complete; she'd salvaged what had threatened to become a sorry routine. "See you around, then."

"Hope so." Taylor leaned forward over the passenger seat, one of his arms supporting the weight of his torso. His head turned; his teeth made a welcome, flashing appearance as he let loose one of his grins. "And hey, for the record? I'm a little bit jealous of that boyfriend of yours." While she stood there, utterly stunned, he nodded and grabbed the open door. "Take it easy now, Bailey."

She didn't remember the door closing, though it must have, nor the truck turning in a tight circle. Later on she had a vague memory of seeing Taylor's masculine profile through the dark glass of the driver's-side window, and of seeing his hand raise in a farewell. Of the small insect flying into her gaping mouth, she had a definite recollection. But nothing remained of her walk up to the house, though she had to have passed by the squadron of beautiful young women practicing their posture and poise.

In fact, she didn't come back to her full senses until she stepped into the house's living room and found her aunts flanking a familiar young woman sitting in an armchair. With Aunt Bubble sitting on a low stool, looking up in the girl's face, and with Aunt Bits standing over her, one arm resting on the girl's shoulder, it was like a scene from an Italian Renaissance devotional painting: two angels supplicating and protecting the Virgin Mary. Only the Virgin's part was being played by a girl with a smear of lipstick that was almost black, a pierced eyebrow, and eyes surrounded with so much dark kohl that they looked like twin bruises. Bailey opened her mouth to speak. "Jeanne?"

"I tried and tried and *tried* phoning you," complained her sister, standing to her feet. "You never return my calls."

Jeanne wore ragged black jeans with enormous flared bottoms that swallowed her feet. Her black t-shirt bore the name of some obscure band that Bailey had never heard of, which was probably its point. It rode high on her abdomen, revealing . . . oh hell. Revealing a few inches of skin swollen in a gentle curve. "You're pregnant," Bailey said. If she'd been stunned in the driveway, that was but a mild doctor's mallet of a blow compared with the giant hammer her sister had shown up wielding.

Aunt Bits's eyes flashed, as if challenging Bailey to say anything negative. Bubble looked up from the stool and chirped, "Isn't it wonderful, dear?"

Jeanne crossed her arms, shifted her weight from one hip to the other, and growled, "Well, *durrrrr*."

Maybe she didn't have a sense of humor, Bailey reflected about herself. But somewhere out there in the ether sat a malevolent deity whose sole purpose was to flummox Bailey at every turn. And was damn successful.

Chapter Eight

"John, pass me that there salt, would you, sugar?" When Mr. Walter Rice talked, it was with a lazy accent that sounded as if he drawled right through his nose. Someone from another part of the country might have heard that voice and dismissed him as a hick, a boob from the backwoods, but Bailey had spent enough time growing up in the South to recognize the sound of patrician Virginian gentility. In its thick vowels she could practically smell the saddle leather, the Old Fashioneds, and the money. The old man sitting next to her elder aunt had more spots on his face than a measles ward, all of them from simple age and too much sun. He had to be a good fifteen years older than Bubble, Bailey thought to herself, but every now and then they would turn to each other and smile with great, secret delight, as if seeing each other after a long parting. Either it was very sweet, or else impending senility had its small advantages. "I say, John," he repeated. "The salt? Would you, please?"

"Oh!" Bailey realized Mr. Rice meant her. His disconcerting habit of addressing anyone younger than himself as "John" might save him the necessity of learning anyone's name, but at any given moment left doubts about whom he might actually be addressing.

"I've got it," said Jeanne. Although she was sitting across the table, on the other side of their mother, she leaned forward, grabbed the salt shaker, and set it in front of Bubble's guest to her left.

"Well thank you, sugar," he said, bobbing his head up and down. "Thank you kindly."

"No problem!" said Jeanne cheerfully, not looking Bailey's way. She was the chirpiest pseudo-Goth that Bailey had ever seen.

"As I was sayin'," Mr. Rice wheezed. "I had to drive all the way into Richmond to see a specialist, and what did I get? A goddamn Eye-ranian doctor. An hour drive to see a goddamned Eye-ranian doctor. And was it cheap? No sir, it was not." He liberally salted his potatoes as he spoke, then picked up his fork and waved it around the table. "An Eye-ranian, I ask you. Used to be in my day a *real* doctor would come out to your house in a Cadillac and treat you right!"

Bailey found it difficult to pay attention to their guest when beside her, her mother's knife hand quivered over her roast beef. She wasn't automatically supposed to intervene, she remembered reading; recuperating stroke patients were supposed to set their own new routines and find their own limits. Watching each painstaking bite, however, was wearying her reserves of patience, which apparently were none too full to begin with. "I remember the days, Walter," Bits nodded. She didn't so much deliver food into her mouth as snap it off the fork, her neck and mouth darting forward to seize fodder from the upturned implement and then rend it to shreds with her teeth.

"I had a fine Mexican doctor when I had to have Majesty put down," said Mr. Rice, shaking his head. "Fine horse, that was. By the time we discovered the cancer, though, his testicles looked like Swiss cheese."

"How dreadful," murmured Bubble, nibbling from a roll she held with both hands.

Bailey had barely been able to look her sister in the face all through the meal. "So have you seen a doctor yet?" she asked the kidney-shaped fragment of beef on her plate, pushing them around with her fork. After Mr. Rice's clinical description, she couldn't bring herself to eat them. When she looked up, all eyes were on her. "I meant Jeanne," she added, answering the unasked question.

Her sister's jaw jutted out. Honestly, Jeanne could be so pretty if she tried a little. A smart bob instead of her long, black-dyed frizz, a little more makeup and some regular exfoliation, and she'd have a rosebud of a face. What was the point of trying to be "individual" by wearing the exact same style of makeup worn by thousands of other people? "I took a home pregnancy test when I missed my first period." When Bailey's eyebrows shot up, Jeanne countered with, "I think it's pretty obvious that I'm pregnant, in case you didn't notice."

Her mom's knife dipped, and for a moment looked as if it actually might connect with the roast beef. Bailey didn't know what emotion was making Jeanne so stubborn; she stared at her mother's progress while she spoke. "That's kind of irresponsible, isn't it? Prenatal exams are essential for the health of both the baby and the mother. There's ultrasounds, and fetal heartbeat monitoring, and all kinds of tests. Protein and sugar levels," she ventured, trying to dredge up all the details from other women's pregnancies that she hadn't followed with much attention when they'd talked about them. "It's important."

Jeanne sat back in her chair and crossed her arms. Bailey could tell her sister looked right at her. "Not all of us have the money for doctors."

"But there's free prenatal clinics for low-income patients," Bailey insisted. She couldn't stand it any more.

She twisted slightly in her seat to try to assist her mother with the knife, but before she could reach across the plate, her mother had pulled away. Somehow, the refusal fueled her slow fire. "That includes no-income patients."

When Bailey flickered her glance at Jeanne's face, she found it reflected by her sister's flinty eyes, so like their mother's. "We know of a marvelous prenatal doctor, dear," said Bubble consolingly. "Last year, right before the pageant, one of our girls. . . ."

"And the less said about that, the better." Bits rattled her utensils onto her plate. "Honestly. I'm not at all certain this is a fit topic for the dinner table!"

"But we can talk about horse testicles?" Bailey wasn't about to be blustered down.

"Those goddamned testicles were like Swiss cheese, they were." Mr. Rice sighed. "It was a goddamned shame. Is there any more asparagus, Myrtle?"

"I do enjoy the company of a man with a hearty appetite!" Bubble enthused. "And Jeanne, don't you worry about a thing. We'll set up an appointment for you with Dr. Marcus. You are staying for a while, aren't you?"

"Of course she is," snapped Bits. "She just arrived. We haven't seen her in years. She's won't be haring off again at the end of the week like some people."

Bailey grit her teeth at the remark so obviously intended for her. "Unlike Jeanne, I have a career."

"Never said you didn't."

"I'd be happy to stay." Jeanne smiled at her aunts, and as her lashes lowered in a slow blink, shot a glance in Bailey's direction. Evil, sheer evil. "It's been so long."

"Lovely!" Bubble clapped her hands together with pleasure and began rising to her feet. You could practically hear the bones creaking as she hefted her considerable weight on the table for balance. "I'll get some more asparagus."

Bailey's chair clattered back as she beat her aunt to

the punch. "I'll go." She needed the space. Merely sitting across from her sister was more effort than she cared to exert at that moment. Grabbing the bowl, she attempted to sound merry as she made her exit. "Anything else you all need while I'm down there?"

No one said a thing. It wasn't until after Bailey had pushed through dining room door and into the hallway that anyone spoke. "Another thing about so-called goddamned modern medicine," said Mr. Rice. "They don't *fix* any goddamned thing!" Once she stepped onto the staircase down to the kitchen, the screeching old stairs drowned out his voice.

Running from the dining room felt a little like deserting a battleground in the heat of combat. When Bailey had been young, her mother used to give her quarters for the vending machines outside the pharmacy. Sometimes, instead of the usual gumball or hard candy, she'd find behind the machine's shiny silver door a transparent capsule, inside of which were two plastic Scottie dogs, one black, one white. They would be barely the size of a thumbnail, and were affixed at their bases to gently curved magnets. The magnets had always fascinated her. There was nothing electrical or mechanical about them—only natural forces caused their poles to attract and resist. For long minutes she'd put the Scotties face to face, so that their same poles would repel the other. South to south. Between her fingers, she'd feel them push away. When she'd let go, they'd rock on their magnets and shudder back. On smooth, slick surfaces like a polished table, one of them might spin until it faced the opposite direction, if the magnets were strong enough.

That day, she and Jeanne were like those toy Scotties, facing south to south. Bailey had been the one to turn away. What was it that angered her so about her sister? Was it the pregnancy? Typical of Jeanne to let something like that happen. She'd probably galloped her way through the Triple Crown of Taboo—no birth control, unprotected sex, and God only knew who the father was. And then to show up here, like that, unannounced, unapologetic, not even seeming to care about either her own health or the baby's! What had Jeanne been *thinking*?

She hadn't been, of course. Planning ahead had never been Jeanne's strong suit. Her little sister simply played her hand according to whim, without any thought of the end game. You couldn't live a life simply for *fun*. It was short-sighted and harebrained! Worst of all, it was hard on those who actually had a sense of responsibility. Who kept bailing out Jeanne at the end of every month, when she couldn't cadge enough money for her share of rent in that dank little walk-up share in Brooklyn? Bailey, that's who. Phone call after phone call she'd endured this month alone. Or she would have, if she'd bothered to answer them.

And when, exactly, was the last time she had bothered? A scolding intonation very like her mother's sounded in Bailey's head.

Great. Her mother might not be using her voice, but apparently it wasn't actually necessary for the woman to open her mouth to make herself heard. Bailey had her implanted in her superego or conscious or whatever was that center of trampled nerves in the core of her brain that sent out snotty little messages like that one. A few remaining asparagus stalks remained in the saucepot atop the stove, wilted and soggy. She fished them out with a slotted spoon and let them curl into the bowl's bottom. Every vegetable Aunt Bubble touched somehow got rendered into mush. Bailey stared at the bowl of green stalks with distaste, wishing she were back home again. She missed her nest of an apartment. She missed the sight of her great-grandmother's quilt lying atop her bed. She never should have come on this trip.

If she had been a petulant person—or, as the stern

voice at the back of her mind whispered, a *more* petulant person—she would have tossed the asparagus in the old dumbwaiter and sent it up to the dining room without returning. Wouldn't that surprise them all? Though it had been a posh conceit of the farmhouse's original humble builder, no one had ever used the darned thing once in all of Bailey's memory. During the years the Rhodes had lived in the house, Bailey had broken it by wedging Jeanne inside and trying to haul her up. It had been a good thing that when the rope had given way, it was a mere four inches from the bottom.

Odd how a funny memory of her sister made her more irritated with the woman she'd become. Bailey slid up the door experimentally. Her aunts appeared to be using the dumbwaiter to store oversized pans and, curiously, a four-foot knitted scarf wrapped around a rolling pin. Oh, she was being silly. Even at her most overblown and dramatic, Bailey couldn't ever seriously contemplate such a display of pique. Much as she wanted to act like Jeanne and do something spectacular to pull all attention on herself, Bailey would take the high road.

Or, as Mr. Rice might call it, the goddamned high road. He was playing raconteur once again when she reentered the dining room. "All right," he chuckled. "It's a good story, but it's a bit off-color."

"They're the best kind!" Jeanne leaned over and flashed him a big smile. Didn't the old man notice her ugly makeup? Or the eyebrow ring? Bailey set down the asparagus dish before him without comment, not expecting thanks, and not receiving any.

"Well, John, I agree. I agree with you on that one. They are indeed the best kind. But ladies?"

Bubble appeared undecided. "Will I be shocked? Is it shocking, Walter?"

Mr. Rice tilted his head back and patted the few remaining wisps of gray remaining atop his head. "Well, I don't rightly know about that, Myrtle. I was hoping you might find it titillating!"

"Oh, Walter!"

Bits apparently couldn't stand her sister's girlish giggling any more than Bailey could stand the way her own sister joined in. "Walter, no matter how much you protest, you know you're going to tell us, so spare an old woman who hasn't much time left in the world the formalities and get on with it."

Amen, Bailey thought to herself. She might be less than half her aunt's age, but it felt as if she'd spent half her lifetime trapped in the dining room that night. When she heard the sound of her mother finally releasing her silverware onto her plate, Bailey looked over. Mom had barely eaten any of her roast beef, or the asparagus, though she'd finished nearly all her mashed potatoes. Everything was cold by now, surely. Bailey felt a pang of sympathetic disappointment at her mother's stubbornness and pride.

Mr. Rice cleared his throat. "All right, then. There was a boy, and he was a *beautiful* boy. Well-built boy. Broad shoulders and everything." He made a shape with his hands like an inverted triangle. "And so he made up his mind to be a goddamned model. So he went to the modeling agency and he said, 'Hey, I want to be a model, hot dawgit!'"

"Hah!" Jeanne snorted in amusement. "I'm liking this one already." Barely taking her eyes off the old man, she casually reached over and seized hold of her mother's fork. For a horrified moment, Bailey thought her sister might be helping herself to their mom's portion of roast beef, but instead Jeanne leaned a little farther to reach for the knife, pulled the plate a little closer to her, and from the beef separated a bite-sized piece. And then another.

"And the modeling man says, 'Well, we gotta see you nekkid, boy. Strip down! Take off them goddamned clothes.' So the boy, he strips down and he's beautiful. Hooooo! Bronzed!" Mr. Rice let out a long, low whistle.

Bailey tried to warn her sister in a low voice, "She probably won't let you." Jeanne gave her a quick glance before returning to her cutting. Why wasn't Mom saying anything? She watched Jeanne without expression.

" 'But there's a problem, you see,' the man tells him. 'You got this white strip across your middle.' " In a tone of delicacy, he added to Aunt Bubble, "You know, *down there.* Anyway, so the boy says to himself, 'Aw hell, that ain't nothing. I can take care of that!' So he goes down to the beach, and he digs a hole in the sand, and he covers up everything with sand save that white strip across his middle, so it'll be the only part to get all tan. He covers his head and everything!"

"Good lord," muttered Bits. "In front of the children, no less!"

"Hush now," her sister chided. "They're adults."

The fact that one was pregnant indicated at least a journeyman's knowledge of the male anatomy, Bailey mentally added. Jeanne had finished carving the beef into little squares and moved onto the asparagus, efficiently dividing each stalk into inch-long segments. Fine, thought Bailey. When her mother refused to react, let Jeanne see for herself how useless a task that was.

If Mr. Rice had noticed Bits's objections, he showed no sign of it. He was already relishing the joke with little chuckles of his own, clearly anticipating the punch line. "So a little bit later, along comes this woman, and she's walking her dog, and she says—heh-heh-heh— 'Fido, what'cha found, boy?' Then she sees what she sees, and she puts her hands on her hips and she says, 'Y'know, when I was twenty I didn't know what to do with it. When I was forty, I couldn't get enough of it. When I was sixty, I even paid me a little for a bit of it. Now that I'm eighty and don't give a good goddamn, I'm finding it growing wild on the beaches!' "

Bubble let out a shriek of shock and horrified amusement, as phony as the girls Bailey had known in high school who let the boys tease them so they could return the attention with coquettish protests. Jeanne let out a belly laugh. Even over the noise, when Bits crossed her hands in her lap and let out a long-suffering sigh, it was plainly audible. "I can see why you like him, Aunt Bubble!" Jeanne said, forcing Bailey to stifle the impulse to mimic her with a sneer. Part of Bailey knew how juvenile her impulses were, but she couldn't help herself. Why did sitting at the old dining table with both her mother and sister suddenly make her feel—and want to behave—as if she was once again in the fifth grade? She kept her mouth shut when Jeanne replaced the knife and fork in their proper places on the plate, keeping in mind her mother's left-handedness, and slid the whole thing back onto her placemat. "He's a keeper!"

"Why, thank you kindly, John," said Mr. Rice. He seemed almost embarrassed at the attention. Bubble patted and squeezed his hand where it rested atop the table, beaming at him, but Bailey couldn't watch. She had heard a clink of metal against porcelain. "Mrs. Rhodes, that's a fine, fine daughter you've got there."

Her mother had picked up her fork and, using her shaky left hand, jabbed at one of the little squares of meat. She paused once she'd accomplished the task, and looked up. Her lips trembled, then parted. Words worked themselves out like maple sap through a tap on a chilly spring morning, slow and steady. "Thank you, Mr. Rice." Before Bailey could assess the complex, seething emotions seeming to paralyze her, her mother turned and in a much softer voice, added, "Thank you, Jeanne."

"No problem, Ma." Jeanne barely seemed to notice what had happened. Already she was stuffing more red meat into her mouth and leaning over to talk to her aunt's gentleman friend. "I heard this one joke from my friend Tag. But it's really *dirty*. You'd probably like it. Okay. So there was this guy with an enormous *you-know*, and he went to a plastic surgeon, and he said to the plastic surgeon, 'Hey, I've got this big you-know.' So the doctor says. . . ."

Had that moment really flown so swiftly over Jeanne's head? For three days Bailey had attempted to get some kind of conversation from her mother. Some kind of appreciative credit for having come all this way to spend time with her. Crap, she would have welcomed some kind of acknowledgment that Bailey was in the immediate vicinity. And in waltzed Jeanne, pregnant with some stranger's baby, to snatch away the first words of thanks she'd heard her mother say since the stroke. Had Jeanne been the one who'd come down to Richmond on the weekends, after that calamity? No. Had Jeanne talked to the doctors and the nurses and the insurance people? No. Then why in *hell* did she get that thank-you?

"Who's Tag?" she asked suddenly. Her neck felt stiff, as if turning it might shatter her spine into a thousand chilly pieces. "Is he the father?"

Jeanne broke off the joke in its middle. For the first time that evening, they really looked at one another. Bailey saw in her sister's eyes a fire that quickly dampened, its embers completely smothered to cold dust in a fraction of a second. "No," Jeanne .replied in tones equally as frigid. "He's a friend."

"You know what, Mom?" As the words fell from her mouth, Bailey knew how ugly they sounded, no matter how many good spirits she forced into her voice. "I've been thinking about that trip you wanted to go on. The one to Carverton?" That had gotten everyone's attention. Bailey looked around the table and saw the aunts staring at both her and her mother with unreadable expressions. Bubble slowly raised a hand to her mouth. Bailey turned back to her mom. "Now that Jeanne's here and you two are such chums, maybe she could take you."

"Carverton!" Bits lifted the napkin from her lap and threw it onto the table. "Polly Whigfield Rhodes! Is this true?" Without waiting for an answer, she turned in her chair and leaned over the table to face her oldest sister, sitting at its head. "I can't believe you'd want to go back to that place! Bubble! Tell her!" Aunt Bubble shook her head, but the gesture was tenuous, the merest back-and-forth motion. Both of Bailey's aunts seemed absolutely horrified at the bombshell she'd dropped. Bits went back to cross-examining everyone in the vicinity. "Polly, who told you about what they're doing in Carverton? Was it you, Bubble? I can't believe—after I told you not to."

"What's happening in Carverton? What trip?" If Bailey could have taken satisfaction in her sister's confused protest, she would have. Jeanne's uncertainty at being an outsider, though, was a hollow victory, far outweighed by their mother's expression. Frightening as it had been to see that face in the hospital, impossibly slumped from the stroke that had taken control of its left half, the slackness there now was worse to behold.

Her mother had specifically asked her not to tell the aunts about her request. Bailey had ignored that, and hefted the issue straight onto the massive oak table for everyone to observe, as out of place among the willowware, the plastic placemats trimmed with fake lace, the roast beef dinner, and the fussy bowls filled with sugar cubes, as would be a Viking's double-bladed axe still dripping with the gore of the day's plunder. Even Bailey was appalled by how inexcusably she'd behaved. In a sudden panic, Bailey looked around the table at the angry faces of her aunts, Mr. Rice's blank countenance, her sister's bewildered and silent pleas for explanation, and last, her mother's stony, somber stare. "Mom?" she appealed in a very small voice.

It was too late. Her mother's chair clattered back over

the planks as, with immense dignity, she rose in one fluid motion. Both the aunts and Jeanne leapt to their feet to help her steady herself, but it wasn't necessary. No matter what blankets of silence she had wrapped around herself since the incident, her mother still knew how to command attention. Only her fingertips lay on the table, and it seemed more as if she rested them there to keep the table from moving than to prevent herself from falling. The right side of her mouth trembled first, then opened as words came out. "I want to go home."

"She does know she's home, right?" Jeanne asked.

"She means where we grew up, dear," said Bubble, who had graduated from shock to a nervous wringing of her napkin.

"She means nonsense," Bits spat.

"I want. . . ." Bailey bit her lip as her mom tried to raise her voice. Her mother took a deep breath and continued. "To go home. One last time." The effort to produce more volume increased the slurring, so Bailey noticed the sibilant sounded more like a *zh* than an *s*. As if reading her mind, her mother skewered her with a terrible look. "And I intend to go."

She had nothing more to say. She turned in place and, once facing in the right direction, began walking for the door. Both Bubble and Jeanne ran to stand beside and slightly behind her, to escort her wherever she intended to go. Bailey thought of standing up and offering her own help.

Yet she didn't want to find out how she would react, when her mother rebuffed the offer.

Like some trio of strangers, she and Bits and Mr. Rice remained at the table, silence settling upon them more thickly with every passing second. Bailey remained perfectly still, staring at her mother's mostly uneaten dinner plate, fearful that the slightest motion might loose the tears that had been building up since the moment her mother had spoken. Bits stared at the table, her arms crossed, refusing to break the sulk into which she'd fallen.

When Mr. Rice spoke, it was with the practiced sincerity of a true gentleman trying to smooth over a crisis by pretending he'd never witnessed it. "Well, John," he told Bailey, patting the table with hands so gnarled from age that they resembled ginger roots. He paused, as if trying to muster words of kindness with few to choose from. "That was one fine dinner. One fine goddamned dinner indeed."

Part Two
Second Chance
at Love

Chapter Nine

"Ow . . . ! Holy . . . ! My G . . . ! *Ow* . . . !" There was a certain rhythm to the curses, as if they were being recited as a mantra. At the same time, there was enough authenticity to each that Bailey knew there had to be ample cause for them. She simply didn't want to find out what it was. To get from the house's front door to the driveway, though, she would have to pass the sunroom, from where the shrill cries came. She tiptoed forward, trying to tread carefully over the porch's narrow white floorboards.

"Norelle Springfield!" Bits's voice came from right inside the window. "I swear, my sister has never had anyone so noisy in her chair."

"But it hur-ur-ur-ur-urts!" said the girl with a mighty sniffle.

"Don't be silly. Sit up straight! Smile! She's only doing a little teasing!"

Exactly what kind of chair had Bubble set up in there? Did Bailey even want to know? Ever since the night before she'd crept around the house and tried to attract as little attention as possible, spending most of the evening in her room fanning herself with an ancient copy of *Southern Living* magazine. She'd tried to read the darned thing, but someone had gone through and scissored out so many of its recipes that most of the magazine's pages were gaping absences held together with unclipped bylines and gardening tips. She would have slept, but from Jeanne's room next door she'd been treated to the sounds of her sister trying to find an acceptable radio station on the old tabletop radio receiver, at last settling on a classic rock station from Newport News, liberally garnished with static.

Oh, and the voices. First Bubble's, low and concerned and babbling on like a steady stream, barely letting Jeanne get a word in edgewise. Then Bits joined them, breaking into Bubble's torrent like sharp rocks along the falls of the James River. On and on had gone the river of voices, their words indistinguishable through the house's thick walls, until at last Bailey had fallen asleep, waking in the middle of the night to hear the subdued sounds of guitar rock still drifting from the radio next door.

No wonder Bailey's head felt like an eggshell stuffed with hot hatpins that throbbed with pain whenever she moved too quickly. The screaming didn't help. "Ow . . . ! Miss . . . ! *Stop . . . !*"

"I'm barely touching you, dear!"

Bits's voice moved closer to the open sunroom window. She must have been standing right beside it. "You're lucky you came to us, Norelle. Lucky! Because my sister and I are far more forbearing than your alternative. Do you think that Shirley Jones would put up with this nonsense? If you'd been accepted—and that's a mighty big if!—Shirley would send you back home with your tail between your legs if you'd dared shed a tear, and don't think you'd be welcome to try again, after that! Once Shirley Jones blackballs a girl, she can't enter a . . . a . . ."

"Wet T-shirt competition?" supplied a semifamiliar voice.

"Yes, a wet . . . no, CeeCee, not a wet T-shirt contest. I'm surprised you're conversant with such a thing."

A voice cut through the squabbling. "Being beautiful requires sacrifice. Sometimes it hurts." Bailey recognized the confidence in that voice, bordering almost on the lazy: Larkin Merino. She pressed her back against the bricks and peered around the window shutter. Sure enough, Bits was inches away, her arms crossed. Several of the other girls sat in chairs around the room's edge, but all Bailey could see of them was their crossed legs, or their feet dangling shoes from the toe. "Look at those girls in that plastic surgery show on TV. It takes hard work and a lot of liposuction for them to look good, but it's totally worth it, to transform from an ugly duckling into a swan."

"Yeah, and those women all end up being Barbie dolls in long blond wigs, cinched into corsets, looking like they were all stamped from the same mold." Bailey startled to hear a voice so close by, though not in the sunroom. A pair of eyes looked at her through the fence posts, roughly level with her ankles. Careful to backtrack a few steps so that she wasn't standing right in front of the window where the Butter Beans congregated, Bailey stepped to the railing and looked over at the girl who stood there. Strands of smoke from the girl's cigarette drifted up and into Bailey's hair. "Every time Larkin watches that fucking show, I tell her to turn it off. It's a strike against diversity. There's no effort to convey to the television viewing audience any sense of acceptance or understanding. Just a message of 'you're not good enough so we're going to turn you into a better person through plastic surgery.'" The girl took another drag on the cigarette, then looked back up at Bailey and said, curlicues of smoke issuing from her mouth, "It's total bullshit."

Bailey took in the girl's long, shaggy hair, today streaked with vermillion, her green khakis with the legs cut off below the knee, her Doc Marten boots with textured gray socks spilling over their tops, and her ratty T-shirt with the words *Southern Womyn's Music Festival* and last year's date. "You're the one who was sitting with my mom the other day."

The girl looked a little uncomfortable. "Yeah. About that? I didn't know she was your mom. Larkin kinda clued me in later."

"Your hair was blue, then."

The girl's hands flew up to her head. For a second, Bailey caught a quick glimpse of the self-consciousness behind the girl's booted facade. "Maybe," she said, trying to sound vague. "I don't keep track of that kind of thing."

Bailey didn't buy it for a moment. In her experience, girls who aimed at bold statements with their clothing, footwear, and hair were the ones who kept mental track of everything—what they'd worn and when was the last time they'd worn it, what created maximum effect and who had noticed—and spent too much time pretending that they didn't care. They were also usually the ones who longed the most to be seen. "You live with Larkin?" she asked, wondering how anyone could survive with someone whose head was swollen enough to fill an entire living room. The girl's eyes squinted with suspicion. "You're her . . . ?"

"Friend," said the girl, almost too quickly. "I'm not her sister or anything. I'm Fawn," she added, sticking up a hand. "Lennox. Fawn Lennox."

Bailey leaned over the railing and shook. "Fawn?" What an odd, soft name for such a blunt young woman.

Instantly Fawn looked suspicious. "And what's wrong with that? I'm thinking of changing it."

"Nothing. I like it. I'm Bailey Rhodes." She hadn't thought short, buxom Larkin and this tall, flat-chested girl had been at all related. In fact, given the Womyn's Music Festival T-shirt and the rainbow flag belt buckle on the belt barely holding up the khakis, she'd been wondering about a relationship of a completely different kind. "So, what, you hang around here all day while Larkin's with my aunts? Isn't that boring?"

Fawn spun around and leaned against the railing, her back to Bailey while she sucked on the butt between her thumb and first two fingers, then stubbed it on the porch. After a long exhale, she said, "Hell, no. I don't hang around here *all* day." She accompanied the declaration with a roll of the eyes. "As if. Associate with *these* chicks? Who can't think of anything better to do than play dress-up for a patriarchal society that regards them as disposable and interchangeable? I think not. I'd rather stay among the lesser beings. That's what Larkin calls us."

"You have what my mom would call an abundance of opinion," Bailey told her, with a great deal of sympathy for what it must be like to live with Larkin. When Fawn looked up and narrowed her eyes again, she added, "No, I like it. It's a good thing."

Fawn regarded Bailey steadily for a moment, then turned away again. She shrugged. "Well, you're the only person around here to think so."

"Bailey Rhodes!" Aunt Bits's yelling, though Bailey was a mere eight or nine feet away, seemed to shake the chinaberries shading the driveway. "Get in here, girl! I need you!"

Either Bailey was imagining things, or Fawn chose that moment to smirk. "Good luck," she said, slumping down until her Crayola-colored hair vanished from few.

Sighing, Bailey loped back to the sunroom window, hoping against hope for an interruption. Even one of the girls' awful impromptu songs would have been a godsend. She had no such luck, however. "You swore to me that you wouldn't ask me for help."

An earful she'd certainly expected. To hope otherwise was like riding a log flume and praying not to get wet. What Bailey hadn't anticipated was her aunt grabbing her upper arm and yanking her through and across the window's sill. Luckily, its lower edge was a couple of feet from the ground, but she still grazed her left shin on the trip. Barely was Bailey steady on her feet when her eyes and nose were assaulted by a vapor so sour and astringent that it immediately set her into a coughing fit. Whatever it was stung, within mere seconds reducing her to blindness. "Help? You? I'd sooner turn my girls over to Shirley Jones! And believe you me, that's not going to happen save over my dead body, and even then I'm sure the good Lord would allow me one last dying gasp to reach up and grab the ankle of any of my girls who decided to go over to the dark side."

The words seemed intended more for the Butter Beans sitting around the room's edge. Bailey took the moment to clear her eyes of the sticky, stinging substance clogging her vision, then blinked and looked up to find Bubble wielding an extra-large aerosol can of Aqua Net and a scythe over a decapitated head. "Whoa!" she yelled, jumping backward into what felt like an octopus.

Several voices protested at once. Hands pushed at her hips and rear. Bits crossed her arms. "Bailey, what *has* gotten into you this morning?" She disentangled herself from the nest of legs into which she'd stumbled in her haste to get away from the horrible, awful . . . beehive?

She blinked to clear the last of the hairspray residue and quickly dispelled any lingering doubts she might have had about Bubble being some kind of Blackbeard. Aunt Bubble was merely dressed up in some sort of odd pants suit with a matching cape that would have been darling on Doris Day during the *Pillow Talk* years, but which on her resembled nothing more than an over-large set of pajamas fashioned from an oilcloth table cover. The scythe was nothing more than a large, curved plastic comb. And the decapitated head belonged to a very pretty black girl sitting in a stylist's chair wearing a plastic drape. The girl stared back at her from under one of the most enormous, distended heads of hair that Bailey had ever seen. "You send girls into your pageant looking like *that?*"

"Looking like what?" asked the girl, suddenly panicking. Despite Bubble's mild protests, she tried to turn around to see herself in a mirror.

"What's wrong with the way Norelle looks?" Bits wanted to know. From behind her, Bailey heard other murmurs, equally curious.

"She looks like. . . ." Turning her head, Bailey took in the three girls closest by. They, too, boasted masses of hair teased and sprayed into puffy clouds that looked like spun sugar, but which were probably as hard as reinforced steel. "A Marvelette!"

"A what?" asked one girl.

"It's a candy?" Bailey heard CeeCee say. "Marshmallow on the inside and chocolate on the outside?"

"Chocolate on the . . . oh, no she didn't!" said Norelle, glaring at Bailey and struggling up and out of her chair.

Bits squashed any notion of a good old-fashioned girl fight by striding to the chair where Bubble was attempting to do her bouffant magic and clamping down on Norelle's shoulder. "Well, of course this isn't the *final* product. Part of our two-week program in charm and beauty coaching includes sessions devoted to finding the right individual pageant-style hairdo for each of our girls."

Yet Bailey's impression, when she turned around and around in the long room in which the eight girls perched on white wicker furniture so dry and ancient it had probably been woven by the Israelites right before they'd whipped up a reed basket for the baby Moses, was that every single one of the girls had been afflicted by the same bad hair disease. There were would-be white Supremes with swept up-dos, Dusty Springfield imitators with shiny bouffants, and a Lesley Gore with an It's-My-Party flip who held a sieve and a towel in her lap while she snapped green beans—probably for Bailey's own dinner that evening. CeeCee Jackson wore a fabulously feminine concoction of upswept waves and a cascade of curls around her head that made her look like a singer from *The Lawrence Welk Show*. Larkin Merino, in the meantime, read a copy of *Pageantry Magazine* in another hairdresser's chair with her hair tightly wound around little black rollers that looked like miniature birdcages, waiting to be brushed out.

If God had created these young women in His image, He was obviously a fan of oldies radio. "That's a lot to do in two weeks."

Bubble set down the Aqua Net and looked as if she were about to say something, but Bits cut her off. "The girls aren't allowed to seek coaching until the day the applications are made available, and they're not made available until two weeks before the pageant. *Some* coaches were found guilty of year-round cultivation that, if you ask me, bordered on extortion. The fees alone!" Bailey tried to keep the glance at her watch surreptitious. She was sure she was in for yet another lecture about the Evils of Shirley Jones—she'd already developed a picture of the woman as a modern-day Cruella de Vil, swanking around in puppy skins.

"The committee found us in contempt of the very same rule ourselves," said Bubble, unfastening the apron snaps at the back of Norelle's neck. "I think two weeks is plenty. It's enough time to make sure. . . ."

"Bailey didn't need to know that," Bits carped, hustling Larkin into the chair. The girl settled onto it as a young Queen Elizabeth might have on her throne, as her elderly lady-in-waiting, Lady Bubble, scurried to drape around her a clean apron. "Though obviously she has something to say about your competency at hairdressing." Bits crossed her arms once more and stared at her niece. "Well?"

Even the girl on the cover of Larkin's *Pageantry Magazine* didn't have such an exaggerated, stylized hairdo. In fact, the model's black hair was as long and straight as

any Hollywood starlet's—an infinitely more natural
look than the hair-in-bondage styles Bubble had summoned from the distant past of when she'd first started
hairdressing. Bailey had no idea what the famed Ms.
Jones's students looked like, but almost anyone would
have an edge over what was looking like a road show of
Valley of the Dolls. She opened her mouth to say as much.
Then she paused, seeing the challenge in her aunt's
eyes. Stepping in with her opinions would mean having to justify them, which would lead to more arguments, and before you knew it, Bailey would be
standing behind the chair with bobby pins in her mouth
and a hot iron in her hands, playing nurse to Bubble's
hair surgeon. "They're lovely." She smiled pleasantly
and glanced down at her watch again. She'd hoped to
be halfway to Taylor's farm by now. "I wouldn't change
a thing. Now, if you'll excuse me. . . ."

"I do not. I didn't ask you in here to talk about hairstyles. I wanted to talk to you about your mother." It
was the last topic Bailey wanted to tackle at that moment. After the bludgeoning she'd taken, she was still
feeling tender about the previous night's dinner. Why
in the world did Bits insist on airing the family's dirty
laundry in front of all her girls? Just last night, Mr. Rice
had been witness to the most colossal Rhodes war in all
memory—larger than the time Bailey had declared her
intentions to move to Manhattan. Hell, bigger than the
time in high school when Bailey had been asked to her
senior prom by a Young Republican and her mother
had spent so long debating him on his party's failing
economic policies that they were nearly three hours
late. Apparently Bits had some of the same reservations
about discussing the matter in front of her pupils, because she glared around the room before speaking
again. Seven heads that had been turned in her direction immediately bowed down over their magazines
once more. "This idea she has in her head about going
to Carverton is nonsense," she whispered.

"I know," said Bailey.

"You can't take her."

"No, I can't."

"It's ridiculous. You've got to make her see that."

Bailey tilted her head. "You do realize that I'm not arguing with you, right?"

"Tilt your head a little, dear," Bubble told Larkin. Using the pointed tip of her comb, she deftly speared and unspooled one of the girl's many curlers. Not since the age of nine had a single curler touched Bailey's head. She hadn't realized that they came in so many different sizes, nor that they'd been laid out in a strategic pattern, instead of the random formlessness she'd assumed. Each rolled plait conformed perfectly with the next, so that as Bubble brushed them into shape, they formed a luminous stream. Larkin, her eyelashes prettily fluttering low, seemed to accept the natural crown of gold as her due. "Tell Bailey what you told me, Bits." Bubble didn't seem to notice her sister's head whipping around, nor the look of dislike that followed. "About Carverton. Ettlestone Road, in particular. Apparently," she supplied when Bits didn't answer immediately, "Our entire old street is being . . . what's the word? Renovated."

"*Bulldozed* will do," said Bits. "Polly's obsession is useless. She'll be disappointed."

Of all the things Bubble might have said, that was the most unexpected. "Bulldozed?" Bailey asked. The idea made her feel slightly sick at the stomach. Her reasons to avoid the trip had seemed perfectly logical moments before, but this new urgency was an element she hadn't expected. She'd thought her mom wanted to visit solely so she could see the hills, the almost Eden-like tranquility of the sleepy road covered with a blanket of red pine needles, and the old sights, like the spot where once stood Bailey's grandmother's feed store, or the little schoolhouse where the Whigfield girls had all learned to read and write. In other words, the boring, familiar old stuff that Bailey had grown up hearing about. The mere fact that paradise was about to be paved to put up a parking lot threw her motives into stark relief. Who in the world was she to deny her mom a last chance to see what might not be there in another six months, or in a few weeks?

"So you agree." Bits seemed to think the matter settled, but Bailey felt as if she were being bulldozed herself. "Your mother needs to learn the past is in the past. We can't go haring off to Georgia. Not now."

"I should say not!" Larkin's lip pouted at the notion. "Why, Miz Oates, you've got a duty!"

"Hold still, dear." Bubble's hands darted to capture a plait that flopped as Larkin's head darted in appeal from one girl to another.

"Miz Whigfield, I cannot hold still when there is beauty at stake! Beauty comes before family!"

"Don't be silly." Bits's snappish retort exactly voiced Bailey's own annoyance.

"But it's true! Families come and go, but beauty endures! 'Juliet's beauty makes this vault a feasting presence, full of light!' That's Shakespeare. 'Beauty excels each mortal thing upon the dull earth dwelling!' That's Shakespeare, too. Beauty—"

Before Larkin could summon any more quotes from the Bard, Bubble interrupted. "Nothing's more important than family, dear. Don't be silly."

"But Miz Whigfield, it's true! Think about all the great legends!" From time to time, Larkin's plastic apron suddenly lifted into the air, as if the girl were making rapid hand gestures beneath it as she talked. "Cleopatra! Helen of Troy! Juliet! The Lady of Shalott! They outlived history because of their great beauty."

"Juliet and the Lady of Shalott are fictional," Bailey pointed out, tired and anxious to be on her way.

Larkin ignored her. "Think of *me*," she announced. "I'm destined to win that pageant, and if you go, I'll never fulfill my destiny!" Wasn't anyone else outraged by Larkin's sense of entitlement? It had rubbed Bailey the wrong way right from the first. A Bed, Bath, and Beyond stocked with nothing but cheese graters couldn't have reduced her nerves to shreds any more quickly. When Bailey looked around the room, however, none of the girls seemed outraged. Maybe they were used to Larkin's airs.

Aunt Bits, however, was immune. "Girl, I swear, if there was a brain cell in that pretty head of yours, a troop of Boy Scouts armed with flashlights and compasses wouldn't be able to find it. And what did I just get through saying? Nobody's going anywhere, least of all until after the pageant's over." She threw her hands up in the air, then crossed the room to take the finished colander of snapped beans from the Lesley Gore lookalike. "And this talk about beauty is absolute nonsense. With a bit of effort, anyone can be beautiful. Posture, poise, and presentation is all there is to it."

The smile gracing Larkin's face would have been better suited on a smug little six-year-old who'd been told by her parents that Santa was bringing her everything she wanted for Christmas. It aroused in Bailey a perverse desire to be the bigger kid who told her that there was no jolly old Saint Nick. "Oh, get real. That's what we tell lesser beings so they don't get discouraged."

"Oh my God," Bailey exclaimed. "You did not actually say those words aloud." When Larkin looked up, her pretty, pouty face a blank, she could have squeezed it for a shot glass of Concentrate of Smug. "People don't actually *say* those things."

"Sugar, I don't know what you're worried about." Larkin seemed surprised. "It's not as if you have to worry. You're a pretty girl. We're all pretty girls in here. I didn't mean you!"

"Yeah, but you can't . . . !"

"It's a simple fact, isn't it?" Larkin appealed to the group around her. "Genetics. Some people are born gifted. Most people aren't. All of us are very lucky!"

Not all the girls seemed to be in agreement with Larkin's opinions, though a couple of them nodded their heads. CeeCee and Austyn, in the room's far corner, looked positively uncomfortable. Bailey had a sneaking suspicion they'd been on the whip end of Larkin's decrees at some point. "And the rest are lesser beings?"

"Yes!" The room seemed to grow brighter from the would-be beauty queen's two-hundred watt smile, bestowed upon Bailey as a kindergarten teacher might beam at a slow pupil making progress. "Exactly! There's nothing *wrong* with them. It's a pity, that's all."

"Well, that's one of the most ridiculous things I've heard." There was more than Bits's usual cantankerousness weighing down her words. She seemed genuinely displeased. Even Bubble was shaking her head as she worked. "Of course there's genetics involved, but there's more to beauty than genes."

"Is that the kind of bullshit you tell your—" Bailey stopped at the very last word, before she said either something untrue or unkind. "Roommate?"

"Language," tutted Bubble.

One might have thought that Bubble had touched her hot iron to the back of Larkin's neck, by the way the girl startled forward. "What?" she asked. Then, settling back, unease marring her brow's smoothness and the perfect curve of her lips, she allowed Bubble to resume her ministrations. "I don't have a roommate."

"Fawn?" It was fun to poke at what was obviously one of Larkin's few vulnerable spots. "She seemed to think you find her one of the pitiful ones."

"Who's this Fawn? Larkin, what garbage are you spreading, girl?"

"Fawn's a very nice young woman who—hold on." The spiky glances Larkin kept shooting her way were reward enough for what she was about to do. Bailey ducked out through the window and stepped onto the porch, locating the vermillion-haired girl by the column of smoke rising through the hydrangeas. A few moments later, she was dragging a protesting and surly Fawn back through the window. "Here she is," she announced.

"Hi, Fawn!" From across the room, CeeCee waved. "Isn't your hair sweet?"

It had been difficult enough to get Fawn to stub out half a perfectly good Camel and accompany her onto her aunts' porch, much less convince her to enter a room full of girls she probably thought of as her worst enemies, but the sight alone seemed to have repaid the effort. Fawn stared around the sunroom, taking in the enormous hairdos, the photographs of Miss Tidewater Butter Bean former contestants hanging on the walls, the enormous old-fashioned hair dryer, the hairdresser's chair, and what looked like a practice tiara hanging on the back of the door, and blinked. Her amazed eyes looked like enormous pools of white; after a moment, she actually snorted with laughter. "Oh, jeez!"

"Oh, you meant *Fawn*. Fawn is my mother's best friend's sister's daughter from Ashland," explained Larkin, her soft Southern accent suddenly having developed hard, defensive edges. "She's been living with me for only a few weeks or so."

"Four months!" Fawn rebutted.

"I don't know what she's doing here at your gracious abode, Miz Oates. She follows me around like a puppy dog sometimes."

"Yeah," said Fawn, studying Larkin as if seeing her for the first time. "Woof woof. I don't know what I'm doing here either, now that you mention it."

Bailey honestly hadn't meant to spark a face-off between the two. Making Larkin uncomfortable was nothing to her. The girl would get over it, sooner or later. If she had to take sides, though, Bailey was firmly on that of Larkin's outcast friend; if Fawn had some kind of crush on the beauty queen, she was sorry for it, but she wanted to make a point. "Okay, Bits," she said. "Look beyond the crimson hair. You could make this girl into a beauty queen every bit as beautiful as most of these girls. Including Larkin, right?" Bailey ignored the look of hatred that crossed Larkin's face.

Fawn, on the other hand, seemed genuinely baffled and, for a few milliseconds, actually frightened. "Hey, hey," she protested. "Hold on here."

Bailey placed a hand on the girl's shoulder. "I'm just asking a question," she said. "You don't have to do anything."

"Yes, Fawn." Larkin sounded as if she was spitting bullets. "Don't do anything."

"Good," Fawn said, trying to shrug back on her persona of indifference. "Because I'm not entering a . . . I'm not doing it."

Bits, in the meantime, had been considering the raw material at hand. "Her posture's atrocious, of course," she criticized, walking in a circle around them. Beside her, Bailey felt Fawn straighten up slightly in a way that was meant to be imperceptible. "Her teeth are quite good." Fawn drew shut her mouth. "She stinks of tobacco. I don't know how she manages, but her skin's quite good. I mean, someone would have a lot of work on her hands, but of course it could be done."

"She couldn't be in a pageant!" Larkin said. Though she sat still and compliant so Bubble could continue fixing her tresses, she had crossed her legs. One golden sandal peeked out from under the edge of her apron; it bounced up and down on her toe in a manic, almost frantic rhythm. "She can't! For one thing, she's a *lesbian!*" If Larkin had expected the bombshell to cause mayhem when it exploded, she was in for disappointment. The revelation was little more than a squib. None of the Butter Beans seemed surprised. There were no sudden giggles, no shocked faces, no more of a hushed silence than there had been a moment before. Bits turned around, crossed her arms, and peered at her star pupil. "Well, she *is*."

"Yeah, that's right," Fawn said softly, as if making up

her mind about something. "I'm a big lesbian. What about it?"

"You can *see* she's not pageant material!"

"I don't know why not, dear," Aunt Bubble said through several bobby pins held in her mouth's corner. "Aren't you a lesbian, too?"

Now that, Bailey thought, was how one delivered a bombshell. Larkin's mouth opened and closed silently, like a fish stunned to find itself out of water. All the girls looked up from their magazines and photograph albums, unblinking and barely daring to breathe. Even Fawn resembled her animal namesake, caught in the headlights of an oncoming car. Bubble, in the meantime, kept unrolling hair and combing it out into its stylized shape. "Several of our best girls through the years have been highly talented lesbians. I always hoped several of them would go on to Hollywood."

"Bubble, you butt-ignorant twit," growled Bits through her teeth after a moment's pause. "There's a world of difference between a *lesbian* and a *thespian*."

Fawn, in the meantime, still looked as if she expected to be mowed down by the aunts' massive combined wills. "I'm not entering the stupid pageant," she said. "You can't make me."

"It's not like you'd win, anyway." Reassured of her supremacy, Larkin settled back in the chair, allowing Bubble to remove the last few curlers above the nape of her neck. "Really, it's best to spare yourself the disappointment."

"Oh?" Fawn's jaw jutted out to the side. "Miss Oates, how much are your coaching lessons, anyway?" she asked suddenly, her eyes never leaving Larkin's face. "I work at the dog groomer's and I don't get a lot of money."

Before Bits could open her mouth, Bailey spoke up. "I'll be your sponsor." Any amount was worth the satisfaction of seeing, at that moment, the horrified roundness of Larkin's eyes, and the small *O* of her lips. "The sponsor covers all entry costs, too, if there are any. And I'd spring for some nice clothing."

"Oh gee, that's awfully nice of you, Bailey." Fawn seemed to be enjoying her moment of triumph. "It's so nice to have a real friend who stands up for you. Should we go outside and discuss it?"

"Yes, let's," Bailey said in the same breezy air.

"If you're serious, you'd best start with us today," Bits called.

Fawn had already stepped over the sill, her arms still clutched around her chest. Bailey followed, trying to keep a straight face until she was out of eyeshot. She heard her aunt shouting out her name, and turned to find Bits's head sticking out at waist level. "I don't know what's gotten into you," she scowled. "All I can say is that you'd better not get people's expectations high when you don't intend to follow through. You did it with your mother, and now you're doing it again." The woman peered around the corner to where Fawn slouched against the bricks of the house. "And you, girl! Take a shower if you intend to come back here. And wear a dress. If you have one." Bailey had a feeling that Bits would have loved to have slammed the window shut at that point, but it was too hot. She settled for letting the Venetian blind cascade with a rattle until it collided with the sill.

Bailey looked at Fawn; Fawn looked at Bailey. They both collapsed into silent giggles at last, barely able to control them until they'd reached the end of the porch. "Oh my God," said Fawn. "Your aunts are so twisted."

"Hello!" said Bailey. "Tell me about it. I had to grow up with them."

"You know there's no way in hell I'm entering that pageant, right? I was only trying to scare that fucking hag. I can't *believe* her." Fawn dug into one of the deep, capacious pockets of her pants and withdrew her packet of Camels with trembling fingers. "I'm talking about La Merino. Not your aunt. In case you were wondering," she added, through lips clamped down on the cigarette.

"Ah." Bailey had, in fact, been trying to figure it out.

There were more suspects for the role than there had been murderers on the Orient Express. She knew it was intrusive, but she couldn't resist a last question. "So you and Larkin. . . ." Fawn looked up, wary. "You aren't. . . ."

Blink, blink. Fawn stared at her for a moment before realizing what Bailey was trying oh-so-tactfully to imply. "No. God, no! Can you imagine me and her . . . ? No!" She lit the cigarette and inhaled deeply, seeming to regain some composure from its toxicity. "I kinda hoped. . . ." She abandoned that thought completely, and in the space of a few seconds, visibly hardened. It was like watching the walls of Jericho spring back up from the rubble, hiding what had lain vulnerable moments before. "I thought she was more tolerant than that. That's all."

The last glimpse she had of the poor girl, as Bailey hustled down the driveway, was of Fawn leaning against the house, cigarette in mouth, her head inclined toward the sunroom window. It looked for all the world as if she was eavesdropping on a conversation in which she longed to participate, but for which she didn't know the language.

Chapter Ten

"You would think by now I'd have learned that I'm apparently not essential to anyone," Bailey muttered to her companion, punching the end-call button on her cell phone. "I mean, it's not as if I haven't put in a half-dozen years at the network. You'd think that the first time I took a week off—a real week off, and not one of those working vacations that involved going out to a shoot and pretending that wiping the butt of so-called talent whose last solid credit was standing on a rotating platform gesturing at muscle cars at the Detroit auto show but who now believes she's a full-on celebrity chased by paparazzi, when she can barely scare up a ten-year-old with a disposable camera. . . . Where was I?" she asked. "Oh. You'd think that someone might notice I'm not at my usual desk. You'd think that someone might miss me. You'd think that *someone, somewhere* would say, 'Where's Bailey? We need Bailey. Why isn't Bailey here?'" She sighed. Speaking of butts, her own was losing feeling from sitting on the curb for so long. "Have you ever felt unnecessary?" she asked. "No, of course not. You live the life. Everybody loves you, don't they? You've always had a home to go to at the end of a

hard day. Someplace you belong." When her companion didn't answer, Bailey followed up her monologue
with a look of accusation. "Don't deny it."

The golden Labrador simply wagged her tail, briefly
licked her chops and closed her mouth, then resumed
her happy panting, drool dripping down onto the hot
sidewalk. "I knew it," Bailey said with affection, ruf-
fling the animal between her ears. "Lucky bitch."

A voice spoke from immediately behind her. "Well, I
do declare, I've always heard that when the temperature
soars, people do strange things, but I can honestly say
I've never seen someone talking to a hound dog before!
Well, there was my second cousin, once removed, Phyl-
lis, but she was a queer old thing!"

Something about the accent triggered instant recognition; perhaps it was the way the man said the word *dog*
as if it had three distinct, yet melded, syllables. Bailey
craned her neck and caught a glimpse not of the vision
in white she expected, but of her short, squat friend
dressed from head to toe in canary yellow. Everything
was the same shade—the patent-leather shoes, the
pants, the jacket with the wide lapels, the shirt with the
pimp collar, the festive, wide-brimmed Stetson. He
looked as if he'd been dipped in a leftover vat of Easter
egg dye. Even the man's necktie matched the rest of his
clothing, though its vibrant hue was interrupted by
polka dots of the palest imaginable pink. "Oh, hi!" A
numb butt didn't help Bailey's struggle to her feet. She
felt miserably un-put together compared with the natty
attire of her weird little friend—not to mention the cool
elegance of his female cohort, who wore a simple sundress and white sandals as if it were designer chic. "This
is Kitten," she said, gesturing to the panting dog. When
the man's eyebrows shot up, Bailey realized her statement wasn't exactly recouping any points with him in
the mental stability check column.

"What a darling name for a dog. Isn't it a darling

name, Sapphire?" he asked his young friend. Wait. The different name startled Bailey. Was this the same girl as the last time? Apparently not, though the differences between this model and the last were so subtle that Bailey would have sworn they were the same dark-haired, long-limbed, victim of ennui. Who was this guy? Was he running some basement cloning operation? "It's a darling name. And don't let anyone tell you different! I was taking my midday constitutional and thought I saw you sitting here, sugar!" The man's voice was as sweet and friendly as could be, like a big sticky slice of Aunt Bubble's pecan pie covered with ice cream and drizzled with caramel. "And I said to Sapphire, 'Why, it's that lovely Bailey Rhodes! Let's go over and wish her a hearty good day.' Didn't I, Sapphire? So here we are." The girl answered the question with the same unruffled stillness of her predecessor, but the little man beamed so broadly that Bailey could see a gold molar glinting from the back of his mouth.

"That's so nice. It's nice of you to be so, um, nice." Bailey stopped before she made herself sound any more foolish, but it was nearly impossible not to gush. The man made her feel so warm and fuzzy and *welcome*. "How are you? How's . . . work?" Part of her hoped the man might drop some hint to clue her in to his identity. At this point, after all his compliments and flattery, she would be making enemies with a blunt, *Who are you, exactly?*

"Oh, my, that trifling business? That doesn't interest me at *all*, nor should it you, sugar. Aren't those the cutest little loafers you're wearing? Aren't they adorable, Sapphire?" he asked his sighing companion. "Are they Stuart Weitzman? I just knew it! I've always said to myself about you, 'That Bailey Rhodes is one girl who knows her shoes!' The crocodile embossing is absolutely the living end. I bet it's all the rage in New York . . . you certainly don't see it out here in the sticks, hah-hah! And how are your aunts?"

The man had a smooth way of gliding from one subject to the next. "Oh, they're fine!"

Before she could add anything to her basic statement, he had taken a step closer and was leaning on his shiny brass cane. "Are they?" he asked in a tone of concern. "Because I worry about the poor dears. They really contribute so *much* to the community, don't they, Sapphire? And you know how it is with people who give and give and give . . . sometimes they feel underappreciated and overworked. I do hope the pageant coaching isn't tiring them out?"

"Not at all!" said Bailey, laughing at the idea. "You know how they are. There could be anthrax and nuclear war and a new ice age, and they'd be wearing gas masks and radiation suits and earmuffs while laying out new housecoat patterns and baking." The man's hilarity was a little out of proportion to the quality of her joke, but Bailey wasn't about to let the moment pass without a little riff. She adopted Bubble's vagueness and said, "Bits, do hand me that Geiger counter, dear, so I can check the pie tins for gamma rays." Then, in her other aunt's more stern tones, she replied, "Do it yourself, you old bat. Can't you see I'm making snowshoes from my John's old tennis rackets?"

It took fully a minute for the man's throaty chuckles to diminish so that he could reply. "Delicious!" he said at last. "Honey, you can quote me on this one, but you have missed your calling! You are the funniest thing this poor old man has seen since Wally Cox was Mr. Peepers! And don't ever let anyone tell you different!" After fanning himself with a pair of canary yellow gloves, he replaced them in his coat pocket, then pulled out a matching handkerchief that he delicately applied to his brow. "Honey, you are going to give me apoplexy if you keep that up! What a pistol! Now, tell me, honey, how are the pageant contestants looking this year, hmmm? Are there any future Miss Americas among the fine young fillies those gracious women have taken under their tutelage? Hmmm? Is there anyone of special note in whose splendor I will revel from my lowly seat in the audience, come pageant day?"

"Well. . . ." Bailey didn't mean to sound as if she was prevaricating. She simply didn't know how to answer the question.

"You can tell me, sugar. I'll be silent as the proverbial tomb!" The little man pursed his lips into a moue, raised a finger, and pretended to be shushing himself. "Won't I? And Sapphire too, of course."

A promise from Sapphire to be silent as the tomb would have been fairly redundant. From all the evidence Bailey had, the young woman might have been mute. "There is Larkin Merino," she said. "I think everyone considers her to be the front runner."

"Oh yes, Larkin!" The man seemed to be playing with his fingers a game of here-is-the-church-and-here-is-the-steeple in front of his lips, so deeply was he concentrating on what Bailey had to say. "A truly beautiful, vivacious girl. I won't hear a word said against her, will I, Sapphire? I'm sure your aunts can work wonders with her. A pity they can't do anything about her height—a truly beautiful girl, don't get me wrong, sugar, but if she got a stocking job at the Food Lion, everything would be on the bottom two shelves, am I right? I'm right, aren't I, Sapphire?" It was the one time that the girl allowed a smile to cross her face, a smile that even on a sunny summer afternoon would have deep-frozen an entire case of Slimfast. "Do tell me though," he said, moving right along, "What is that delicious girl doing for the talent portion of the show? No! Don't tell me!" he commanded the instant Bailey's lips parted to answer. "Juliet! Am I right? Tell me I'm right!"

"You're right!"

It was as impossible to keep the surprise from her voice, apparently, as it was for the man to keep a smug smile from his face. "I knew it. She's been stagestruck since she was in high school, that girl. She's been in love with *Romeo and Juliet* since the drama club tackled it her senior year."

"She was Juliet?" Bailey couldn't help but ask.

"No, she was Juliet's nurse. A much *taller* girl was cast as Juliet. And I don't care what anyone says, as the nurse, Larkin was completely and utterly—memorable, shall we say? Every time she was on the stage, my attention simply flew to her. Even when she wasn't talking. Mostly because she was mouthing the lead's lines." When Bailey laughed, he asked, "And how do you like her Juliet?"

"Well!" Okay, *now* she was prevaricating. "It's certainly—memorable, shall we say?" she ventured at last.

After a momentary pause, the little man laughed again, his head rolling back with enjoyment. "My dear, you are the soul of tact! Well, well, well, I dare say that our theatrical performances are nothing like what you are used to, living on the Great White Way, but we are grateful for every little bit of culture we get out here and do tell me, my dear, where did you get that cunning necklace?"

"Macy's?" she asked, caught off guard.

"It's lovely, truly lovely. I'd steal it from you if my neck weren't so thick, hah-hah!" He indulged in a self-deprecating laugh. "And the other would-be winners? Of course, they might not be able to compete with Larkin—lovely girl, really, just a lovely girl—but I'm certain they're all beautiful in their own ways. Am I right? I know I'm right."

"Oh, sure," Bailey said, seeing a way to be funny once again. She then launched into a vivid description of her aunt's outdated hairstyles from that morning, soft-pedaling her horror at how out of touch they seemed to be with current pageant styles, but making certain to tickle his ribs with a description of the procession of outdated flips and the sheer size of her aunt's whipped-up creations. The retelling lightened her own mood. It felt good to laugh with someone who seemed to understand. The guilt she felt at her disloyalty to the aunts was nothing, little more than the slightest tickle at the back of her throat.

"You are a positive terror to my health, sugar!" he exclaimed at the end of it. "There's a streak of mischief in you, isn't there, Sapphire? A veritable streak of one hundred percent unadulterated mischief!"

She grinned at him. "I did kind of try to convince a strident lesbian to enter the pageant."

He held up his hands in mock horror. "No! Wait! I've heard there's quite an *odd* character living with our Larkin. Is she . . . ?" Bailey's nod sent the fat little man into paroxysms of rapture. "Oh! Oh! Perfect! Well, I can see that when you're around, I am definitely going to have to keep my eye on *you*, young lady! But I shan't take up any more of your no-doubt precious time, my dear, though it was delightful, as always, to see you!" When he extended his crooked arm, Sapphire automatically reached out to clutch it with her elegant hands. "One of these days, you and I are going to have a sit-down and a good, long talk, do you hear?"

"Well, if you have to go . . ."

"I'm certain we'll chat again, my dear." The man had already backed away when he bowed and made an elaborate flourish in the general vicinity of his hat brim. "I adore your stories!" Before he scuttled down the street with the much taller woman gliding at his side, he kissed his fingertips and waggled them in Bailey's direction.

She watched him go with a certain disappointment. Days and days had passed since she'd had a good dish; a little bit of gossip reminded her of the friends she missed and the hours misspent in the pointless swapping of celebrity scandal, coworker hearsay, and the ever-popular tittle-tattle about mutual friends—the stuff of life that made her feel vaguely guilty, no matter how oh-so-enjoyable it felt. Where did that lingering sense of wrongness come from, anyway? Probably her mother, Bailey considered. Through most of her life, her mom would have thought anything vaguely entertainment related to be unworthy of pursuit. Though she'd never come out and said it, Bailey knew her mother hated the years Bailey had spent chasing an acting career. She probably thought the fluffy travel-and-nature documentaries of the Expedition Channel were unworthy of great minds. And Bailey was fine with that, really. At least, 95 percent of the time she managed to convince herself she was.

"Hey," she heard from behind where she was leaning against the streetlight. When she pulled away, her arm was indented and red from where the hot metal had pressed into her flesh. Taylor stood there, an enormous plastic bucket of paint hanging from one hand, and a plastic-wrapped bunch of flowers in the other. Kitten, in the meantime, greeted her master's return with increased panting and tail-wagging. Bailey blinked. Who were the flowers for? Surely not for her. Taylor knew better. Right? "Make all your phone calls?"

"Well, I made them. No one answered them. Get your paint?" Thinking about her mother had driven from her mind all the glee she'd derived from her conversation with the round little man, but she attempted to sound not as glum as she felt.

"I didn't come for paint," he told her. Okay, that was an odd statement to make when it was pretty obvious that he was carrying a ten-gallon plastic pail bearing the description of *ceiling white* on its outside, but she wasn't about to argue the obvious. Or did he mean that the flowers had been the main purpose of his trip into town? She stared at the cheap bouquet of baby's breath and colorful daisies, quirking her mouth. If that was the rural way of wooing a girl, it was ham-handed at best and embarrassing at worst. Where had he bought it, at the 7-Eleven? She could practically smell the refrigeration. "What do you mean, no one answered them?"

"No one seems to know where Chandra—my assistant—is." She watched him swing the paint bucket into the truck's bed. "My friend Sidney's in a meeting. My friend Euan's on the set of his soap, or something. Steve—that's my boyfriend," she said, emphasizing the last word, "is unavailable."

"Unavailable for you?" Taylor was wearing the same ratty baseball cap as the day before, but his jeans were clean, and his short-sleeved shirt seemed to have been ironed. "Hard to imagine."

How could he simply stand there and not mention the damned bouquet in his left hand? She couldn't stand it any longer. "Nice flowers. Are they for me?" she asked, following it up quickly with a joking, "I'm not sure Steve would approve!" When she turned them down, she would at least have a solid footing for it.

"Thank you. They're not for you. Your Steve doesn't have to worry," he said smoothly, giving her an odd look.

Taylor shifted the bouquet from one hand to the other and backtracked to the passenger side door. The handoff felt as if he was revoking a gift. It stung a little. She should never have said anything. But who was getting the flowers, then? While in Bailey's big head she'd been assuming that she was the center of his universe, had Taylor been hiding a sweetie of his own?

That was fine. Good, considering. But somehow she couldn't help but feel a little chagrined, when she took her place in the front seat of his pickup. She waited until he opened his own door and slid in before replying. "For your girlfriend, then?" she asked, when he wedged the bouquet in the console between them. In the back seat, Kitten circled around and around until she found a comfortable place to sit and pant.

He didn't reply to her question, instead asking one of

his own. "So if you were in Manhattan right now, what would you be doing?" She was so taken aback by the incongruity that she couldn't answer until after he'd started the ignition. Taylor pulled his lap belt around his waist, then remained facing her. "Seriously. What would you be doing right this moment?"

"Well, let's see," she said, glancing at the dashboard clock. "It's noon, so I'd probably be reading the Deals Daily. That's an e-mail about network deals with talents. They send it out every day at about noon."

"Uh-huh," he said. "What else?"

What in the world was he trying to get at? "I'd probably be . . . I don't know. I usually do all my hardest work in the morning, before the people on the West Coast make it in to their offices. Plus I'm kind of a morning person." She waited for the inevitable wince she received from almost everyone else to whom she made that confession, but he nodded, pulled into gear, and released the brake. Of course. He was probably a morning person himself. Didn't farmers get up at the screech of dawn so they could milk cows or churn butter or whatever it was they did? Or was she creating false assumptions from memories of the *Little House on the Prairie* books? "Okay. So. Twelve-ten. I'd probably have finished looking over a bunch of contracts from legal. Maybe given Chandra some errands to run. It seems that half my job is thinking of stuff to keep her busy." He nodded again, encouraging her to continue, though she still didn't have the foggiest notion of why he was so interested. "Then I'd probably give a call to my friend Sidney to see what she was up to, and once that was done, I don't know. I'd flip on CNN and listen to what's going on around the world while I organize my desk for the afternoon."

The truck picked up speed as they reached the outskirts of Crestonville. "What else?" he insisted.

"What is this all about?" she asked, puzzled beyond tolerance. "Why are you so interested in my job?"

His voice was teasing in reply. "Aw, come on. There's

got to be something else you do at this time of the day back in the Big Apple."

"What?" She thought furiously. "I don't deal with that many big celebrity names, if that's what you're trying to get at. I review contracts, talk to managers, make phone calls, get Chandra to arrange limo service and catering, ask—"

"I'm a little curious, but don't you ever plan for a midday meal in that *That Girl* life of yours? Lunch," he explained, once he saw her baffled expression. "Don't you have lunch in the big city? Don't tell me you're one of those types who skips meals to keep trim."

"Oh, lunch," she said, aware that in her mouth the word sounded foreign. So he thought she was trim? Or was he suggesting that she was anything but? And why in the world was she overanalyzing? "Of course, lunch." Once again, she was painfully aware of the bouquet in the console between them, wedged between the cup holder and the emergency brake at an awkward angle. "Sure, I eat lunch."

"Good," he said, the mischievous quirk of his lips blossoming into a full-blown grin. There was something in that broad smile of his that could instantly set her at ease, if she'd let it. It was warm; it felt genuine. "Because that's where we're going."

"Going where?" she wanted to know, surprised. Was there a restaurant in town she didn't know about? Someplace where she wasn't likely to contract ptomaine?

"You'll see." As if to comfort her, Kitten leaned over from the backseat and slurped Bailey's ear.

You'll see had always turned out to be a portent of disappointment when Bailey had been growing up. If her mother had ordered her into the car and replied with those two words when Bailey asked where they were headed, it usually meant that the old Dodge Dart would shortly be pulling up in front of a campaign headquarters where her mother was volunteering, and that Bailey and Jeanne would soon be spending their afternoon stuffing envelopes with promotional fliers instead of snuggled down in front of the TV. Or it might mean that they'd stop somewhere near the Surry power plant to join other picketers, and that Bailey would have to spend hours at a time holding up a homemade sign on poster board stapled to a stake that boasted an anti-nuclear slogan. So although her hopes automatically weren't all that high, when Taylor eventually pulled the truck into his own driveway rather than the parking lot of some roadside pit advertising the best pork rinds in the county, she was slightly relieved. "You're cooking?"

"I'm not likely to subject anyone to that right off the bat," he chuckled. "No. You'll see."

Again, those words. Instead of driving all the way to the house, however, her aunts' neighbor stopped fifty feet from the road and turned off the motor. She didn't wait for him to open her door. As much as she appreciated the way he automatically played the part of a Southern gentleman when it came to the car door, she wasn't entirely helpless. Kitten bounded out after her, immediately galloping in the direction of the house, barking at the top of her lungs. Taylor, in the mean-time, ambled around to the truck's rear gate, reached over, and pulled out a folded bundle of cloth that proba-bly had once been a bedspread. "You take this," he com-manded, tossing it so that she caught it with a little fumbling. He hauled out the enormous paint bucket with one hand, and then a small cooler with the other. He paused for a moment to reach into the front seat of the truck once again, withdrawing the flowers. The truck door slammed. "This way," he said with a jerk of his head.

Bailey followed him off the drive and onto the grass, where it sloped at a gentle angle down to a narrow strip of oversized bushes, wild-looking, the tips of their long stems heavy with a flat, blackish berry. "Pokeweed," Taylor warned her as he held back a cluster of branches.

"I keep trying to clear it out of here, but the mocking-birds eat the fruit, then poop out the seeds, and they come up somewhere new. Watch out for the berries," he said.

"Why? They're poisonous?"

"Yes, but I was more worried about them staining your duds than you eating them," he joked. "Just a little bit farther." Beyond the brush and bramble was a narrow footpath, obviously much-used, that first dipped and then led upward. Within half a minute's walk, Bailey found herself standing atop a small hummock of perfectly grassy earth that overlooked Taylor's fields, shaded by an old oak. "What do you think? Perfect spot for a picnic?"

For one of the few times in her life, Bailey was sincerely happy to discover that the words *you'll see* hadn't contained a nasty coda at the end. "It's beautiful!" Taylor honestly couldn't have picked a better place for a picnic; the road wasn't at all visible through the dense flora surrounding the little mound. "You can see the house from here." She pointed in the direction of the horizon below, where amid a huddled collection of trees stood the old homestead, looking as if it had stood there for centuries and planned to stand for centuries more.

"I thought you might like it," he said, taking from her the old bedspread and unfurling it. Together they shook it out and laid it over the ground. Rather grandly, he gestured for her to sit. "I didn't bring any pillows. But I could run to the house if you wanted."

"No!" She honestly didn't want Taylor to go to any trouble for her, yet after the weirdness over the flowers, she was absurdly pleased he offered. "Really, this is fantastic. Overwhelming." Did she sound too enthusiastic? "Okay, anything would be better than eating mayonnaise sandwiches on Wonder bread with the aunts. But this is great. One question, though." She watched while

Taylor, using the giant container of paint as a stool, flipped open the lid of the cooler. "Is there any food?"

"We shall come to that. First, mademoiselle, the finest vintage Crestonville has to offer!" With a flourish, Taylor withdrew from within the cooler's depths two cans swirled with green. Shaved ice still clung to the aluminum; small fragments of it sprayed into the air and melted to droplets the moment they touched Bailey's skin.

"Mountain Dew?" she said, recognizing the label.

"And . . . Diet Mountain Dew!" he said, offering both. She took the non-diet can, for some reason hoping he wasn't the type of guy who automatically expected her to want the no-calorie version. "Excellent choice, mademoiselle. Is there food, you ask? A fine question." It was the first time she'd seen Taylor deliberately acting silly. He wasn't outrageously funny, like Euan could be during their improv exercises. Taylor's antics simply put her at ease in what could have been a very awkward situation. "Indeed, there is food. But first, a question. Does mademoiselle enjoy Italian? The pasta, the chicken marinara, the cannoli?"

"Well sure! Who doesn't?"

"She does! Delightful! Unfortunately, this establishment, she have no Italian. But tell me, does mademoiselle enjoy Thai food? The spicy noodle, the chili chicken, the curry soup?"

Bailey couldn't help but laugh. "No, I love Thai. Seriously."

"Ah!" Taylor made another mock face of sorrow. "Unfortunately, this fine establishment, she is not serving the Thai food this afternoon. One more question. Does mademoiselle enjoy the Mexican?"

"The burrito, the spicy chimichanga, the *donde esta la casa de pepe?*" Bailey said, laughing outright by now. "Let me guess, this establishment, she doesn't have that either?"

Taylor's dark eyebrows rose with triumph. "But this

is where mademoiselle is wrong! For Mexican is exactly what this establishment, she is serving!" With that pronouncement, he sprang off the paint can and pried open its flexible lid with the corner of his fingers. Once he'd tossed the lid aside, he reached into the depths and withdrew a blue bag. "Los Corn Chips del Frito!" he said, jerking at its top to open it.

"You put food in a paint bucket?"

"It's clean. With no girly basket, I had to improvise. So shush up." Once he had gently lowered the bag onto her lap, he reached into the bucket again. "Queso de Nacho!" Off popped its plastic seal cap, followed by the flip-top metal lid. "Dippo de bean! And not lima beans, either." Another flip-top lid followed the first onto the ground. He pulled out twin packages of white globes and displayed them as if they were prizes on *The Price Is Right*. "For dessert, Snoballs de la Hostessa! And finally, for our main course, la *pièce de résistance*, and yes, I know that's French and not Spanish, we have. . . ." He withdrew a plastic container. Steam was condensing inside its top. "Taquitos de siete-once!"

"7-Eleven taquitos?" she asked, nearly wincing. "The kind that roll around on the warm hot-dog griller all day?"

"You act like you've never had one," he commented, placing the last of their picnic on the ground and sitting cross-legged opposite her. "You must go to fancy restaurants or something."

"At the last lunch I had, the restaurant served a twelve-herb chicken that is said to be magnificent. I adore *haute cuisine*." It was a statement she could have pulled off much better had she not been chewing on a mouthful of Fritos and cheese dip.

"Today you're getting hot cuisine. Anyway, they say that it's all in the presentation. So I thought that since I had crap to work with, I'd emphasize the presentation."

"And you get an A-plus." She hadn't realized how hungry she actually was until all the food had begun to appear. Even the taquitos looked edible. She released their plastic top with a snap. "Seriously, thank you. A junk food feast is what I need right now."

"You looked a little down," he conceded. "So I thought I'd make an attempt at cheer."

"I am a little down. You called it right." If he was going to present her with those flowers, now would be the time. They sat there at the far end of the blanket, nestled in their shiny cellophane, waiting. Now was the perfect opportunity.

But Taylor didn't reach for them or look in their direction. Instead, he helped himself to a taquito, bit into its cardboard-brown crust, made a slight face at the taste, and chewed, waiting. "You can talk to me."

"Talk to you? No, my thing is . . . it's stupid." It was obvious she could wait until the end of time and those dry and wilted daisies would never find their way into her hands. "You know, when I started acting school, one of the first things my teachers told me was that I'd have to lose my accent. 'It's charming,' they'd say. 'It's really quaint.' Then they'd gently tell me to lose it, unless I wanted a career playing hicks and idiots. And I was fine with that. I'd already tried to change my accent during high school. The other kids would stare at me whenever I opened my mouth. I mean, seriously, I'd call out the right answer in class and when I'd turn around, there would be Denise O'Bannon, repeating exactly what I'd said in a drawl so thick and heavy. . . . I could've given the most intelligent answer in the world and it would have come out sounding like I was a blithering idiot, in her imitation."

"So what'd you do?" he asked, holding out the bean dip.

At first she demurred, but then gave the Frito a tentative swirl. The bean dip had a smoky flavor and a processed smoothness that wasn't totally unpleasant. "It's easy to modulate vowels with practice, but for a long time I was so self-conscious about all the flaws in my speaking that I barely opened my mouth. I was afraid

I'd leave the G's off my -ings, I didn't want to be heard saying *y'all* instead of *you guys*. I had to cut out all my *honeys* and *sugars*. You know how common that is down here? I can go to the drugstore and buy Preparation H and lice medicine and an ointment for a rash and the man would put it into a bag for me and still call me *honey*. No one does that anywhere else. They'd think I was crazy if I used it."

"I'm charitably going to assume you're using hemorrhoid and lice and rash medicine merely as a random example," he joked.

"Please do. Then there's stuff like *carry*. You know how when someone wants a ride, they'll come up to you and say, *Can you carry me to the grocery store?* Like that?" He nodded. Of course, he probably used it all the time without thinking. "You should see the looks you get when you say that outside the South. 'Carry you!' they'll say. 'You're too heavy for me to carry you!' It's the funniest thing in the world to them."

"Every region has its little quirks, though." Probably Taylor hadn't expected such an outburst from her, poor guy. He looked thoughtful.

"Yeah, and that's exactly the point. Every section of the country has little things like that, and you don't hear people calling open season on Midwestern accents. New Jersey accents get made fun of on television sitcoms, but usually the people using them are thought of as annoying. Anyone with a Southern accent, though . . . they're automatically assumed to be *stupid*. Anyway." She was working herself into too much of an upset over the wrong thing. "I thought that erasing the accent would make my life easier. All it did was make my family think I was ashamed of where I came from."

"They don't think that," he chided. "It takes more than an accent to ruin a family."

"Does it?" she said, bitterness seeping in. "I'm sorry. You made this nice picnic for me, and I let loose. I'm a bad guest." Before he could protest—though she was very happy it was obvious that he intended to—she looked up from the taquito she was considering tasting and asked her next question. "How hard is it to learn to drive?"

"What?" If he was flustered by the sudden change in subject, at least he had the grace to minimize it.

"Sorry again. I'm skipping all over the place today. Is it difficult? Driving?"

Taylor's brow crinkled in a way that reminded Bailey of a bloodhound. "It's not difficult, no, but it's the kind of thing that needs practice."

"Like, how much practice? In high school, it seemed like the kids who learned to drive were in Driver's Ed for three months or more. At least that long, right?"

"It could be. My dad taught me. I think it was two months between the time I got my learner's permit and my driver's license, and then it was with me nagging my dad to get out there on the road every day. Why?"

"So it's ridiculous of anyone to expect me to figure out how to drive before Friday, right?" She encouraged him with a nod, to let him know that it was okay to agree she was no Mario Andretti. "Right?" At last he rewarded her with agreement. "Thank God."

"What's Friday?" he wanted to know.

"When I leave." She'd totally lost him. Small wonder. If she'd been guiding him through a forest, she would have been the girl charging ahead without a compass and running into a wolf in grandma's clothing. "For some reason my mother's got this notion in her head that she wants to go to Carverton. Carverton, Georgia. It's a little town outside Atlanta where she and the aunts grew up."

"Is she well enough?"

The taquito was as tasteless as she feared—a vaguely crunchy amalgam of salt and dough with a chewy filling that could have been anything from beef to chicken to Soylent Green. How in the world could she answer

that question? There were the doctors' encouraging answers, and then what she'd seen with her own eyes
every day that week. When you had a living shell of a
relative, what constituted "well enough"? Honestly, if
there came a time in Bailey's own future when she was
reduced to a vegetative state, staring at nothing, caring
about nothing, she hoped someone would have the decency and the courage to . . . well, do something. Was
Steve the kind of guy who could be counted on to do
the right thing for her in a medical emergency? She
didn't know. She could imagine him rubbing a hand
over the wisps of hair on his head, rubbing his red eyes,
and saying, *I just don't know. I just don't know.*

What a funny quality to look for in a potential mate.
How did you ask someone something like that? *Hey, I
know we just met, but if, you know, I take you home tonight
and we hit it off and started to see each other, twenty-five
years down the road, would you be willing to pull the plug on
me if I ended up brain-dead? And by the way, what's your
sign?*

She chewed while considering how to answer. "Physically she's recuperating fine. They told me she whizzed
through the in-hospital physical therapy. She's been doing exercises at home to get back the precision she lost in
her hand. But she's not. . . ." There was no way she could
finish the sentence. "She'd have no problems with a trip
South, but I don't know how in the world she expects mir-
acles from me. How could I learn to drive in two days?"

"Plus there's the matter of a car, and a driver's license, and insurance," Taylor pointed out. His finger
managed to pull corn chips from their bag without so
much as a rustle. How in the world did hands so large
and coarse manage to maintain the silence when her
own, narrow and slender, could not?

"Yes! Exactly!" She felt more validated. "It's impossible."

His right eyebrow rose into the air, boomerang-shaped.

"Though you could take the bus. Or see if Amtrak stops anywhere near. No, sorry," he added, when her own brow furrowed. "You were right at first. You couldn't do that. It's impossible."

"One thing about me," she said, trying not to crack a grin. He was right, of course. "When I'm on a rant? The common sense thing? Not so pleasant to the ears." She let the smile escape, simply to let him know she wasn't seriously upset. "I know, you're totally right, but I don't want to expose her to all that public scrutiny. She's too proud to let me cut her food for her." Though not, apparently, too proud to let Jeanne do the same. "So I know she'd be mortified about having to be assisted onto and off of a train or a bus. Or the restroom, or eating, or any of the things that slow her down. Even if I could arrange the trip there and back before Friday. Which I can't. So it's impossible."

Her words floated out over the little hummock and out into the fields, off toward her family's house in the distance. She couldn't decide whether they sounded defeated or relieved. It was a lose-lose situation. If she took her mother to Georgia, her aunts would be furious with her; if she didn't, her mother would be devastated. If she did, she'd have to take more time away from a job that was a nightmare from afar. If she didn't, well, she'd have to live with herself, after. Everything would be so much easier if circumstances simply prevented her from having to make choices. "I could drive, you know." Bailey turned away from the house to face Taylor. His hands were empty, and his expression almost apologetic. Sheepish, even. "To Georgia, I mean. I could . . . you know. Drive."

She could only stare at him for a moment. What was he doing? She barely knew the guy, and all he'd done was set deed upon good deed for her—a veritable brick wall of kindness, one favor at a time. One for each trip to and from the airport. One for taking her into Crestonville, another for bringing her home. One for having a silly picnic, another for making a picnic basket out of a paint bucket. An entire layer, simply for that offer, mortared and set into place. But why? "You . . . I . . ." she stammered, unable to find words.

"I know. It's impossible," he repeated, looking down at the grass beyond the bedspread's edge. He seemed to be braiding it in his fingers. Though he hadn't eaten much, it was clear he was through with his lunch. "So. Anyway. I thought I'd offer. In case it, you know. Wasn't. Impossible."

"Taylor," she said, putting a hand on his forearm. His skin twitched at her touch, but she left it there. At least he'd given her a moment to regain her mental balance. "That was a handsome suggestion. Thank you. But you've got, you know. A life. And work." She couldn't let the proposal go without acknowledgment, but it was too grand a gift to accept.

When he replied, his voice was low and level. His eyes avoided her own. "I remember you have a boyfriend. This isn't that."

"I know. It's just . . ."

"Seems like he's 'unavailable' a lot. When was the last time you spoke?"

"That's not your . . . I'm not . . ." By now she was utterly confused. What was she supposed to believe? "Is this a boyfriend thing or not? I was only saying that you've got, I don't know, cows to milk and chickens to egg and . . . What?"

Taylor had abandoned his hurt, distant expression and now stared at her with absolute disbelief. "I don't have any chickens or cows," he said. "What do you think I am?"

"A farmer?" If this was a pop quiz, it wasn't all that difficult.

"What kind of farmer?" She'd seen the annoyance in his eyes once before, the previous afternoon, after she'd insulted his crops. "What kind of farmer?" he repeated.

"I don't know. A bean farmer?" She felt helpless, not knowing what he expected.

"I'm an agronomist-botanist," he told her. "I don't

raise chickens. I create hybrids. I research their resistance to disease and drought and a hundred other factors. I didn't grow up birthing cows. My dad was a banker. My mom did office work. I have a master's degree. I supervise two employees. Publications and a list of strains I've developed are available upon request. That's my résumé, any of which you could have asked about at any point. Probably your aunts could have told you, too." He sat erect, then struggled to his feet.

"I'm sorry." She disliked upsetting him. Somehow it was a task she accomplished without trying. "I didn't mean anything."

"It's a profession, like any other. But somehow, when people see a guy with a few acres of land, they start making assumptions about how he lives and how much he knows. Some people might even think he's stupid. Sound familiar?" Bailey started to protest. She didn't have to think back very hard or far to realize that perhaps she'd come off sounding superior. Hadn't she tried to explain to him yesterday what a cell phone was? "When you finish up here, why don't you put the stuff in the bucket and fasten up the top," he said, his voice detached. "That way I won't have to have an ant swarm."

"Please don't go," she said, but it was too late. He was in motion; she'd prompted his exodus and sheer momentum would keep him going back to the house. "I'm sorry."

Maybe the apology worked. He turned before stepping off the covering, swooped down, and scooped up the flowers. Their covering crackled in his big hands. "Oh hell," he said, facing away from her. "I'm sorry, too. I said you could talk to me, then I end up chewing you out. Maybe—maybe this is a boyfriend thing, after all. Shit, Bailey, if he's not making any effort to. . . ." Sunlight cast golden highlights across his waves of dark hair. She didn't dare say a word. To interrupt might break the spell. "Here," he said, his voice soft and low. She thought he was going to toss the flowers at her, and instinctively her arms flew up to catch them. Instead, though, he simply held them out in her direction. "I bought these for your mom. I hope she keeps getting better."

The daisies hadn't been fresh to begin with, and a half hour in the heat hadn't helped their curled petals. They'd been for her mom all along? She accepted them solemnly in a silence in which she could almost hear another square of red clay settle into the wall he'd been building, brick by brick. "I'll be sure she gets them," she said. It was impossible not to feel sad. Things were so much easier with Steve—they never had these kinds of misunderstandings. *Except over drawers*, a voice from within reminded her. *And walking out of shows. And ignoring you at parties.*

Maybe the parallels weren't as cut and dried as she liked to imagine.

"Come by tomorrow if you need to go into town and you don't hate me too much," he told her, halfway glancing over his shoulder. He shuffled forward. "I'm sorry it was a crappy picnic."

"I don't. It wasn't," she murmured. But he had gone, striding off down the path, leaving only the rustling of pokeweed as reply. "It wasn't at all."

•

Chapter Eleven

Bailey had always thought it odd how quickly the human nose became immune to certain aromas. She could enter a bakery, drawn by the overpowering, sugary scents of frosting and cookies and cakes, comforted by the smell of fresh bread. Yet after a wait in line, she scarcely noticed it anymore. A month ago, every time she'd entered the downtown Richmond hospital where her mother had been recuperating, she'd recoiled from the odors of urine and age. The moment the elevator doors opened onto the fifth floor, feces and disinfectant warred to conquer her nostrils. Yet after twenty minutes by the bedside, even they and Aunt Bits's vinegary perfume receded from notice, forgotten until the next morning when she would step through the sliding elevator doors and into another invisible wall of ammonia and human waste.

For over an hour, though, she'd been aware of the attic's peculiar smell. The dark space where the main house's roof peaked was no different from anyone's attic, she supposed, but the odor of old wood and grime and neglect had settled over the room like a thick woolen blanket, topped off with a lacy coverpane of soot. No matter how much she tried to ignore it, the sharp odor prickled at the very back of her nasal cavities, irritating her throat and making her sniffle. It probably hadn't helped that the slate roof had been baking in the sun all that afternoon. Now, close to midnight, the temperature up here still had to be in the mid-eighties. She could feel heat from the flat, black stones seeping through the wooden planks above. When eventually she walked down the staircase, her little bedroom would feel like a cool oasis.

What was she searching for up here, exactly? Bailey couldn't have named the impulse that had led her up to the attic. Restlessness, perhaps—an unwillingness to sit down in the den with the aunts as they clucked and disapproved over whatever was playing on one of the four channels their little television set received. There were a limited number of times she could take walks around the grounds, or flip listlessly through the pages of the novel she'd bought at the airport, or lie on her bed and wonder where in the world Chandra might be, or Steve was, or what Euan and Sidney were probably doing together, and whether any of them were thinking about her. Restlessness, hell. She needed to face facts: She was bored beyond belief, and needed something to do.

The attic, however, proved to be filled with things that were . . . well, if not interesting, at least she hadn't seen before. Thick layers of soot cascaded to the floor every time she pulled back one of the old sheets or baby blankets covering the piles of old possessions huddled in the middle of the floor. She'd pawed over suitcases that wouldn't have looked out of place on train platforms in old war movies, and round boxes containing hats that had been worn with care and lovingly repaired over the years until they were too long out of style to be any use. There was an old *Encyclopedia Britannica* that dated back to the mid-1940s, and which had probably been secondhand. One stack, close to the chimney nearest the front, revealed a number of half-empty boxes of

Christmas ornaments. Those on the top had been crushed by a carelessly laid plank from a bookshelf, but the remaining globes still sparkled under the 40-watt bulb hanging from the ceiling.

Eventually Bailey had come to sit cross-legged on the floor, leaning against the chimney and letting its bricks warm her spine. It was good for her, right? She'd paid for hot rock treatments at spas before, to cope with far less stress than she'd experienced in the previous few days. True, the carefully planned aromatherapy offered by the Chelsea Lomi Pohaku Massage favored frangipani and jasmine over mold and cobwebs and baked antique castoffs. And the reading material in the waiting room there tended to be more magazines of the *Food and Wine* and *Vogue* ilk, with an *Utne Reader* thrown in for variety. Not these old books that had caught her attention.

She'd discovered the stack of children's books when she'd knocked a couple of them over after closing a flute case. Only a few were loose-standing. The rest had been tucked into cardboard boxes sometime in the past and left up here to molder. Perhaps she had some sort of recessive librarian gene somewhere in her makeup, for she had automatically sorted the books into stacks as she examined them. They might be worth something, one of these days. Like the Christmas ornaments—those classic designs sold for a lot of money in vintage shops. And the hats. She could probably even get something for the old dresses and coats hanging at the attic's other end. Bailey snorted. Textbook psychology at work—she felt so estranged that she wasn't looking at the old possessions as nostalgic relics of her family's past, but as booty to be plundered for eBay.

From the staircase, she heard a snap of the floorboards that immediately roused her back from her dozy distraction. "Is someone up there?" she heard, thin and reedy.

Jeanne. Fantastic. The attic was fairly large. Its pyramids of rubbish cast odd, angular shadows across its floorboards and onto the low-hanging roof. Bailey could probably get away with hiding behind one of the mounds, or under one of the coverings, if she could stand the closeness and the grime. But why did she feel compelled to hide? She wasn't breaking any family rules up here in the attic. Her sister would probably turn around once she saw who was up here, anyway. She wiped the hair from her face, sat back, and waited.

"Is—oh." At the top of the steps, Jeanne stood in silhouette, one hand resting on the gentle swell of her belly. Unconsciously or for effect, Bailey couldn't tell, though she wouldn't have been surprised at the latter. Christ, why was she so bitter, when it came to her sister? "I heard some moving around downstairs and thought there might be raccoons up here," said Jeanne, by way of explanation.

"I was sorting things." It was a lie, of course. Bailey might have set the books into separate piles, but it wasn't with the intent of being helpful or replacing them in order. She could lie more easily than tell the truth, though—that she resented her sister's presence, that she resented her pregnancy, that she absolutely hated the way she'd sprung it on the family. On *her.* Yet Jeanne wasn't going away, as she hoped. She strolled over slowly, her black hair swinging, studying her surroundings as if she'd never been in the attic before. Then again, maybe she hadn't. Bailey tried to sound brisk and efficient, like the job-holding, tax-paying, responsible, self-maintaining good citizen she was. "It's a mess up here. I should hire someone to come in and help take care of some of this old junk."

"I like it." Jeanne lifted one of the coverings, peered underneath, and let it drop. "It's kind of like a haunted house. Spooky, but cool. Hot, though. Aren't you hot?" She wandered a little closer, lifting another sheet so that the dust atop it tumbled down practically into Bailey's lap. "Sorry."

"Not a problem." So typical of Jeanne, to blunder around without considering what might happen to anyone else. At least she wasn't wearing any of that ridiculous goth makeup. In a T-shirt printed with a slogan too small to read, and in sweat shorts that must have dated back to her high school years, she looked halfway normal. Was she intending to hang around all night? Bailey couldn't simply walk back downstairs, not now that she'd made a point of staking a claim to be there. "What're you looking at kid's books for? Or are you hiding from the great Whigfield sisters versus Shirley Jones smackdown?"

Jeanne's belly was unavoidably close; all Bailey had to do was look up and there it was, round and bulging. She looked down at the books surrounding her instead. "It's funny, how you can tell which book had belonged to which Whigfield," she said, trying to make polite conversation. A ridiculous concept. Who made polite conversation with her own sister? She held up one of the blue-covered volumes. "How much do you want to bet these Nancy Drews belonged to Aunt Bits?" When Bailey glanced up, her sister stared down at her as if she were nuts. Maybe she was. She opened the front cover anyway. Sure enough, at the top of the page over Nancy's sleuthing silhouette, in a child's attempt at perfect Palmer handwriting was the signature, *Elizabeth Katherine Whigfield*. "I was right."

"You looked before I got up here," Jeanne said, skeptical.

"Nope, I swear." That, at least, was the truth. "It doesn't surprise me in the least, that's all. She should have been a detective herself."

"Because she's nosy, you mean." Jeanne snorted. That was pretty much what Bailey had meant, all right. "You wouldn't believe all the questions I had to put up with over dinner. Which you skipped." Was that an accusation? Bailey simply pretended she hadn't heard. The leftover taquitos were burning a hole in the lining of her stomach. "Okay," she added, after a pause. "I'll play. What's next?"

Bailey reached out and pulled the second stack a little closer, picking up the volumes one by one for display. *"Five Little Peppers and How They Grew.* And *Pollyanna."*

"Say no more," said Jeanne with a grin. "God, that crap has to be Bubble's. Do you remember her trying to read *Five Little Peppers* to us one time?"

"I remember they were awful, and that one of them dies. Or is that *Little Women?"*

"Beth dies in *Little Women.* The Little Peppers were the ones who were so poor that all they ever had to eat was a single cold potato! They were so fucking cheerful about a cold potato that it made me want to stab out my eardrums with a screwdriver so I wouldn't have to hear about it ever again."

Bailey smiled at the memory without meaning to. Jeanne had always been sarcasm-laden; when she was heaping on the scorn, it was difficult not to grin. She cracked open the spine. Right at the top of the first page, in careful looped cursive, it read, *Myrtle Whigfield.* "I remember that now. Pollyanna's not much better, you know. She's the one who's glad about everything after she gets crippled, and brings tears and smiles to her Aunt Polly's face."

"Holy crap, I remember that one. I would've done a Tonya Harding on the little simp myself if she'd showed her freaky little face around me." Jeanne bent over with an agility that surprised Bailey, and picked up a couple of the other books in Bubble's pile. *"Maida's Little Shop. Maida's Little Boat."*

Bailey read the next pair of titles. *"Maida's Little School. Maida's Little Island."*

"Maida's Little Theater. Shit," said Jeanne, handing them back. "That Maida bitch had it good. Tell me the next one's *Maida's Little Whorehouse,* or I'm going to

yack." The laugh that erupted from deep inside Bailey's diaphragm wasn't forced or fake. She'd been thinking along similar lines. "What's in there of Mom's?"

"*A Girl's Guide to Etiquette*," said Bailey, pulling over the third pile and reading the top title.

"Mom? Etiquette?"

Jeanne sounded incredulous, and Bailey couldn't say she blamed her. It wasn't that their mother had ever been a boor or a slob, or the kind of woman who picked her teeth in public or cut lines—but she had never exactly been a kid-gloves, no-white-after-Labor-Day, speak-when-spoken-to type, either. For a volume over fifty years old, it was in remarkably good condition. Almost as if it had never been opened, in fact. Bailey riffled through a few pages until she reached an inscription beneath the title. "*To my daughter Polly, on her tenth birthday, with the hope that she grows up to be a gracious and cultured young lady. Sincerely, Carzella Olive Whigfield.*"

"Sincerely?" If Jeanne had struck a note of disbelief a moment before, she positively caroled it now. "That's Grandma Whigfield, isn't it? What kind of mother writes *sincerely* to a ten-year-old?"

"I don't remember her being a very nice person, do you?" Weird, how she had slipped into a normal conversation with Jeanne, so quickly. She shouldn't have done it. Watch. Jeanne would take advantage, and suck Bailey into one of her dramas.

Jeanne shook her head, then took a few steps to retrieve and drag over an old wicker-bottomed chair that poked out from under a sheet. The seat had rotted through in places, but after Jeanne took a ginger perch on its edge, she settled back. "I don't remember her at all, really."

"My memories are pretty vague," Bailey admitted. "Mostly I remember her scowling a lot and complaining about how no one ever appreciated anything she'd done for them. And I remember one time we'd driven all the way down there—"

"Shit, I hated those long drives," Jeanne interrupted, her hands moving uneasily over her belly.

"—and we stepped out of the car, and she took one look at me, and then one look at Mom, and said, 'You're letting her get fat.'"

"No way!" Jeanne seemed appropriately outraged on her behalf. "You? You've always been a rail. Me, now." She patted her stomach. "At least now I've got an excuse."

Bailey averted her eyes, embarrassed. She couldn't comment. Instead, she picked up another book. "*A New Guide to Modern Domestic Science,*" she read. Inside the cover, in the faintest pencil imaginable, was a crude, unformed predecessor to her mother's slapdash penmanship: *Polly Whigfield.* "*Teach Yourself Touch Typing. Hygiene and Popularity. Social Rules for Young Moderns.*" She flipped rapidly through the last book in the stack until she found another inscription. "*Given to my darling daughter Polly on this Christmas day,*" she read aloud, "*in the hopes that she will continue on the path to being an upstanding young woman who will never forget the sacrifices her mother made for her. Sincerely . . .* Sincerely, again. Yeah, that sacrifices thing is pretty typical of the way I remember Grandma Whigfield."

"You have *got* to be kidding me." Jeanne craned her neck to see. "It's like a blueprint for a little girl's future, back then. Good manners, good secretarial job. Holy shit, no wonder Mom ran away."

"Mom never ran away," Bailey said, confused. "What're you talking about?

"Sure she did. She clawed her way into college and got married to Dad immediately after, so she could move up here instead of walking through life in the strait-jacket her mom had picked out for her. I mean, wasn't Mom the one working at Grandma's feed store or whatever to help make ends meet?" Jeanne was right, of course. Their mother had been too responsible, too early. "Christ, who signs something to their kid with *sincerely*? I'll never do that. Serves Grandma Whigfield right that after she married that second husband of hers, he drank his way through her money." During her sister's outburst, Bailey had been watching her face—the anger in it, particularly. Since when had Jeanne ever regarded her mom as more than a convenient alternative source for rent and Christmas gifts? Once again, her sister's hands drifted to her midsection, stroking it. "You haven't said a thing about this, you know."

Bailey began replacing the books into their boxes, one by one. "About Mom?" she asked, unable to admit to the other subject for some stubborn reason.

Jeanne's hair fell from her shoulders and hung in a thick curtain when she cocked her head. "About my baby. I know you have an opinion."

Bailey supposed it was too much to wish that the whole situation would simply go away. "What difference would my opinion make?" She pretended to be flipping through the Maida books to prolong storing them. She needed something to do with her hands. Otherwise she'd have to focus on the conversation. "Who says I have one?"

"Oh, don't even." Jeanne crossed her legs at the knee, wriggling her naked toes. "Just go on and let me have it. You think I'm irresponsible. You think the father's some crystal meth addict off the street or something. You think I can't support a baby, that I'm too young, that I'll drop it on its head or something, that I won't take care of it right."

"Well, it's not as if you've been on top of the prenatal care, now, is it?" Bailey said, angrily flopping a Maida book into the carton. Her sister was right, of course. She'd been thinking every single one of those things.

"See? I know you've got this crap in your head. It doesn't do any good to bottle it up."

"If you know what I'm going to say, Psychic, then

why do you have to hear me say it?" Bailey sat back against the chimney once more, arms resting on her knees, her nose twitching not only from the attic's smell, but with exasperation. "Don't come looking to me for some kind of validation, Jeanne."

"Why can't you say what you feel?"

"Why say it?" Bailey threw her hands up in the air, aware that her voice had risen, both in pitch and volume. Fine. Jeanne should know she was upset. "What good will it do? You run around the way you want, regardless of what I think or Mom thinks. You always have, you always will." In her gesticulating, she had scraped the back of her knuckles against the bricks, hard. She didn't care. "You want to know what hurts? The way you sprang it on us all. You couldn't give anyone any warning. You had to show up here out of the blue, big and gravid. God knows where you got the money for the trip down."

"I borrowed it," Jeanne interrupted. "From a friend."

"The baby's father?"

"No!" Bailey had obviously poked a sore point. Her sister sounded hurt at the suggestion. "Not him," said Jeanne. Then, eyebrows furrowed together, she shot back, "He doesn't know, okay? And before you start jumping to conclusions, yes, I know who he is. He's a nice guy. He's the kind of guy you'd approve of," she said, making a grimace. "But . . ."

But what? Not nice enough to know about his baby? Not nice enough to take responsibility for his actions? What? Bailey needed to know, and would have jabbed away with her questions had Jeanne not looked so vulnerable. She paused, and waited, not daring to move or breathe.

The words came out in a tumble. "He's a Columbia student, okay? I was kind of seeing him for a while. His name's Charlie. And he's a little bit better off and a lotta bit younger and a whole lot smarter than me, so he doesn't need this shit hanging over his head." Jeanne fiddled with the hem of her T-shirt. Bailey read the words printed across her sister's chest in orange letters: *I'm one big fucking ray of sunshine, aren't I?*

"A lotta bit younger? What are you going to be, like Grandma Whigfield, robbing the cradle for a second husband when you're in your sixties?"

Jeanne rolled her eyes. "He's eighteen. He doesn't need the hassle, trust me. And I don't need a husband I have to get a baby-sitter for."

"I wish you'd told me first, that's all. Then I could've broken it to Mom and the aunts and it would've been a lot—"

"Bailey." Jeanne said her name with such derision that Bailey shut her mouth. "When is the last time you answered one of my phone calls? You don't pick up at home."

"I'm hardly there!"

"You don't answer at work!"

"I know you've never had a real job," Bailey said, trying to suppress the reality that she could have answered any one of those pink slips Chandra had given her in the past six weeks, "but I'm very, very busy at work."

Jeanne didn't seem to care. "And your cell phone stopped working." That would be, of course, because Bailey had switched providers and not given her sister the new number. She kept her mouth shut. "Anyway, I don't know how else I was supposed to tell you. It's not like I planned it. It's not like I knew about it until about three weeks ago, and when I found out, I didn't want to think it was true. And I *can* take care of my baby."

"How?" Bailey couldn't help the skepticism in her voice. She could have made a list of all the lacks Jeanne had in her life—lack of funds, lack of job, lack of experience, lack of roommates who weren't crackheads—but before she started in, Jeanne mumbled something. "What?"

"I said . . ." Jeanne ducked her head. "I'm moving back home." Bailey could only blink. Jeanne must have misunderstood her shocked expression for incomprehension, because she repeated herself for a third time. "I'm moving back home. I brought all my stuff. I don't have much, anyway. I'm here to stay."

Oh, Bailey had understood, all right. She simply didn't believe it. "You're kidding," she said, her voice leaden. "And they're letting you?"

Jeanne's chin tilted up and jutted out, defensive. "If you'd have come down to dinner, you could've heard how happy they are."

She barely noticed the attic's stuffy heat, so intense was the burning knot in her own intestines. Not all of it was caused by the leftover taquitos, either. Why was Bailey feeling so angry, right then? "So that works out well for you," she said, the words squeezing through her clenched teeth for escape. "Everything bought and paid for without a lick of trouble on your part."

Jeanne's legs uncrossed. She leaned forward, obviously offended. "What's your *deal?*" she wanted to know, her face looming close enough to make Bailey recoil. "For your information, I went to a lot of licks of trouble. Giving up all my friends. My roommates are probably going to sell all the CDs and DVDs I left behind to make the rent I didn't pay them, not to mention all the clothes I left behind. I don't know a single person in this hole who's not family, and this is so totally not my scene, so don't give me this shit about me having it easy. Are you jealous, or what?"

"Yeah, sure." Bailey tried to sound ironic. She couldn't stand Jeanne hovering over her, so she grappled with the bricks and floor and struggled to her feet. "I'm jealous. No, you want to know how I feel? I'm *pissed* that you get to come home with the prodigal daughter routine and everyone's *so* happy to see you. . . ."

"I haven't been to Sunday school in like, forever," Jeanne broke in, "but I remember enough to recall that God or Jesus or whoever wasn't on the stay-at-home brother's side on that one."

"Fine. Then yes, I'm jealous. That's what I am. I'm only the one who actually called Mom from time to time and didn't open each conversation with the words, *I need some money*. I'm only the one who came down to the hospital after the stroke. I'm only the one who talks to the doctors and the therapists and who makes sure Mom gets the very best care. I'm only the mean, jealous bitch who took a whole week off at a very busy time at work so she could come down and make sure Mom was settling in okay."

"And who never, ever, ever lets anyone forget the sacrifices she's made," Jeanne retaliated. "No wonder Mom doesn't like you doing stuff for her. All you do is talk about it for years after."

The accusation stunned Bailey into silence. All she could do was stare at Jeanne, horrified. Her sister's eyes shone with triumph for a moment, but the look quickly faded when Bailey's lower lip began to tremble. She sucked it in, willing herself not to cry, but the blow had wounded her deeply.

"Girls?" Despite the voice from the stairwell, the Rhodes sisters couldn't seem to stop gazing at each other. Bailey's neck trembled. She wouldn't have been surprised if her head had popped off and rolled across the floor like one of the old Christmas ornaments. "What are you doing up there?"

"Nothing," called Bailey and Jeanne simultaneously, as if they were both children and their aunt had caught them reading in bed after lights-out.

"I thought I heard voices . . . oh, there you are, dears!" Bubble, in one of her old flowered housedresses, pulled herself up the last of the stairs and waddled across the attic floor. "Whatever are you two doing? Oh my!" She clutched at the back of Jeanne's chair to steady herself. "It's stifling, isn't it? Jeanne, you shouldn't be up here, dear."

"Why not," said Jeanne, sounding defensive. She turned her head away and then, with much softer tones, smiled and said, "I'm okay."

"It's not healthy for the baby, dear! My goodness, with the trouble Bits has had with her uterus, you'd think you girls would pay a bit of care . . . oh my." Bubble stopped, seeing the books that still lay on the floor. "Oh my! I haven't thought about those in years!" Before Bailey could stop her, Bubble knelt down and picked up one of the volumes that had been her own.

"I'm sorry. I was sorting through them," Bailey told her, rubbing her face on the back of her arm. She was tired. She wanted nothing more than to go back downstairs and bury her face in the pillow with the lights out, and let the cotton sheets cool the flames dancing over her skin.

"Oh, don't be silly, dear. No need to apologize. *Maida's Little Shop.* How I loved that book as a girl!" Enraptured, Bubble opened the book and flipped through the first few pages, then tucked the volume under her arm. "It's about a little girl whose father is very, very wealthy, and because she's sick and listless, her father buys her the most darling little shop, where she sells ribbons, and candy, and colored paper, and pickled limes. You could read them to your daughters someday! Wouldn't that be sweet?" Bubble was living up to her nickname, at that moment—she was practically overflowing with a goodwill that Bailey wished she could feel herself. Jeanne seemed to have softened under the aunt's influence. She smiled and brushed her hair over her shoulders while Bubble continued talking. "There's a whole series! She had a little boat, and a little school, and a little theater, and a little. . . ."

"Whorehouse?" Jeanne shot Bailey a complicit glance, pleading for her to laugh.

"What, dear?" Bubble asked, vague. "Why, yes, I do believe she had a wee house. Now, come back downstairs, both of you. You'll catch your death up here. I know they say that mostly in cold weather, but heat can be as dangerous as. . . ." Still prattling, she clutched on to Jeanne's arm and led her in the direction of the stairwell. "Bailey, you, too," she called out, as she took the first step down.

"I will," said Bailey. There had been apology in Jeanne's eyes a moment ago. She was sure of it. And yet, she couldn't bring herself to accept it. Jeanne always expected things to come her way too easily—money, family, forgiveness. Shouldn't some things be earned, rather than assumed? Messes couldn't be glossed over. They had to be cleaned up.

Speaking of which. Bailey bit back the unspeakable sadness weighing her down, and knelt down to return the books to their cartons. *Maida's Little Island. Five Little Peppers. Social Rules for Young Moderns.* What had it said in her grandmother's inscription? *In the hopes that she will continue on the path to being an upstanding young woman who will never forget the sacrifices her mother made for her.*

Bailey shut the book with a snap. Jeanne was right. Small wonder her mother had run away.

Chapter Twelve

"Chandra, I don't understand a word you're saying." The proprietress of the secondhand store—no, strike that, *consignment* shop—was so blatantly staring that Bailey felt compelled to turn away from the counter for privacy. Plus there was the fact that the middle-aged woman's pancake makeup and black Chinese bun, complete with chopsticks inserted through the knot, were so outrageous that Bailey couldn't stand to look for a moment longer. Not when the woman had been giving her the hairy eyeball ever since she and her companion had walked into the establishment. "No, it's not the signal. My signal's fine. Yes, I'm sure. It's that you're not making sense." She ignored the shop owner's cleared throat. "Slow down and start again."

"How about this?" Fawn stepped out from behind one of the racks holding a hanger draped with a long magenta spangled dress with more fringe than fabric. Bailey, still trying to listen to her assistant, made a face. Fawn raised her eyebrows. Bailey drew a finger across her neck to get the point across. "What's wrong with it?"

Chandra was still at the babbling stage, so Bailey put a hand over her phone's mouthpiece. "Get serious," she hissed. "It's obscene. The bouncers at a hooker's ball would tell you it's too slutty."

"I *beg* your pardon!"

How old was the shop's owner? Fifty-five? Sixty? When Bailey looked over her shoulder, a broad and apologetic smile plastered across her face, she tried to show respect. "You're right," she said pleasantly. "They'd probably let her into a hooker's ball in that."

"I think it would be ironic," said Fawn from across the room, still clutching onto the hanger. "Kind of a, you know, sardonic, self-referential statement on the tawdry male expectations of beauty."

"No." Fawn stared at the dress again and seemed about to say something else in its defense. "No!" Bailey said again, meaning it. She pointed at the rack. Of all the crap in this store, why the girl in calf-high Doc Martens, boot socks, camouflage shorts, and an orange T-shirt emblazoned with the legend LESBIAN should pick the one gown with the most spangles and the least amount of coverage, Bailey had no idea. Not with racks and racks of the most bland and inoffensive stuff she'd ever seen outside of a Gap fire sale, ready for the plucking. Shopping for a dress with Fawn was like taking a child to Toys 'R' Us and telling her to ignore the flashy dolls and the bleeping electronics and to pick out something educational for herself.

Fawn shrugged, sighed, and went back to browsing. "I think you're overlooking the possibilities of making a caustic statement of the paradoxes inherent in enfeebled Western archetypes."

Make that a very wordy, opinionated child.

"Bailey, have you heard a word I've said?" Chandra complained in her ear. "Are you there?"

"Yes, of course I'm here," Bailey said, turning around once again and, upon seeing the stern shopkeeper standing there in her Chinese-print wrap and those awful plastic chopsticks protruding from her hair, immedi-

ately regretting it. The woman scowled as if she was a
public health inspector and Bailey a venereal wart.

"What are you doing?" Chandra wanted to know.
"Are you driving or something?"

"No, not at all," said Bailey. "I'm in a secondhand
store, looking for . . ." There was no way she could finish that sentence gracefully, was there? *Looking for a suitable dress for a militant lesbian to wear so she can practice for
a butter bean pageant* was accurate enough, but didn't roll
trippingly from the tongue. *Looking for something inexpensive worn by someone under the age of a hundred* was as
precise, but Julie Chen's white grandmother might take
offense. ". . . my sanity," she finished uneasily.

"This," the storekeeper reminded her for the fourth
time that morning, in tones so icy they could have
chilled enough Budweisers for a year's worth of frat
parties, "is a *consignment shop*." Bailey had never been a
fan of the all-purpose dismissal of *whatever*, popular
with everyone from surly teens to shoving matrons at
every Barney's sale, but if ever a woman deserved to be
whatevered, boy, was it this one.

"But Bailey!" Chandra's plaintive voice caught her attention again. "What about the shoot?"

"The shoot?" Crud. Somewhere in the morass of excuses that Chandra had been giving for being away
from her office for two days, there had been something
of import that Bailey had obviously missed. "What
shoot?"

"The Jessica Munford shoot? I was telling you—"

"But there shouldn't be a shoot," Bailey said, panicked. "You told me she still hadn't signed the contracts." That much she had picked up on, anyway. "No
contracts, no shoot."

"But—"

"No buts! That's the way it works, Chandra." Her assistant had canceled and rescheduled the shoots, right?
As she'd asked?

"But. . . ." Chandra was dithering so much that if Bailey interrupted again, chances were the girl would never spit it out. She tried to bite her lip. While she watched, Fawn pulled another hanger from the rack. Apparently Cher had blown through town on one of her multiple farewell tours and decided to discard a white feathered Bob Mackie pants suit suitable only for disco remakes of "Half Breed." Honestly, who in this godforsaken neck of eastern Tidewater bought and discarded outfits like the ones Fawn seemed to find attractive? She certainly hadn't met anyone with that kind of fashion sense—even using the word *sense* in the broadest interpretation. She marched over and made Fawn replace the horrible outfit, then began flipping through the rack herself with her free hand while Chandra talked. "You see, I was trying to *tell* you, Bailey, all about the miscommunications, and how the shoot started, and how I went to Connecticut to get Jessica's signature—"

"*What?*" A parrot with a copper larynx couldn't have outshrieked Bailey.

". . . thought I could get her to sign before the crew took any footage, so I said to myself, *what would Bailey do?*, and then I went out there, and. . . ."

Bailey would not have allowed the shoot to proceed, that's what Bailey would have done. With less than twenty-four hours' notice, she would have had no qualms canceling and rescheduling, even if it had meant giving up picturesque Essex, Connecticut, and finding some other quaint locale. She wouldn't have allowed a single foot of tape to roll! "Crap," she mumbled, more to herself than anyone. Then, when Fawn reached for the feathered monstrosity again, she repeated more firmly, "No."

"No? But they'd already caught a whole day's footage and she still wouldn't sign, so—"

"Chandra." Bailey had to keep the girl from another monologue of self-recrimination and babble. Of all the angers she'd experienced this week—the tiny piques to the large, hurtful grudges she held against Jeanne—today's was surely the most infuriating of all. The formula was so simple! "This is exactly why I keep telling you, no contract, no shoot!" she said. "Do you know what a liability it is for us when we have footage on talent, but no contract? It's like handing Munford and her people a blank check! At this point her demands can escalate and she'll have us bent over a barrel, ready to screw in nine different—"

In a very small voice, Chandra asked, "You mean, like ask for her three kids to be put up at the bed and breakfast, too, and be taken to a local racetrack and be given rides in a Lamborghini and then be given free passes to Hershey Park?"

It felt as if someone had replaced Bailey's blood with frozen Cherry Slurpee. A guttural gasp escaped her. "Those weren't theoretical!"

"No," Chandra admitted in a very small voice. "But what made the second inn back out was when they found out she wanted them to cancel all the other reservations and give her family the run of the entire . . . Bailey? Are you there?"

"No." Her voice sounded weak. Fawn had chosen that unfortunate moment to hold up a perfectly good sundress that actually appeared to be in her size. She scowled in disappointment at what she thought was Bailey's refusal. Bailey snapped her fingers to get her attention once more, and then nodded to let Fawn know that she actually did approve of the garment. The girl shrugged, sighed, and slumped off in the direction of the changing room in the back. "I can't believe you let this happen," she breathed.

"I knew you were going to be mad!" Chandra wailed. "That's why I went down there to try to fix things! So you wouldn't look bad!"

Instantly Bailey's self-protective instincts leapt into

action. There was no way she could come out of this
predicament looking good, now. The buck for this sort
of thing stopped squarely with her. If the entire series
was canceled because the Munford's demands couldn't
be met, all the wasted footage and labor and squandered
money would be blamed on her—not on her assistant.

If Chandra had somehow managed a coup, though . . .
oh. That would have been rich. She would have had a
whole week, nearly, with Bailey out of the picture, to let
everyone at the Expedition Network know how she'd
saved the day. She could practically hear the story Chandra must have rehearsed in her head. *So I asked myself,
what would Bailey do? And I went to Connecticut, and oh, Jessica was really such a sweetheart about it. It's a good thing I
was able to clean up Bailey's loose ends!* That devious little
wench. Maybe it was fortunate she hadn't succeeded.
"How much footage did they get?" Bailey asked, her
mind frantically scrambling around for a solution.

"They got all of the Essex material they needed,"
Chandra said, sounding just as panicked. "It only took
yesterday and today."

Not bad. Not too bad . . . that was money down the
tubes if this all fell through, but enough to be controlled. "And the inn in Maryland canceled? The one
that was supposed to be the second week's shoot?
Okay," she said, thinking aloud. "That's good. There are
plenty of little inns and B-and-Bs around that would be
more than happy to have the Munford and our crew
tramping around in exchange for some free publicity.
We can find another one easily. That gives us a week of
leeway to clean up this mess." When Bailey thought she
heard a little gulp of relief at the other end, she decided
it was time to play Bette Davis to Chandra's Anne
Baxter—and Bailey felt certain that Euan would be
proud of her for remembering both female leads in his
favorite movie that wasn't *Showgirls*. "But Chandra, you
and I are going to have to have a little talk about this
when I get back. Understand?" When the girl whim-

pered, instead of protesting and running off at the
mouth, Bailey felt she'd done her job. She added with a
few more admonitions for Chandra to do nothing until
she returned, Saturday, and some lofty, yet noble, proc-
lamations about how she had wished Chandra had
done what she'd said, instead of haring off on her own.
Best to end with the upper hand, right?

When she finally pressed the end-call button, she
found herself shaking slightly. Crisis averted for now—
but it was essential she get back to New York as quickly
as possible so she could clean up this mess. As she'd
predicted, everything fell apart without her to supervise. Yet she got little satisfaction from the realization.
"What?" she snapped at the shopkeeper, whom she
found glaring between the circular racks with her arms
crossed.

"If your friend leaves a smell on that dress," said the
shop owner with a nasty edge to her voice, "there'll be a
laundering charge." She placed a peculiar emphasis on
the word *friend*, as if she'd read Fawn's shirt and had
her own interpretations of their relationship.

"What are you implying?" That lesbians didn't wash?
That they had pit odor? Fawn hadn't struck her as exactly an Irish Spring and-I-like-it-too! girl, but in Taylor's
truck a little earlier that morning, on the ride into town,
she hadn't seemed any stinkier than Bailey herself.

"Cigarettes!" As the sleigh bells hanging on a leather
strop over the shop door jingled, the woman pronounced
the word as if she were mouthing the proper name of one
of the more acrobatic and unspeakable acts from the
Kama Sutra. "She reeks of tobacco."

"So she's doing her bit to keep the Virginia economy
afloat. Well done, Fawn!" she called loudly enough to be
heard over the top of the dressing room door. The shop
owner glared.

"What?" she heard the girl reply.

Before she could answer, another voice cut in. "Well!
As I live and breathe! If it isn't the most fashionable

woman to grace Crestonville with her presence since Miss Crystal Gayle stopped on a trip from Richmond to Norfolk and bought a Coca-Cola at the Pick and Save!" Bailey almost startled out of her skin to find her Truman Capote lookalike friend standing nearby with the inevitable female companion on his arm. Outdoors, his voice had certainly been loud enough, but inside, it was positively overwhelming—almost as if cupped around his shining, small lips was an invisible megaphone tuned to project the slightest nuance to the top balcony seat in Lincoln Center. "Bailey Rhodes, don't you look a positive vision in that that *sweet* little halter dress. Is that Diane von Furstenberg? No? I could have sworn it was. It's adorable, though. Isn't she adorable, Dolly? Hello, Dolly! So nice to see you!" Apparently he was addressing the shopkeeper who had materialized at his side, suddenly all smiles.

"Back where you belong?" The hand that Bailey lifted to her face was as much to keep from giggling at what she thought was an intentional joke, as to shield her corneas from the squat little man's eye-popping suit. It was the palest shade of green imaginable, color-coordinated from his shiny pastel shoes to the wide brim of his green cowboy hat. He resembled a walking lime supporting a statuesque brunette. Was it the same girl as last time? When neither Chopstick Dolly nor the man laughed along with her, she stopped chuckling. "Hello, Dolly? It's so nice to see you back. . . . Never mind."

"Charming," said the man, his broad smile unchanging. "And don't ever let anyone tell you different, honey. So," he said, as if moving on to a more pleasant topic. "I see you've found your way to this fine, fine establishment. Why am I not surprised? India, tell me why I am not surprised?" he asked his female companion, who for reply disengaged herself from his elbow and disdainfully began flipping through the racks.

"This is the crème de la crème of consignment shops in the entire county!"

Bailey's first instinct was to reply with a heartfelt, *I'm sorry?*, but under Dolly's watchful gaze, she stammered out, "I bet."

Not that anyone noticed. The man's attention lay squarely on his companion, who had pulled out the Cher feathered pants suit off the rack and held it up for display. "Why, Dolly," he exclaimed in a voice laden with surprise. "What in the world is my old Mardi Gras costume doing on the *women's* side of the store?"

"I don't think this dress is right for me." Bailey and the others all turned to find Fawn standing in the entrance of the dressing room, barefoot and nervous, wearing the sundress that Bailey had picked out. Although the girl had at least removed her ratty shorts and her boots, the garment's straps still rested on the orange fabric of her T-shirt. She fidgeted from side to side, instantly hardening her face when she saw not one, but four people staring at her. "This was a *stupid* idea." The shop's owner let out a noisy exhalation of long suffering, souring at the sight of her clothing being mistreated. The sigh annoyed Fawn more. "Who licked the red off *your* candy?" she snapped viciously enough to send the woman scurrying back across the room behind the counter.

"That'll be enough of that." Bailey marched over and, ignoring Fawn's half-hearted protests, yanked the straps up and off the girl's shoulders. "What was stupid was thinking you could try on a dress with your shirt still on. Honestly, Fawn!"

"Oh God, it's sooooooo much trouble!" she complained. "I'm going to have to put it all back on again!"

"I don't know why I had to think I could be Henry Higgins to you," Bailey growled. By now she had nearly succeeded in yanking the neck of the T-shirt over her Eliza Doolittle's chin and nose.

She would have completely removed it right there in front of everyone, had her protégé not struggled away and stalked back into the dressing room. "I'm old enough to undress myself, you know!" she growled, slamming the door. A moment later, her T-shirt flew over the top of the booth, landing on the floor with the softest of thumps. Anyone who hadn't read the word LESBIAN by this point could scarcely fail to notice it, now.

"My goodness, what a firecracker!" said the man, blinking as he stared at the bold print. "Such spark and life! Oh!" He gasped, crooking his fingers and holding them in front of his mouth in a way that signaled not only *I've been struck by a sudden notion!*, but also *I'm a huge drama queen!* "Don't tell me *that's* the girl you've convinced to enter the pageant! India, did you hear that? I told you, didn't I? I said to India, 'That Bailey Rhodes, she's a mischievous little imp to tease her aunts so,' didn't I, India?" The dark-haired girl could have been chiseled from marble, for all the change in expression she betrayed at the question. "So," said Bailey's round little snowman in green. "Tell me. How are your aunts reacting?"

Bailey sighed. "They don't know it's official yet," she confided, dropping her voice low. "Fawn made up her mind to enter this morning. She wasn't at all serious about it yesterday. But apparently she and Larkin had some kind of major falling-out last night, and ... well ... somehow it made her determined to follow through with it. Out of spite, I think. And now Larkin's pretty upset, from what I hear." *Upset* probably wasn't the right word for someone who had telephoned the aunts at seven in the morning, shrieking at a volume that could be heard from Bailey's perch across the kitchen, where she'd been trying to nurse herself awake with coffee.

"Oh my," he said, drinking in every detail. "Can't you envision the high emotions? Juliet and Punky Brewster in a showdown for primacy! Oh, if you and I had been flies on the wall, my dear. What a spectacle that would have been. Wouldn't it, India? Can't you imagine it, honey?" Personally, Bailey didn't think that India could have envisioned so much as a Pepperidge Farm Milano cookie, even if one had been held up in front of her face along with a flash card. "Delicious! So you're here to . . . what, exactly?" he asked, enthralled.

Bailey couldn't help but be flattered by his interest. It was kind of a funny story, after all. Taylor had been hard-pressed to conceal his amusement at Fawn's long list of complaints about Larkin in the truck a while earlier—most notably the revelation that Larkin often practiced her Juliet standing on the next-to-top rung of a wooden stepladder while wearing a gauzy white curtain on her head, capped off by a plastic Christmas wreath, for full medieval effect. "You know," she said, conspiratorially. "Clean her up a little. I thought it would be easier to get the aunts to take her as a student, especially this late in the game, if she wore something that made her look—"

"Human?" The man fluttered his eyelashes as if his tart interjection was intended merely to be innocuous.

"Softer." His criticism had unsettled her. A bitchy edge was one thing. Until now, though, it hadn't been used against her or anyone she cared about. At least, she didn't think so. "You know. A pretty dress. So she looked like the rest of the girls."

She'd lost his attention. The man stared in the direction of the dressing room. When Bailey swiveled around, Fawn stood outside the swinging door, her posture awkward and her bottom lip firmly clamped between her teeth. At the sound of Bailey's exclamation of pleasure, Fawn pulled her face into a scowl. "If you tell me I'm pretty or something unimaginative like that," she growled, "I'll bite you."

Yet Fawn was pretty. Okay, her hair was untamed and could have used a good conditioning, and her skin tone was a little uneven thanks to the sun, and she was still much closer to crunchy granola young womyn than lipstick lesbian, but it was quite clear that beneath all the bluster and words lurked a handsome young woman reduced to shyness by having to appear before a group of people in a simple sundress. More remarkably, she didn't seem to have any visible tattoos or piercings. "It's much better without the T-shirt." Bailey tossed it at her. "She'll be wearing this out," she added in an aside to the shopkeeper. "So there won't be any *cleaning charges*."

"I am not . . . !" Bailey knew how to turn on the silent air of authority when needed; she'd squelched more determined personalities than this one before. Chandra, for one. Fawn saw her expression, shut her own mouth, and glowered. "Fine. I should take off my shorts then. They only go right back on, when you're trying on clothes!" she added, when Bailey opened her mouth to squawk. "I don't buy into this entire culture of consumption, you know."

Taylor had appeared out in the street, his day's groceries in hand. Through the shop's front window she caught a glimpse of him acknowledging her gaze with a nod, as he lifted the tonneau and hauled his plastic bags into the truck's bed.

Bailey pointed her finger at the dressing room door. Like a teenage girl—a stage Fawn had barely grown out of, Bailey had to remind herself—her pupil dropped her arms, sighed as if she was being put upon for the hundredth time that day, and shuffled back to the enclosure. The dressing room door closed quietly behind her. Bailey felt like sighing, herself. At least Fawn hadn't put up too much of a fuss. "She's charming!" the man mouthed, his voice barely audible. Then, a little louder, "I don't care what everyone else says, she's absolutely charming, don't you think, India? My goodness, won't your aunts have a handful? Well, I'll let you two girls get on with your shopping. I've errands to run. So much to do, this week! I'm sure you understand, dear."

"Of course, but—"

"Come, India!" said the man with a snap of the little pink stubs that were his fingers. The woman glided to his side, her expression serene and unbroken. "Dolly, we'll talk. So glad to see you. And *so* glad to see you, Bailey Rhodes. I don't know what I would have done without your help this morning. You're a fine young lady. And don't let anyone tell you different!"

"My help? What did . . . ?" Bailey might as well have asked her questions to the air. The man had scuttled so quickly across the secondhand store's carpeted floor that when he touched the metal door handle, she was surprised the entire door didn't light up from the static electricity. Bells tinkled as the door swung open and shut. Such a hurry he seemed to be in that she wouldn't have been surprised if he'd whizzed off down the street like the cartoon Tasmanian devil, a short little blur of dust and motion. Yet outside the shop door, he and India both paused by Taylor's truck to exchange a greeting. Bailey returned her attention to the dressing room. "How are you doing in there?" she called.

A mournful little voice replied, "I look stupid."

"You do not." Bailey kept her voice level and plain. "You feel awkward because you haven't worn this kind of thing in a while." If ever. She cleared her throat. "Pretend you're Larkin. You've seen her swan around. Imitate her."

"Hmmmm," said the girl, thoughtful.

It was a very different sort of Fawn who flounced out of Dolly's shop a few moments later. She'd grabbed a floppy white sun hat on their way to the counter. It sat on her head now, holding her hair close to her face so that it hung in straight lines to her shoulders. "Why, thank you ever so much," she said in an exaggeration of Larkin's thick accent. "Aren't you the sweetest, honey?" she told Bailey, who couldn't help but grin. "Well *hi*, sugar!" she enthused in Taylor's direction. "Aren't you a big, strapping hunk of man? It's a shame your entire gender doesn't do a thing for me, honey, or I'd be all

over you like a fly on a peanut-butter-and-jelly sandwich?" She handed an amused Taylor the shopping bag
containing her old clothing, then hopped up onto the
running board and into the backseat with a flip of her
skirt.

"She's laying it on a little thick," Bailey explained.
"But for my aunts' purposes. . . ."

"Gotta admit, she looks a lot different," said Taylor,
still rubbing his jaw. Bailey had feared that today's en-
counter with her aunts' neighbor might have been awkward after the botched picnic, but he was as polite and
friendly as ever. She reveled in his smile. "Nice work."

Down the street, the forms of India and her squat escort still raced toward some unknown destination.
"Hey, do you know him?" Bailey asked, pointing toward his retreating silhouette.

"Who? Jones?" asked Taylor, peering down the busy
avenue. "Sure. Everyone knows Jones."

"Oh, thank God," said Bailey, considerably relieved.
"Have you ever been in one of those situations where
someone thinks you know their name, and you don't,
and the more you talk, the less appropriate it is to
ask. . . ." She paused. Cold prickled at her skin. "Jones?"
she asked. "What do you mean? His name is Jones?"

"Yeah, Jones. Jonesy." Taylor nodded back down the
street, but the lime green Boris and his dark Natasha had
disappeared. "Kind of an eccentric. He—"

Fear seemed to have seized control of Bailey's larynx.
Her words came out raspy and harsh, like a crow's call.
"Is he married? To a woman named Shirley?"

"Shirley?" Taylor wrinkled his brow. "No, that's his
own name. Shirley Jones."

"Shit!" The paralysis had spread to her legs, her arms,
her lungs. "But Shirley is a girl's name!" she croaked
out. "Isn't it?"

How in the world could Taylor stand there and be so
calm? Because he didn't know how horrified Bailey was
with herself, that's how. She'd told Shirley Jones so

much. *Everything*. Her aunts were going to kill her. No, not just kill. Eviscerate, followed by drawing and quartering, and then a touch of flaying, concluding with a dip in brine before granting her oblivion. "I guess most people think so," he said slowly. "But it's not uncommon for men in the South, you know. Like Marion. Or Kelly. Or how sometimes Southern girls are named Michael. Or Taylor, too, I guess . . . hey, are you okay?" His hand touched her shoulder with concern. "You look like you're going to be sick."

"Nothing that a little cyanide wouldn't cure," she gasped out, trying to claw her way through the open door onto the passenger seat. "I need to get back home."

"Are you going to vomit?"

"Now!"

Afterward, she never remembered the door closing, or Taylor's door opening, or the sound of the ignition. All she could hear was the rush of blood in her ears and the impending sound of doom, like the largest bass drum ever built, struck by mallets made from redwood trunks. At the very least, the one thing on that terrible drive back home she did notice was that Taylor rubbed her shoulder with concern the entire way, and that not once did he seem to care that she might be sick all over his truck's expensive seat leather.

Chapter Thirteen

Growing up, Bailey had never envisioned Hell as a fiery pit or a river of lava, populated by countless demons and awful creatures by way of Hieronymus Bosch. In her imagination, eternal perdition wasn't accompanied by an unending arid heat unbearable to the soul or by the stink of brimstone. She had always pictured Hell as more like her Grandmother Whigfield's parlor—a sterile place that had smelled of disinfectant and lavender sachets and of windows never opened to let in the smell of the pines surrounding her house. A place where, when they visited, on Sundays she and the aunts and her mother and Jeanne would sit still for hours in their tight church dresses, knees together, hands crossed in their laps, maintaining a long silence broken only by suppressed sighs and the crackle of the plastic slipcovers over the settees.

In the house across Ettleston Road that Bubble and Bits had shared and where the Rhodes would stay when they visited, Bailey and Jeanne could play anywhere. Her grandmother's parlor, though, was *verboten*, a no-trespass zone to anyone save the family's matriarch, and especially off-limits to children. Sundays were the one day anyone else was permitted into the parlor, though her Grandmother Whigfield spent at least a half hour every morning dusting the framed portraits of family members long since passed over, the photograph albums, and the enormous family Bible. She kept the upright piano polished and gleaming, just as the slipcovers kept the upholstery pristine. Yet though neither the piano nor the settees ever betrayed any signs of use, over the years the former had grown more and more out of tune and its hammers had, as Bailey discovered shortly before a reprimand for daring to press the keys, lost many of their felts. The cushions, even with a mere one afternoon a week of use, had gradually flattened throughout the years, so that their padding was compressed and squashy. Even Grandmother Whigfield, unamused and controlling old woman that she was, couldn't fend off decay. Though God knows she tried, armed with a can of Endust and a duster made of an old cloth diaper.

A small photograph of Grandmother Whigfield sat on an end table in her aunts' den. It was one of those postwar posed glamour shots of a creamy-faced young woman, unsmiling and serious, gazing at some spot above the camera. Odd, Bailey realized. It was the sole photograph of their grandmother in the aunts' house. There were none of them as she remembered the woman, old and crabby and with her head covered by a dense cap of set gray curls—only this one of a girl scarcely any older than Bailey herself, gazing off into the future. Did she ever suspect it would end with a husband dead long before his time, three daughters, then later a second husband much younger than herself? Doubtful. At least this den wasn't as stuffy and spirit-dulling as the old parlor. Her aunts were devotees of fresh air and didn't mind a little clutter.

Thud, she heard from outside the window, followed by a strange shuddering noise and the subtle *pitter-patter* of a rebounding tennis ball. Her mother had been out there all afternoon, exercising.

"I see," said Bits from her perch by the telephone, one of the two handsets in the entire house. Like the kitchen phone, it had been hardwired into the wall decades ago. Whenever it rang, it was with a strident clanging that could have roused the dead. Bits sat erect, her posture prim and unforgiving. Whenever she looked Bailey's way, it made her spine curl. "Yes, that's very interesting." Bailey curled up a little more when Bits's glance flickered over to her.

From the other end of the couch, her sister spoke quietly. "It'll be okay." When Jeanne was expressing sympathy for her, Bailey knew she was in trouble. "Oh, that Taylor guy said to say he hoped you felt better."

"Did he?" Bailey leaned her chin on her arm, already resting across the back of the sofa on which the aunts usually watched television in the evenings. Barely had she arrived back to the house that morning than Bubble and Jeanne had hijacked Taylor's truck and chauffeur services so that Jeanne could see a doctor. They'd not arrived back until nearly dinnertime. Bailey hoped Taylor didn't despise her family and the way they monopolized practically all his time. "That's nice."

"He's nice, you mean." Jeanne absently picked at her toenails from the other end of the sofa. "Aren't you going to ask me about my doctor's visit?"

"Mmm-*hmmmm*," Bits said with meaning. "That sounds like her."

Bailey quivered. She, who had stood up to the wrath of faded former movie queen Faye Marvelle mid-shoot during a whale documentary, answering the woman's threat of a walkout with a counterthreat offering the narration to her biggest adversary; she, who had once told a network executive to bite her, when he disagreed with the extra money she wanted to offer an especially personable do-it-yourself handyman before he was snatched up by the Discovery Channel—she was actually frightened of what her aunt might do when she finished this phone call. "How was your doctor's visit?" she asked, keeping her voice low.

"I saw the baby on radar." Though her sister tried to sound cool and disaffected, she could tell Jeanne was excited. Despite the snub left over from the night before, it softened Bailey slightly.

"Ultrasound, you mean?" With every passing hour, it seemed Jeanne was shedding more and more of her tough New Yorker skin and showing a softer, pink Southern underbelly. She and Bubble had gone shopping, as well. Jeanne was wearing a decidedly new polo shirt in a soft pastel blue, and white mid-thigh shorts like those worn by every girl between the age of seventeen and twenty-four from Virginia Beach to the Skyline Drive. Apparently, conformity was the new black.

"I thought Bubble was going to have a heart attack," Jeanne confided, a little shyly. She clutched her chest and rocked back and forth in place. "Oh my goodness!" she mimicked. "Oh my goodness! That's life inside you, dear!" She rolled her eyes. "Then she cried."

"Unacceptable," said Bits, her voice so dry that both sisters looked over guiltily, then fell silent at the sight of their aunt's scowl. "This is completely unacceptable."

Though Bailey was fairly certain that Bits had been speaking to whomever was at the other end of the line, the remark sounded directed at her. She rested her chin on her hand and gazed out the window, avoiding looking at the patio where her mother sat, slowly and grimly tossing ball after ball. Instead, Bailey focused on the patch of grass running beyond the house, where woods separated their property from Taylor Montgomery's. Aunt Bubble and Mr. Rice were strolling along the grass, hand in hand, talking. Was Bubble actually carrying her slippers? She was walking barefoot, like a young girl. Watching them felt almost like an invasion of privacy; it was plain the pair were sharing an intimate moment. Not an intimate moment of the icky-to-think-about, exchange-of-bodily-fluids type, but really, it was clear that although they were doing nothing improper, they honestly thought themselves to be alone.

"Yes, Maryann, I'm *very* glad to have talked to you. Mmm-hmmm. Indeed. Good-bye." The sound of the handset colliding with the cradle was worse than the prospect of a root canal performed entirely with a rusty old Victorian dental drill with a single children's aspirin for anesthetic. "Well." Bits cleared her throat. "That was an interesting telephone conversation."

The remark seemed unusually dry and restrained, even for Bits. Bailey didn't dare say a word. "Oh yeah?" Jeanne asked, returning to picking at her toenails. Bailey wanted to reach out and slap her sister's hand, but she kept still. Jeanne wouldn't be able to reach those toenails, soon enough.

"Mmmmm," said Bits, noncommittally. "It would appear that Larkin Merino is no longer one of our protégés."

"She quit?" Bailey couldn't help but squeak out.

Bits didn't relax at all from her rigid position in the telephone chair. "Apparently," she drawled, "she showed up at town hall two sizes short of a fit, and demanded that certain contestants be disqualified from the pageant." Bailey gulped. "And when that didn't work, she called the editor of the *Weekly Bugle* and attempted to convince him to run a *Sixteen Minutes*–type story on the fact that the newest contestant in the Miss Tidewater Butter Bean pageant was of an alternate sexual persuasion, shall we say."

"*Sixty Minutes*," Jeanne corrected.

"Oh, shit!" groaned Bailey, appalled. She hadn't at all thought about Fawn being dragged into this mess. That was all the girl needed, her name and private business splashed all over the front page of a publication best known for its used truck parts classified ads.

"Luckily or not, our Mr. Banks at the *Bugle* wanted Fawn's phone number. And not, I fear, for an interview." A cool wash of relief flowed over Bailey's skin, from fingertips to the prickling back of her neck, unstoppable even by her sister's bark of laughter. "It is *not* funny," Bits announced with the snap of a testy piranha.

"Sorry." Jeanne stopped playing with her toes and made a face.

Get used to it, Bailey thought with irritation. Jeanne was going to have to cope with an awful lot of *auntitude* if she stayed in this house for any amount of time. She tried to steer the conversation back on track. "But if no one is listening to Larkin. . . ."

"Oh, I didn't say that." Bits folded her arms and followed the move by crossing one leg over the other, obviously settling down for a long, serious conversation. "One person was *happy* to talk to Larkin. One person went out of his *way* to talk to Larkin."

Squeezing her face into a ball only eased the mental discomfort for a moment. *Thud*, she heard from outside, followed by the odd noise of a wooden shutter flapping in the wind. Then, *thunk-a-thunk-a-thunk*. Bailey turned her head to look outside again. "Who?" she asked, miserable.

"Why, someone who, only this morning, had all of his rivals' secrets spilled to him by their ungrateful niece, that's who." Bailey would have opened her mouth to protest, but she could tell Bits was merely warming up. "Someone who ran right home and telephoned Larkin and suggested she come to him for coaching before the pageant next week, instead of us. Someone who, thanks to his wealthy mother's speculation in the garment industry after World War II, is able to invest substantial amounts of nylon stocking earnings in his contestants' wardrobes. Someone who, thanks to his evil, spiteful machinations, has seen his contestants win ten of the last ten pageants!"

No matter what she'd done, Shirley Jones's past track record had nothing to do with Bailey. "Maybe he's just *better*?"

She hadn't meant it as an insult, but that didn't stop

Bits from taking it as one. "Girl, who blew out your pilot light?" The verbal slap made Bailey turn her head away again. Through the window, she watched her mother pull her hand back, ready to throw. She was nowhere near as unsteady as she'd been at the beginning of the visit; when the ball flew from her hand, it traveled swiftly across the courtyard and struck the bull's-eye dead in its center. The target board recoiled against the bricks from the impact. Ah, so that was what had made the shuddering sound, earlier. Bailey watched her mom sit back with a look of satisfaction on her face while Bits kept talking. "He's not *better!* Shirley Jones doesn't have a fraction of the foundation in charm and poise that Bubble and I have! What he does have, though, is cash for his little hobby, and an unending supply of super-models to walk the runways. According to pageant rules, the contestants are supposed to be from a thirty-mile radius around Crestonville, but these girls—well, Bailey, you've not seen them. All I can say is that if they're from around here, there must be a lot of farmers out there raising Maybelline crops and Elizabeth Arden orchards."

"I've seen them," Bailey mumbled, thinking back to India and Sapphire and Marjorie. "So you think he's importing them from somewhere? If he's cheating, then why not call him out?"

"Call him out! You think it's that simple? It would look like sour grapes if we made accusations! And now, for the first time we had a candidate who might have possibly won. . . ."

"Larkin?" asked both Jeanne and Bailey simultaneously, with varying degrees of surprise.

"Yes, Larkin!"

It was amazing how ramrod straight Bits's spine could stay for long periods of time. It was as if she wore an invisible brace, like that girl in Bailey's ninth grade class who'd had scoliosis. What was her name? She yanked her wandering mind back to the conversation.

"Larkin Merino?" she asked skeptically. "Even with scissors and a flashlight, she couldn't act her way out of a soggy cardboard box that had one end open."

"Yes, I know Larkin is a horrible actress," said Bits. "I'm not blind. But she's cute, she has nice hair and teeth, she can approximate a saccharine quality somewhere in the neighborhood of sweetness, and what's more, she and her mother are very popular in Crestonville. She was tap-dancing before she could walk, and she was voted Most Prettiest Baby in the *Bugle* photography contest three years in a row. She'd be a sentimental favorite with the judges!"

With every passing moment, Bailey felt lower than low. "You've got plenty of other pretty girls!"

"And that's all they are, girl! Pretty! Larkin was the best shot we had at winning this year, and now she's gone over to the dark side. She told Shirley Jones she'd be *glad* to have him as a coach. Well. That's it." With sudden decision, Bits stood and shook her head, as if trying to free her hair of invisible demons trying to nest there. "It's over. We might as well get out of the business, now."

Jeanne had simply been sitting back with her arms crossed, watching her sister and aunt have at it. "You're kind of being a drama queen," she told her aunt. Bailey felt a little bolstered by support from such an unexpected source. She thanked her sister with a nod.

What was more scary, Bits's flaring nostrils or her deadly calm at the accusation? "I'm being practical. We're washed up, after this, thanks to Bailey's betrayal."

"And it's not like I did it deliberately!" Bailey reminded Bits for what felt like the hundredth time since she admitted her mistake late that afternoon. "I honestly didn't know who he was!"

Bits stabbed at her temple with a forefinger. "Did you think to *ask*? No, you started blabbing away. Oh, look at me, I'm Bailey Rhodes, I can't keep my mouth shut about sensitive topics! Ask me anything! I'll tell you all the family secrets!"

"You don't understand a damned thing." Bailey had been cowering in the corner of the sofa long enough. Wrong as she knew she'd been, she resented the implication that she was some sort of brainless wonder, almost as much as she resented her aunt's unsteady imitation of her as some kind of vacant-eyed bobblehead. "Yeah, so I didn't know the guy's name. He didn't volunteer it. I bluffed. It's my *job* to bluff. I get paid to do it. I have to bluff that I like people I dislike, right to their faces. When someone's lawyer comes up to me in a restaurant, I have to bluff and pretend I remember deals I've negotiated three years ago. I bluff about the network's finances to talent who want more money than they deserve, and bluff to execs at other networks that we're not really interested in has-beens we'd sell our souls to hire. So yeah, when this total stranger I should've known came up to me and started talking like we were best buddies, bluffing my way through was my knee-jerk reaction." She paused to judge her aunt's response. Nothing. "I wasn't that great an actress, Bits, but the one thing I'm damned good at is pulling on a blank, friendly face, pretending I know what's going on, and making it work for me."

Thud, she heard from outside. Bailey couldn't help it. She turned her head again to look out the window, and caught the sight of another old tennis ball rebounding from the target board. As if aware she was being scrutinized, Bailey's mother turned her head and looked up at the window, meeting her daughter's gaze. It almost seemed as if that stare carried a jolt of electricity—it was so full of life and defiance, and such a contrast to the frightened, almost dead appearance it had held a month before. *I told you I could do this*, her mother seemed to be saying.

Bits, in the meantime, marched over, glanced out over the patio, and apparently saw nothing to keep her interest. She sat down on the sofa between the two girls, positioning herself toward Bailey's end. "Pretend away, then," she said in a voice that Bailey dreaded. Bits had used it from time to time when she and Jeanne had been girls, particularly when they'd been caught doing something spectacularly stupid, such as the incident with Jeanne in the dumbwaiter. It was one of those tones that mingled instruction and superiority in a way that left no doubt who was in charge. "But as you seem to have forgotten, when you are in this house—my house—you are not part of a television network. You're part of a family. Your problem, Bailey Rhodes," she said, pointing an index finger that Bailey had an irrational yen to snap at with her teeth, "is that you think you can simply descend on the house and be treated as the prodigal daughter. . . ."

Which was exactly what Bailey had felt about Jeanne, of course. She felt hot tears prickling behind the bridge of her nose. "That's not true." She didn't dare look at her sister.

"When the fact is, you've one more day left here and then you'll be back with all your other Yankee friends and you'll never have to come back down again until the next medical emergency, or when someone passes. . . ."

"Or when I have the baby," said Jeanne. "You'd come down for that, wouldn't you? Your own niece?"

"It's a girl?" Bailey asked, batting her eyelashes to keep the tears from flowing. Jeanne nodded. For some reason, the information made her want to cry more.

"We all know you want to get back up to the fine life you've carved out for yourself. Dandy. Go back where you belong. Hurricane Bailey! Leaving all kinds of wreckage in her wake! Hmmfph. And it's the rest of us who are going to have to clean up after you, watch. What in the *world* are you doing? Get your hands off his . . . !" Both Bailey and Jeanne looked guiltily at first their hands, and then at each other, until they realized that Bits was staring out the window. Not at their mother, but at Aunt Bubble who now stood on tiptoe, her head tilted back, her lips on Mr. Rice's, and her hands firmly planted on the seat of his pants. "Well, that's it. The butter has finally slipped off Bubble's biscuit. Though I shouldn't wonder, given all the stress you've put her under." The last remark, of course, was directed squarely at her older niece.

Jeanne leaned forward to see around the curtains. "I think it's kind of sweet," she said, once she sat back. She picked up the photograph of Grandmother Whigfield and began to fiddle with it.

"See how sweet you think it is when *you're* the one picking up the pieces because. . . ." Bits interrupted her tart commentary abruptly, then pulled closed the curtain, despite the near-sweltering evening temperatures. With a flick of her fingers, she retrieved the photograph from Jeanne and held it to herself in her lap. "That's not a toy."

"Sorry," said Jeanne. "You should get a new frame for that."

"Absolutely not!" For a moment, Bailey thought her aunt might start to yell. Instead, she took a deep breath and regarded the photo as if trying to see some expression in her mother's face that might tell her what to say next. At last, her lips parted again. "Let's say that your Aunt Bubble does not exactly have the greatest track record when it comes to budding romance." She took to her feet, smoothed down the crisp cotton of her skirt, and sighed as she walked toward the hall door. "I'd best fetch the hose and separate them. Like dogs in heat!"

Bailey was too miserable to respond, but Jeanne's stubborn streak made her protest. "Let her have a little happiness. Just because she had a bad breakup decades ago doesn't mean she's going to fall apart again."

Bits paused by the door so she could place her mother's framed photo on a shelf there. She angled it out with a small nudge. "Yes, I suppose this time the chance of Bubble's suitor dumping her to marry our mother for what money she has is slim to none, isn't it?"

Bailey felt as if Bits had whacked her in the middle with a two-by-four. She heard a gasp from Jeanne at her side. Seriously? Bubble's faithless old suitor had been Grandmother Whigfield's younger second husband? "Oh, my God," she murmured, her hand over her mouth.

"So now you know." Bits's superior tone was as cutting as a fistful of carving knives. "And Bailey, in case you're having problems distinguishing between what's acceptable to talk about in public and what's not? That particular family gem? Not for discussion."

Bailey's voice was quiet when she replied. "I've said I'm sorry a hundred times."

"It's too late for sorries." Bits pivoted to walk down the hallway.

"I'll make it up to you, then!" Bailey called. She grabbed the pillow she'd been leaning against and pulled it to her stomach, as if clutching the fringy pad with all her might could somehow ease the hollowness she felt.

"How, Bailey?" she heard from the hallway. "How?"

Bailey buried her chin and mouth into the fabric. That was a question to which she had no answer.

In her dark mood, she'd almost forgotten that her sister was in the room until Jeanne spoke. "Holy crap," she said. "That was a bombshell."

"Yeah, well," Bailey mumbled, getting a mouthful of dusty fringe from the pillow as a reward. "This family's good at that particular little party trick." The sigh that followed should have been deep enough to expel both lungs.

"Yeah, but shit! When you find out your grandfather was nearly your uncle!"

"That man wasn't our grandfather," said Bailey. *Thud*, she heard from behind the pulled drapery. The sound of her mother connecting with the target once more made her lift her head up and speak more clearly. "I don't remember ever meeting him."

"Me neither," said Jeanne, quiet in the gathering dusk. "But holy hell! It's like some soap on TV, isn't it?"

"Television," said Bailey, inspiration slowly coming to her. Across the room sat the aunts' thirteen-inch set on a metal stand, its twin antennas stretched to the limit and sprawling in different directions. Only a moment before she'd been feeling completely bleak, but the sight of that familiar round-edged screen made her feel on solid footing once again. Television was her life. Television was what paid her bills. Television was also the constant pain in her ass, but with one blinding, illuminating flash of light she'd seen a path to the end of the labyrinth through which she stumbled. Television would save everything. "Jeanne, you're brilliant."

"I am?" It was the cry of every younger sibling who suddenly found herself entrusted with an unexpected compliment. "What'd I do?"

"It doesn't matter," Bailey said, leaping to her feet. "What time is it?"

"After eight," Jeanne said. "Where're you going?"

"Out," was all Bailey would tell her. She was going out. For the first time since she'd arrived, though, she actually felt as if she had a destination.

Chapter Fourteen

"I aw Google wight 'ow," said Sidney.

"What's in your mouth?" Bailey wanted to know. She curled up onto the broad leather chair in the unfamiliar room and tried to imagine herself back in Manhattan, in Sidney's tiny apartment filled with the clutter of Expedition Network souvenirs. For someone so cynical, it was surprising how sentimental Sidney could be. There wasn't a show she'd been involved with from which she hadn't snatched a memento. Snow globes, shooting scripts, autographs, a former host's toupee—they were all fair game.

She heard her friend swallow. "Cheese Doodles. Don't judge. Listen, I'm on Google right now. I typed in *what in the water in Virginia can make you crazy*. I'm only concerned for your mental health, here! And okay, the first link is to some George Michael lyrics and then there's a bass fishing guide. But after that, there's this article on benzenes that says ingestion, even in trace amounts, can lead to hallucinations and other mental ailments. . . ."

"Sidney." Bailey couldn't help but laugh. "Let me reiterate what I told you earlier. Strange man's house. Strange man's phone. Long distance."

"Is this the sexy farmer with biceps for days? He can't be that strange if you're ogling his arm muscles."

"He's a botanist-agronomist. Or agronomist-botanist. And I don't ogle. Much. Anyway. What do you think?"

"Well . . . I guess it sounds like he has a degree, when you put it like that."

"About the *idea!*" growled Bailey. Kitten took the rare opportunity of a visitor lying feet-up in her master's living room chair to wander over and give Bailey's face a doggy-scented lick. Bailey didn't flinch. Then again, why was she assuming it was a rare opportunity? Taylor could have dozens of girls over a week, for all Bailey knew. In this very chair, many a young woman could have been licked. Ew. That didn't come out right. She made a mental reminder to take a shower when she got back to the house. "It's good, right?"

"It's do-able," said Sidney, begrudgingly. "I'll check out those two Crestonville-area inns you gave me to see if either of them is available for a shoot. I wish you'd told me about Chandra, earlier. Right from the beginning I told you—"

"I know, I know, you told me she was nine kinds of nuisance," said Bailey, giving credit where credit was due. "I'm not entirely sure she meant to be malicious, though. She could have been trying to help, in her own bumbling way."

"The first bullet you take might be an accident, Bail." Sidney crunched into a Cheese Doodle with such vigor that it sounded as if she were snapping through bone. "If she fires a second one into you, that's intentional. If she goes for a third . . . well, that's your own damned fault, by that point. Now tell me about the hunky agronomist."

Although she was alone in Taylor's living room—save for Kitten, who had flopped down into a dog bed by the television, where she lay happily beating her tail against the floor—Bailey lowered her voice. "Not here," she murmured. "Not now. He's sitting outside."

"Can he see you? Is he looking at you through the door, his thumbs holding up his overalls? Wink at him, Bail. Just kind of wet your lips and wink at him, so that he reaches up and takes off his ten-gallon hat."

"I'm not at Southfork Ranch, ass," Bailey growled.

"Trucker hat. Whatever."

"I'm hanging up on you now."

"Okay. Euan's on his way over so we can watch a repeat of *America's Next Top Model* together, anyway. You know Euan . . . no such thing as too much *America's Next Top Model*. Can I update him on everything? Including the hot farmer boy?"

"You'll do what you want anyhow, Sidney. Why bother asking?"

"It's polite. Miss you. Bye."

Sidney had already hung up on her end when Bailey said with sadness, "Me, too." She missed Sidney dreadfully. She missed her apartment, the quilt on her bed, the restaurants, the dark coffee that could be had so easily and plentifully from almost any street corner shop. She missed being able to look out her window and see the city's twinkling lights after sunset. The absolute darkness out here in the country, where the nearest streetlights were miles away and where she'd had to use a flashlight to find her way down Taylor's long drive, made her feel empty inside. Frightened, even, as if the dark vacuum beyond the living room windows had sucked out some essential portion of her insides and left her acutely feeling their loss.

Taylor sat in a folding lawn chair a few yards beyond the front door, his left leg supporting the weight of his right at the ankle. At the sound of the screen opening, he craned his neck back. "All done?"

"Would you mind if I made one more call?" she asked, already knowing that he wouldn't mind at all. "I feel badly about kicking you out of your own house."

"You're not kicking me out at all," was his reply. A single can of Labatts sat on the ground. He reached down to pick it up. "I usually sit out here by myself on nice eve-nings like this. Listen to the cicadas. Think about things."

"Sounds lonely," she said, leaning against the door for a moment.

"Nah. More like, 'meditative.' Helps me to sleep. Makes me feel settled." He took a sip from the can and replaced it on the ground. "It's a nice, quiet time at the end of the day. No television. No cars. No machinery. No aunts," he added, softening it with a grin to let her know he was joking. "I don't know how I could live without quiet time."

"Well," she said, not certain how to respond. "Let me make my call? I'll be done and out of your hair soon."

"No rush," he said, looking out in the direction of the road. "And my hair's not going anywhere." He ran a few fingers through the thick mat atop his head. "I hope."

Despite the fact that Taylor's perch was a good few dozen feet away, once she was back indoors, Bailey took the cordless receiver to the living room's far end and settled down on the sofa there. The other line rang five times before, with a great deal of fumbling, someone picked up the receiver. "Hello?"

Hearing Steve's voice after nearly a week wasn't the great rush of relief she thought it would be. Why had she called him? Or more to the point, why had it come to a point where she was forced to call? "Did I wake you?"

He exhaled directly into the receiver. For a moment, his voice sounded muffled, as if he was already lying down and in the process of turning over. ". . . guess so," he said. "What's up? How's your trip? Or are you home?"

"No, I'm still down here. I'm staying another week. A lot of stuff's been happening." It was an effort to speak without launching into the diatribe she wanted to make. But why was she so itchy to tell him off? On any other trip, she simply wouldn't have worked herself into a tizzy over whether her boyfriend was constantly calling her or not. Before she'd become so busy with her mother, they'd gone for longer periods without making

THE MILE-HIGH HAIR CLUB

contact, both busy with their work and own lives. She was supposed to be evolved, wasn't she? And not clingy and possessive? "It's chaos down here, more or less. Something happens, and it sets off all these chain reactions. I feel like I'm spinning out of control, a little." She silently pleaded with him to reel her back in. Maybe she wasn't evolved, after all.

Bailey heard him yawn into his hand. "That's basic economic principle," he told her. "A system seeks its own equilibrium and maintains it through a number of forces. When something sets an individual unit or several units of the system in motion, it immediately reacts to bring itself into equilibrium again."

"Don't you think that's depressing, Steve?"

"Depressing?" He fell silent for a second. "We're talking about economic theory, here. It's just theory. It doesn't have a value like 'happy' or 'sad' attached to it. Why would it be depressing?"

"Because nothing ever changes," Bailey said, her voice dull and lifeless.

Steve sounded much more awake, now that he was warming to his favorite topic. Good old Steve—he could be trusted to expound on economics in terms she would be sure to understand. "Of course things change. Change is a given. Equilibrium doesn't happen around a single point. The forces at work can nudge the system in a number of directions, if you envision it as reposing in a three-dimensional set of axes. But a system's natural tendency is to be at rest, and to remain that way." Good old Steve, indeed. It was a shame that he had to say words she didn't care to hear. "Hello? Are you still there?"

Bailey couldn't respond immediately. Her throat was too choked with conflicting emotions to answer. "I'm still here," she said at last.

"Oh, I thought the connection dropped, or something. I don't know how your cell reception is, down there."

"No, you don't, do you?" She slipped her fingers into the shoulder of her blouse and used the fabric to wipe the corners of her eyes. She didn't want him to hear her crying—either Steve or Taylor.

"What're you calling for, anyway? Are you upset about something?" Again, she couldn't answer right away. Maybe she was giving him less credit than he deserved for sensitivity. That is, she was willing to believe it until his next words. "Is this about the drawer? Because listen, good news. I've thought it over. I've thought over the pros and cons, and the pros win every time. So yes. I'll take the drawer."

He wanted equilibrium, she realized. Her offer, that night a week ago, had been the wild, random force that had set everything off-kilter. They had been a system, neat and closed, at rest in the way that a system should be in his universe, and she had set it reeling and spinning. In her mind she could see him so clearly thinking out those pros and cons, typing them into an Excel spreadsheet, mulling over the ways he could bring their relationship back into balance. "Oh, Steve," she sighed.

"What?" he sounded baffled. "The offer's still open, isn't it?"

It was hard enough on a daily basis being Bailey Rhodes. She didn't want to be a system. "We need to talk," she told him gently.

When she stepped outdoors again a few minutes later, she was grateful for the dark outside, and how it concealed her red-rimmed eyes and a nose raw from sniffling. The night air felt cool on her face; the breeze smelled of trees and moss. Kitten's collar made a slight jingling sound as she clicked her way across the floor to investigate the slamming screen door. In the faint glow of the light streaming through the windows, Bailey could see Taylor turn once more. He jerked his chair around across the ground so that he half-faced her. "All done?" he asked.

The dark seemed more frightening and empty from inside the house, Bailey realized. Out here, basking in it, she forgot to be lonely. Above her head, in the perfectly clear sky were more stars than she ever could have imagined. Her eye picked out a few constellations she remembered from her youth. Orion. The Big Dipper. The Pleiades. "All done," she said, crossing her arms. Despite the warm evening, she felt a chill.

"Guess you had to arrange your ground transport and stuff for tomorrow," he commented. "For when you get home."

"I'm not going home tomorrow," she admitted. "I'm extending my visit."

"Oh?" The clatter of his chair against the drive brought her attention back from the heavens down to earth. Taylor had risen to his feet and, with long strides, walked to where a hose lay coiled up against the house. He returned carrying something rectangular that, with a single motion, he popped open and set down for her. Another chair. "That's good, then?" he asked, sitting down.

"That's good." She took the seat, not caring whether the webbing was dirty or not. It felt good to relax in the dark, with Taylor beside her, and nothing to look at save for the stars above. "I made some mistakes," she explained. Her words didn't carry any farther than Taylor's ears. "So I thought I'd bring work to me, instead of going home to work. And I'm going to get the aunts on television, if I can."

"Their own show?"

"Good God, no!" The very idea was almost enough to make Bailey laugh, but she couldn't manage more than a shrug of her shoulders. "Just enough so they stop hating me."

"Nobody hates you." If only she could believe Taylor's words. They sat in the stillness for a moment more before he spoke again. "What about . . . the boyfriend?"

It was a question she'd both anticipated and dreaded

in equal measure. She'd thought hearing it aloud might make her resent Taylor for intruding, but instead, she found herself answering quietly, "As of a few minutes ago, that's not an issue anymore."

He didn't answer. Had she made a mistake in telling him? Taylor might be one of those men who enjoyed a good flirtation, but reared like a frightened stallion when opportunities presented themselves. She'd made a mistake, Bailey was almost certain. He was no doubt practicing excuses not to see her again. She should say something to let him know that what had happened really had nothing to do with him. She began to muster the words, and was working her lips when she heard him speak.

"I'm sorry." She closed her mouth. "Do you want to talk about it?"

"No."

"Do you want to meditate some?"

In the darkness, she felt his warm touch, first on her wrist where it lay on the chair's arm, then tracing down to her hand. Their fingers entwined somewhere between them, a connection she could feel, but not see. "Okay," she told him, squeezing. "Yeah. That would be nice."

If she had to be at equilibrium, this was where she wanted to rest.

PART THREE
THE LONG TRIP
HOME

Chapter Fifteen

The moment Bailey Rhodes saw her friend Euan cup his hands around his mouth and yell at the top of his lungs, "Girl, you're walking like Betty Rubble on the rag! Work that booty like you're selling it and the rent's due tomorrow!" she realized that there *was* such a thing as too much *America's Next Top Model*.

CeeCee stopped at the front edge of the plywood boards set up in a circular pattern around the driveway and peered at him. "Beg pardon?"

"Mis-ter O'Reilley!" Bits sat ramrod straight in her seat behind the table. Her right hand clutched a pencil that she tapped on the clipboard where she was making notes. Her left rapidly waved an old church hand fan in front of her face. "Did you *hear* that, Bubble?"

Bubble only giggled.

"Ms. Oates," said Euan, a smile across his face. He, too, picked up one of the fans from the table and, with the exquisite grace of a geisha, tried to cool himself down with miniscule rapid motions. "Have I mentioned what a good job you've done with the girls so far? They're fabulous. Absolutely gorgeous. You can tell by their posture alone. So much like yours, in fact. Were you a pageant girl in your youth? No? Get out!" All the way back from the airport, Bailey had carefully coached Euan on how to deal with both her aunts. She wasn't at all sure Bits would buy her friend's reassurances, but apparently Euan was managing to play it on the safe side of smarmy. Bits's expression could have been fossilized, for all it had changed while he talked, but at least it wasn't completely soured. "Girls?" he called to the group. They had been hovering over by the porch, waiting for their turns to walk down the mock runway before the mock judges. "I hope you've been paying attention to this woman's posture. It's superlative. Observe the proud carriage, the . . . Ms. Whigfield, would you oblige?"

It was the moment of truth. Had Bits been mollified? For a moment, they all sat in suspense until at last, slowly, regally, Bits stood from her seat. She sidled behind Taylor, who occupied the chair next to Bailey, and took a few steps away from the table. Finally, her practical shoes met the plywood, and she took a few steps— tentative at first, and then bold, as she walked back and forth.

"Exquisite. Like a queen!" Euan breathed. He broke out into spontaneous applause. Bits, trying in vain to hide the proud smile that had crept onto her lips, stalked back to her seat. "And trust me, I know queens. *Thank* you, Ms. Whigfield. Now. You. What's your name?"

"Me?" CeeCee looked around as if there might be other blondes on the runway. She looked a little frightened of Euan.

He leaned in and waved a hand in front of her eyes. "Darlin', can you spell MGM backwards? I bet you can't."

If it had been possible to glimpse a cutaway of the activity in CeeCee's brain at that moment, it would probably have revealed mismatched gears unsuccessfully trying to mesh and turn as she thought about the question. "MGM?" she ventured.

Beside Bailey, Taylor let out a bark of laughter. She stared at him. "Sorry," he apologized. "*Showgirls.*"

"Oh my God," said Bailey. What was this fascination people had with what was possibly the worst movie in the world? Was it a cult? "You're a *Showgirls* fan? Please tell me you're not gay."

He leaned over and, in her ear, breathed out a reassurance. "Straight men like the movie, too. Though mostly for an entirely different set of reasons from the gay guys."

"Try again," Euan demanded, a few feet away. He stepped back so the others could see CeeCee's stumbling path across the plywood. Her walk was self-conscious and stiff; she barely bent her knees. When her feet connected with the ground, it resembled more closely a cat trying to cover its mess in the litter box than any natural walk that Bailey had ever seen. Euan tried encouraging her along the way. "And *work* it! And *work* it! And . . . oh hell," he muttered, returning to his seat. "I give it a three out of ten. Judges?"

"Four," said Jeanne, from where she lay on the ground beyond the table's far end. She wore ear buds connected to some kind of portable radio, one of which, from time to time, she would remove so she could hear better.

Bubble cleared her throat and addressed an expectant CeeCee. "I think you did a lovely job, dear, and as always, I think you look lovely as well. But you were a little unsteady on your feet, and I think you could put a little more . . . what is it that Euan said earlier?" She appealed to the rest of the judges. "Oh yes. A little more junk in your trunk. I gave you a five!"

Taylor suddenly was overcome by a wild coughing fit that Bailey suspected was a cover-up for hilarity. While he doubled over, trying to clear the laughter from his chest, she pretended not to notice. "I gave her a four," said Bailey. At the disappointed look on CeeCee's face, she tried to soften the blow a little. "You look like you're thinking about it too much." As if that was possible. "But your hair looks nice!" That won a smile.

It was nothing, though, compared with the vast expanse of teeth that CeeCee displayed at Taylor's score. "I gave her a seven," he said.

"Seven!" said Euan and Bits, simultaneously.

Taylor shrugged. "She's a pretty girl in a bathing suit. That's all a man needs to know."

Euan leaned forward to argue. "She's got the grace of Paris Hilton in a pair of cement wedgies," he protested. Bailey winced, and suddenly felt very protective of CeeCee's feelings. After all, she'd been the first contestant of this bloody contest that she'd met. Judging from the girl's giggling, though, she seemed to think the Paris Hilton comparison was a compliment.

"Posture: deplorable. Decorum: passable. Smile: nil. Attention to instruction: none. CeeCee, take this as a challenge, but I give you a two." The girl's smile vanished once more. Aunt Bits lay her clipboard on the table with a clunk and turned to face Taylor again. "Seven!" she marveled.

Bailey leaned over. "He's given all the girls sevens and eights," she reminded her aunt. Then, whispering, she added, "I think he's afraid to disappoint them."

"I think I'm a little more easily satisfied than the rest of you all," said Taylor, sitting back with his arms crossed. "I keep telling you. Pretty girls. Bathing suits. Enough for me."

Euan shook his carefully tousled and pomaded head, mirroring Bits, who shook her sprayed and set wave. For once, they were in exact agreement. Poor CeeCee, in the meantime, stood in front of them still, shuffling her weight from one high-heeled leg to the other, while she waited for instruction. "Just . . . just go," Euan said at last, shooing her away.

"Thank you?" CeeCee didn't seem at all sure whether she meant the two words, but at least both aunts nodded with approval while she clomped away. Apparently thanking judges for ripping you into shreds was good pageant etiquette.

"Lennox! Next!" Euan yelled at the cluster of girls in front of the house. He leaned over and looked past the three other judges to Bailey, at the table's other end. "You so owe me combat pay after today," he said, shaking his pencil.

"You're getting paid?" she asked innocently, pretending to know nothing about it. Then, simultaneously, they broke out into smiles. Man, she had missed her friends. When she'd called him two nights before to beg him to come down, she couldn't believe how anxious he was to help. It was one of the slower weeks at the studios and he had vacation time coming, he'd assured her. Bailey hadn't let him pay for either his expensive last-minute plane ticket—though she did wish she could have afforded first-class accommodations—or for his room at the hotel in Crestonville's downtown. If he wanted to help out as a lark and for the stories he could tell his other friends back in Manhattan when it was all done, that was fine. But she'd be damned if he had to go out of pocket over any of it.

His smile didn't last long. "*Lennox!*" he bawled out at the top of his lungs, sounding like a drill sergeant with a four-day case of constipation. He rose from his seat, stepped over Jeanne where she wagged her foot in time to the music, and wandered out from the shade of the maple tree into the sun. "Which of you is Lennox?" he demanded, shading his eyes from the sun.

"She's coming?" CeeCee called out. "She's looking for something in the house?"

"Lordie," grumbled Euan. "As if I don't have enough to put up with." He snapped open the fan and looked as if he might bat someone around with it.

To be fair, none of the other Butter Beans looked happy with the delay, either. It was a hot, muggy day—

the Tidewater area at its worst, with a temperature that had to be hovering around ninety. At least a light breeze kept everyone from sweating like pigs, although Bubble had stopped fanning her face and now employed her energies in sending wafts of air up the bottom of her housedress. Bailey, seeing that Taylor's glass of water was nearly empty, leaned forward to refill it from a pitcher that seemed to have more condensation on its outside than actual water within. "*Len*—!" Euan started to cry out once more.

Bits interrupted him. "She's a bit of a special needs case," she said, then added darkly, "Bailey's special project. She'll . . . oh, here she is. What in the world!"

Fawn was walking—shuffling, really—across the front lawn in the direction of the tree, not bothering to keep to the plywood catwalk. Around her shoulders was draped . . . what was it, exactly? A blanket? A shawl? No, it was too shiny. Once the girl stepped out of the sunlight and into the shade, Bailey recognized the red-and-white expanse of vinyl that Fawn had wrapped around herself as one of Bubble's novelty kitchen table-cloths. When spread out, it depicted all the famous statues of Richmond's Monument Avenue, in case someone wanted a little historical instruction along with her morning Coco Puffs. When Fawn opened her mouth in that determined fashion that meant a diatribe was certain to follow, Bailey shrank down in her seat. Her "special project" was something she'd already come to regret a thousand times over. "Do you know what a desecration of the female form this is?" she asked, glowering at the judges one by one.

Bits sighed deeply. "I believe you've quite clearly made your position on—"

Fawn interrupted her with sparks of fiery speech. "Stereotypical images of female beauty are used against women to subject them to second-class citizenship! What about all those women out there who don't have the time to waste on prettifying themselves because they're *working* or *studying* or *caring* for other people? Why should they be expected to live up to some vapid, Miss America, Miss Universe, *People* magazine paragon when there is an infinite variety of—"

Aunt Bits could give as good as she got in the interruption department. "Fawn," she announced, "take off the tablecloth and walk around in your swimsuit like a good girl."

"But why should we enforce rigid standards for beauty? I refuse to let my body be used as a tool for oppression! Am I the one person here with a conscience?" Arms outstretched, though not so far that she actually lost hold of her vinyl wrap, Fawn appealed to the crowd. The collected judges shifted nervously in their seats. "Am I the one person here with a soul?" she asked in the direction of the girls sitting on the porch steps, all of whom were listening with bored expressions on their pretty faces.

Pity that Fawn hadn't committed to memory Shylock's famous "Hath not a Jew eyes?" speech; she could have done Shakespeare a damn sight more convincingly than her rival. Bailey had only one weapon in her arsenal she could use at moments like this. So far, she'd employed it sparingly, afraid it might lose its potency if wielded too often. She cleared her throat, catching Fawn's attention, and said the magical four words: "Larkin would do it."

Fawn's jaw instantly jutted out while she thought it over. Her eyes narrowed. Then, without a word, she turned and stomped back in the direction of the porch and the beginning of the catwalk. Everyone around the table heaved sighs of relief that collectively should have been audible from as far away as the road. Euan leaned over and, in Bailey's direction, mouthed the words *thank you*. Then he stood up and clapped his hands. "Okay, let's do this right! And now, ladies and gentlemen," he said, changing his tone so that it sounded more like an announcer's voice, "we have another lovely contestant in our contest, the mighty fine . . . Miss Fawn Lennox!" As they had for the other girls, everyone clapped politely, if not enthusiastically.

Whoosh. As if she were a supermodel at a Milan fashion show, Fawn tossed off the tablecloth like it was a tiresome old girlfriend, and walked out onto the runway. Euan bit his lip. Bits immediately threw up a hand in front of her horrified face and peered through her fingers at the approaching spectacle. Taylor grinned and whistled. Jeanne sat up onto her elbows to gawk, pulling the stereo buds from her ears.

Fawn stalked her way around the circle, taking step after long step until she reached the front, where she turned and walked clockwise in the opposite direction, a totally insincere smile plastered to her face. If she'd left on the plywood scorch marks in the shape of cloven hooves and a pointy tail, Bailey wouldn't have been in the least surprised. "Nice!" Taylor called out, when Fawn reached her second stopping point on the right hand of the imaginary stage. For a brief moment she broke the pouty, angry character she had assumed to thump around in, and a glimpse of the mischievous young woman underneath poked out. Then, like a guillotine, her reserve lowered with a boom. Stone-faced, she was back to circling around to her first stopping place, looking all the world like a bitchy runway model wearing a pair of shoes two sizes too small.

At long last, it came to an end. Bailey wondered if she looked as stunned as the rest of her fellow judges. Judging by the fact that she couldn't bring herself to look at the staging area, she probably did. After what seemed like an eternity of waiting, in which glaciers surged forward and receded and streamlets grew and flourished and left behind grand canyons in the rock before they vanished completely, Euan spoke. His voice sounded dry and crackly in his throat. "The attitude was perfect," he said. "But . . . two."

"Three," said Jeanne, her mouth still hanging open in awe.

Bailey cleared her throat. "I thought you had quite a walk," she said, trying to be as tactful as possible. "Very high fashion."

"Mmm," agreed Euan. "That's true. Very high fashion."

"At the same time, though, I think you were a trifle out of place. So I gave you a four for this time. Sorry." She couldn't look at Fawn to check her reaction. She couldn't look at Fawn at all.

Taylor, however, didn't have any problem checking her out from top to bottom. "Nine," he said without any prompting. "A nice, solid nine. What?" he added, when Bailey gaped at him.

"Are you trying to encourage her, or provoke me?" she asked.

He appeared to think carefully before he answered. "Which one is working?"

"Am I the only one?" Bubble asked, voice plaintive and reedy. "What *is* that story? They read it to you when you're young. The fairy tale, the one about the king?"

"King Midas?" Jeanne speculated. "The one who turned things to gold when he grabbed on to them?"

"No." Bubble sounded fretful. "The one with the small boy."

What did it say, when Bailey had known where Bubble's mind was wandering right from the start? "The emperor's new clothes," she said, tapping the eraser end of her pencil onto her own clipboard.

"Thank you, dear! I knew you'd know!" Bubble leaned over, peered at Bailey through her thick spectacles, and bestowed her with a sunny beam. "But now that we've established that, is it just me? Or is she not wearing anything?"

Again, someone could have driven a convoy of semi-trucks through the resulting silence, and still had time to escort past a small flock of waddling, slow-moving ducklings. There was no denying it. Fawn had taken the runway absolutely, unabashedly, stark naked. Not only that, she had reveled in the way her nudity had reduced everyone to uncomfortable silence. Everyone, that is, save for Taylor, who kept nodding abstractedly while he stared. Bailey wanted to swat the chucklehead.

Her teeth clenched together, Bits growled, "I think the bottoms have boiled out of all your grits pans. Of course the girl's got no clothes. Are you all *blind?*"

For the first time since she'd made with the Lady Godiva act, Fawn crossed her arms. When Bits immediately dropped her hand and looked as if she might continue with her harangue, Fawn bared her breasts once more and stood with her hands on her hips. "This is what I wear when I go swimming," she declared.

"I weep for the public pools in Ashland." Bits averted her gaze. "Zero," she said, grim and not at all amused. "Zeros across the board. Zero for decorum. Zero for smile. Zero for attention to instruction. And most of all, zero for making a mockery of something that I take very seriously. You know, it may be *your* intention to create havoc in the name of—" Bits usually did better in the face-to-face approach when giving someone a tongue-lashing, but since she couldn't bring herself to look in the direction of the naked contestant on her lawn, Fawn had her at a distinct disadvantage. Bits did manage to rise to her feet, though, her impressive posture lending her more height than she actually had. "For heaven's sake! CeeCee! Somebody! Cover her up!"

Everyone sat awkwardly while Austyn trotted over in her swimsuit, obediently bearing the tablecloth. Fawn's serene unawareness of her nudity—or her simple lack of concern about it—made her look like Botticelli's Venus, formed from foam and blown in from the sea upon a clam shell. And Austyn's ministrations, as she wrapped the covering snugly around Fawn, reminded her of the nymph in the famous painting, cloth billowing as she attempted to conceal her mistress. Only Bailey was fairly certain that in *The Birth of Venus*, the goddess of love wasn't being swathed in vinyl images of Robert E. Lee and Stonewall Jackson. "The last time I checked, this was a free country," said Fawn, ruining the illusion of tranquility. "I am trying to express my disdain for this—"

"What you are trying to do, young lady, is the Scottish Reel on my last nerve." Without any bare breasts or buttocks to offend her eye, Bits was now free to march over and speak her mind directly in Fawn's defiant face. "We're going inside to have a nice long talk, you and I."

"Oh, are we?" Fawn asked, trying to shuck her tablecloth again.

Only Bits grabbing the vinyl by its edges kept it from flying off Fawn's shoulders. "Yes," she announced. "We are." With a firm fist, Bits yanked the girl forward, practically lifting her from the ground as she marched to the house. Fawn squawked and flailed and tried to jerk away, but Bits's will was too strong and besides, she moved too quickly. Fawn had to scramble to keep up with her.

"Oh jeez," said Jeanne. "I'd sure hate to be her right now."

Euan shook his head. "The girl needs a lot of work. Then again, they all do."

Taylor shrugged. "I thought she was great."

"Hah!" said Bailey. She'd seen a certain glimmer in his eye when he'd said that. "You *are* trying to provoke me!" Truth be told, she was relieved; she liked the idea of Taylor the Playful much better than Taylor the Pig. "Maybe we could . . ."

Whatever *maybe* she wanted to share would have to wait, because Bits tossed back one shrill word at the top of her lungs, as she marched into the house. "*Bailey!*"

"No reprieve for the hard-working," she muttered.

Chapter Sixteen

Aunt Bubble happened to be humming to herself when Bailey stepped down the stairs, aspirin in hand, on the way to the kitchen sink and a glass of water. What was the tune? It sounded tantalizingly familiar. An old hymn, perhaps. She smiled at her aunt, who sat at the round wooden table set next to the old cooking hearth. A teapot rested before her, and she riffled through an old recipe box. "Oh, hello, dear!" she murmured. The soft folds of her face pulled back into a sunny smile. "Going out? I do hope you have a good time."

When the Rhodes had lived in the house before ceding it to the aunts and moving North, the kitchen had always been a dark, forbidding place. Bailey's mother had never been much of a cook, admittedly—her specialty had been quick, one-dish meals made out of boxes and bottles, usually featuring not-quite-foods like Rice-a-Roni or dehydrated potatoes. It hadn't been until her teens that Bailey realized that pasta's sole source wasn't Chef Boyardee, or that green beans could be snapped and simmered instead of slopped from a can.

To be honest, Bailey hadn't noticed the loss. Children didn't care about those things. She and the other kids she knew growing up took prepackaged, processed foods as normal and thought bizarre anyone who didn't follow suit. When one girl in New Jersey had revealed that her mother made her own mayonnaise, she'd been ostracized from the more popular lunchroom tables and forced to eat with the undesirables, near the leaky window. For her mother, boxes and cans and the microwave oven had been a convenience that let her dispense with mealtimes quickly and efficiently, so she could spend her evenings attending League of Women Voters meetings, or stuffing envelopes at Democratic headquarters, or throwing herself heart and soul into whatever cause was near and dear to her heart that month.

Under Bubble's reign, though, the kitchen had almost immediately changed. It had always been a soft, feminine room, warm and cozy in the winters and because of its location in the lowest part of the house, cooler than the other rooms in summer. It certainly wasn't a Food Network set, by any means. The cabinets from which Bailey took an old jelly glass had been installed sometime during the 1940s. They had a rough-hewn charm, as did the sink from which she drew her glass of water. Yet the cabinets bore painted-over dents, and the sink's white enamel had been eroded by time and scarred by decades of pots and pans.

Bubble had made the room homey. Her cross-stitched samplers decorated the walls. Bouquets of plastic fruit tied atop slotted spoons hung from below the window sill. She'd clipped advice columns and panels of *Family Circus* from the newspaper and affixed them to the refrigerator, and hung dried flowers from the backs of the door. Bailey downed her aspirin, left the glass in the sink, and took a few steps in the direction of the back door. "Have a nice time, dear," Bubble said. "See you tomorrow, I hope?" She began humming again, as if Bailey were already gone.

The simple dismissal made Bailey stop dead in her tracks. There was no denying the fact that Bailey had hoped she could ease through this spell in Virginia with a minimum of fuss and bother. Bubble treated her as if Bailey had, moments before, punched her time card after a day's work so she could scoot out as quickly as possible. With a pang of guilt, Bailey realized the analogy wasn't too far off—she *had* been treating interactions with the aunts as if they were work. No, not work. She usually tackled work with relish. She'd spent the entire week treating the aunts as if they'd been chores, more arduous than rinsing dishes yet less loathsome than scrubbing out a dirty toilet. Bits at least had the nerve to call her on it. Bubble, on the other hand, merely accepted the bad treatment as her due, smiling after each little sting. The realization made Bailey swallow hard, turn around, and retrace her steps to the table, thoroughly guilty. "I'm not in a hurry," she said, reaching the table and pulling out a chair for herself. "I was going over to Taylor's place to . . . well. Maybe you'd like a little company?"

"Oh!" Bubble immediately sat up. The quality of her attention changed; she seemed to focus and actually see her niece. Maybe, Bailey thought ruefully, because it was one of the first times she'd really been there. "Isn't that sweet of you? I don't want to distract you from your fun."

"Nonsense. Mind if I . . . ?" Next to her little teapot, Bubble had set out a plate of cookies to work through.

Bubble beamed and pushed the plate a little forward, so that Bailey could help herself. "I hope Bits wasn't too hard on you, honey," she sighed. "I could hear her voice from up here."

It took a great deal of restraint for Bailey to refrain from pointing out that Helen Keller, wearing a pair of earmuffs, could have found her way across the country to Crestonville using Bits's voice in the den upstairs as her sole guide. For close to an hour Bits had ranted and railed, while Fawn had sat sullenly on the sofa and stared at the ceiling. Although Bailey certainly

hadn't played any role in Fawn's stunt, it seemed as if
most of Bits's lecture on tradition and decorum had
been aimed her way. After all, hadn't it been a varia-
tion on all the lectures she'd ever gotten from Bits,
growing up? Responsibility, blah blah blah. Showing
old customs respect, blah blah. Hygiene, blah. Bailey
decided understatement might be appropriate here.
"She was a little upset."

"There's always one." Bubble reached for another
cookie. How many had she eaten already? Sometimes it
seemed as if Bubble existed on cookies and pies and
other sweet tidbits. A freshly iced coconut cake, made
that morning, sat in a cake cozy on the kitchen counter
for that evening's dinner, a single slim slice already
missing from its side.

The cookies were good. Bailey had to give her aunt
that. Sweet and crunchy on the outside, their insides
seemed laden with some kind of chewy fruit. Raisins?
"One what?"

"One rebel in the bunch. Mind you, they don't usually walk around in the altogether. Very few do. In fact,"
Bubble said, nibbling around the edge of the cookie as
she considered, "I'm certain this might be our first girl
who has." Behind her thick glasses, she blinked rapidly. "Oh! You have no idea how hard it was to keep
from giggling all morning, knowing what was coming.
But I had to see the look on Bits's face when it happened."

"Mmmm," said Bailey, eating the last half of her
cookie. Then, after she thought about what her aunt had
said, she added, "Wait a minute." Bubble peered at her,
her expression pleasant. "What do you mean, knowing
what was coming?" Surely Aunt Bubble couldn't
have—she wouldn't have! "You didn't know ahead of
time, did you?"

Waiting for an answer was close to torture, but Bubble was occupied in searching for something in her
recipe box, humming to herself under her breath the en-

tire time. At last she found the weathered old clipping she needed, set it aside, and smiled. "Well, dear. All I can say is that for nearly a half-hour this morning I had to listen to your friend talk about how she didn't believe in beauty pageants . . . which is silly, because it's not like believing in Santa Claus, when he really doesn't exist. Because beauty pageants happen all the time, whether you believe in them or not. So I said, don't be silly, Fawn, it's not like believing in Santa Claus, when he doesn't really exist, because beauty pageants. . . ."

Bailey had no idea which was a more dangerous place to wander—the thorny hedge maze of Bits's barbed tongue, or the wandering, roundabout circumlocutions of Bubble's brain. "And she said?"

Luckily, her aunt didn't seem to mind the nudge at all. Like an old record player stuck on a scratch, she jumped ahead into the groove and talked as she searched for another recipe. "And she said, well, I don't *own* a bathing suit like the other girls have. And I said, well, we can get you one, dear. And she said, well, what if I don't want one? And I said, if that's the case, dear, then why don't you wear what you usually wear to swim?"

"Oh no," Bailey breathed, both horrified and delighted at what she was hearing.

"And *she* laughed and said, you wouldn't like to see what I wear to swim, and I paid her no mind and *I* said, then wear what you like, dear! Because I had so many girls to think about, you see. I can't be expected to mind only the one." Was that a smirk on Bubble's lips? Bailey leaned in more closely to inspect. "I can't say I was *entirely* surprised when she appeared *dishabille*, as they used to say."

"But!" Bailey didn't know how to frame her protest. "*You* were the one who pointed out that she was naked!"

"Well, dear, I didn't know for *certain* what was going to happen, did I?" She paused in her recipe search to give Bailey a wink. "Besides, if I hadn't pointed it out, I think Bits would have kept on pretending it wasn't happening. Stubborn woman."

"Oh my God." Bailey absolutely could not believe what she was hearing. An unexpected burst of laughter flew from her lips. "Bubble, you are one wicked old hag!"

"Thank you, dear!"

Over the kitchen table they looked at each other for a moment. Finally, Bubble's lips pursed, pleased with herself. Once Bailey could shut her mouth, she mirrored her aunt's expression. There was so much she wanted to say, but she didn't want to rend the delicate spirit of confidentiality between them. All she could do was revel in delight at the discovery of her aunt's mischievous side. How long had it lain dormant? Or had it been there all along, and Bailey simply had never realized it? Perhaps she'd never looked past her aunt's sugar-coated exterior to the chewier morsels underneath.

Overwhelmed with a sudden affection for the old woman, Bailey sat and watched her for a silent minute as she rummaged through the old cards and clippings. The recipe box had sat atop her aunts' refrigerator since the day they'd moved in, a plain metal card holder that once had been white but now was a distinct shade of smudge, beneath which could be seen a stylized illustration of a rooster. "Do you want me to help look for something?"

Though obviously pleased with the offer, judging by the smile on her face, Bubble shook her head. "I know where everything is in this box." She probably did, too, judging by the way her fingers expertly danced over the recipes wedged tightly within. As if to prove her point, she fished out a small fold of paper covered with antique handwriting. "I didn't mean to put you off. I don't even allow Bits to go through Mother's recipes. Not that she can cook more than a boiled egg, poor dear," she murmured, pulling shut the box's lid. It didn't quite close. With its interior so cram-packed with recipe cards, the lid gave an impression of barely restraining everything from popping out at any moment, like some sort of culinary jack-in-the-box.

"Mom didn't turn out to be much of a cook either."

"Oh, she used to be quite good in her teen years! She used to cook for Bits and me when we were children, you know. Oh yes," she said, seeing the surprise in Bailey's expression. "Mother was always busy at the feed store, and she relied on your mother quite a lot, in those days. Polly would make pail lunches for us before we woke up, and walk us to school in the mornings before heading off to her own school. Then she would meet us in the playground, afternoons, and take us on the long walk up the hill back home. She'd baby-sit us and help us with our homework, and play games. When we were older, she made sure we went to our piano and dance and charm school lessons. She did laundry and kept the house clean and made dinners . . . using many of these very same recipes," she said. From the way she stroked the old metal box, a casual observer might have thought it contained priceless jewels instead of recipes culled from newspapers and countless old magazines. "Chops and vegetables and side dishes and biscuits—the lot. Then after we ate and she sent us off to bed, she'd have a little while to do her own homework before Mother came home, and she'd have to sit with Mother while she ate."

Bailey leaned onto the table with both elbows and propped her chin in her hand. "She must've hated that," she said, biting into another cookie. She couldn't imagine her mom as a young domestic goddess.

"Polly? Oh, didn't she just!" Bubble made a series of clucking noises. "With all her heart and soul! From the time I was eight until Polly went away to college when I was—let's see, fifteen?—she was more mother to us than our own mother. And you're right, she absolutely despised it. I remember. . . ." Bubble looked off in the direction of the window over the sink, where rays of sunlight slanted through over the grass and gravel at eye level outside, and onto the flagstones of the floor. "I remember that she used to keep count every night of how many more meals she had to cook. *Only one thousand, two hundred, and twenty-seven meals,* she'd say. Then the next night, *Only one thousand, two hundred, and twenty-six!* Of course, shortly before she went off to school—and weren't we proud of her, getting that scholarship with all she had to do—it became a game, really. *Only thirty more to go!* Then ten, then two, then one, and she was gone, and I don't believe she ever cooked much again after that. And I took over from her at home."

All while Bubble had been talking, Bailey couldn't help but think about those books she'd found in the attic. With all those expectations and responsibilities placed on her, she was surprised her mom hadn't exploded under the pressure. "Did you mind? Taking over, I mean?"

"Oh, no. Well, it wasn't the same after she left, of course. Bits and I are only two years apart, so taking care of her wasn't the same as taking care of very young children, as Polly had to. And we could split most of the chores between us—I did the cooking, and Bits kept house. Of course, that's when Mother started losing money on the feed store, and both Bits and I had to help out there after school, too, so she could let go of the paid employees. People simply weren't keeping as many livestock in those days, especially as Carverton got more suburban. Oh, we were still out in the country, don't you get me wrong, but it was getting to be like around here . . . so many people living in the country and commuting into the city, and fewer actually farming or keeping animals."

"People commute from here?" Bailey wanted to know,

intrigued. "To where, Richmond?" She supposed it was less than an hour's drive; people in greater New York commuted for longer than that every day.

"Richmond, yes, and to the District of Columbia, too. My goodness, they couldn't have renovated Main Street without the tax money from Crestonville's commuters!" Bubble took another cookie and began chewing around its edges, taking a squirrel's miniscule nibbles. "Where was I? Oh yes, working in the feed store. It wasn't a bad life, certainly."

"Mom never talked about her life growing up, I guess," Bailey said, studying her aunt. "I didn't realize much of this stuff about her. I thought she hated Georgia. I didn't realize she had a reason."

"Oh, she doesn't hate Georgia! She loved Carverton!" Bubble's rejoinder was so astonished that Bailey was taken aback for a few seconds. Her mom didn't love Carverton. She'd visited once every eighteen months at most, and then only gritting her teeth and swearing about her mother the entire time. And those visits had stopped for good, right before they'd packed up and moved to New Jersey. "She loved that little town more than anyone could love a place, I think. When we were young, she always knew where all the wild berry patches were in the woods. I used to wake up in the middle of the night to find her sitting in our window, watching the moon cross the sky. She liked the quiet of it, she would tell me." Bubble sighed. "I thought that was a lovely phrase. The quiet of it. After she married, she would write and tell me how flat it was there, and how she missed the smell of the pines and the winds in the hills. Poor Polly. Moving away was one of the biggest sacrifices she could make, but of course, she had to protect herself. Mother would have had her running the feed store single-handedly if she hadn't gone away to school . . . and don't think she didn't try to get Polly to come back, when she needed the help!"

"So why did she hate going down?"

"Well. . . ." In the moments of silence that followed, Bailey could count the passing seconds by the tick of the mantel clock sitting over the old hearth. "She had college, and then, of course, she married your father. Such a sweet man, he was. I cried when he passed away, with you children so young. But that's neither here nor there. Mother . . ." Bubble's lips worked, unable to summon the necessary words. Bailey felt guilty about pressing the issue. They were probably treading too close to a territory her aunt didn't want to revisit. She was about to change the topic entirely when Bubble finished the sentence. "Mother remarried," she said, softly. "A much younger man. It was . . . unexpected. He—he had been a particular friend of mine." Bailey swallowed, appreciating the euphemism for what it was. "No one approved. They all said he was after the money she'd made from selling the feed store. Of course, after that. . . ." Bubble paused again. For a moment, Bailey thought her aunt had become overwhelmed. "After that, I couldn't live with Mother any more. I—I couldn't forgive her for a long time. I'm not certain I ever did. Anyway. Bits had married John Oates by then, and they'd moved into a house across the street and a little bit down. . . ."

"The house we used to visit you in," Bailey said, trying to soften the pangs Bubble must be experiencing. She remembered it well.

"Yes, that's the one. And of course poor John passed on before he and Bits had been married a year, poor man. It seems as if Whigfield husbands never last long— your grandfather, your father, Bits's John. You might want to remember that when you marry your economist, dear." It was difficult not to stiffen at that remark. "Only Francisco survived." At Bailey's raised eyebrows, she explained. "Francisco. Your grandmother's second husband. My—my friend. Your mother was furious with

Mother after she married, of course. We all were. That was the main reason she didn't come back often. When she did, it was mostly to visit Bits and me." Bailey waited politely for Bubble to finish sighing, and to let her take a sip of tea and nibble her way around the rest of the cookie. "And then Mother died, and Francisco had her cremated immediately, so none of us could pay our final respects. When the will was read, we found out that Francisco had managed to talk her into leaving everything to him. All the money, all the heirlooms, all the furniture. Everything. Oh, it was so hard, going to the memorial service knowing how evil he was." Bubble's hand rose from the tea cup to the recipe box once more, wiping the top of what few dust motes had accumulated in the past several moments. "This is all I have of Mother's. And I was lucky to get that."

"I don't remember any of this. I don't remember going to Grandmother's memorial service." Surely she had to have gone. "I don't remember this Francisco guy at *all*," Bailey said. Her recollections of her grandmother were largely a bundle of cutting comments and prickly reserve. "I remember sitting in her parlor, but you know, I don't think I could tell you at all what the kitchen looked like, or where she slept, or anything about her house. Yours, I remember perfectly." The kitchen of the aunts' Georgia home had been smaller and whiter than this one, but was well-kept and clean and cozy. The aunts had held Easter egg hunts for Jeanne and Bailey in a backyard she remembered well, and she could have diagrammed how the furniture had been arranged in every room of the aunts' house, down to the color of the chenille bedspreads and the pattern of the curtains. But a man, living in her grandmother's house across the road? It seemed inconceivable.

"You probably never went to any part of Mother's house save for the parlor, dear," Bubble said. It seemed as if she were trying to console Bailey, which seemed odd. If anyone needed consoling for this sad episode of her life, surely it was Bubble. And Bits. And her mom. "Bits and I would sit in the parlor after taking Mother to church, but that man . . ." Her lips twitched with decades-long anger. "We saw as little of him as possible, which meant never going beyond the parlor. That was Mother's room, of course. And then after Mother died, and the will—well, we saw even less."

"I'm sorry." Bailey felt compelled to reach out across the table and take her aunt's hand in her own. Bubble's skin was soft and dry to the touch. Squeezing it felt like squeezing a scented sachet, the sort tucked into dresser drawers to keep them fresh. "Is that why Bits is so against Mom going back to Carverton a final time? Because of everything that happened?"

"Oh, Bailey, dear. There's nothing to be sorry about. There are plenty of people who have much worse lives! And yes, that's why Bits is so—well, you know how Bits can be. There's more, of course, but. . . ." Bubble smiled, and placed her own hand atop her niece's. "Listen to me, boring you with stories about people long gone!"

"Bubble?" Bailey hadn't felt connected to a family member in some time. Funny. She'd spent an entire week trying to wish herself part of something more, somewhere else. The night before, she had simply sat with Taylor, looking at the stars and listening to the sounds of the night. And that afternoon, she'd sat down and listened to Bubble's stories. Staying still and quiet had brought her closer to people in shorter periods of time than years and years of trying to do the right thing. More than trying to do her duty. She had to know something, though. "Are you . . . happy?"

For a moment, Bubble seemed to retreat into what, before now, Bailey had thought of as her natural state: wooly-headed, distracted, and vague. Now that she knew about Bubble's mischievous side, though, exactly how much of that persona was an act? And how much was she going to have to revise the way she looked at

her older aunt? "Bailey," she said, shaking her head and
squeezing her niece's hand once more. "What a silly,
silly question. Of *course* I'm happy! I have a lovely
home, and my health, and oh-so-much to do. And now
your sweet sister will be living here and there'll be a
baby, and there's. . . ." She trailed off, her lips forming
into a private smile.

"There's Mr. Rice, you mean." Bailey supplied, instantly rewarded by Bubble lifting her hands and making little shooing motions, as if she were embarrassed at
hearing it said aloud. She'd worn the same expression
the evening before, in the back garden, walking with
her beau. "I think it's sweet," Bailey said, laughing
when Bubble became more embarrassed than before, if
possible. Her aunt giggled like a girl of fifteen, upon
hearing the dreamiest guy in class was planning to take
her to the sock hop. And Bailey felt like the best girlfriend who'd delivered the news. "No, seriously! I think
it's wonderful!"

"Well, you're a sweetheart for saying so," was all the
acknowledgment Bubble would give. "And I won't
stand for you staying indoors on such a lovely day for a
moment longer. You should be outside in the sun!"

"No one goes out in the sun anymore," Bailey told
her, taking her cue and rising from the table. "These
days, it's all about the SPF."

"I don't believe we get that station, dear," Bubble said
placidly.

"No, SPF. It's . . ." Suddenly, Bailey narrowed her
eyes. Was Bubble having her on? Damn it, she made it
impossible to tell!

Bubble began pouring herself another cup of tea.
"And don't worry about your young friend, dear. I told
you, there's one in every group of aspiring beauty
queens. There hasn't been a single year Bits hasn't had
to take one of the girls aside for coming up with some
new brand of naughtiness!"

"Thank you. Really. Thank you." On impulse, Bailey

scooted around the table and gave her aunt a great big hug—longer and more meaningful than any of the embraces they'd shared in the airport drop-off and pick-up lanes in the last month. "I'll be back for dinner," she promised. "One of your mother's recipes?"

"Cubed steak with mashed potatoes and fried onions!" The description alone practically hardened Bailey's arteries. She was nearly halfway across the kitchen when Bubble spoke up again. "Your mother was one, too, you know."

Bailey smiled and turned. "A rebel?" That had been the point of the entire conversation, hadn't it?

"No, dear. A beauty queen." Bubble seemed to take a particularly sadistic pleasure in shocking people, it seemed, because while Bailey stood there, absolutely flabbergasted, the older woman sat back and helped herself to another cookie. "First runner-up, Miss Bartholomew College, her sophomore year. Ask her yourself if you don't believe me."

"*My* mother?" It couldn't be.

Apparently it could, though, because Bubble nodded. "She was always the prettiest of the three of us. Not just the bravest, you know."

What was it that Taylor had said, earlier in the week? That every family had stories? The Whigfields and Rhodes were the freakin' library of Alexandria.

Chapter Seventeen

Bailey would never have known the greenhouse was there. It wasn't visible from the road, or from the front of Taylor's house. She hadn't noticed it through his back windows when she'd been lounging around in his living room. Yet there it lurked, stretching in a long narrow line perpendicular to his home, a high-tech, gleaming corridor, like a bullet train into the agriculture of tomorrow.

Or something like that. It was the impression Taylor wanted to give her, she was pretty certain; he took great care to explain the theory of hydroponics and let her examine the root systems of some of the plants he was more interested in. A setup like this would look great on an Expedition Network documentary, she realized. Maybe a series—a whole set of programs about today's agronomists. They could give it a catchy title, like *Botany Bay*. . . . No. How about *Tales from the Farm*? No. It sounded too *Hee-Haw*. Okay then, *Frontline: Agriculture*. Or *From Seed to . . .* something else beginning with the letter *S*? *Salad*?

His deep voice interrupted her musing. "Too hot?"

They walked down the long lines of tables and low-lying platforms where greenery sprouted from constantly circulating troughs of water. The greenhouse was indeed more than a little warm, even with vents ajar at the glass apex above them, and doors open at the front and back and along the sides for circulation. Not unbearable, though. "No, I'm fine," she told him. If anything, it was the intense odor of green that was more difficult to bear than the heat. The smell of growth and plant life and the burgeoning of leafy vegetables was so concentrated within the four walls and the roof of glass that it made Bailey's nose twitch. "This place is great," she told him, plotting in her head a pitch for the series at the next biweekly meeting. "I mean, really. This is cutting-edge stuff, right? So what happens, you come up with hybrids in here, and then when you have enough seed, you plant them in your fields?"

"In a general sense, that's how it works. I did most of my college work in corn—trying to come up with some specialized varieties of supersweets, backcrossing some alleles into some hybrids of. . . ." The more technical Taylor became, the less Bailey understood, but she listened and nodded to his lecture until she got the gist: the sweeter the corn, the longer the shelf life, and some of that same type of research had somehow transferred over to his current interest in flat beans. "Oh heck," he laughed. "Your eyes are glazing over. We can get out of here if you want."

"No, not at all," she exclaimed, sniffing to clear her nose. She'd been paying attention! Her brain had simply been hard at work during the talk, though, trying to think about how broad an appeal all this might have to her network's audiences. "Seriously. So your beans are different how?"

"How about I give you the short version?" He raked a hand through his hair and rubbed the back of his neck. Genuinely interested as she was in what he had to say, she found herself distracted by the smooth curves of his tricep as his bent elbow tilted up in the air. "My beans have higher protein levels, which is good for consumers, and the higher levels of certain sugars enhance taste and shelf life, which is also good for consumers. I'm trying to work on improving disease and insect resistance, too. And it's all thanks to some genetic manipulation."

"Genetic manipulation? Like, putting frog genes into vegetables?" Now, *there* was a good television program. Give it a title like *Bizarro Farming*, or *Freaks of Nature*, and it could pull in some respectable numbers.

"Yes," he replied smoothly, without breaking stride. "Exactly like putting frog genes into vegetables or crossing corn with bats and extracting firefly DNA to make glow-in-the-dark zucchini so that night harvesting is a hundred times easier." He dropped the poker face and raised his eyebrows. "Why is it that whenever I talk about genetic manipulation, everyone thinks of these Frankenstein vegetables, tromping all over the place and killing the cows, or getting into the food supply and turning people into zombies?" When Bailey made a face, he laughed. "Oh don't look distressed. It's not your fault. There is a lot of genome microbiology involved in agriculture these days. But I meant the good old-fashioned kind of genetic manipulation that mankind's been doing to its crops for centuries. Cross-breeding and hybridizing."

"Sorry," she said, almost laughing at herself as well. "You see all this stuff at the movies and on television, though, and—" she shrugged "—you get weird ideas."

He stopped and leaned against a broad table on which, in shallow troughs of soil, grew seedlings. He crossed his legs at the ankle and relaxed. "Look at it this way," he said. She cocked her head. How would Taylor look on camera? Easy answer: damned good. "You know maize. We call it corn, right? Thousands of years ago, those big yellow ears of corn looked nothing like they do today. They looked like green beans, no bigger than this." He measured out the first two joints of his index finger. "Segmented, too, with a single kernel in each hard-shelled pod. Totally inedible, except for the kernels, which were hard to get to because the maize plant had too many tassels and the multiple ears were hard to harvest. But the natives of Central America had plenty of this wild grass growing around and not much else. So they harvested only from the plants with the biggest pods and cultivated them, and from later generations picked those . . . are you sure you're not bored?" He folded his arms, seeming embarrassed about how much he had gone on.

"No. Go on," she grinned. She could absolutely picture him in front of the camera, especially those biceps that popped out whenever he crossed his arms. If he could make ancient crops sound sexy, he could appear as a guest speaker on one of their shows . . . or maybe cohost one, with the right B- or C-list talent. "You're doing great."

He resumed the story from where he'd left off. "You've heard of natural selection? What we do in agriculture is unnatural selection, in a way. We select the characteristics we want in a plant, and encourage it. So from later generations, the natives would pick and cultivate the maize fruits with more rows of kernels and fewer tassels and thinner and thinner pods. It took a long time, but we ended up with the modern-day ear of corn—which on this continent we raise more than twice as much as any other crop. I mean, how could 7-Eleven make its taquito shells without the corn plant?"

"I think those taquitos we ate had a flour tortilla shell."

"Work with me, a little," he suggested. "I'm trying to make my mini-lecture relevant. And exactly what did you mean, I'm *doing* great?" He looked around, peering up at the roof and down the long rows. Only one of his employees, putting away some equipment at the greenhouse's far end, prevented them from being completely alone. "Are there spy cameras in here? Am I on the Internet?"

She laughed, a little mortified to be caught out. "No cameras. I was interested!"

"Interested because I'm naturally fascinating, or interested because you've got some idea in that devious head of yours? Don't deny it," he commanded, when she opened her mouth to protest. "You've got that look Donald Trump wears right before he's about to fire one of his apprentices."

"No! Fine, I'll come clean," she said, when he appeared not to believe her. Somehow the heat in the greenhouse made her unwilling to stand too close to Taylor; she stood across the aisle, resting the small of her back on the table opposite. "I was kind of wondering how you'd look on camera."

The gloating *a-ha!* elements of his triumph seemed to be dulled quite a bit by the withdrawn, shy *aw, shucks!* side of his immediate reaction. What won out in the end, though, was a baffled sort of crunched-eyebrow, wrinkled-nose, *Huh?* "Why?" he wanted to know.

Immediately Bailey assumed her talent producer's mantle, remaining briskly professional despite the heat and the humidity and the fact that when Taylor looked awkward, his eyes crinkled at the edges and made him look adorably like a kid abashed about his new haircut. "You have an ease in expressing complex scientific concepts with well-selected examples." She ticked off a finger. "I mean, I can only manage the *New York Times* crossword puzzle on Mondays, so. . . ." He didn't get the reference. She simplified. "It's the easiest one of the week. What I'm saying is that if I can understand genetic manipulation from your explanation, *anyone* could."

He narrowed his eyes, as if he didn't quite believe her. "I'm sure there are lots of people—botanists, molecular biologists, agronomists—who could do the same thing."

"Well, maybe," she said. Boy, it was kind of hot in the greenhouse. It seemed as if flames were licking her face. Or was that her embarrassment at being pinned down? "You've got the smarts, like a professor, but you're accessible."

"So you mean I'm like Carl Sagan. And I could talk about billions and billions of seeds and bring an understanding of the cosmos of farming to the American people."

"No. Not like Carl Sagan." She was bluffing. She had no idea who Carl Sagan was. He sounded like someone on PBS. "What I'm saying is that you've got a certain kind of. . . ." She cleared her throat, hyperaware of his scrutiny. "Look. A certain kind of look. A kind of. . . ." Bailey cleared her throat. Taylor had raised his eyebrows, waiting for an answer. "Kind of like a professor, yes, but . . . one who's, you know. Not totally bad looking or anything. Anyway, it's—"

"Like a professor who's not totally bad looking," Taylor mused, rubbing the back of his knuckles across his chin. The slight cleft there made his hand bounce up and down slightly. "Oh," he said at last, light dawning. "Like the professor from *Gilligan's Island*!" He almost seemed to enjoy flustering her. "So you think I can build a radio out of coconuts?"

Bailey's lips twitched. "No," she said, trying to keep her voice level. "Not like the professor from *Gilligan's Island*. I meant that you have a certain level of . . . comely good looks that wouldn't look entirely out of place on the television screen."

"Ohhhhhhhh," he exhaled, at last seeming to understand. Then his lips stretched out in what looked dangerously like a leer. "You think I'm purty," he drawled.

"No!" she almost yelled.

"Oh yeah." He definitely wore a leer. Not just a leer—it was practically a smirk. "You think I'm real pur-ty!"

Was her face red? It felt the color of ripe tomatoes. "Listen, Big Ego, that's not what I'm saying."

Taylor's assistant had been walking in their direction from the back of the greenhouse. He was younger than Bailey had realized—probably a high school kid earning some extra money over the summer. "Hey, boss, I'm taking off for the day," he called as he passed.

Bailey turned her head away, so the boy wouldn't notice how flushed she was—a fruitless gesture, as it turned out, because Taylor said, "Hey, Matteo. Bailey here thinks I'm pur-ty."

"Taylor Montgomery!" Apparently sometime over the past week, Bailey had learned to channel her aunt Bits. That certainly was Bits's voice that had issued from her mouth, anyway.

"Give her a flash of your lady-killer smile," Taylor suggested to the boy. "Maybe she'll think you're purty, too, and put you on TV."

Without hesitation, Matteo displayed his pearly whites. They certainly were white, too, a perfect set of blinding teeth that offset the natural darkness of his skin. "Anyway," she stressed, trying to ignore the puerile hijinks, "it's a long shot, and I'd have to pitch the idea back at the network, but I thought, you know, if it flew, you might be interested, and then I'd be able to, like, visit the aunts when I came down to. . . ."

"She thinks I'm purty, and she wants to see more of me," Taylor gloated.

"Listen," she growled. "If you say *purty* one more time, I'm going to do something so drastic, you'll never produce seeds again, ever. And I don't mean bean hybrids."

"Hit dog howls loudest." He winked.

"See you tomorrow, boss," grinned Matteo, waving farewell as he stuffed a dirty pair of gloves into his back pocket. He was a purt—a *pretty* boy, probably the heartbreaker of the junior class.

But he wasn't half as pretty as Taylor. He'd nailed her. No, that was an unfortunate choice of words. He'd been right in all his guesses so far. She did think he was attractive. Deny it as she tried to him, she couldn't lie to herself. "Okay, fine," she told him. "You're good-looking. You've got television looks. You're hot. You're a hottie. You're Hottie McHottentot and when I get back to my room I'm going to lick purple and gold stars all over my geometry notebook and spell out the words *Taylor Montgomery is sooooo fine* and then the rest of the first violins and I are going to paste your yearbook photo in our lockers so we can look at you every time we go there to get out textbooks and tampons." His nostrils flared with amusement. "You're pretty. Satisfied now?"

For a moment she thought she'd talked him into a corner, but before she knew what was happening, he licked the tip of a finger, raised his hands, and pretended to smooth back his hair. "Do you really think so?"

"Shut up," she commanded, wanting both to shake him for being naughty and to squeeze his cheeks for being so adorable.

"Yes'm," he complied, feigning meekness. "Hold on a sec. Let me get the doors. Oh, and Bailey? I think you're pretty keen, too," he told her, his voice magnified by the planes of glass overhead, as he took long steps in the direction of the back opening.

Pretty keen. That was just great, she told herself. It wasn't that the words didn't make her feel—well, alive. They did, arousing inside her an anticipation she hadn't felt in years. Taylor had a habit of making her feel the way she had when she'd been younger, when she'd woken up on a cold morning and discovered a coating of snow on the ground. Or on the last day of school, when there was a palpable excitement in counting down the final minutes of sixth period.

But was she second-guessing herself today? Breaking up with Steve had seemed the right thing to do. Her friends had all recognized the stagnation into which they'd fallen, long ago. It had taken her longer, but she'd known them to be right, this week. She hadn't broken up because she was fooling herself into believing that she and Taylor could have a future, had she? She hadn't tossed away something good because of pique and a tingly feeling, deep down in her stomach, right?

No, she told herself. The relationship with Steve hadn't been *good*. Stable, yes. Predictable, definitely. Fun, never, and good, almost certainly not.

Taylor returned from the far end of the greenhouse after making detours to shut the side doors as well. "Come on, let's get out of here," he suggested. Bailey was happy to comply.

Outside, the late afternoon heat felt like air-conditioned comfort after the sweltering conditions of the greenhouse. Bailey had known it was hot in there, but she had no idea exactly how sweaty she'd gotten until she felt her own blouse, damp beneath the shoulder blades, clinging to her skin. "Ick," she said, trying to peel off the wet fabric.

Kitten had been circling around the greenhouse entrance ever since they had walked in; apparently she knew it was strictly off-limits for the likes of her. Now she jumped onto her hind legs, plainly overjoyed her master hadn't gotten lost and disappeared for good in the wilderness of inch-high seedlings. Her barks echoed between the barn and the house. She had saved some of her enthusiasm to dirty Bailey's shorts. "Kitten!" groaned Taylor. "Behave!"

"I don't mind," Bailey reassured him.

"It's one thing with me, but it's another with other . . . Kitten!" Taylor's admonishment came out as a growl. The dog paused, instantly dropped down to the ground with droopy ears as if frightened, and then to show that she was joking, raced off in the direction of the driveway with her tongue flopping from the side of her mouth. Bailey couldn't help but grin. Dogs had a certain freedom that she envied—like that of small kids, before they started to trade free expression for acceptance by other kids. "So," Taylor said, crossing his arms and watching the dog run around in circles, chasing her own tail. "About this television thing."

She was about to take it all back—explain that it wasn't really an offer, that she was thinking aloud, that program ideas got pitched in television all the time and never picked up. "It's not for me."

"Oh," she said, surprised. That hadn't been the answer she'd expected at all.

"I'm flattered, of course. And I don't want to sound like I'm shooting you down. But the work I do is what I enjoy. And appearances to the contrary, what with my freelance chauffeuring lately, it keeps me pretty busy." He studied her reaction for roughly the same amount of time it took her to decide what it was. "That okay?"

"Oh, hey," she said, feeling a rush of concern. Had he honestly thought he'd hurt her feelings? To be truthful, she was so used to dealing with personalities who'd do anything to get on television or to prolong their fame in thirty-second increments, that it was a relief to discover Taylor wasn't one of them. If he had been, she might have questioned his motives, past and present. "No, it's fine. Really. Seriously. It's hard for me to turn off the business mind, sometimes," she explained. "I'm always trying to think of new program ideas, new personalities, that kind of thing." Since she wasn't in charge of programming at the network, it was a slight fib. But at least it allowed her a graceful dismount, particularly as he didn't seem inclined to argue it with her.

He'd been kidding, of course, with the whole thing about her finding him purty and wanting to see more of him, but he hadn't been far off the mark. But what the hell was she doing? She didn't believe in long-distance relationships, and he couldn't pick up his beans and plant them in Manhattan. Or could he? No, she thought, shaking from her imagination the vision of a hydroponics network atop an uptown rooftop. It was impossible. And yet she wanted to spend time with him. She wanted to be able to look at his face at whim. For now, she rationed out little peeks here and there, afraid to let Taylor see how much her eyes starved for glimpses of him. Whenever he flirted, it hurt. She wanted it to continue, but she knew it had to stop before she became too addicted. Maybe she was crazy. Not addled: stark raving lunatic insane. It was the one explanation she could think of. And having to spend a week with family? The perfect cause for the onset of symptoms. Or maybe Sid's theory about benzenes in the water carried weight. "I had something to ask you," she told him, finally working up the nerve to address what she'd come for.

"Oh?" He didn't turn his head at the words. What did that mean? He didn't want to look at her? He'd gotten so used to her family's pathetic reliance on him that he'd already assumed she was here to demand his services? She was overanalyzing. He was merely getting a kick out of watching Kitten act like an overgrown whelp on puppy uppers.

"You offered to do something once. Something big," she started to say. A rush of fear shot from some unknown core of ice in the middle of her chest, up through her lungs and across her shoulders, trickling in the direction of her fingertips. What if he'd not meant it at the time? What if he'd said it to be kind? Was she pressuring him into agreeing by bringing it up? Crap. "I'm going about this all wrong. I should have. . . ."

"Yes," he told her, without so much as a hesitation. Reacting to her surprise, he turned his head and looked at her. "What?" he asked.

"You couldn't possibly know what I was going to ask!"

"I could. And did. And I already said yes. So how about them apples?" For a moment she thought it had to be one of his jokes. It would have been like Taylor to get her goat by pretending to be a mind-reader. It was only when she saw a trace of sadness in the way he looked at her—the tentativeness of the down-turned corner of his mouth, the way he frowned slightly—that she realized he wasn't joking at all. "I don't make proposals like that lightly," he told her in a quieter, gentler voice. "If I said it, I meant it."

"It's too much, tho—" she started to say, only to be silenced when he shushed her with a finger to his lip. He shook his head. "But it is! There's. . . ."

"Bailey." She quieted at the sound of her name. "It's not too much." She could barely look at him for more than a few seconds at a time, afraid to become too accustomed to the quality of his gaze. "You only had to ask."

She turned her head. "I didn't get the chance to ask!"

"You asked a few days ago." He stood beside her, now. When she felt the pressure and warmth of his hand on her shoulder, she almost flinched. How could anyone not be soothed by that touch? She kept her focus on Kitten, who trotted up with her tail wagging and a look of canine adoration in her eyes to sit expectantly at their feet. That was the kind of esteem she could handle, right now—the kind with expectations that ended at a simple can of Alpo. "That was all it took."

"I don't know what to say," she murmured, capturing quick glances of his big, blue eyes.

"I was kind of thinking that *thank you* was the usual thing," he drawled.

They were back in funny territory again. That was fine; she knew the topography here much better. "Ha, ha, ha," she said with what she hoped was a comic roll of her eyes. Then, in a smaller voice, she added, "Thank you."

"You're welcome."

She dreaded the moment he would have to leave her, but much to her surprise, after he fed Kitten and locked her into the house, he drove her back to the aunts' house, and he was still at her side when she led him around the house so they could deliver the news. Her mother and sister sat on the old concrete patio in their lawn chairs. Jeanne hummed to herself as she listened to her portable radio through her earphones, and her mother simply sat there. She looked relaxed, Bailey thought. They both did.

Though she wasn't actually holding Taylor's hand as she approached the pair, it nearly felt like their fingers were intertwined. He was there. That's what mattered. If she got too badly off-track, he'd help her navigate back. "Mom?" she said, alerting them both to their presence. "I wanted to tell you something."

Jeanne, hearing her sister's voice, removed her earphones and blinked. The surprise on her face at Bailey directly addressing their mom was fairly palpable. That was okay, though. Bailey more or less deserved it, after the way she'd been skulking and slinking around the house the previous few days. Her mother looked wary in her own way. Her neck rotated stiffly, as if it hadn't turned in weeks. Bailey felt a brief moment of doubt. Had it? She couldn't remember how much motion her mother had lost in her neck. She should have paid more attention. She should know things like this.

Her hesitation must have shown. "Hey, Taylor. What're you two doing here?" Jeanne wanted to know. She still hadn't dropped her guardedness. If she'd been Kitten, she would have had a tail that was thumping softly, but a growl brewing behind her bared teeth.

In her head, Bailey had pictured announcing this news with only her mother present, and not with an audience of two. She wished Jeanne was somewhere else. "He's part of the reason I'm here," Bailey said.

"How's the target practice going?" Taylor wanted to know.

"She can hit the target nine out of ten times now," Jeanne told him. Bailey blinked. She'd no idea her mother had gotten so good at her exercise. "I moved it about ten feet farther and she's still hitting it. I'd say that's pretty good."

She looked at Bailey in a way that seemed to indicate she was grabbing all the credit for herself. Or maybe it was a simple *no thanks to you*. Or maybe, just maybe, Bailey was projecting her own guilt and insecurities on the whole thing. "I'd say that's great," Bailey announced.

"Absolutely," said Taylor.

It was time. "Mom?" Bailey knelt down so that when she looked into her mother's eyes, she had to look up. Her hope was that the position didn't seem overbearing. "You know I'm staying a few extra days because I've moved one of the network shoots here. But I don't have to be here the entire time. As a matter of fact, once everything's set up, I'm pretty much dispensable, so I was thinking." So far, so good, she thought to herself. She seemed to be avoiding a patronizing tone or sounding self-congratulatory. "Let's take that trip to Carverton." For a few seemingly endless moments, Bailey watched her mother's face for a reaction. She would be devastated if, at this point, her mother didn't agree to the idea. "Taylor's said he would drive us. He doesn't mind." Still no reaction. "If you could stand the long car ride, we could leave Wednesday, get down there in the early evening, spend the night, visit Ettleston Road Thursday, then be home late Thursday night. I promised I'd be here for the pageant, Friday. How's that sound?"

After a long, long pause, during which Bailey waited in a suspense that approached torture via pointy sticks beneath the fingernails, her mom nodded. "Yes," she said, her voice sounding stronger than it had all the previous week. "That sounds . . . that's what I want."

"Wait," said Jeanne, surprised. Had she been expecting their mother to refuse? "I'm going." Before Bailey could open her mouth, her sister began arguing. "I don't remember anything about Carverton. I'm not staying here. And I want to be able to tell my baby about it someday." She smiled smugly at the last reason, obviously thought up right at that moment. It was her trump card. "So I'm going."

"Sure. You should go." Bailey kept her tone light, as if she'd been planning to invite Jeanne all along. "It's okay, isn't it?" she asked, checking with Taylor, just in case. If he had a reason for not including Jeanne, well . . . at least it wouldn't be on her head.

"No, that's fine," Taylor said, not shifting from his solid, amiable stance.

"It is?" Obviously it wasn't the response Jeanne had expected. She rallied, though. "Well then. What about the aunts?"

Now, that threw Bailey for a loop. She looked to Taylor for support on this one. "Obviously there's a limited amount of—"

"What *about* the aunts?" she heard from behind her. Bailey froze, then craned her neck around. Sure enough, Bits was at a standstill outside the doorway, eavesdropping. "What's going on?" she demanded, marching over and around the boxwoods to confront the small group.

"I—I. . . ."

Bits was a skinny woman with elbows like daggers and shoulder blades like sickles, but when she was in full samurai stance, she appeared twice her actual size and ten times as powerful. "I said, what is going on behind my back? Taylor?" The man smiled, held up his hands, and silently surrendered. "Jeanne? Bailey, if you've . . . !" When neither of her nieces dared to answer, Bits clamped her hands onto her hips and squared off with her sister. "Polly?"

When Bailey looked at her mother at that moment, she saw in her eyes a rebirth of the woman she'd always known—someone who might not always have gotten her own way, but who was prepared to move heaven and earth in the attempt.

Chapter Eighteen

In her nylon baseball cap sporting the legend CRES-
TONVILLE, VA in swirly cursive letters across its front,
and with her VIRGINIA IS FOR LOVERS T-shirt on bold
display, and wearing her yellow rubber bracelet
stamped with the word *Virginia!*, Sidney considered the
menu. "I'll have . . ." she said thoughtfully, taking a moment to bite the inside of her lip. "I'd like the crispy
chicken fingers pita sandwich with American cheese
and mayonnaise on a bed of lettuce with tomato, but instead of American cheese I'd like muenster, and instead
of mayonnaise . . . do you have a creamy Dijon?" The
grumpy waitress, who only a few minutes before had
been forced to admit in detail that the Crestonville
Diner did not carry sliced fresh lime for patrons who
chose to drink Diet Coke, stared at her. Sidney looked
up at the woman's tired face and sighed. "American
cheese is fine. And so is mayonnaise. Oh, and I want
some onion rings. Are they Vidalia onions?"

The waitress ignored her and turned to Bailey. "I'll
have the patty melt," she said, and then added to Sidney, "You look like a chamber of commerce's wet
dream."

"Take a photo of me!" Sidney began fumbling in her purse for her camera phone.

"I'll have the chef's salad, no cucumber, dressing on the side," Euan told the waitress, passing her all three menus. Without a word, the woman promptly stuffed them back into the small holder at the table's center, already crowded with a plastic basket of jellies, a jug of artificial maple syrup, salt and pepper shakers, a small glass bottle of Tabasco sauce, fly-specked squeeze bottles of catsup and yellow mustard, a napkin dispenser, and a tiny vase spiked with stained silk flowers. "She's friendly," he commented, when the woman waddled into the back, the flesh-colored support hose on her substantial thighs scraping audibly.

"I hope they're Vidalia onions," Sidney pouted. She set her phone on the table, then with glee announced, "I can smoke! I can smoke in restaurants here, can't I!"

"You told me you were quitting," Euan reminded her.

"I know. It's the idea of it that enraptures me."

Save for the comedown in locale, it felt like old times. When Bailey closed her eyes and listened to her two friends talk, she could practically hear the Ninth Avenue traffic and the crowds beyond the open front door. "I'm so glad you came!" she told Sidney.

"Of course I came. As network production manager, I get some travel flexibility, and an emergency reschedule is a perfect opportunity for me to jump in, get my hands dirty, and make sure the project's going to come in on budget."

"Plus I called her the night I got here," Euan cut in, "and she screamed when she heard how crazy the pageant was."

"What, you thought I'd let Euan have all the fun? And it wasn't just the pageant. He said that he was staying in a hotel where the bellboy was a hundred years old. . . ."

"A hundred and ten, at least."

"And that the woman behind the front desk was way older. I couldn't resist anymore. I had to see for myself!"

"She looks like Norman Bates's mother, post-shower! I'm surprised there aren't vultures circling whenever she steps outdoors!"

"She's not *that* bad," said Sidney. "More like Jessica Tandy in *Driving Miss Daisy*. Every time I see her standing, I want to cradle my arms and offer her a seat."

"*Driving Miss Daisy*! She's more like the Cryptkeeper."

With a rush of affection at their bickering, Bailey sighed. "I've missed you guys."

"Aw, Bailey, we missed you, too!" Sidney reached for one of the little jellies, peeled back the foil lid, and scooped it out with a spoon. "I want to hear all about this pageant. . . ."

"Oh lordie." Euan rolled his eyes.

". . . and your aunts. . . ." Sidney popped the jelly-filled spoon into her mouth and promptly began unwrapping another one.

". . . and the hot hunk of manflesh that made you dump Steve."

She should have protested the misuse of the word *dump*, but it wasn't worth the effort. Bailey knew she hadn't done anything so cold-hearted as a dumping, and both Euan and Sidney knew her well enough to know she couldn't simply chuck one man over her shoulder in favor of another. So she let it pass, and instead cocked her head and looked with meaning at Euan. His initial attempt to pretend innocence didn't pass muster. "What?" he protested. "Oh, come on. How was I not supposed to tell her?" To Sidney, he licked the tip of his index finger, applied it to his hip, and mouthed the words, *he's hot!*

"Oh! And Chandra! Did you see her? She was supposed to get in last night."

"Nope."

After Sidney thrust the third spoonful of concord grape jelly into her mouth, Euan reached out and grabbed her wrist. "I am going to go into diabetic shock if you don't stop."

"I'm hungry!"

"I was too busy at home to get to the hotel last night," Bailey said. "I told her I was having lunch with you guys, and then stopping by the hotel to chat about the Munford's schedule. You know, Chandra's probably sleeping only a few feet away from you guys." They both looked horrified at the thought, which made Bailey want to pique them a little more. "She told me once she slept nude."

"Ew." Euan managed to look horribly offended and yet intrigued at the same time. Then his face changed completely as he turned in Sidney's direction. "Speaking of nude!"

"Oh-my-God-tell-me." Sidney slurred all of her excitement into one word. "Did Bailey's protégé do something else? Is she still refusing to wear a bathing suit? Tell me tell me tell me!"

"This morning we were working on our formal wear walks. Half of these girls take to the runway like virgins who've been told by their mamas never unclench in case their hymen pops out, and the other half are like the Budweiser Clydesdales. So I'm trying to get one of the whinnying wenches to tread a little more lightly, and little Miss Nude Thing comes out and says—"

"Don't tell me she was nude again!" Bailey pulled the jellies out of reach before Sidney could start eating them again, her heart in her throat. Why, of all the people she had jokingly chosen to mess with her aunts' contest, couldn't she have picked one who half-heartedly gummed the works? Why had she chosen Fawn, who actually had the means and determination to screw things up?

"No, she wasn't nude again. Your girl knows better than to try the same stunt twice. What she did do was to march up to little Miss *Amelie* French Bob—I've forgotten her name."

"Mandy, I think."

"And practically ripped the collar and cuffs off her dress because they were fur. We almost had a second nude contestant on our hands."

"Fur in the middle of summer?" Bailey unconsciously clawed at her throat. It sounded hideous.

"Well, anyone who would wear real fur. . . ." Sidney reasoned.

Euan looked pained. "It wasn't real fur. It wasn't even her actual formal wear. It was one of the practice dresses that your aunts have provided from their own wardrobe, circa 1962. Pea-green cocktail dress with black fox trim. Very Jackie, with a hint of Mamie. *Anyway*," he added, before Sidney could make any more inquiries into the other practice dresses, "our little Fawn gave a ten-minute lecture on the evils of fur that nearly reduced. . . ." He groped for a name.

"Mandy," said Bailey, dismayed but fascinated.

"Yes, reduced Mandy to tears, more or less, though most of it was coming from her nose, poor snotty thing. So I said, 'Fawn, this isn't real fur, girl. You're putting your values on the line for a handful of acrylic and a black marking pen.' And she flew off the handle and started talking about how fake fur is worse because. . . ." He thought back and tried to dredge up the exact words. "Because it mythologizes the glamour of real fur and allows the wearer to indulge in the sensations of the actual thing without being made to bear any of its moral or emotional culpability." Back in their acting days, Euan had always possessed a fantastic memory for lines. Bailey had no doubt those were Fawn's own words. She groaned aloud.

"Wow." Sidney gaped. "Just . . . wow."

"I am going to give that girl nine kinds of hell," Bailey growled.

"Hush, Flo from *Alice* is back," whispered Euan, none too softly.

The waitress had indeed returned, bearing on her forearms all the plates their table could possibly want. Sidney rubbed her hands together at the onion rings' appearance, but lost her enthusiasm at the sight of the limp, soggy pita. Euan stared at the enormous wooden bowl filled with a salad that seemed largely composed of processed turkey and ham with a few wisps of iceberg lettuce accidentally tossed in, all pureed in a blender. "I asked for dressing on the side," he told the woman.

"Yeah, and I asked for a body like Catherine Beta-Jones and look what I got," the waitress snapped back. Apparently she'd heard the *Alice* remark. "You gonna eat it, or not?"

"Zeta-Jones," Euan said meekly. "And I'll eat it." Yet he didn't look all that happy about it.

"The patty melt looks delicious!" Bailey's attempt to summon enthusiasm for two charred pieces of toast, a scrap of meat, and a few onion sprinkles didn't do any good. The falsehood was so patent that she didn't pretend to believe it.

"I can take it back, if you want." The waitress's pleasantness was equally as forced and twice as unbelievable. "Fix it up for you real nice."

There was something in her tone that convinced Bailey that the alleged fixing up would involve spit and maybe a dusting of roach powder. "That's okay," she declined.

The waitress's smirk clearly said, *thought so.* "Anything else?"

"I—" began Euan, but the waitress had already walked away from the table.

Sidney attempted to roll up her pita. It peeled away from the plate like bare thighs from a leather car seat on a sticky summer day. "You need to come home," she said mournfully, to Bailey. "I can't stand the thought of you living on Southern cooking."

Euan, having tried a mouthful of the salad, apparently decided it wasn't totally inedible. "This is crap food, sweetie, not Southern cooking. Crap food you can get in any state. Southern cooking, though. Mmmmm."

He leaned over the table and jabbed in Sidney's direction with his fork. "Bailey's Aunt Bubble makes a baked chicken with an *amazing* crust that—"

"Wait a minute. How did you know we had chicken last night?" Bailey asked him, confused, but enjoying the familiar, petty babble of good friends about nothing of importance whatsoever. Over the noise she barely registered the tinkling sound of the bell ringing over the diner's front door.

"Your aunt made a dinner basket for me to take with, since someone didn't invite me to dinner at their table. Anyway, an *amazing* crust and these biscuits that were light as feathers, with a kind of honey butter, and fresh green beans, and coconut cake . . ."

"Oh my God, I'm having foodgasms here." Sidney chomped into her pita.

"Why's Bubble giving you dinner baskets?" Bailey wanted to know. "I would've invited you!"

"Well!" cried a delighted voice. None of the three had been paying any attention to anything beyond their own perimeter; they hadn't seen the rotund little gentleman approaching, a lady on either arm. "Bailey Rhodes, I do declare, I run into you everywhere. Though let's be frank, it's not *too* difficult in a tiny town like ours, is it? I bet in New York City you can go for weeks without seeing anyone you know. Of course, and I was telling India and Saffron here—wasn't I, India?—that New York City has so much to do, so much to see! It would be too rich a diet for me. Why, I'd gorge myself until I was fat as a hog!" He beamed around the speechless table. "You must be from New York, sugar!" he said at last to Sidney.

"Yes." Sidney's lips twitched, and her jaw set to the side. Bailey knew the look; usually Sidney reserved it for Chandra's presence.

"Delightful! Delightful." He looked over his shoulder and waggled his fingers at the waitress. "Looking good there, Agatha!" he called, causing the woman to simper like a girl. "Your friendly face always brings a smile to mine, you know!"

Friendliness wasn't the first thing on Bailey's mind, at this moment. In fact, the first thing she wondered was exactly how much of a mess Euan's salad might make on the man's pastel orange leisure suit, if she were to pick it up, take off the man's matching beret, and dump it over his fat little bald head. "These are my friends, Euan and Sidney," she said in guarded tones.

"And I'm Shirley Jones, and these *handsome* young women are my companions, India, and Saffron. What a charming name for a charming young lady, and don't let *anyone* ever try to tell you different, honey! Nice to meet you, Euan," he cooed, holding out his hand to Sidney.

Sidney, however, regarded the proffered hand in much the same way Bailey had her patty melt. "I'm sorry. I didn't quite catch your name," she said, in tones so frozen they could only be measured in degrees kelvin. "Jones, wasn't it? Sherbet Jones?"

Euan choked; Bailey had to fight back a smirk. No one was more a master of the cold, cutting remark than her best female friend—and it was impossible to deny that in his tight-fitting suit, the man resembled nothing more than a generous scoop of orange-flavored slush, flanked by two ripe tomatoes. How in the world did the man tell the long-haired brunettes apart? Oh yes. Since India was the one who looked as if she'd bitten into a lemon and still couldn't rid the taste from her mouth, Saffron must be the one with the invisible stick rammed up her butt. "Aren't you the funniest thing?" he chortled. "Shirley, actually. *Shirley* Jones."

"Oh, like David Cassidy's mother!" Bailey felt a rush of vindication at Sidney's bland response. Hadn't she said nearly the same thing to Bits? No wonder she'd thought Shirley was a woman.

"I was going to say like the star of *Oklahoma!*" said

Euan, whose worst tendency when nervous was to chatter. "The movie. In Todd-AO. Did you know that *Oklahoma!* was filmed in both Cinemascope and Todd-AO? They'd do takes for one in the morning and for the other in the afternoon. Most people say that because it was filmed earlier in the day, the—shutting up now," he finished softly, catching a raised eyebrow from Sidney.

"And aren't you a dapper young fellow!" Shirley's toothy beam carried the wattage of a klieg light as he turned it on Euan. "Do tell me that's DKNY you're wearing."

Euan's hands flew self-consciously to his flimsy silk shirt, imprinted with trellises of pink and red roses. "Why, y—" His face changed once he registered the memory of Bailey's several lectures the previous day about how he was under no circumstances to spill a single bit of information to the roly-poly man in the Willy Wonka suits. "No," he said. With amusement and approval, Bailey noticed that his voice dropped an octave as he attempted to butch it up. "My girlfriend got it for me at Wal-Mart." After a beat, he suddenly leaned over and put his arm around Sidney. "Thanks, babe."

"Yeah, sure thing." Sidney bit into an onion ring, but didn't remove her eyes from the vision in creamsicle.

"Isn't that adorable? India, aren't they an adorable couple? I won't hear a word said against them!" Bailey was becoming more adept at reading Shirley's subtly veiled insults; he hadn't bought any of it, of course, but was willing to play along for as long as it served his own purposes. "Bailey Rhodes, what charming friends you have."

"Why, thank you, Shirley Jones!" she replied sweetly, determined to give as good as she got.

"Are you all colleagues of Bailey's? Or just visiting the quaint little hometown where she grew up? Why, one of these days, she's going to be so famous that we'll have to change the name of our main street to Rhodes

Street. Or Rhodes Road!" He guffawed, amused at his little witticism. Bailey and Euan laughed politely but without real feeling, while Sidney munched on her onion rings without much of an expression at all. "Rhodes Road. That's . . . well, yes. So is your visit professional? Or personal in nature? Oh, look at me. I'm such a Nosy Parker, aren't I, Saffron? The girls are always telling me that if my nose were any longer, I'd be Pinocchio!"

Bailey would be damned before she let it slip that her friends were here because of their involvement in the pageant. All the shows in the quaint inns series adhered to a rigid formula of fourteen minutes of puffery about the inn's amenities and eight minutes of local color. Devoting two of those eight minutes to the Miss Tidewater Butter Bean pageant and promising, promising, *promising* her aunt that she and Bubble and their contestants would have at least forty-five exclusive seconds of that time was the one thing that Bailey could have done to mollify Bits—and considering how often the directors and producers of the Expedition Network's shows plugged leaking holes of screen time with vanity shots of their relatives and friends and their own kids, God knew it wasn't an ethical breach, by any means. Giving Shirley Jones any indication of what was really going on, though? That was the wedge's thin edge, and Shirley would use it to convince the crew that his glamazon contestants were more worthy of their attention.

She was having none of it. "They've come down to visit," she told him, deliberately remaining polite while seething inside.

"Mama Bear and me was headed to Florida," Euan growled. In the seconds since his last speech, he'd settled into character, making his voice deep and masculine and oddly Jersey-ish, as if he were trying out for a one-shot appearance (so to speak) in *The Sopranos*. "So we could hook up with some biker friends. For a rally. Right, babe?" He gave Sidney a generous squeeze. The look she returned made it perfectly clear that as far as Mama Bear was concerned, Euan was on his own.

"Fascinating! Simply fascinating!" Shirley took in Euan's flowery shirt, his thin frame, and the leg clad in deep crimson corduroy, carelessly sprawled over the diner bench. "Bailey Rhodes, you must live the most interesting life! I have always said that Manhattan city was the absolute *epicenter* of the world, and here you are, surrounding yourself with the *crème de la crème*." He leaned in and whispered, fingers held to his mouth because whatever he was about to say was so naughty, "How you found the world's one male florist turned biker I'll *never* know."

Bailey could only bare her teeth in response. If Euan had to do some on-the-fly character development, she wished he'd dressed the part. "How's Larkin?" she asked brightly.

"Oh, my! You know, it's quite the coincidence—isn't it, Saffron?" For the first time that afternoon, Shirley lost the unbearable smile and looked sincere. Well, not sincere. Just less dishonest. "I was saying to Saffron, this morning, 'Saffron, I hope that Bailey Rhodes and her aunts aren't angry with me because Larkin Merino came to me in tears, begging and pleading for me to take her in. Like an orphan in the storm, she was, knowing not where to turn!' You aren't, are you?"

Somehow Bailey felt surrounded by the punchline of a joke: *how many drama queens can you fit in a small-town diner?* "If Larkin wasn't happy, she wasn't happy," Bailey said soothingly.

"That's so true," Shirley agreed. "No one can do their best when they're not happy. I hope your aunts feel the same way. I would be absolutely desolated if they thought the less of me for it."

"They could never think less of you! Besides." Bailey dropped her voice in volume to force Shirley to lean in a little more closely. "Trust me. If I heard them say you did them a favor once, I heard them say it a dozen times."

That seemed to have unsettled him a little. "Of course, I'm always glad to help out," he murmured, "but why in the world would your aunts feel that way about sweet Larkin? She's such a dear, sweet, talented—"

Bailey's snort of laughter cut short that train of thought. She stopped cold at Shirley's expression of surprise. "Oh!" she said, reaching up and grabbing his hand where it rested atop his white cane. "I'm sorry. You were serious. Yes. Absolutely." With a nod, she agreed with him. "She's dear and sweet and talented. A dear, sweet, talented unwed mother of two, but I'm sure the judges won't mind." She didn't look to see how her friends might be taking this improbable information. She didn't dare.

"Mother of . . . ?" Shirley looked aghast. Saffron and India dropped the pretense they weren't listening, and adopted expressions that would have been quite appropriate if someone had passed gas.

"She wouldn't admit it to the aunts, either, until one of the fathers came banging on the door during coaching and demanded to see his poor, sweet baby girls. You wouldn't believe the amount he was paying in child support. I felt for him, I honestly did, but then when a garbage collector from Newport News showed up the next day with the same story . . . well, the aunts had to question her honesty." She smiled and waggled a finger. "I'm sure she's not getting away with anything under your keen eye, though!"

To India, Shirley fretted, "What was Larkin doing when we left?" The creamy-skinned girl shrugged. When Shirley looked her way, Saffron shook her head. "Well, well!" he laughed, tapping together his fingers nervously. "We'd best get back to training. Such a lot to do, and a mere five short days to do it in!" Bailey feigned disappointment. "Lovely to meet you! Lovely to meet—!" With a waggle of his fingers, he was gone.

"Oh my God. Bailey, you are evil. Evil, evil, evil!" Euan dropped all affectation and went back to his usual expressive tones. "But florist turned biker! I know you told me about the evil old queen, but I didn't know he'd be like *that*."

"He called me fat," Sidney's eyes were mere slits.

"I warned you!" Bailey shook her finger at Euan. "If he finds out you kind of sort of almost have runway experience and that you're coaching the girls. . . ."

Anyone could have told how offended Euan was by the sudden tilt in his nose. "Kind of sort of *almost?*" he sniffed. "You are so unfair."

"Sweetie, helping produce the annual Christmas drag show at Lips in the West Village isn't quite the same as coaching Lacroix runway models during Paris Fashion Week."

"Truth," he proclaimed sadly, "is so cruel."

"He called me *fat*," Sidney repeated. When her friends stared, she said, "He said I had too rich a diet." She savagely sank her teeth into an onion ring. "He said I obviously *gorged* myself. Like a hog!"

"He meant that metaphorically. Sid! He was talking about how he'd overindulge on cultural stuff, back home." Sidney cocked her head at Bailey's explanation, obviously not satisfied. "You know how out-of-towners do!"

"He said that if he were in New York, he'd gorge himself. And then he said, *hoo-doggy, sugar-pie! You sure look like you're from New York!* Meaning, I'm bloated. And gorged. And *fat*." Euan looked at Bailey; Bailey looked at Euan. She'd heard the same dirty implication at the time, now that she was clued into Jones's sneaky way of insult. "And for that . . . I'm going to make him *pay*."

"Very *Mommie Dearest*," Euan commented, digging into his salad again.

"I know." Sidney giggled, ruining the illusion of fierceness she'd been building. "All I need are the shoulder pads. At least it's more convincing than biker boy over here."

"He was the first character I thought of! It was either him or a Cuban waiter."

"Go with the Cuban waiter next time," said Sidney. "Remember the first rule of improv: play what you know, sweetie."

"Apparently Bailey has added Sneaky Snake to her repertoire of things she knows, then," said Euan, impressed. "Because dang, she got Sherbet good!"

"Oh my God, I almost lost it when I called him that. Could you tell?" Sid was back to her usual high spirits. She'd been joking about revenge, obviously.

"Not at all. *I* almost lost it when you did!"

Bailey sank her teeth into the patty melt. It was as bad as she feared, but her friends' familiar playfulness was seasoning enough to make it palatable. She and Euan took the rest of the meal to catch Sidney up on pageant gossip, and only stopped when it came time to pay the bill.

"I love this place," Sidney sighed happily, when Euan rose to pay the bill at the little register. "Not the diner. The diner sucks. But this town! I mean, I couldn't live here if my life depended on it, but I love it. Everything's so . . . *real*. The people are so down-to-earth and *connected*."

"Sweetie, you did see Elton John's eccentric dad and his two hoochie mamas breeze through here, right? Not to mention the waitress who wanted to pee in our coffee?" Bailey asked her. When the bell over the door jangled again, she was aware enough of it to turn her head and see who might be coming in—there was Taylor, his head bowed down a little shyly at the sight of her sitting with her friends, but nonetheless looking at her from across the room. Bailey's lips parted as she nearly called out to him, but Taylor had glanced away to give a curt nod to both Agatha the waitress and to the bald bulldog of a short-order cook behind the counter.

Euan slid back into the booth, grumbling. "One quarter," he announced. "That's all I'm leaving as a tip. One shiny object lesson quarter, and if either of you try to supplement it after I leave, there'll be *words*."

"They're exceptions," Sidney was saying, as she casually opened her purse and put both a handful of sugar packets and more of the jelly containers within. "Isn't that why you're all hot for your truck driver hunk?"

Said hunk was loping down the length of the diner, getting closer with every passing second. "He's not a truck driver."

A roll of the eyes, and Sidney dismissed the objection. "Fine, hunk who drives a truck. Don't argue semantics with me. Aren't you all goose-pimply for him because he's the salt of the earth, with the dirt of the fields beneath his nails and the sweat of a day's labor on his neck?"

"Sidney." Euan cleared his throat.

"That's the kind of *real* I'm talking about. *Real* men, not the gentrified, homogenized, watered-down men you see walking the streets back home. Sure, they might work out at Crunch four times a week, but have those pretty-smelling metrosexuals ever really put those muscles to good use?"

"Sid," said Bailey, reaching out a hand. "Sweetie."

But it was impossible to stop the speeding freight train that was Sidney, when she was on a roll down a steep incline. "Look at that guy who came in a minute ago. I mean, *damn.* You know the kind of city guy I'm talking about, Bail. You dated one for long enough until you had the sense to drop him for this Chippendale's dancer in overalls." Oh, crap. The bottom of Bailey's stomach seemed to fall out when Taylor stopped at the table, his hand resting on the back of Sidney's chair. "Tell her, Euan. Steve was totally useless." When Euan, who was watching Taylor, didn't answer, she made a face of sudden understanding. "Oh, I'm sorry. You work out at Crunch, don't you? I didn't mean anything by it."

She turned back to Bailey, who was trying with her eyes to apologize to Taylor. "So when do I get to meet Mr. Biceps, anyway?"

"How about now?" asked Taylor in his deep voice. He stared down at the top of Sidney's head with a smile. "Hi there."

After a moment, she let her neck roll back and looked straight up into his eyes. "Oh, hi," she murmured. Then, after another moment, she added, "Wow."

If it was true, what they said about one's life flashing before one's eyes right before one died, Bailey hoped to hell that this would be one of the incidents that got skipped. She didn't ever want to have to revisit it again. In fact, enduring it right at that moment was making her wish for a speedier demise. "Taylor," she said, trying to sound patient and humorous. "You remember me talking about my friend, Sidney?"

"Her crazy friend, Sidney," Sid said to the ceiling and Taylor's eyes. "Pleased to meet you."

"Bailey's told me all about her crazy friend Sidney."

"Like what?" Sid was still staring straight up at him.

"Like . . . you're crazy. And you're her friend."

"And that I have diarrhea of the mouth?"

Bailey narrowed her eyes. Was Sid staring at Taylor's pecs? "Can we get out of here?"

"Yes, let's." Euan slid off the bench. "We need to skedaddle before the Wicked Witch discovers her tip and tries to suck our souls out through our nostrils. And *don't you dare*," he warned Bailey sternly, reading her mind. She had intended to palm a couple of loose dollar bills while she searched her purse for an Altoid, then drop them on the table.

Not until they were outside, Sid and Euan bounding ahead, did Taylor address her directly. "You actually ate in that pit?" he asked. "Did you lose a bet or something?"

"I know it's not the *haute cuisine* of 7-Eleven," Bailey told him, "but we needed to eat."

"Oooo, Euan!" Sidney, having shucked her embarrassment of a few moments before, ran to the median in the street's center. Close to the intersection stood a metal pole supporting a veritable pyramid of logos printed on aluminum signs discolored from the passing of the years—Kiwanis, the Rotary, the Good Neighbors of Crestonville, the Crestonville Optimists, the Jaycees, the local Methodist church. "Come look!"

"There's a lot of good little places around here if you're willing to drive a mile or two," he said. "If you were hanging around a while longer, I'd take you. There's a barbecue place out on the road to the interstate that makes a pulled pork that melts in your mouth. And their lemon pie—mmmmmm! So sweet it'll slip down easy, and so sour it'll make you pucker. You like lemon pie?"

She certainly liked the way he described it. "That sounds fantastic," she said, not answering either the question he asked, or the question he'd left unspoken of whether or not she'd go there with him, sometime. Instead, she watched while Euan took a photo of Sidney standing beneath the cluttered signs welcoming strangers—and Rotarians—to town. Those logos had sat at exactly that spot for probably a good thirty years, and Bailey had never paid them any mind. Did anyone who lived here actually notice those things?

"Oh my God, Bail." Sidney ran over with her phone display held outward so that she and Taylor could see the photos. "This place is off the hook. I don't see how anyone could ever leave here."

Taylor grinned. "A lot of us don't feel the need."

Was he looking in her direction? Bailey was almost afraid to turn and see, fearful there might be another invitation in those eyes—or perhaps worried there might be none.

Chapter Nineteen

The collision started when, at the end of the procession of Butter Beans, Regina stumbled slightly at a point where two sheets of plywood overlapped. A light rain overnight had brought down the temperatures, but had also left the runway boards slightly warped at the edges, so walking across them had been an exercise in alertness all morning. Regina reached out instinctively to steady herself, and her fingers brushed against the small of CeeCee's back; CeeCee flinched and turned, and bumped against Austyn. Austyn, in turn, tripped and had to catch herself on Ellie's shoulders, and Ellie knocked into Norelle, who shrieked slightly, which startled Denise, who reached out and caught hold of Mandy, who stepped on Joan's heel. Everything would have been fine if only Joan hadn't reached out and, with the very tip of her index finger, accidentally brushed Fawn's back.

Yet Fawn was but a novice in the art of wearing the high-heeled shoe, and that slight disruption to her concentration caused her first to wobble forwards, then backwards, and then, at the moment Bailey and the other observers were certain she'd caught her balance, her knees buckled and gave way. She fell backward into Joan, who staggered back into Mandy, who knocked against Denise, who disrupted Norelle, into whom Ellie collided with Austyn right behind her, who yelped, grabbed the shoulder strap of CeeCee's dress, and dragged her down to the ground. The whole thing happened in less than eight seconds from start to finish, and by the end, all the Butter Beans save a startled Regina were scrabbling around on the grass and plywood in varying degrees of collapse. From Fawn came a steady and profound stream of profanity.

"Oh dear!" said Bubble, hastening to her feet and running over to help up her girls. "Is everyone all right?"

"Kill me now," murmured Euan, his face buried in one hand while he clutched Sidney's knee with the other. "Just kill me now." On his other side, Bits, her jaw gyrating in angry circles, grabbed her plastic box of wintergreen Tic Tacs, shook one into her hand, and crunched down on it without sucking.

It didn't take Nancy Drew to detect that Sidney had been highly amused by the collision, as she had been by the questions and answers led by Taylor. Particularly when Austyn had revealed, at the question of where she saw herself in five years, her hitherto unknown goal of becoming a cocktail waitress at Harrah's Cherokee Casino in North Carolina so that she could work her way up to Atlantic City or even Reno. And as she had been by CeeCee's rendition of Gilbert and Sullivan, by Norelle's ability to shape long pink balloons into animals that all looked like long pink penises, and by Denise walking around with her evening dress inside out. "Love it!" she murmured after each incident, eyes wide.

Bailey simply sat back, face pained, and waited for the fireworks to begin. Taylor had been watching the proceedings with amused relish as well, but his was of a quieter brand than Sidney's, who all but slapped the table and demanded more. He bit his lip and raised his eyebrows as a private comment to Bailey, who simply shook her head in response. This whole thing had been a mistake. Her aunts' girls were going to look like idiots on television, assuming the camera crews could find any usable footage in which someone wasn't falling down, swearing, or as CeeCee was doing now, trying to retrieve the undone straps of her dress and cover up her bra. If it had been anyone else's disaster, she'd probably enjoy it. As it was, she wished she were somewhere far, far away.

Even if it was only as far as Jeanne and their mom, who both walked at a distance along the pebbly driveway. It was good to see her mother doing something other than target practice after a week and a half. Though slow, there was something vigorous in the way her mother walked, occasionally stooping to pick up something from the dirt before discarding it again. "This was a total mistake," Bailey told Taylor. "I should never have gotten involved."

"You know your aunts are happier that you did."

Down at the table's other end, Bits rapidly tapped her Tic Tacs container so that it rattled like a castanet. She wasn't looking at the carnage onstage. She glared straight at Bailey as if she had stuck out a very long leg and tripped the girls herself. "I'm not so sure about that."

"Why is she still in this?" Taylor asked, keeping his voice low. Bailey didn't have to ask. She knew he meant Fawn. "No offense, she's a firecracker and all, but. . . ."

"I know," she murmured back. Despite the afternoon's soaring temperature, she could still feel Taylor's own body's heat when he leaned over. She cleared her throat, distracted by his closeness, and explained. "I think it's pride at this point."

"Hers?" Taylor raised his eyebrows. "She has some?"

"She's got *plenty*, trust me. She thought spoofing Larkin would be simple, and that gave her enough energy to get herself over the hurdle of entering and enlisting for coaching. Now she's learned that this stuff isn't as easy as she assumed. But she's too stubborn to admit it." Bits was still crunching on the hard-shelled mints, looking Bailey's way as if formulating something cutting to say. Bailey leaned back out of eyeshot, behind Taylor. "And Bits is way too obstinate to give up." She hoped.

"Everyone's all right!" Bubble exclaimed, having helped the last of the girls to their feet. "No bruises! No rips! Now, smile, everyone!" She sounded like the *Romper Room* lady announcing that her kiddies hadn't suffered any boo-boos. "Smile! Accidents happen! We must go on!"

"I don't feel like smilin'?" said CeeCee, whose slight embarrassment with her dress had landed her near tears. "I don't like this? I don't like this at all?"

"Ladies, ladies." Euan, having recovered most of his composure, had risen from his chair and joined Bubble near the front of the runway, where he clapped his hands to get everyone's attention. Nine red faces—eight frustrated and near tears, one defiant and angry—turned in his direction. "Miss Whigfield is absolutely right. On the runway, anything can happen. It is your responsibility to make certain that the consequences are minimized."

"But she *pushed* me!" "It wasn't *my* fault!" "I can't help it if she—" "Well you—!" The peace of the front yard, or what was left of it, was shattered by several shrill, simultaneous protests of innocence.

Euan held up a hand and cut off the outcries with a shake of his head. "Nuh-uh," he told them. "Because once you're on that stage? Those judges don't care about whose fault it is. They don't care about the fact that you were shoved," he said, pointing to Norelle, "or that you got clipped by someone behind you," he added, pointing to Joan. "What they do care about, is that *you* were clumsy." Regina got the pointed finger treatment that time; she responded with a guilty bowed head. "And that *you* can't handle yourself under pressure." Ellie had the grace to look at the grass under Euan's scrutiny. He came to a stop in front of Fawn. "And that you walk like a clumsy ox dressing up in your much more graceful mama ox's clothes and lipstick, and that if you hadn't been so damned slow and holding up the rest of the line, none of this mess would've happened."

"I don't wear high-heeled shoes," Fawn glowered.

"The judges don't care."

Fawn had her answer at the ready, probably memorized since the moment she'd gotten dressed. "High heels are a tool of a male-dominated society to cripple women so that they are forced to be at a disadvantage when it comes to competition in a workplace—"

Euan interrupted her prepared speech with a snap of his fingers. "Don't care."

"But I—"

"Fawn?"

"I—!"

"Don't." He challenged her to say another word.

After a moment, it was obvious Fawn felt compelled at least to try. "You're . . ."

"Care." Euan waited until he was certain that the littlest rebel wouldn't say a word more, then stepped back and adopted a serious expression. "Girls, let me tell you something. Have you seen your competition, walking around on the arms of Mr. Shirley Jones?" Not a single girl shook her head. At the mention of their rivals, they all hushed their petty arguments and listened solemnly. "You've seen them. They're sleek. They're serious. They're evil bitches with one agenda—to claw their way to the top, one beauty pageant at a time. Today, Miss Tidewater Butter Bean. Tomorrow . . ." he stumbled for another example.

Sidney's patriotism had been stirred by Euan's speech. She sat up straight in her guest judge's chair and yelled out, in an attempt to be helpful, "Miss Schenectady Yam!"

". . . . Miss Universe," he concluded, waiting until his head was turned and none of the girls could see before rolling his eyes at his friend. "Do you think any of those girls would waste time complaining about who shoved who?"

"Whom, dear." Bubble stood beside Euan now, with her hands folded. "Keep going," she whispered. "You're doing a lovely job."

Euan blinked, then returned to the task at hand. "But here's a secret, ladies. In my daily work as a casting director for one of my network's premier daytime dramas, I see hundreds of girls like those on a daily basis, all desperate for a shot at the big-time exposure the tiniest appearance on a CBS soap could afford them." Most of the girls were rapt with attention by this point. Only one still sulked, off in her own little Fawniverse. "But do you know what the essential difference is between them and you?" He paused for a moment, as if actually expecting an answer. "The difference . . ."

A growl came from the end of the assembly. "Boob jobs."

"Fawn? Don't care," Euan said, not acknowledging her with a look. "The difference, girls, is that you have souls. Really. They don't. They've given up everything they have to become what they think is an ideal of feminine beauty. Though we all of us know that there's no such thing," he added a little more quickly, to cut off whatever canned speech Fawn might have at the ready. "Ask any of us who are industry professionals." He gestured to Sidney. "Ms. James knows. So does Ms. Rhodes, who at the Expedition Network has dealt with the contracts of many incredible celebrities, from the star of *90210* and *Charmed*, Shannen Doherty, to Andrew Shue, to Ramona from the first season of *Survivor*." In better circles, that particular list might not have impressed anyone, but most of the contestants regarded Bailey with newfound respect. "They'll tell you the exact same thing. Prettiness might catch attention, but it's *character* that wins in the end. Over the course of what time we have left, if you will work *with* me and not *against* me, you will find the inner you shining through."

Ellie raised her hand. "But the judges aren't gonna care about the inner us, are they?" She looked around the group for support. "They're just gonna care about what we look like in a bathing suit." Bailey felt a pang of pain for the girl. No matter how right Euan was about character, weren't beauty pageants about one thing alone . . . beauty?

"Girl, you can't let yourself think that way, okay?" Euan softened his tone. "None of you can," he said, addressing the group. "You've got to think about these girls not as your superiors, but as your *competition*. They're beautiful, yes. But they're clones. Evil clones. Think of them as fembots. Did you all see Austin Powers? Yes? Then think of them as vicious, heartless fembots, the handiworks of Dr. Evil." That got a snort out of Sidney, at least. "And they've been programmed all to flounce and walk and sashay in exactly the same way."

Most of the girls looked relieved and even a little invigorated at Euan's comparison, but Fawn spoke up and interrupted the excitement. "And what about Larkin?" she asked. "She's no fembot."

Euan had never seen or met Larkin before her defection to Dr. Evil's camp. Bailey stood up to help him out. "You're right," she told them, looking especially at Fawn. "She's not like those girls. She was one of you. She turned her back on you all and jumped ship when the going got tough. And now she deserves to be taken down."

"This is like *Buffy the Vampire Slayer*, right before they're going into battle and Buffy's giving a pep talk to her comrades," Sidney commented in an undertone to Taylor.

Bailey ignored her. "You can do this, and do it with style and grace. I've never seen a group of people work so hard toward a goal. And trust me, by Friday... you'll be fantastic, if you believe in yourself."

Several of the girls seemed immensely gratified at her speech by the time Bailey took her seat. Euan began directing them back to the beginning of the runway so they could start again. "Bail," whispered Sidney, leaning over. "Nice bluff."

The words, clearly audible to Taylor as they wafted over his lap, caused her a slight sense of shame. She honestly hadn't thought she was bluffing when she spoke; she thought she'd been telling the truth. Wasn't that why it had come out so convincingly? Or, after years at the Expedition Network, was bluffing so thoroughly engrained in her personality that she couldn't tell when she was doing it any longer? Either way, it didn't look all that good in front of Taylor basically to be praised for being an accomplished liar. "I wasn't," she stammered. But Sidney had already settled back into her chair, and Bailey found her only audience was Taylor himself. He folded his mouth until it stretched across his face, then raised his eyebrows. As an expression, it was impossible to read. "I wasn't!"

"Bailey Rhodes, a bucket under a bull is of more use than your pack of lies," Bits scolded, turning her chair around so it faced Bailey's end of the table. "This is not a game. This is a very real contest, with real prizes, and all the jibber-jabber in the world is not going to get these girls ready for it by Friday. Not with you gallivanting down to Georgia tomorrow and dragging with you the only two people with any experience whatsoever in—"

"Now hold on one minute," Bailey protested, raising her voice over her aunt's. "No one is dragging you anywhere. This trip was supposed to be for Mom. Out of the goodness of his heart, Taylor offered to take the two of us down there so she could get one last glimpse of Ettleston Road. Then Jeanne horned her way in, and next thing I know, you're telling Mom she can't go, you won't let her go, and that if she's going to be fool enough to go, you and Bubble have to tag along. Now poor Taylor's putting up with five women in his truck for five hundred and thirty-five miles. . . ."

Taylor protested, his voice rumbly and amused. "I don't mind."

"This trip is not good for your mother," Bits said. With her arms folded across her chest, she looked hurt, almost vulnerable, despite her spikiness. "What are you trying to prove by carrying her down there?"

"It was her idea! Definitely not mine!" Bailey retorted. This trip was the very last thing she'd wanted.

"Fine. What's the point of revisiting old hurts? Does she think it'll be the magical cure-all for what ails her? Because it won't be." How was Bailey supposed to reply? She had no idea what had motivated her mother's need to return to her hometown. Behind them, far in the direction of the mouth of the driveway, she could hear the crunch of a car's tires on the gravel. Probably one of the girls' parents or boyfriends arriving to pick her up, signaling the end of the afternoon. And not a moment too soon. "You don't know. . . ."

When her aunt couldn't finish the sentence, Bailey took over. "I don't know what, Bits? It seems you're the one with issues about this trip. If you don't want to go, don't. Stay here with the girls and work on their posture. Trust me, I'm great with that."

At first, her aunt didn't answer. Bailey had seen her lips compressed together before, but never had she seen them so tight and white. "I don't feel right, leaving my girls like this for two whole days."

"Bubble, tell her," Bailey asked her other aunt, who

had rejoined the table. "It'll be fine. Euan will be fine. The trip will be fine. There's nothing to worry about. You can waltz back Friday, make the final finishing touches, and enjoy the pageant." Her older aunt, however, merely seemed absorbed in her pad of notes on the table. Had she heard a word? Or was she faking? "Bubble? Aunt Bubble?" She was definitely faking. "Don't you want to go to Georgia?"

"I'm not saying I don't, dear," said Bubble, after a long, nervous exhale. "But I'm not entirely certain it's the best of ideas, either. Don't get me wrong, now," she added hastily, upon seeing Bailey's impassioned reaction. "I don't think it'll do Polly any actual *harm*, but I can't see it doing anybody any *good*."

"Bailey!" Up the slope, from the direction of the driveway, Jeanne yelled her name. When Bailey turned, she saw her sister standing not by one of the ubiquitous trucks come to retrieve a girl, but a shining black limousine that had nosed its way past the brick pillars flanking the drive's entrance, but had stopped there. Her mom was farther down the slope, studying the ground. As Bailey attempted to piece together what might be happening, her mother bent over and, with surprising agility, picked up a pebble, then discarded it once she was upright. Maybe it was some kind of accuracy exercise, Bailey considered.

"What a lovely car!" Bubble exclaimed. "I've always wanted to ride in one!"

Another figure by the limousine leaned forward and held up a hand to shield her eyes from the afternoon's sun, then waved madly. "Oh, shit." Sidney stood up, forgetting the Butter Beans. "Isn't that . . . ?"

"Chandra," Bailey growled. "So she's here, is she?" Bailey had checked on her assistant at the hotel when they'd swung by after lunch, but had been informed that Ms. Ellis had canceled her reservation two days prior.

"More to the point, in a limo? What the—?" As network production manager, Sidney's eye was always on the bottom line. "What kind of assistant rents herself a limo to get around? That's pathological! She ought to know better than that, Bail. You didn't tell her she could—"

"No," said Bailey. She knew she should start walking. The sight of Chandra perkily jumping in place at the sight of her, though, kept her legs frozen. "Of course not. I've never been that irresponsible. You'd kick my ass."

"You're damned right I would," Sidney agreed. Then, for good measure she added, "A limo! If she were one of your bigger names, maybe a town car, but . . ."

That was enough to set Bailey into motion. She suddenly knew who was in that limo. She jogged under the chinaberry tree and across its carpet of yellow straws, up the slope of grass, and in the direction of her sister, who stood with her arms crossed, uncertain of how to proceed. By the time Bailey reached the car, she was tired, a little out of breath, and decidedly sweaty. Was it uncharitable to think that maybe Chandra had planned it that way? Perhaps not, because the girl's first words were a concerned, "Are you okay? You don't look so good."

"Where have you been?" It wasn't easy, sounding tough while leaning on your knees to catch your breath. Finally she stood upright again and heaved out, "You were supposed to call me from the hotel when you got in last night."

"Oh, I didn't have time," Chandra said, pouting in a way that made it clear she thought of her lapse as the merest whoopsie. "Don't be mad. My plans changed. You see—"

"And why are you . . . in a . . . limo?" Sidney was in worse shape from the run up the hill than Bailey had been. She clutched at her stomach and for a moment it looked as if she might topple over. Both Jeanne and Taylor reached out to grab her, but she waved them off.

Taylor? What was Taylor doing here? When Bailey gave him a surprised blink, he cleared his throat. "What?" he asked. Then he shrugged. "I go where the fun is."

"Oh, you don't think this is *my* limo, do you?" Chandra was wearing a plain white blouse that, out of the air-conditioned cool of the vehicle would very soon be soaked with perspiration, judging by the way it was already clinging to her shoulders. She picked at the fabric and laughed. "Oh no! How comic! No, Jess told me. . . ."

So it was *Jess* now, was it? "From *Ms. Munford* to *Jessica* to *Jess* in less than a week. Nice work." The edge in Bailey's voice surprised her. It must have taken Chandra aback as well, because she almost flinched. "So Ms. Munford said you could use her limo? Where is she?"

"She checked into the inn last night," said Chandra, rallying. She straightened her shoulders and pretended not to have been startled a moment before. "She said that she'd prefer me to stay with her."

Bailey thought Sidney might have a stroke of her own with that announcement. She could practically see the dollar signs registering in the production manager's eyes. "Isn't that convenient?" Bailey said, dangerously pleasant.

"Well, it allows me to be near her for the duration of the shoot, of course." Chandra spoke as if she were explaining the simplest thing in the world to a child. "She specifically requested it."

"She requested it of you?" Bailey crossed her arms and waited for the answer. "You specifically?"

"Well, she asked Larry."

Larry. Larry Gilbert! That information nearly bowled Bailey right over, even delivered with a candy coating. The Munford had asked the Manhattan branch's gen-

eral manager for Chandra's personal assistance? "Why
did she do that, Chandra?" Bailey was already dreading
the answer.

Chandra fiddled with the ends of her hair. "Because
he kind of found out that she never inked the contract,
and that the Connecticut shoot had wrapped already,
and since you weren't around . . ."

Bailey didn't have to ask how all of that had tran-
spired. Chandra had snitched. She'd messed up the one
loose strand Bailey had left unfinished and unraveled it,
then pointed out to Larry Gilbert how tattered it was
and left the blame squarely on Bailey's shoulders. She
and Sidney exchanged glances; she knew exactly what
Sidney was thinking. *The first shot might be accidental.
But the second and third. . . .* Her assistant had just un-
loaded several salvos right into her chest, and all she
could think of was revenge. She wanted to slap her. She
wanted to push her in front of the car and run back and
forth over her with both sets of wheels. Yet she couldn't
let the shock and mental bleeding show. Not in front of
Jeanne, not in front of Taylor. And especially not in front
of Chandra herself. It would be her biggest bluff ever,
but she would have to see it through. "And are the contracts inked?" she asked. She hadn't failed to notice the
industry slang Chandra tossed around so casually, as if
she'd used it for years.

"Well, no, but—"

"Where's Jessica?"

"She checked into the hotel last night, but. . . . Oh,
hey, you can't . . . ! Bailey!"

Bailey knew a non-answer when she heard it. Ignoring her assistant's protests, she dodged around her and
headed straight for the limo. The glass was too dark to
see inside, but she rapped on the tinted back window
anyway, thoroughly aware she'd look seven kinds of
stupid if Chandra had actually arrived alone. Nothing
happened. She kept on rapping. Still nothing. Bailey

didn't care if she had to pound until her joints were sore and bloody. Someone was going to answer, damn it.

Nothing. And then, slowly, the glass began to lower. Not much at first—only a crack. "Ms. Munford?" Bailey asked, nearly cackling with delight. Chandra was a novice compared to her. She kept her game face on, though, as she moved her face closer. "Ms. Munford? I'm Bailey Rhodes. We've talked on the phone, but I'm glad to make your acquaintance at last."

Down rolled the window another few inches. A woman with dark, impressively styled hair lounged within, her eyes concealed behind a pair of enormous sunglasses. Her face remained impassive. No sense in beating around the bush; Bailey got right down to business. "I was hoping that we could talk, perhaps this evening, about the matter of the unsigned contract."

For a moment Bailey might have been talking to one of the stone faces on Easter Island, for all the response she got. Then suddenly the senator's wife became very animated. "I'm afraid tonight is out," she announced with authority. "Tomorrow evening, perhaps, if I can clear my schedule."

It was reflex for Bailey almost to agree. With a jolt, though, she remembered that the following night she would be most of the way to Georgia. There weren't enough swear words to express what she felt at that moment, though she rattled off a good two dozen or so in her head, including some new ones made up on the spur of the moment. "I'm afraid that won't work. I'm not going to be here to—"

The Munford cut her off with an icy, "You seem not to be around for much."

Bailey bit back the sharp retort on the tip of her tongue, and attempted to sound as pleasant as possible. "Ms. Munford, I'm sure we can—"

But the woman had already dismissed Bailey and moved on. Her hand reached up to her sunglasses and pulled them down so she could look over the tops.

"Hello," she said, smiling. The window eased down the rest of the way. Bailey turned to see whom she addressed. "Who are you?"

"Hiya. I live next door." Taylor was leaning down beside her now, gesturing to the east. "Don't I know you?" he asked. "Wait a minute, you were on TV, right?"

Inch by inch, the Munford looked over Taylor Montgomery—his face, his eyes, his chin, and then down to his broad shoulders and arms, his chest, and then obscenely lingering around the area below his belt buckle. Bailey could barely contain herself from slapping the woman. "Perhaps you saw me on my talk show," she suggested, inserting a tip of her sunglasses into her mouth and sucking on it. That bitch!

"Oh yeah," said Taylor, nodding. He wrinkled his nose. "I don't watch those so much."

"I've tapes of my highlights back in my room if you'd care to view them," suggested the Munford. From her lurid tone, it was impossible to tell if those tapes were of the actual show, or more personal, filthy, and naked in nature.

Either way, Bailey would sooner rip the older woman to shreds before letting her sink those Elizabeth Ardened claws into Taylor's tender hide. She stepped between them, blocking the view. "Mind if I have a minute?" she asked Taylor, including Jeanne in the request. It was difficult not to want to slap Taylor around a little as well, solely for being attractive enough that other women took notice of him, but in her heart she couldn't assign any portion of blame to him. He didn't know how greedy and amoral these television types could be.

"Sure thing," said Taylor. Before he turned to go, he reached out and squeezed Bailey's shoulder with a wink. She unmelted a little at the gesture. He hadn't been taking the Munford seriously at all.

"Yeah, I'll get Mom," Jeanne said, nodding and crossing her arms.

Bailey waited until the pair of them had begun to amble down the drive before she whirled around again. "Ms. Munford." She'd dropped all pretense of pleasantness. "It's my understanding that the shoot is scheduled to begin Thursday afternoon. There'll be no footage if your contract isn't signed beforehand. If it isn't, I'll be instructing all the crew not to film a single frame. I've been working for weeks in good faith with your legal representation. . . ."

"I'm sure they'll be signed before then." The glasses were back on and the window back up, halfway.

Was the Munford bluffing? It was impossible to tell. Surely it couldn't have been that easy. "Because if they're not, I have the Expedition Network's production manager out here, and she'll be glad to tell you that the network will not assume fiscal responsibility for any of the expenses you have incurred, including both your rooms at the inn and—" she indicated the limo with the hand sweep of a model on *The Price Is Right* "—anything else to which the network has not agreed in a signed contract."

"I'm sure that Chandra and I will work things out, dearie. Come, Chandra." The window swept up into place.

When Bailey turned, her assistant was flushed and furious as she accused, "You didn't have to do that!"

"Oh yeah. I did." Before she could add the lecture she'd intended, Chandra was already flouncing around to the car's far side. "Chandra!" she barked.

"I have to go. You heard Jess." Her assistant opened the door.

"You watch yourself!" Bailey managed to call out, before Chandra disappeared entirely. Slowly, regally, the long car eased its way back into the road, halting suddenly when a banged-up old Dodge truck whizzed by. Its driver yelled an obscenity out the open window as it screeched around the limo's bulk.

"You okay?" Sidney asked, while they watched the limo pull onto the road and drive off. Bailey nodded. "You'd probably kill me if I did the told-you-so dance, I bet."

"That's a bet you'd win." Arms still crossed, Bailey jerked her head and started to make her way back down the drive, kicking pebbles with every step. She had to keep her arms contained. If she didn't, she worried they might do something wild, like claw the bark from every nearby tree, or strangle an innocent bystander, or punch a glass window.

"I had *no* idea she'd gone to Larry." Sidney's attempt at consolation didn't go very far. "I would've stepped up for you if I'd known."

"I know. She's a snake. You told me from the start."

"It's one contract, Bail. No one's going to get fired over one contract."

"Sure."

"Larry has the reputation of being a hard-ass, but every time I've dealt with him, he's been a pretty good guy."

"Whatever." She knew that she was being curt with someone who didn't deserve it, but she couldn't help herself.

"I'm sure that if you explained—"

"Did you *see* the way that mantrap looked at Taylor!" Bailey exploded, then shut her mouth before it did any more damage.

"Oh." Sidney's tone was so curious, so shrewd, that Bailey felt compelled to glance over. Sure enough, there was a knowing smile on her face. "So you're angry at what, exactly?"

"Don't," Bailey warned her.

Bailey's legs were much longer than her friend's; Sidney had to scurry along to keep up. "I'm wondering what you're madder at, Chandra, or the way Jessica—"

"Seriously. Don't." Again, she was being unnecessarily harsh to someone whose sole fault was playfulness. She hated it. Bailey knew Sidney had more than an inkling of what was most bothering her. Sidney probably knew Bailey knew. Why in the world did they have to speak aloud about something so hopeless? "I don't mean to be a pain," she amended, trying to soften her hard edges. "I don't want to talk about that, though."

"Do you want to do something about it?" Sidney asked, slightly out of breath.

"I don't know." They were fast approaching the plateau on which the house had been built, moving off the driveway with increasingly swift steps. One of the girls was walking toward them, her high heels clutched in one hand while she rubbed her feet in the grass as if she'd never before felt it with her bare soles. Fawn, of course. Her hair was a mess, as if she'd leaned over and shook it out and then dragged it through a thorny hedge. The very sight of her messing herself up when the other girls were back at practice made Bailey angrier than before. Every little thing she'd touched while she was down here had failed to bear any fruit. "Let's table it for another time," she suggested diplomatically, not trusting herself to say anything else.

Sidney raised her eyebrows. "Your call," she said, separating from Bailey and striding in the direction of the table, where Euan and Bits were visibly arguing over something. Bailey was a little surprised at the sudden desertion, but maybe it was deserved. Or maybe it was simply a good move on Sid's part, because without any warning, Fawn changed vector and began a course that would intersect with her own.

Before they were within close earshot, she could hear the girl complaining. ". . . should have known better. I'm quitting! Nothing you can say's going to change my mind, you know."

"So quit," Bailey called out to her. A moment more, and they were face-to-face. Between the two, Bailey had an advantage in height. "Seriously. Drop out."

Plainly Fawn hadn't expected any response other than Bailey attempting to talk her back into the lineup. She took a moment to recover. "I am!"

"Fine!" Bailey didn't give a damn. Over by the table, she saw Sid sit down next to Taylor once more and make some casual conversation, her gaze only once shifting in Bailey's direction. That woman had better not be saying anything about her.

"You can't talk me out of it!"

"What part of *quit* didn't you understand?"

Fawn looked sheepish. "I thought you were trying reverse psychology on me."

"Nope. Quit if it's too much for you."

"Oh, see?" Fawn returned to her smug, superior state, as if she'd caught Bailey in some vital inconsistency. "Don't bother following up. I know how reverse psychology works. *If it's too much for you, drop out. Obviously you're not good enough.* When we both know damn well I'm more than good enough." Bailey waited. If the girl was going to argue with herself, why waste the energy? Sure enough, she kept talking. "I don't have to prove anything to anyone, you know. I know I could get through this pageant if I wanted to. I could even learn to walk in these fucking high heels! But just because I can doesn't mean I have to."

"No, you don't." Asking Fawn to participate in the pageant on a moment's whim had been like setting loose a moose in a ladies auxiliary high tea—you'd never train the thing not to crack the porcelain and poop on the scones. She'd totally done Fawn a disservice by getting her mixed up with this mess. In the practice dress they'd bought together at the consignment shop, she looked constrained, like a caterpillar captured in its chrysalis. The moth waiting to emerge might not be as flashy as the butterflies below, but she would be a thing of wonder when she emerged. "So, quit." She honestly meant it.

"I don't want to be a pretty girl," Fawn complained. "What happens to pretty girls? Nothing!"

How could Bailey refute that? If Fawn didn't want to spend her life wallowing and exploiting her prettiness, fine. Let girls like Larkin spend their lives bartering their good looks for smiles and praise and free drinks at the bars. Fawn wanted something more than playing dress-up. That should be commendable, right?

And then she looked at the group still collected on the lawn. Euan had split away from Bits and was herding the girls into their places. They primped and smoothed their dresses, looking like there wasn't a thought in their head save preparing themselves to walk forty feet across the lawn. "My mom was a pretty girl," she said, not expecting to hear the words from her own mouth. Fawn's head jerked in the direction of where Jeanne and her mother sat at the end of the folding table, hunched over something that Jeanne sorted through with her fingers. It looked like a pile of rocks from the driveway. "Bubble told me she won a beauty pageant. And she did a lot with her life." And, God willing, she'd do more, once she'd shaken off whatever specter of the past haunted and depressed her.

"Huh."

Whether Fawn was genuinely impressed, or merely unwilling to say anything bad about her elderly mother, Bailey didn't know. "Fawn, you already are a pretty girl." The anger she'd felt inside dampened a little, and although she could feel the girl bristle and ready herself with retorts to the contrary, she kept talking. "You don't have to be in a pageant to prove it. You're smart enough to know that pageants don't make you pretty. You're smart enough to know that dresses and makeup and high heels don't do the trick either. So you should be smart enough to know that you don't have to prove your intelligence, either. Quit if you're not enjoying it. Seriously. Forget about trying to impress Larkin. Forget about trying to impress me or my aunts or your parents or whoever it is you're trying to prove a point to. Walk away and do what most pretty girls do.

Live your life the way you want." Like her mom had done. Or Bits, or Bubble, or Jeanne, or Chandra or even the Munford, or any of the pretty girls she'd known, young or old.

"Yeah." Fawn shuffled her bare feet on the grass, quiet for once. "Do what I want?"

"Do what you want."

Bailey hadn't intended the words to be a benediction, but Fawn smiled wryly, took a few steps away, then wound up with her arm and in one tremendous swing, let her heels fly into the air. One shoe parted from the other, its own peculiar arc blinded by the sun's brightness. Once she'd blinked the tears from her eyes, Bailey saw them both fall to earth, a dozen feet apart.

Fawn had already run halfway up the hill, abandoning her shoes in a sprint for Cedar Pass Road. As if knowing with certainty that Bailey still watched, she turned and waved, jogging backwards and slowing down before once again she spun and picked her way across the stony driveway before vanishing. Neither of them had spoken the word good-bye, but the quality of the moment was enough. The moth had been released from captivity—and of all the girls in the pageant, Bailey felt certain this one could survive in the wild.

Chapter Twenty

Bits's lemon drops. Taylor's deodorant. Air freshener. Bubble's cloud of hairspray. And then, following a crinkle of cellophane in the backseat, the vaguest whiff of something familiar also tickled her nose. The scent reminded Bailey of waking up on a winter's morning and smelling breakfast from downstairs—toaster waffles, covered in . . . was that it? Maple syrup?

When she turned around to investigate, Jeanne pulled an enormous candy bar from her mouth. "What?" Though Jeanne's mouth was full, she kept her voice low. Their mother leaned on her shoulder, breathing deeply as she slept. On her mom's other side, Bubble sat with her head lolled back, occasionally letting out a sudden, startling snore. Bits slumbered as well, her spine's one concession to sleep being a slight incline of the neck forward. Otherwise, she sat perfectly erect behind Taylor, her legs crossed at the knee and her wrists folded over her purse.

"What're you eating?" Bailey asked softly. Bubble breathed heavily and her head rolled to the other side. Her body shifted uneasily, trying to find more space for itself. Her older aunt was the largest of the four women sitting in the truck's back seat, but as Bits and Jeanne had the same family tendency to boniness, the four were more close than cramped, Bailey knew that from experience. She'd ridden in the back most of the day, and had gotten her turn in the front passenger seat less than an hour before.

Chewing and drooling slightly, Jeanne held up the nut-studded candy bar. A red-and-yellow slanted Stuckey's logo had been stamped in the middle of the clear wrapper. Beneath it, in old-fashioned blue letters, read the words PECAN LOG ROLL. Although she'd eaten both breakfast and lunch and had indulged in most of a bag of low-fat wheat chips that Bits had pronounced inedible before finishing the remainder, Bailey found her stomach reflexively rumbling at the smell and sight. "Where'd you get it?"

"When we stopped in Kenly, earlier."

Bailey had to think back through the grueling hours. She remembered a Stuckey's at every exit when they used to make the Virginia/Georgia trip in her childhood, but they'd only stopped at one that day, back in North Carolina. "Ugh. They're nasty, aren't they?"

Jeanne pulled back the wrapper and exposed another bite. "I like them," she added, while she took another mouthful. The sweet smell was almost overpowering. Why was it that it roused none of the sleeping women? "Bubble bought me, like, a twelve-pack."

Typical Jeanne, thought Bailey, mooching off her aunts for something as insignificant and unnecessary as candy. Crap. There she went again, taking the high-and-mighty stance. Hell, she was being a candy snob when she wanted nothing more than a whole bar to herself. Her own hypocritical reaction made her wince. Why was her immediate instinct, whenever it came to her sister, to think the worst? Wrap her hair in curlers, frost it, and hang a pair of reading glasses from her neck and

Bailey would be Bits, plain and simple. The thing of it was, she didn't *want* to be Bits. She swallowed, hoping it wasn't audible. "So can I have a bite?"

Was Jeanne actually having to think it over? With eleven more foot-long pecan logs in her bag? Seriously? It appeared so, but after a very long pause in which Jeanne seemed to be studying her, she held out the bar.

Bailey turned around in her seat and skinned the wrapper down like a banana peel. A few of the pecan chunks fell onto her blouse. She paused to retrieve them before they could tumble down and litter Taylor's floor. "You can put those in the ashtray if you're feeling tidy," he suggested, breaking through the silence. "I don't mind either way." He reached down and flipped open a little compartment in the console, then returned his attention to the seemingly never-ending I-95.

She felt a little uneasy, biting into a honking big pecan log while Taylor shot amused glances in her direction. Candy bars were kid stuff. Not at all surprising that her sister would want to stuff her face with them. Hell, with that pink T-shirt she'd let Bubble pick out for her, imprinted with a giant Sanrio cartoon bunny on the front, Jeanne looked like a child herself. Bailey needed something in her mouth, though—scratch that thought. She needed the boost a little rush of sugar would give her. With one hand self-consciously cupped so that Taylor couldn't see her voracious chomp, she sank her teeth through the outer layer of nuts. "Oh crap," she exclaimed. "It'sh shweet."

"Isn't that the point?" Since she'd never herself driven, Bailey wasn't certain how much concentration it actually took to steer a car down an interstate in moderate traffic, but at that moment it felt like Taylor was looking more at her than at the road.

Anyway, Bailey couldn't answer him, not with the

sticky, maple-laced caramel adhering her teeth together more effectively than any superglue. She turned and returned the confection to Jeanne, who immediately inspected it to see how big a bite was missing. Bits stirred in her rest at the sound of the crinkling wrapper.

"I din' know it wash gonna be thish shweet," Bailey eventually managed to say, her mouth still full. It felt as if her salivary glands had kicked into overtime, producing an equivalent volume of drool to the amount of pecan sludge she'd bitten off.

"You don't have to eat it!" said Jeanne.

Taylor still stared over, amused. Her mouth worked furiously for a moment to clear itself. Finally he took pity. "You know, a few months ago I bought a Charleston Chew. Did you ever eat those when you were a kid? Big, honkin' huge bar of taffy covered with chocolate? I used to love those as a kid. Spent darned near all my allowance money on them. I thought when I died and went to heaven, the roads would be paved with Charleston Chews. Hadn't had one in years, though." Over the rumble of the road and Bubble's gentle snoring, she could barely hear his voice, but she nodded. "That thing nearly freakin' pulled out all my teeth and tasted like pure cane sugar. Another of my fond childhood memories shot to hell."

Bailey had started laughing midway through the reminiscence. She couldn't help it. She knew exactly how he felt. "You know those Hostess Snoballs you bought for that picnic?" she asked, a little shy because that particular meal had ended so badly. "I had them for dinner that night, and oh my God. Coconut? Marshmallow? And a cupcake in the middle? Who *invented* that crap?"

"Slim Jims," he countered.

"I ate those like *crazy* when I was a kid," she exclaimed, excited at the memory.

"I used to eat them by the box. Remember how they

had that skin on the outside, like plastic? I used to peel the skin in strips and eat those first, then I'd finish off the beef jerky and move on to the next."

"You," she declared, "are a freak." For a moment, when the truck zoomed beneath an overpass, she caught a glimpse of her reflection in the car's windshield, her teeth gleaming in a smile. She couldn't remember the last time she'd seen herself so gleeful. Then the image vanished, replaced by the steady rhythm of the highway's white lane dividers. "Did you ever do the Pop Rocks thing?"

"Too scared," he confessed. One of his hands slid down along the steering wheel.

"Too scared?"

"After that kid exploded from eating them with Pepsi, sure," he joked.

From the backseat, Jeanne sighed. "Well, I *like* Snoballs," she announced, as though hers was the one opinion that mattered.

"What?" The chatter had woken Bits, who came to with a start. She couldn't sit up any more than she was already; only her open eyes and her neck's sudden stiffness indicated any difference between her awake and napping state. "What's going on? Where are we?"

"Go back to sleep," Jeanne suggested, her voice softer and less petulant than Bailey had expected.

"Still in South Carolina," Bailey told her.

"Rest area," Bits announced, her finger following a green sign as it passed. "Pull over in here, Taylor," she announced, as though the car were hers and Taylor her servant. "I need to stretch my legs."

"Yes'm," he called back, flipping on his blinker.

"Bits, you had to take a walk an hour ago," Bailey complained. "We're never going to make it to Georgia tonight if we keep stopping."

"Girl, have the kernels fallen off your cob?" Bits growled. "I *have* to *stretch* my *legs*."

Taylor cleared his throat, his hands crossing as he

steered off the exit. "I was kind of assuming she was using it as a euphemism," he said. "For peeing."

"Mr. Montgomery! Really!" said Bits, outraged.

Some perverse impulse made Bailey say, "Oh, so when she says she wants to stretch her legs, she means she has to wee?"

"Oh yes, your aunt definitely means that she has to take a whizz. Or maybe a number two." Taylor steered the truck down the lane intended for small vehicles, and aimed for one of the parking spaces.

Though she could hear her aunt gasping from the backseat, Bailey nodded solemnly. "I feel like I've learned something today. Stretching the legs? Apparently means needing to squeeze one out."

"And that will be quite enough of that sort of talk," Bits announced, her tone indignant. She had the door open and her feet out before Taylor had turned off the ignition. "Honestly!"

"Well, dear," said Aunt Bubble, stirring from her sleep. "I know that I could certainly go for a tinkle." Anything Bubble said these days that sounded both innocent and vaguely off-color, Bailey instantly suspected. She craned her neck around, peering for any sign that would betray her aunt's real intentions. "Come with me, Jeanne. Let's go punish the porcelain, as they say." She gave Bailey the faintest hint of a wink as the two of them slid from the bench and out Bits's door.

"She is *so* nailed," Bailey muttered, undoing her seat belt.

"I kind of need to stretch my legs, too. You mind?" asked Taylor.

"What do I look like, the Pee Police?" Bailey wanted to know. "Go stretch."

"Need anything from the snack machine while I'm there? Soda? Snoball? Snickers bar? Syringe with corn syrup to inject straight into your veins?"

Bailey opened her door and stuck out her legs. "I'll pass on that."

"Okay then. Back in a bit." A moment later, and he was following Jeanne and the aunts up the sidewalk to the circular building housing the facilities. Set in a quiet area of the Carolina countryside, the rest area was quite a pretty little nook; several picnic tables sat on a stretch of grass near an area designated as a dog run, where the land ran down to a small, pebbly stream. Save for the huge, idling eighteen-wheeler blocking the view toward the exit back to the highway, it was nearly perfectly picturesque and tranquil.

Her mother was still in the truck, Bailey realized. The other four had vanished so quickly to take care of their bladders that they hadn't given a thought to the last person sitting. Or was it a conspiracy? And why the hell was she so nervous all of a sudden? The woman was her own mother! Before her stroke, Mom might have had the ability to hit all Bailey's buttons with the accuracy of an old-fashioned Bell telephone operator, but . . . there was no but about it. It was simply the first time she'd been left alone with her mother in days and days. To feel nervous was stupid. "Do you need to use the restroom?" she asked.

Apparently her mother had been looking out the tinted side window at the landscape before Bailey opened the door and asked her question; to suddenly find herself face-to-face with that blank face and those staring eyes was a little unnerving. After a moment, her mother shook her head. "Get out and stretch a little bit? It's got to be cramped back there." At first, Bailey wasn't certain that she'd been heard. An eternity seemed to pass before her mother nodded, leaned forward, and sank her hands into the rear seat pocket. After a bit of rummaging around, she produced a paper bag—the Stuckey's bag holding Jeanne's stash of pecan logs, in fact. Her left hand was steady as she upended the bag on the seat so that the bars went bouncing. She folded it into quarters. "Yeah, let's get rid of some of the trash in here," Bailey suggested, grabbing an empty Stuckey's wrapper and an aluminum can.

Only when her mom had stowed away the folded bag in her pocket did she ease herself down. Bailey made several attempts to assist, first ready to help navigate her legs onto the running board, then straightening back up to offer a hand for balance. Yet her mother was surprisingly nimble, both for someone who'd suffered from a stroke the month before, and especially for someone who'd been sitting in the same position for a little over an hour. "Walk with me," she said.

It was more command than request. Already her mother had made headway across the parking lot in the direction of the green stretch beyond, her posture dignified, her pace surprisingly swift. Bailey shut the truck door and followed. "Yeah, that's probably a good idea. Exercise the muscles a little." She caught up and slowed down her pace to match her mom's. "Looking forward to seeing Carverton?" Her mother acknowledged the inquiry with a shrug. "I guess I am." She couldn't let the question remain unanswered. "I haven't been since, what, when I was twelve? Right before we moved to Jersey? I don't remember it that well. I guess—"

"Bailey." The unexpected interruption startled her. "You're making noise."

She knew instantly what her mother meant. Bailey wasn't making conversation. She was filling the air between them with sound, simply so that there wouldn't be silence. Like a frightened person leaving on the television in one room and the stereo in another so that she wouldn't feel alone in an empty house, she had been surrounding herself with the most comfortable and familiar noise she knew—of her own voice, talking about herself. What a fantastic daughter she was, she thought to herself. This monologue has been brought to you by the Corporation for Rampant Egotism, and the letter *I*.

So she simply made up her mind to walk, remain quiet, and see what her mother needed, reminding herself that she was doing remarkably well in her recovery. No shaking in the hands, no pronounced limping, no balance problems. That was what mattered, right?

Only Bailey paused by the metal garbage can to empty her hands. Her mother continued in a straight path in the direction of the small creek, hell-bent on the water ahead. Recent rains had left the ground slippery underfoot; Bailey had sudden horrific visions of her mother tumbling down into the creek, a fear that was exacerbated when they passed a sign warning against bathing in, fishing from, dumping in, or drinking the water.

"Mom," she said, unable to bite back the warning. But her mother was sidling down the incline. Though her footing fumbled a little bit near the muddy slope's bottom, she made it to the little rivulet's side with no problems. It was Bailey who had to find her way to the bottom ass-backwards, her cute white sneakers garnering brown streaks on their sides from trying to find a foothold. Grappling for balance, one of her hands tore off a handful of grass, leaving the insides of her fingers sticky with their juice. When she managed to get herself upright and turned around once again, she found her mother holding out the Stuckey's bag. "What?" she asked, confused. What in the world were they doing here? "Do you want me to hold it?"

That must have been the right answer. Her mother flapped the bag impatiently until at last Bailey grabbed it. While she unfolded the paper, shaking it out and staring at the logo on its exterior, her mother began to walk down the creek bank, her eyes to the ground and one hand clutching her left cheek. Was she in pain? Bailey looked back in the direction of the truck—could she get back there quickly if her mother suddenly collapsed? Would anyone hear her if she called? No one had yet returned from the restrooms, as far as she could tell. Hell, would they even be able to see where she and her mother were?

Her mother fell forward. Bailey sprang into action, ready to sprint so she could close the gap of several yards between them. As suddenly as her muscles tensed for action, however, she arrested them. She'd completely misread the situation. Her mother wasn't collapsing, but bending over from the waist so she could grasp something she'd found on the ground. With her back still toward Bailey, she stood up once more and examined whatever it was she'd retrieved. Her elbows sawed in and out while she cleaned it off.

Bailey ambled over to her mother's side, trying not to appear too solicitous. This whole charade of having to pretend not to be concerned, simply to save her mother's pride, was insane. But she bit down hard and swallowed the lecture she wanted to give, and instead inhaled deeply. She could bluff her way through this one, too.

Without warning, something heavy landed in the bottom of the paper bag she had been holding open with her thumbs. Her mother returned to scanning the bank, leaving Bailey to reach into the bag and withdraw . . . a rock. A round, smooth rock that fit perfectly in her hand, its bulging surface matching exactly the curve of her palm.

Over and over she turned the rock, as if trying to read upon its gray granite surface the answers she needed. Then again, what were the questions she needed to ask? She scarcely dared to formulate them in her own mind; weaving together the tendrils of her thoughts was far too painful. Within a moment, her mother returned with two more rocks, and then another two. She pried the stones from the mud as if she'd made a business of it, discarding most and keeping those few that met whatever standards she had set. Only when she had used the flats of her fingers to wipe the worst of the debris from their surfaces would she let each new find clatter atop the others in the bag.

Within three or four minutes, her mother had collected over a dozen stones. She peered into the bag, then nodded, apparently satisfied. Close to where the rest area clearing ended was a gentler slope than the one they'd descended. Clutching the bag to her chest, Bailey followed her mother up the incline and in the direction of the truck. Through the paper and through her own blouse, she could feel the stones, each as cold and heavy as the tears Bailey had to blink away with every step.

Though Jeanne was still straggling back from the restroom station, both the aunts and Taylor were clustered around the truck, drinking Cokes from plastic bottles. Bubble beamed broadly at the sight of them, but Bits gulped down a mouthful of soda and launched into a harangue. "We were worried sick. What have you been doing with your mother, Bailey Rhodes?"

"I told you they were down by the stream," Taylor protested mildly. Was that a look of concern he gave her, despite the light-hearted and reassuring tone? She wiped her cheek on her forearm, in case there was any lingering moisture there.

"You saw them yourself, Bits, don't be silly," Bubble chided.

"Polly, look at you!" scolded Bits, who had grabbed her oldest sister by the wrists. "How'd you get your hands so filthy?" Her mother's hands were nowhere as dirty as the look that Bits shot her, right then. "Let's go get you cleaned up. With all the disease and germs running about these days . . ." The fussing continued as the pair walked in the direction of the restrooms, with Bubble clucking and following once again.

Which left Bailey standing there, holding a sack full of her mother's stones. What in the world was she supposed to do? "What's wrong?" Taylor asked, recognizing immediately how out of sorts she was.

Bailey said the words she'd been frightened to think to herself moments before. "I'm worried that my mom's . . . crazy," she confessed. Once said, it sounded ridiculous. It was a stupid, traitorous thing to think, right? At the same time, giving the notion voice lent it a gravity too weighty to bear. "I mean, what if there's something wrong in her head? She hasn't been the same since . . ."

"Since the stroke." Taylor finished the sentence she couldn't.

"Is that the way it happens? Is that the way it's going to be from now on? Is she going to get any better? Am I going to have to put up with . . . ?" She halted, unable to continue, while her mouth and heart betrayed her with every word.

"I'm not a doctor. I wish I could tell you."

Taylor seemed so helpless. She hadn't done him any favors by battering away with questions. "I know. I know," she apologized, still clutching the bag to her chest. Her sister was approaching and was probably already within earshot, so she dropped her voice and tried to change her demeanor. "It's been tough, that's all."

"I know." His voice soothed the ragged edges of her nerves. "Bailey, if there was anything I could—"

"What're you doing with my pecan logs?" Jeanne asked, obviously suspicious. Taylor stopped whatever he'd been about to say and turned to welcome her back, a smile on his lips but not in his eyes. "You're not eating them, are you?"

"No, I'm not eating them," Bailey said. She didn't want her sister to see the evidence of their mother's mania, but Jeanne plainly felt that anything in a Stuckey's bag was hers to inspect. She marched up and seized it, and Bailey surrendered almost immediately so that the paper wouldn't tear.

"Oh," Jeanne said. Almost immediately she handed it back. "More of Mom's rocks. What'd you do with the pecan logs, then?"

The information took a moment to process. "What?" Bailey said, not comprehending.

"What," Jeanne repeated, with the utmost patience, "did you do with my pecan . . . ?"

"No. About the rocks."

"Mom's been collecting rocks for the last few days. Didn't you know?"

"No!" Almost immediately, Bailey had a recollection of seeing her mother picking up pebbles from the driveway the day before. Knowing she'd been at it a while didn't help convince her of her mother's sanity. The woman had never once expressed an interest in geology. "Why?" Jeanne shrugged. She apparently didn't know and didn't care. "Didn't you ask?"

"No. Did you?"

"No!" Without an argument to sustain it, their face-off was bound to collapse. Bailey attempted to feed the fire with indignation. "Then what am I supposed to do with these?"

"I don't know!" Jeanne acted like the victim of an unwarranted tongue-lashing. "Put them with the others!"

"What others?" both Taylor and Bailey asked.

"The ones in the back?" When neither of them showed any inkling of understanding, she sighed heavily and walked around to the truck's gate. Taylor obligingly opened it and pulled up the tonneau. "There." Jeanne pointed to a large circular tin the size of a hatbox that had once held Charles Chips, back before either she or Bailey had been born. Bailey lunged to pull it closer, and found it heavy. When she pulled off the lid, inside were dozens of stones. Gently rounded stones no more than three or four inches in length, flat enough that they could fit in the palm of the hand. They weren't all the same color or shape or the same type of rock or mineral; there was no sense why they'd been plucked from the ground. "Those are from the woods," Jeanne explained. "There's another one somewhere with some from the drive and around the house. Oh, there it is. That cereal box."

Bailey didn't need to see any more. She dropped the bag of creek stones on top of those already in the potato chips canister and snapped back on the lid, not wanting to see them again. "This is insane." Taylor looked unwilling to deny it. "Didn't you think it was insane? Why in the *world* did you help her?" she accused Jeanne.

"It keeps her occupied! She enjoyed it! And what harm does it do? Lots of people collect stuff, you know. And besides," she added, "It's not like you've been exactly available."

"I've been—" Bailey clamped down on the excuses bubbling to the forefront. This whole trip to Georgia was supposed to have been about being available. "This is insane," she ended repeating.

"Maybe you could talk to the aunts about it," Taylor suggested. They were coming now, hands presumably clean enough to pass Bits's tests for contagion.

She considered. She could ask. And then for the rest of the trip she'd have to endure Bits's angry accusations, Bubble's fretting, Jeanne's protestations of innocence, and her mother's silent anger. Oral surgery without anesthesia sounded more pleasant. Honestly, if Jeanne had—but now wasn't the time for that. "No," she said. "When we get back, I'm taking Mom straight to a doctor. A psychiatrist. I don't care if I have to miss the damned pageant. Until then we'll bluff our way through it. Don't let her know we're worried."

Jeanne said, "She's not . . ."

"I don't want to hear it from you," Bailey snapped at her sister. "No more stones."

"But. . . ."

"Why bluff? Why don't you ask your mom what she wants them for?" Taylor wanted to know. Her unfortunate first response was a hostile glare from which he backed off, though she tried to soften it with a mumbled apology. "Your call," he said. Without waiting for an answer, he withdrew his key ring from his pants, twirled it around his finger, and walked to his door.

Yet how could she have answered him? Bailey knew that had she asked, she would never have received an answer. Was there anyone in there to reply? All that seemed left to her mother was a cipher, an unknowable undefined x in an equation that no longer included any of her family.

Chapter Twenty-one

The bathroom mirror was too tiny. Miniscule, really. The only way she could judge how her dress looked was to jump up and down in an attempt to glimpse something other than her shoulders. She would have had a better chance of checking out her makeup from the highway shoulder in the side-view mirror of a passing semi.

At least she'd treated herself to a long shower, freshening those parts of herself that felt not-so-fragrant after five hundred miles of travel, and cooling herself down on what had to be one of the hottest summer nights she'd experienced in some time. What was it about travel that wore one out? She hadn't had to concentrate on the road ahead, or look for signs, or exercise, or actually steer the truck. She hadn't done anything all day save sit on her ass and listen alternately to the sounds of gossip, complaint, and sleep, so why had she felt like road kill when they'd pulled into the tiny motor court, two hours before?

And why, for that matter, had they let Bubble pick out this damned hotel? No, motel. Not even a good motel, though it hadn't yet devolved into the sticky mess of a by-the-hour no-tell. "My high school friend Gloria Weller used to run it," she'd insisted, when they'd pulled off the interstate and down a rural route road populated solely by gas stations, peach orchards, and the occasional convenience store. "The Maple Leaf! Like the Rag. Or the hockey team. Isn't there a hockey team? It used to be so quaint! I always wished I could have a motor court of my own, after I saw how sweet the rooms were, and how much fun Gloria had with her duck pond right in the middle of the courtyard, not to mention all the interesting people that you could meet every day. . . ."

"*Maida's Little Motor Court*," Jeanne had said, leaning forward to murmur it into Bailey's ear.

What had been quaint thirty or forty years ago was now dated and shabby. Old linoleum stuck to her feet as she walked around the room, looking for the watch she'd removed and for the little travel bag in which she'd stowed a necklace and several pairs of earrings. The flooring felt like it might be pried up simply by taking quick steps from one end of the cinderblock room to another. Tepid air spit from a window air conditioner with such fitfulness that Bailey felt sure it might cough, sputter, and die at any minute. At least there was a table fan to circulate the air, though it meant that the faint odor of must tripled in intensity and made Bailey sneeze like crazy, every few minutes.

It didn't matter though. Unhappy as they might have been with the dilapidated state of the Maple Leaf Lodge, none of them had the heart to stuff themselves back into the truck and drive at least a half hour to find another pit stop for the night. Bailey could easily have afforded separate rooms for them all, at the rates the Maple Leaf was asking, but Bits's constant eye on cost-cutting could have earned her a prize spot on any Presidential cabinet. Or as Sidney's assistant, for that matter. After Bubble and Jeanne had agreed to share a room, and Bits announced that she'd be watching after their mom, Bailey had found Taylor staring at her with raised eyebrows and an impish twitch tugging at the corners of his lips—followed by mock disappointment when Bits announced that, of course, they'd have separate rooms of their own. Yet there had been one brief, hopeful second . . . no, it was silly to contemplate. There was no way that she'd spend an entire night in a centipede-infested hotel room with a strange man, even for the sake of saving twenty-four dollars.

Visiting him after dark, though. That was an entirely different story. Were earrings too fussy? She discarded the long, dangly pair she'd picked, and closed up the travel bag. Bad idea. Who dressed up out here in the middle of nowhere, where the most popular nocturnal activity would be walking down the hill to get a YooHoo from the Piggly-Wiggly? No, she wanted to look casual. As if she'd merely freshened up a little, without needing it at all. Although after sitting across from her at dinner, he would have seen those strands of hair stuck to her sweaty forehead, the mysterious smudge on her cheek that had appeared midway through the afternoon and only was first noticed in the privacy of her own room, and the spasm of irritation that crossed her face when Aunt Bits launched into a monologue about her digestive system. Best to spray on a little scent, then, and hope for the best.

She'd scarcely spritzed her cleavage and the back of her legs when someone knocked at the door. That brief flurry of sound made her intestines roil and her breath quicken. Was Taylor coming to her room? Why? Was it for the same reasons she'd intended to visit his? What if it wasn't? Worse, what if it was? Did she know what the hell she was doing, playing around like this? She wanted to flirt. She badly wanted to get her rusty eye-batting skills back into practice and prove that she still had the knack.

But of all the people in the world, why Taylor? Why not schmooze the guy who wore the beer-logo baseball caps behind the counter of the Crestonville 7-Eleven? Why not wink and leer at the gas station attendant, or the nice male nurse she'd met when her mother had been in the hospital, or the manager of the greasy spoon where they'd all had dinner not an hour before? It wasn't as if Taylor was her only choice.

As her mind went into hysterical convulsions, Bailey knew she was overanalyzing. There was a simple answer to the question of why Taylor. Taylor was the one she wanted. Of that much she was certain. Or at least she had been until the knock had thrown her into a panic.

Again, the knock sounded at the door, insistent and to Bailey's imagination, masculine. Unless it was the desk clerk who'd rented her the string of rooms all together in a row, come to say that Bailey's credit card had been rejected, it had to be Taylor. Taylor, for whom she'd showered and dressed up, and then dressed down again. Taylor, who made her slightly giddy despite being on the other side of the—

"Our TV's not working, Bubble's in curlers, and I'm not ready to go to sleep," Jeanne announced. She looked her sister up and down as she brushed by, eyebrows raised. "What're you smiling for?"

She'd been smiling for Taylor. Bailey's utterly studied look of casual surprise wasn't fooling Jeanne at all. What wasn't at all fake was her new expression of chagrin when Jeanne flopped down on her bed, legs sprawled to catch a breeze from the air conditioning unit whirring away in the window. "I'm not smiling!" Bailey told her. Typical of Jeanne, to barge in and assume she'd be welcome. Typical Bailey, too—thinking the worst of her sister. "You guys actually have a TV?"

"This place is a pit," She fingered the fringed edge of the bedspread. "Can you catch crabs from linen?"

"Jeanne."

"I'm asking because there was this girl I knew back

home—back in New York, I mean—who said she got this rancid case of crabs from some sheets she bought at the Salvation Army. What?" asked her sister, when she became aware that Bailey only stood there with crossed arms and a stony expression. "I didn't think you could. I think she got them from this asshole she was seeing. He was fucking around on her something fierce. What?" she repeated. "I'm not talking about *me*."

That particular thought had crossed Bailey's mind for a moment. "I was about to go to bed."

Jeanne flopped over onto her stomach—was she supposed to do that?—propped her head up on her elbow, and crunched her eyebrows together. "Wow," she said at last. "You don't know how to lie at all, do you? Not the big ones," she added, seeming smug at having made Bailey's jaw drop open. "You do okay with those. It's the little ones you have trouble with. Like, *I was about to go to bed*, or *Oh, did I forget to give you my new cell phone number?* Or maybe, *I'm happy about your baby*." She rolled back over again, swung her legs over the edge of the bed, and looked ready to heave herself up and out of the room. "I'll go."

Bailey wanted to bend herself over and give her own ass a good, swift kick. How was it that Jeanne always, always, always managed to make her feel like the wickedest stepsister, hell-bent on keeping Cinderella from her glass Ferragamos? "Jeanne!" she protested. It was obvious that no matter how much Bailey wanted to get out of the room, they had to talk. She slowly perched on the edge of the bed. "I'm not unhappy about your baby!"

Anything it was possible to roll, Jeanne rolled. Her shoulders, her head, her eyes, her jaw in a grinding circle. "Do you remember that first play you did after you moved to the city?" she asked. "I don't remember the name. It was a one-act workshop in some basement somewhere. About people on a subway. It smelled like piss. The basement, I mean, not the play." Bailey didn't remember the name of the play, but she had an embarrassed memory of the piece, an artistic mess that was supposed to have been stitched together from actual interviews with homeless people who rode public transit all day during the winters, to keep warm. She'd played the only non-homeless role in the entire damned thing. "And you remember that review that got you so upset?"

How in the world did Jeanne come up with these things? Even a reminder of that review had sent Bailey into a deep flush of embarrassment. "Yes," she admitted.

"What was it?" Jeanne assumed a snotty, patrician *Masterpiece Theatre* voice as she more or less quoted the reviewer. "In the role of the social worker, Ms. Bailey Rhodes . . ."

". . . Is not unpleasant." Bailey spoke the words along with her sister. Odd, how no matter how far in the past that one review had been, it still had the power to sting. Her spine slumped a little. She looked at her sister, ashamed.

"You were so mad after that! I thought you were going to move back home, you were so upset."

"I was thinking about moving home! Everyone else got great notices in that review, and that one little line felt like a slap in the face!" Bailey leaned on the bed, remembering it like yesterday.

"Yeah, and then we came to see the play that night and I came backstage and told you how fantastic you were. Remember?" Of course Bailey remembered. It was one of the last times she could remember Jeanne doing something nice without some kind of ulterior motive.

"Yeah, well, mostly that was because after you'd made such a fuss I was afraid you'd make good on your threat and I'd have to give up the bigger bedroom after I'd gotten all my stuff moved in. I would've said it if you'd stunk." said Jeanne. As if sensing she'd shot down the altruism theory, she reached out and put her hand over Bailey's own. "But you didn't. You were good. Seriously. Both Mom and I thought so."

Strangely, Bailey didn't at all mind the confession. She probably would have done the same in Jeanne's place. "Saying I'm not unhappy about your baby isn't the same as saying I'm happy," she conceded. "That's why you're bringing it up."

"Yeah."

She'd been checkmated by someone who barely knew the game. Taylor could wait. This issue had to be attended to. "I'm a rotten sister."

"Oh, don't get all drama queeny about it. I was saying it because . . ."

"I know it sounds dramatic, but I mean it." She had been a totally crappy sibling. Thinking back on all those messages she hadn't returned mortified her further. What if Bailey had talked to her sooner? Could she have done something before it had gotten this far? "I've said the wrong things. I haven't been there for you. I don't keep in touch."

"You eat my pecan log rolls," Jeanne prompted.

"I eat your pecan log rolls. I yelled at you about Mom for no reason this afternoon."

"You aren't happy about my baby."

There was a certain sadness in Jeanne's voice that didn't simply tug at Bailey's heartstrings, but swung from them like Notre Dame's famed hunchback. "I *am* happy about your baby. Really." When she looked into her sister's eyes at that moment, all she could see there was raw hope. "I just—it's all so *big*, Jeanne. You, having a baby. A real *life*, half you and half this other guy. The major decision of my day is what bagel I'm going to get with my coffee in the morning, not what development skill I have to teach that day to the life I've brought into the world. Here you are doing something *enormous* like having a baby and raising it and possibly screwing it up for good, like Mom did with us." She hoped that Jeanne wasn't taking that the wrong way. There seemed to be a certain wry humor to the way she pulled her lips to the side, though. "I'm scared for you. It makes me say crazy things I don't really mean."

"Me, too," said Jeanne in a small voice. "I'm scared for me, too."

She looked at her older sister with such big, wide, frightened eyes that Bailey couldn't help but reach out and brush the hair from her eyes. The eyebrow piercing was gone, she noticed, vanished with the kohl and the mouth-bruising lipstick. Even her sister's dark hair was betraying its mousy roots. More than anything, the sight of that quarter-inch of light brown convinced Bailey that Jeanne must have been anticipating this transformation for some time, well before she threw herself on the mercy of the aunts. Sometime in the last few weeks, Jeanne had somehow decided on her own that a change was what she needed. Bailey had been the one person to whom she'd attempted to reach out—and what had she done? Turned her back. Shunted all Jeanne's calls to Chandra, who reduced the pleas to scribbled notes on pink message pads. And when Jeanne had uprooted herself and returned home as the absolute last resort, Bailey had resented every moment of it. "Hey," she said, trying to be comforting. "It'll be all right."

Jeanne sank into the hug she offered like a small child who'd exhausted herself with crying. Small wonder she indulged in sweets and in allowing herself to be pampered like a kid—these were the last months she'd spend being someone's niece and child, instead of being someone else's parent. "I know. I don't mind being . . . an unwed mother."

Bailey responded to the little tremble of her sister's lower lip with a squeeze. "Hey, you chose the right family to do it in. You've got one aunt who'll pamper you and the baby with food, another aunt who'll . . . well, I don't know what good Bits will do you, but she'll do a lot of it."

Jeanne chuckled slightly. "I thought she'd be the one to blow her top. Even more than Mom."

"Well, Mom! You can't do any wrong with Mom, it seems. I mean," she added hastily, in case that sounded wrong, "with her, being an unwed mother validates her liberal values. If the father had been a bum from the streets, Mom would have been telling everyone how at least *one* of her daughters was able to cross socio-economic boundaries in making a love match."

"Hah. She would've been happier if the baby's father had been black or Hispanic," Jeanne said.

"Or gay."

"Or if I'd been a lesbian and had given myself a turkey baster baby." Jeanne wiped her nose on the back of her wrist. "Instead we both had to go and get mixed up with straight white guys."

Almost reflexively, Bailey said, "I'm not seeing Steve anymore."

"I know." She did? Bailey's arm drifted away from Jeanne's shoulders. "Bubble told me last week. That's okay, I didn't like him."

"Apparently you weren't alone in your opinion." The comment came out as a mutter.

"Oh, no offense, but wasn't he like, fifty?"

For all her sister's helplessness, Bailey couldn't help but feel a stab of irritation. It was of the sort she felt when, after she'd changed her hair color or style, people came out of the woodwork to tell her that they liked it so much better the new way. A milk-chocolate compliment covering a thorny center, in other words. "He was balding a little, but he was only a couple of years older."

Now that she was on a topic other than herself, Jeanne had more or less completely recovered her composure. "I didn't mean the balding thing. I'm not sure I ever noticed, actually." She wrinkled her nose. "Ew. No,

I meant that he always seemed more like a dad than a boyfriend."

Bailey felt she knew what her sister was blathering on about. Right from the beginning, Steve had always treated Bailey like a fixer-upper. He lectured. He pointed out her faults and explained how they could be solved by paying attention to economic theories. She knew exactly what Jeanne meant, but at the same time, she didn't care to hear about it. "Having a boyfriend isn't all about going to clubs and. . . ." She let the words trail off, suddenly realizing she didn't have a damned clue about what her sister might or might not consider an appropriate date. "It's not all fun. There's responsible times, too."

"I know that." Jeanne's superior tone seemed to imply that she'd performed a coup and taken over the role of Older Sister. "But it's supposed to be fun, too. It's supposed to make you feel good. Not embalmed." When Jeanne put an arm around her, Bailey realized with some shock that now she was the one being consoled. "Anyway, Taylor's better for you."

"Excuse me?" Bailey pulled back, wary. "What's Taylor got to do with anything?" Jeanne was now bestowing upon her the same skepticism that Bailey earlier had given her; she crossed her arms and assumed a mask of slyness. "We're not . . . !"

"I'm not *stupid*."

"No, but. . . ." It was impossible to resist the intrigue of her sister's comments. "Why do you think . . . I mean, what is there that makes you. . . ."

"Oh, come on." Jeanne flopped back on the bed again, making herself comfortable with one of the thin pillows that had yellowed so badly it was visible through the pillowcases. "All you have to do is look at him."

"Really?" Suddenly Bailey was back in tenth grade and in her New Jersey bedroom, putting on pink lipstick at her junior vanity and talking to Jeanne while she played with her stuffed toys on the bed behind her. "You think he likes me?" Before her sister could produce a reply Bailey wasn't certain she wanted to hear, Bailey held up a hand. "No, wait. Do you think he likes me, kind of like the way I like popcorn at the movies, or do you think he *likes* me?"

"How much do you like popcorn at the movies?" Jeanne cringed and shrieked when Bailey pounced to swat her. "No, no," she said between laughter, once the feint had passed. "I think he likes you. And I know you like him. So what's the big deal?"

"Big deal?"

"Yeah, why aren't you two . . . ?" Jeanne waggled her eyebrows with meaning. "Single man. Single woman. I mean, this cheap motel alone is *mucho* classier than ninety-eight percent of my dates. You're all dressed up and smelling good. You should be down there right now. Oh, but wait," she added, when Bailey opened her mouth. "I forgot. You're *tired*. You're *going to bed*. Maybe I should let you get your *beauty rest*."

Jeanne pretended she was going to rise from the bed, but she obviously knew she wasn't going to be allowed to progress far. Bailey had been thoroughly out-bluffed. "Whatever." She regarded her younger sister with pretend distaste. "You suck."

"No, *you* suck."

"You."

"So you haven't done it with him yet?" Bailey's eyes flew wide open at her sister's suggestion. "He looks like the kind who's big into oral. Giving oral, I mean. I hope you're ready for that?"

"Jeanne Rhodes!" A shiver tingled up Bailey's spine. "How can you *tell*?"

"Oh, you can," she replied, cultivating an air of mystery. "I mean, that Steve guy? Totally not into it, I bet. He looked like the type who would give it a go because all the books told him he should. But you could tell he wouldn't be into it. Am I right?"

Visions of Dippy Birds flew unbidden into Bailey's mind. "None of your business," she announced. Then, as a consolation prize for everything she'd learned from her sister so far, she added, "But yes."

When she stood from the bed, she felt light-headed. Giddy, even. "Go get 'im, tiger!" Jeanne growled. "Rawrrr!"

"Jeanne," said Bailey in all seriousness. "Don't."

"Fine," she grumped, throwing herself back down on the bed. "But if you're going to go do the slow seduction thing, can I borrow your cell and call some people back in New York? I won't use up all your minutes, I swear. I mean, God, I didn't think it could get more boring than Crestonville. When we get back, the aunts and I are going to have a serious talk about getting cable or the Dish Network or *something*, because. . . ." Jeanne's miniature rant was interrupted when Bailey's phone landed on the bed. "It's cute!" she cooed. Then, right before Bailey closed the door behind her, she heard an enthusiastic, "Good luck!"

Right. So Jeanne thought Taylor liked her, Bailey thought to herself, trying to ignore all the visions of steamy oral sex her sister had conjured. It was a good thing that a breeze was stirring the night air, because she needed a cooldown. The motor court was silent and dark; a solitary light over the Maple Leaf's office at the far end cast long shadows over the parking lot and the tiny circle of bricks, now cemented over, where the famous duck pond had once stood. Bailey's excitement quickened as she stepped past first her own window, and then the one beyond. Behind that window's drapery of yellow-orange plastic thicker than a shower curtain and more like a hanging giant slice of American cheese, Bailey caught a quick glance of a shadowed head, enormous in proportion, covered all over in bumps. Bubble in her curlers, she guessed.

After that came Bits and her mom's room, where the window had been darkened. Her mother had been exhausted after the long trip. She easily could see Bits insisting on an early night. And then, a few feet farther down, where beyond another of the Kraft Slices curtains, glowing orange from the light within, lay Taylor's room.

The sound of metal against concrete brought her hastening steps to a quick halt. Someone was outside. In the dimness, silhouetted against the window, she saw someone lean forward. Another scrape followed—the sound of a chair being dragged over the walkway. When they'd checked in, Bailey had noticed a number of ancient sun chairs, the sort that would be painful to sit in after baking in the sun, with perforations in vague shapes of flowers for design. Was Taylor outside, looking at the sky as he did at home?

Was he maybe waiting for her? Hoping she'd venture out of her room to his?

There was one way to find out. Bailey smoothed down the front of her dress and pretended to stretch, acting as if she'd stepped out of her room for a little breath of evening air. From the way the dark shadow occupying the lawn chair turned in her direction, she knew she'd caught its attention. "Hi," she said, once she'd sauntered closer. "I thought I'd come visit."

Only when she'd come within a few feet of the person did she realize that the silhouette didn't match Taylor's at all. Where his head was broad and rectangular and his hair thick, this figure had a narrow, oval skull with hair swept back in a . . . oh, shit. Set wave. "Bailey Rhodes, don't you turn around. I want to have a word with you," announced her Aunt Bits.

Honestly, the woman's voice could cut through the night like a surgical scalpel through silk. "What're you doing out here?"

Bailey must have sounded more harsh than surprised, because Bits instantly went on the defensive. "Of course I'm out here! I have a perfect right to be out here! Goodness. Why shouldn't I be out here? The idea."

"Sorry." Beyond Bits lay the warm glow of Taylor's

room. He was in there, right this minute, lying on his bed or sitting in the sticky vinyl chair. Maybe he was contemplating paying her a visit. "I thought you were Taylor. Since you're in a chair outside his room," she pointed out. Did she sound as stupid as she felt?

"I suppose I am, but gracious, child. It's a free country." When Bits settled back, the chair bounced slightly. The way her outline bobbed up and down made Bailey feel slightly anxious. "Besides, Taylor and I were having a good talk a moment ago."

"About me?" she squeaked.

"Good heavens, girl, have you burned out every bulb in your chandelier? Of course it wasn't all about you! Not everything's about you! Honestly . . . you've always been a self-centered child, doing what you want without any care for your poor mother or the rest of your family, God knows, and always dominating the conversation. . . ."

Given the chance, Bits could have hosted several episodes of *Jerry Springer* entitled *Wild Nieces Gone Wrong!* and never once give any of the guests a chance to talk. Bailey didn't take any of her carping personally, however. If there was anything she knew, it was that Bits regarded complaints the way most people regarded chewing gum after the flavor had run out—as mere exercise for the jaw. Interrupting was only doing her a favor. "Yeah, dominating the conversation. Hard to know where I got that one from," she said, not without a touch of irony. "What were you two talking about?" Would Taylor know to take anything Bits might say about her with a grain of salt? No, strike that. A whole ocean full?

Although it was too dark to see her aunt, Bailey could imagine the pinched, prim expression on her face simply from the way she spoke. "You make it sound as if I dragged him out of bed to talk his ear off!" she protested. "As a matter of fact, I stepped out of the room and walked over to that pit they call the office—honestly, Bailey, I hope you washed your hands after you were in there, though there's nothing wrong with that room a bucket of kerosene and a few good matches couldn't solve—and then when I came back with a can of Coke, he was sitting in the chair and called out. He thought I was someone else, though I can't imagine who. He's an odd one, that Taylor Montgomery." Clichéd as she knew it was, Bailey's heart fluttered a little at that information. Had he hoped Bits was Bailey? The thought that Taylor could confuse for Bailey a scrawny woman wearing a shapeless dress was slightly appalling, but she clung to the notion he'd hoped it might be her. A shadow from within Taylor's room briefly flickered over the curtain, darkening its yellowy intensity for a second. "Anyway, what are you doing out here?" asked Bits, suddenly suspicious. She still bounced back and forth in her chair as if trying to burn off energy.

"I . . . I . . ." Now was not the time to start stammering. Bailey had a perfect right to be out here, after dark. "I thought you wanted company."

"Hardly!" The word exploded like a bullet. "I know why you're here."

Bailey froze at the accusation. Had she been obvious? Too obvious? Is that why Taylor was shut into his room, with her aunt standing guard like . . . what was the name of that dog that guarded the gates of hell, in Greek mythology? The one with three heads? Not that Bits had three heads. One was quite enough. Oh, hell, she realized in a panic. Taylor must think she'd been throwing herself at him. She was a Slutty McHo, the kind of girl she'd always scorned for flashing her cleavage at the bars and clubs, and he'd appointed Aunt Bits to fend her off. "You do?"

"Of course I do. I'm not blind!" What could Bits see in this darkness? Regardless, Bailey folded her arms over her breasts in case there was too much of them visible. "You're trying to get away from that sister of yours. We saw her go into your room. Honestly, Bailey, when are you going to grow up and accept your sister for who she is and not for who you want her to be?

Now, sit down. I want to talk to you." She saw her aunt's silhouette lean forward and pat a chair next to her.

To say that she was relieved was an understatement. She let her breasts loose from the hold she'd placed on them and sidled to the area where she thought the chair might be. Its back felt rusted; flakes of paint crumbled beneath her grip as she lowered herself down. "Cerberus," she said, finally remembering the three-headed dog's name.

"What? There's no call for that kind of language. Now Bailey, you and I have to have a serious talk here. It's about your sister."

"Bits, Jeanne and I. . . ."

She had been all set to reassure her aunt that she hadn't been running away from her sibling, but Bits apparently already had a speech prepared. "Sisters should be there for each other," she announced. "Sisters take care of each other. That's what they're for." Was it Bailey's imagination, or was there a touch of defense in Bits's voice? She spoke as if she were trying to justify something. "I've always taken care of Bubble, God knows. The woman would be helpless without me. You've seen her. She's no Mensa member. Hoo! She probably thinks Mensa is what used to happen to her once a month before The Change!"

Bailey, who had other ideas about which sister took care of which, cleared her throat. The odds of her entering Taylor's room while her aunt sat outside were roughly comparable to her winning the state lottery, so she settled back and prepared for a long, grim wait. "Jeanne and I are fine, Bits. Tonight, anyway."

Bits acted as if she hadn't heard. "I took Bubble in to my house after Mother married that—well. You know the story."

"Barely!" she exclaimed. "This Francisco affair isn't something that any of you have been exactly forthcoming about!"

"Exactly my point," said Bits.

"You're not making sense."

"I always make sense. You're not listening," snapped Bits. Hurt, Bailey leaned back, refusing to rise to her aunt's bait. "Sisters stick together. They're there for each other in rough times. They keep each other's secrets. *That* is my point."

"You three have entirely too many secrets," Bailey accused. When Bits didn't immediately respond, she knew she'd hit home. She sat there for a moment and listened to the tree frogs' songs filling the night air, before speaking again. "*The X-Files* was less complicated than you." Realizing her aunt might not get the reference, she tried another. "You're like the freakin' CIA."

"You don't know what we've been through." Bits's voice was, for once, small. Tiny, even.

"You're right, because none of you all will tell me. What secrets are you talking about now? Is it about Mom?" Bits's stillness signaled that she was on the right track. "It's about Mom, then. What is it? Is it something the doctors told you that they didn't tell me? Is it about the fact she's gone absolutely crazy?"

"Polly is not crazy," said Bits, rebounding to normal.

"Oh no? Then that's not what you and Bubble wanted to warn me about last week when I first got home?"

"What in the world are you going on about?"

"She's collecting rocks, Bits!" Bailey's words were coming out louder than she'd intended; she modulated her volume so that she wouldn't be heard screeching like a madwoman herself, up and down the hills. "She's got a mania for rocks. There's buckets full of them in the truck. Before that it was tennis balls. What's it going to be next?"

"That's not crazy," said Bits.

"Don't minimize this!" Torn between anger and sadness, Bailey didn't bother to attempt hiding the shaky way her words were coming out now. They burned raw in her throat. It felt like she could choke on them.

"Keeping it a secret isn't going to make it go away! You're not doing her any favors!"

"You think your mother's crazy because she's collecting rocks?"

Why wasn't Bits understanding anything she said? Was the old woman honestly that stubborn? "She's not the same! And . . . it's frightening me."

The last three words she spoke came out as barely a whisper that trailed off into the night and disappeared. In the dark, she could almost pretend she'd never said them. "Don't be stupid," said her aunt after a long pause. The words felt like a light slap. "Of course she's not the same. She's had a stroke."

Bits couldn't use that as the conclusion to every argument! "That—!"

"Your grandmother died of a stroke." The words silenced any protest on Bailey's lips. "Several strokes, all in quick succession. That husband of hers—Francisco—should have taken her to the hospital after the first of them, but he didn't do anything until it was too late." Without benefit of enough light to see Bits's expression, it was impossible to tell how she intended for Bailey to receive this information. But she sounded angry. "How do you think it felt for your mother to know she was being afflicted with the very same thing that killed hers? She was scared to death inside! Of course that's going to change her!"

Her aunt seemed to require some kind of answer, but Bailey was so confused that she could only stammer, "I—I didn't know Grandmother Whigfield died of a stroke."

"Well, stop thinking about your own problems for once, and think about how it felt for your poor mother when it happened. To suffer from the same ailment, after all she'd been through! After all she'd sacrificed! If anyone has the right to act a bit eccentric, child, it's your mother. You leave her be!"

Once again, Bailey had hit that infamous invisible

wall of protection that the Whigfield sisters had erected for themselves. Face first, as usual. Softly, she said, "I know you're trying to protect Mom."

"I always have!" Bits rocked and rocked in the chair.

"I know. I know." Bailey wished there were something she could say to heal whatever was hurting Bits at that moment; she knew there was something bothering her. "Because she took care of you?"

"You don't know everything she did for us." The chair's metal frame creaked, protesting at the rough treatment. "You don't know."

It sounded as if Bits was talking into her knuckles. "I know how much she gave up to take care of you and Bubble when you were younger," Bailey told her, reaching out. It took a moment to find Bits's knee, and her aunt flinched as if unused to displays of physical affection outside of the arrival and departure lanes of the Richmond International Airport, but she stopped her tireless rocking at least.

"That was just the beginning." Bits sighed as if she had more to say.

Bailey waited. Despite her hand on her aunt's knee, she felt alone in the dark. Sad, too. With Steve or with other lovers in the past, she hated those disembodied conversations that took place in the blackness, after the curtains had been drawn and the lights turned out. Secrets seemed to gain a significance they didn't deserve, without benefit of the light. Spoken at night, they seemed so unreal, so dreamlike, and yet so important— but for Bailey there was always the fear that when the sun returned, all those personal thoughts whispered into the gloom might be exposed as the trivialities she feared they might be. "Tell me, then," Bailey whispered at last.

"I promised." Bits's voice cracked with emotion. "I promised I never would."

"Promised what?" Again, she rammed against that

transparent blockade. Bits mashed her fingers as she planted her elbows on her knees. When she moved her hand to her aunt's back, Bailey could feel how difficult it had become for her to breathe. In shuddering spasms, Bits's chest expanded and contracted while she tried to fight off tears. "Promised who?"

"Promised your mother!" Bits snapped. If she wanted to take out her frustrations on the closest person possible, fine. Bailey didn't give a damn about that. She waited, knowing Bits's nature abhorred a conversational vacuum. At last she straightened up, trying to shrug off her niece's hand like she might a horsefly. "This is all ancient history. It's over and done. We should never have come on this trip."

They were back to the beginning again, returned to Bits's Cassandra-like prophecies of doom. "Why?" Bailey insisted. "You keep saying that, over and over. What happened?" Bits's muscles tensed and relaxed beneath her fingers; the old woman was shaking her head. "What in the world could be so bad?"

"Your grandmother's funeral!" The words came out as a hiss, so vicious that Bailey nearly shrank back. She waited for another long pause until Bits began talking again. "Not funeral. Memorial service. That—that *man* had her cremated immediately after she passed."

"What's wrong with cremation?" Bailey asked.

"Nothing. But he didn't even let us have the service first! Mother used to keep a list of all the hymns she wanted at her funeral. When I was a girl, she kept it in the family Bible, tucked right in the front, in case something happened to her." Bailey found the notion a little morbid, but she kept her mouth shut. "It had Scripture readings, too. All our lives we knew that she had very specific intentions for after she passed. Very specific intentions," she repeated quietly. "And that man wouldn't let us into the house. We couldn't get the list. And none of us could remember what was on it. Oh, Lord, I need a tissue."

"I can—"

"I've got one right here." In the dark, it was difficult to tell where *right here* might be, but from the way Bits moved around, Bailey suspected the tissue was stuffed down the front of her dress, in that handy storage area that both her aunts seemed to make of their breasts. "Oh, my," she sniffed. Impatient as she was to see where this might be leading, Bailey kept quiet until at last Bits calmed down enough to keep talking. "Your poor mother," she said, this time putting her hand on Bailey's knee, after a little fumbling. "By the time she and you girls got down here, after we phoned with the news, it was all over."

"The service? Because I don't remember going to a service."

"Not the service, girl. The cremation! Your poor mother didn't have a last chance to look at our mother in repose. Well, none of us did, really, but at least Bubble and I saw her when she left the house, living down the street as we did. All that your mother had to remem-

ber her by, by the time you all got down here, was a little tub of ashes sitting on a table at the Macon Family Funeral Home, and a truckload of bad memories." Much as she didn't appreciate what she remembered of Grandmother Whigfield, and as much as she disliked what she'd learned in the past week, Bailey couldn't help but feel stabs of sorrow for what her mom must have felt, on coming home, that week—everything irrevocably changed, and helpless to do anything about it. How angry she must have been. "We'd all lost someone by then, of course. I'd lost John—he was such a good man, Bailey, you would have loved him, too—and your mother had lost your father. I suppose even Bubble had lost someone, though he wasn't dead. I wish he had been. I reckon that sounds wicked to you. But I wish he'd died instead of Mother, I honestly do." There was a flurry of motion as her aunt wiped her nose once again. "I'm sure your mother wishes the same, since it's all his fault you had to move to New Jersey."

Talk about your *non sequiturs*. All Bailey could do was blink and ask, "What?" One thing didn't seem to follow from another. "What did he have to do with us moving?" Her aunt wouldn't answer. "You're not making sense. How in the world did this guy I don't remember seeing make us move to Jersey?"

Bits's fingers were as spindly as bird bones, but when they dug into the flesh above Bailey's knee, they brought tears to her eyes. What was going through her aunt's head? What was causing the struggle within? After what seemed like an eternity, Bits gasped out, "I promised your mother. We both did."

"Promised her what?" Bailey was desperate to know.

Was her aunt crying? The one person she knew who was always tougher than old leather and harder than nails? "I can't," she said, breathing heavily. "We keep each other's secrets."

"Then let me help," Bailey breathed. She was afraid that anything above a sigh might counteract her aunt's weakening resolve. "Let me help you keep it."

"But Polly. . . ."

"She'll never know that I know," Bailey promised. "Nobody will."

She reached for and squeezed her aunt's hands, and felt those skinny fingers curl around her own with a strength that would have surprised her, had they not moments before been shredding the flesh from her thigh. "You have to promise," she whispered.

"I promise."

Then her aunt spoke. When it was over, several minutes later, and Bits had risen from her chair and retired to her room, sad and hunched, Bailey thought she understood a little better.

She sat in the chair for a while, her head raised to the heavens beyond the overhang. Dark, streaky clouds filled the sky overhead, making the world feel like a much smaller place. Something about Bits's tale had stirred a feeling in her . . . what was it, exactly? She felt as if time had doubled over upon itself, the way one fold of her aunt's skirt could touch a spot further along the hem and reduce the space between them to nothing. She felt twelve once again, watching with sleepy eyes the moon setting behind the house in Crestonville; she felt twenty-seven and stranded at a cheap motel in the middle of nowhere, tired and wanting something more for herself; she felt sixty, looking back at how she'd spent her years so far and wondering what her health might let her do in the future.

What would she do? Now? Here? That was the question.

She stood up and crossed to the door nearby. The chair beneath her scraped when she shifted her weight. A second later, the light went off in Taylor's room, causing her to hesitate. She had been about to knock. Had he gone to sleep? No, he couldn't have.

She had raised her hand when the door suddenly swung open, its hinge emitting a treble cry. Taylor raised his hand to the top of the door's frame and leaned against it, not at all surprised to see her standing outside. Outlined in the dim light from the bathroom, she could see that his chest and feet were bare; his Levis hung from his hips. Did he know the effect that all that skin and muscle was having on her? "I could hear you two talking outside the window," he said, answering the question she hadn't asked.

"Everything?" She felt frightened. She shouldn't feel frightened, she realized.

He shook his head. "Just the voices." He cleared his throat. "I have to know," he said, his voice blending in with the hum and buzz of the distant tree frogs. "I have to know you didn't come out of obligation, or because you felt you owed me something."

Maybe she wasn't frightened because of Taylor's tightly knitted frame of muscles and masculinity, she realized, or because she feared he would shake his head and not let her in. Maybe she was frightened at what she might want to do if she enjoyed what happened, once she walked through that doorway and let it shut behind them. "I didn't," she told him. "I came because I wanted to."

"No lies, no bluffing?" Dark as it was, his eyes never left hers for a moment. "Your friend Sidney told me you've got quite the reputation at work for being able to convince people you're something you're not."

"It's hereditary, apparently." Taylor didn't understand, but Bailey hadn't expected him to. "No bluffing," she told him. "Are you sure you want to take up with the daughter of a Whigfield girl? We're lethal to the ones we love."

"That's a risk I'm more than willing to take."

"Then let me in."

He paused for a moment, then stood upright and let his arm fall to his side before standing out of the way. She would be in those arms in a moment, she knew, and as new and as strange as they would feel around her, she hoped they would be somewhere she wanted to stay. "I'm glad you came," he whispered.

"I am, too," she replied, barely breathing. "Now, shut the door."

Chapter Twenty-two

Bailey didn't remember Ettleston Road being so hilly. She would have hated to be in any car trying to navigate its steep grades during a snow or ice storm; every time the truck's intermittent wipers erased the light drizzle speckling its windshield, she experienced a heart-stopping twinge, in case the two-lane winding road should suddenly dip too far, too fast.

Slow morning traffic had already reduced their trip through downtown Carverton to a crawl. Bubble and Bits, in particular, seemed amazed that their old home actually had a downtown. Carverton had long ago been an outpost of civilization where every day her mother had walked her younger sisters two miles to a schoolhouse that even in the 1950s was merely one room. It had been a town that at one distant time had consisted of Bailey's grandmother's feed and general supply store, a few scattered farms, and a handful of polite churches. In Bailey's memory, Carverton had existed as the dictionary definition of the sticks—smaller than Crestonville and with none of Crestonville's fabulous amenities, like a library or an actual fire department.

And now it was an oasis of subdivisions, strip malls, and shopping centers, of Macaroni Grills and Home Depots and Thai restaurants and national bagel chains, of Jiffy Lubes and Dunkin' Donuts and Old Navys. Its hundreds of streets, none of which shared with the original town any resemblance whatsoever, were clogged with commuters in SUVs and upscale imports, all attempting to reach their jobs in the city. Atlanta's sprawl had reached farther and farther with every passing year until it found Carverton within its grasp. It seized the small town and remade it into the image of every other American suburb, a maze of commerce and services where every corridor looked the same. Bubble's enjoyment of the scenery had been marred with constant doubt: "I *think* that's where the schoolhouse used to sit," she would say, pointing to a Panera Bread sitting next to a bridal shop and a Mexican grill.

"Don't be silly," Bits would tell her. "We haven't passed the post office."

"But is the post office the same post office we knew, dear?" Bubble pointed out, quite reasonably. "I *think* that's where the mill used to be."

"Your noodle's overcooked, old woman. This was all farmland, when we were here."

As the aunts squabbled like children beside her, Bailey could see her mother looking through the window in the front passenger seat, eyes shining and alert. She didn't say a single word until they reached the foot of Ettlestone Road, an incline too steep to anchor more than a single Shell station at its bottom. Pine trees lined both sides, and although the asphalt had been refreshed sometime within the last year and looked almost new, Bailey could almost see it as it had been decades before, before the cookie-cutter businesses had surrounded it on every side. "It looks the same." Her mother's words should not have been audible over the sounds of the engine or the tires running over the fresh pavement, but Bailey could hear every syllable.

She remembered this roller-coaster ramble of ups and downs where the road climbed in fits and starts up the mountain's side; Bailey remembered the thick pines towering high overhead and the banks of clay so red it looked like the earth was bleeding. The aunts seemed to have been overcome with the serenity of the mountainside as well, for they grew solemn and quiet, as if they'd moments before entered a church. Despite knowing that at the hill's foot lay a wasteland of traffic and illuminated signs, Bailey thought it was beautiful.

Yet there were warnings of the destruction to come. Where once had stood a house nestled in the pines, there was an empty lot overrun with massive tread marks and fallen tree trunks. Bubble touched Bits's arm at the sight of it. "Minnie English," she whispered, to be answered by Bits's shocked nod.

A few score feet up the road on the other side, another empty lot lay exposed, the blank red earth beneath seeming naked and cold where rain sprinkled atop it. "Do you remember?" Bits asked, holding a hand to her mouth. She had gone pale; she looked old. Bubble nodded in rejoinder.

A bulldozer had been parked outside another home, ready to reduce it to memory. Farther up the hill were ghost houses, abandoned and forlorn, their doors boarded over and their windows dark and unmoving, like eyes of the sightless. "Up and over this next hill, to the left." Bits leaned forward and addressed Taylor in the soft tones of a mother afraid to waken her children from their sleep. Passing house after deserted small house did feel like a dream. Bailey couldn't for the life of her remember what any of these houses had looked like when she was younger. She couldn't remember who lived in any of them, or what cars had parked in their drives. She did know, however, that what had been here was about to be lost for good. The lots would be filled with large, luxury homes five times the size of the original houses. The families who had lived and thrived and argued and lost here would be forgotten all at once. If she'd postponed this trip, her family wouldn't be witness to the final few days of one of the last remaining traces of Carverton as it once was.

"Here we are." At least Taylor's voice was the one firm foundation on a mountainside where everything seemed to be slipping away. His words broke the spell holding all the women in its grasp. They shifted in their seats and began unbuckling their belts as he pulled in front of Bits's old house. Bits unfolded from her purse a plastic rain cap that she arranged over her hair before fastening the crinkly ties under her chin.

Like the others, the house had been surrounded by yellow tape warning them not to cross. After Bits had followed Bailey out of the truck's backseat and onto the spongy ground, she ignored the warning, lifted the tape, and stood beyond its perimeter, arms crossed. "Oh, my," said Bubble, joining her. "Someone added dormer windows."

"I don't like them," Bits pronounced, evaluating the house as if she were in the market to buy it again, rather than looking at a shell of a home with plywood boarded over the doors and strips of wood blocking the windows, where she hadn't lived in fifteen years.

"Oh, I do. Your second floor was always so dark."

"Well, you'll remember that John bought it from old man Henderson and finished the second floor himself before you moved in. It used to be nothing but attic. We didn't have a call for fancy dormers back then." For someone who had been so apprehensive about this trip, Bits sounded brisk and matter-of-fact about the sights. Until, that is, she added with a sigh, "Poor John."

Taylor, standing in the driveway next to Bubble with his arms folded over his broad chest, turned to her and called out, "Exactly how true is that Whigfield curse thing?" Bailey couldn't help but crack a smile.

Jeanne, standing beside her next to the truck, had heard the comment as well. "So how'd it go with you two last night?" she murmured. "Good?"

"I'm not at liberty to say." Bailey was at her most lofty with the statement. The words were practically zeppelins of dignity and decorum.

"Bullshit. Come on. Come *on*. Did he . . . ?" When Bailey teased her by raising her eyebrows to their highest peaks, Jeanne twisted in place and dug her elbow into her sister's ribs. "You know! Come on!"

He couldn't have heard them, but Taylor chose at that moment to swing around himself, his eyes searching the area behind him until after a few seconds he found Bailey again. The faintest of smiles that he shared with her was private. The wink he left before turning back to answer one of Bubble's questions was not. "Never mind," Jeanne said. "I think I've got the answer to that one, now."

"Just you hush," Bailey grinned.

"Where's Polly?" Bits whirled to see where her oldest sister might be and spied her still in the truck. "Polly, don't you want to get out and look?" she fussed, pulling the tape back up and performing a stiff-backed limbo underneath. "We came all this way for you, you know."

Bailey knew her mother could have gotten out of the car, if she'd wanted. Bits's old house wasn't what she'd come for. She'd never really lived there, like her sisters. She'd been a visitor at times, sleeping in Bubble's room while Bailey and Jeanne bunked in the pullout sofa in the den, but it wasn't this structure of timber and shingle that held any memories for her. She sat in the front seat of the car like an elderly queen of old on her litter: unmoving, regal in posture, her eyes seeing all.

Bits had described her to a tee last night, sitting on the motel verandah. *"She was always so strong, Polly. When Mother made a decision, Bubble and I always fell in line. But not Polly. If she didn't like something, she let Mother know.*

My, how they used to butt heads! You don't know how she could be when she was fierce. A will like iron, Mother used to say about her. She didn't mean it as a compliment. Mother never gave compliments."

But Bits was wrong. Bailey did know how her own mother could be. She'd watched her crusade, issue after issue, for nearly her entire life. Her mother had always seen the world as imperfect and strove to make it conform to her own high standards, letting nothing come between her and that iron will—at least, until the stroke. Even after then, though, barely speaking a word, hadn't she managed to make the entire family do what she wanted? Isn't that why they were here?

"I've had enough," said Bits. She walked back to the car.

"It's funny, isn't it?" Bubble asked, returning to the truck and wrinkling her nose against the fine drizzle. "It doesn't feel like we lived there. It's someone else's house." Like Lot's wife, she turned to look one more time. "Though I suppose it's nobody's house, now."

"How much of this do you remember?" Jeanne asked, as she and Bailey joined the mass trek to the truck.

Bailey's immediate instinct was to reply that so far she didn't recall much, if anything, of Ettleston Road. It wasn't true, though. The scent of pine that had assaulted her nostrils the moment the car doors had opened had been instantly familiar, more readily recollected than any perfume, more evocative to her nostrils than baking bread or cookies in the oven. All the pine-scented products in the world couldn't match the clean, brisk fragrance of those masses of coppery needles covering the ground. She remembered the lay of her aunts' house, though not its details. She remembered an Easter egg hunt held in the backyard, so steeply graded that it was dangerous to run across. She remembered the banks of clay, rich terracotta red in color, with sprigs of green adorning its top. "More than you, probably," she admitted.

"Nothing's familiar. I thought I would. I thought I'd be able to tell my baby about it."

Jeanne sounded so mournful that Bailey put a hand on her shoulders before they separated. "You can tell her about today. It's a great story. Five Little Whigfields, and How They Grew."

"Yeah." When Jeanne smiled, it was an unexpected ray of sunshine on a gloomy morning. "Yeah. I like that. Come on, Bubble. Let's get you into the truck," she announced. "Oopsie-daisy!"

Ettleston Road was already silent, save for the sound of birds and woodland squirrels rustling the branches, but once all the truck doors shut, Bits's voice still echoed in Bailey's head. *"I still remember how your mother looked, that day you all arrived. She got out of your old car—that beat-up junker we told her to get rid of for so many years."*

"The old Dart," Bailey had said.

"It could have been. I never knew cars. John would have known," Bits had sighed. *"She got out of that old car, and she was so tall and so angry. 'Take the girls inside,' she told Bubble. Then, when you all had gone in, she marched up the street. She hadn't unpacked or freshened up or anything, but she didn't care. She meant for me to follow along, of course. And the first thing she did was walk straight up to Mother's house and bang on the door."*

"I don't remember any of this."

"How could you, child? You were too young to understand anything that was going on."

"So what happened when she banged on the door?"

"Nothing. He wouldn't answer. Francisco knew he had an opponent in your mother. And of course he'd convinced Mother to change the locks a long time before, so she couldn't barge in. So she banged and banged, and made such a ruckus that eventually he came to one of the upstairs windows and threatened to call the sheriff on her."

"Oh my God." Totally sucked into the story, Bailey had gasped with shock. How was it that she never knew any of this until now?

Bits had nodded. "She was so upset about the will and the cremation—and not so much about the money, as far as the will went. But the things we'd grown up with. The furniture that had been our grandmother's, and the old photos, and the family Bible. He intended to keep it all, even when he didn't care for it and it wasn't worth anything. He wanted to spite us, because we'd been so against the marriage from the start."

"That's horrible!"

"I'm not ashamed to admit it, Bailey. I was afraid your mother might kill him that day. I wasn't the woman I am now, back then. I was nearly in tears, watching them go at it. I might not have liked Mother very much, but all that cater-wauling! I thought it was disrespectful of the dead." Bits had sighed heavily. "It ended when he threw one of Mother's vases out the window at her. It wasn't a valuable vase—not one of the Wedgwood. It wasn't even particularly pretty. Polly and I had saved up our pennies and given it to her as a Mother's Day present back in the days when your grandfather was still alive, so you know it couldn't have cost much. It was pink and covered with roses, though, and sat on her bedside table since we gave it to her. He picked it up . . . and chucked it out. Just threw it at her! It missed your mother by only a couple of feet. Well, it splintered into a million pieces on the drive and I did, too, at the sight." She had grown quiet for a moment, then, as if picturing the wreckage. "I don't rightly recollect what happened after that. They yelled some more, but Polly didn't stay long. I remember her telling him she wouldn't be at the service, because she was going back to Virginia. 'Good,' he yelled. Then I remember her dragging me back to the house, and the two of us putting cold water on our faces in the bathroom, and then all three of us trying all afternoon to pretend that nothing was wrong, so you girls wouldn't worry. It was the longest afternoon ever, waiting to go to the funeral home that night."

"But I don't remember a funeral," Bailey had said. She'd wracked her brain the entire time Bits had been speaking, trying to bring up the vaguest of memories that might match the events as Bits narrated them. She had kept coming up blank. "You'd think I'd remember a funeral."

"Of course you don't remember the service," Bits had told her. "That's because you didn't go."

Grandmother Whigfield's house was probably a mere seventy-five feet up the road from where Bits had lived with Bubble for so long. Mistiness hung over it like a shroud. From her bottomless handbag, Bits produced a wad of plastic that matched her rain cap, which she proceeded to unfold until it became a capelet that she draped over her shoulders. No one else bothered. The rain falling was so fine that it felt more like a cool cloud of fog than actual precipitation.

Jeanne and Bailey exited the backseats first, followed by the aunts. Taylor had already walked to the drive and, with a penknife he carried in his pocket, cut through its protective boundary. The separated lengths of yellow tape fluttered to the ground and lay there.

It was a house much like any other. Adorning the second story were small windows like those on many houses built before the second World War. Its shingles were covered with a tracery of scratches and dirt marks. Bailey could easily imagine them covered with ivy or whatever vine had once clutched to their surfaces. Like the other houses on Ettleston Road, the front and side doors had been boarded up. Someone had spray-painted the words GAS OFF on the front. Whatever trees had decorated the lot had been cut down and cleared, and whatever grass once grew there was long trampled to nubs. Bailey sympathized with Bubble—the house looked sad, and aged, and a mere skeleton of a former memory that Bailey could barely resurrect. Where had her grandmother's parlor been? She couldn't have picked it out had she tried. Jeanne walked around the front yard and to the side, as if trying to find anything that looked at all familiar.

The aunts, however, stood with reverence before their childhood home, acknowledging its special significance. With her foot, Bits traced a circle in the drive's grime. Was she seeing there a memory invisible to everyone else, of a pink vase broken and in shards? Bubble reached out and took her sister's hand, reassuring her with a pat and a squeeze. What memories did she relive, standing there?

"We tried to talk her out of it," Bits had said. Between them, the darkness seemed to take on weight, becoming a burden they both had to bear. "We told her that maybe he was grieving in his own way. Maybe he'd soften up and let us have a few keepsakes. All we really had were our old books and a few presents she'd given us through the years, but nothing of hers to remember her by. We didn't want anything valuable. We didn't care about the money in the bank, though there was precious little of that by the time Mother passed. We just wanted something personal. Anything, really. But Polly said no, that he'd never give in. Of course," she'd said, her voice changing, "she was right about that. After the service the next day, we never saw Francisco again. He didn't disappear or anything, mind you. But he never talked to any of us, or made any effort to get in touch, or to ask us if we'd like any of Mother's things. I don't even know what happened to them all. All those photographs, all her brushes, her clothing. Destroyed, probably. Or sold. He was a bastard. So your mother turned out to be right, as always, and I don't think she ever regretted what happened next."

"What happened?"

In the funereal mood, Bailey had almost forgotten about her mother until the moment she heard the last of the truck doors open. Taylor was there, helping her out of the front seat. Bailey's legs, which had felt rooted to the spot, found themselves moving to his side. "Mom?" she asked. "Are you going to be all right?"

Her mother nodded, then waved them off with her left hand. She knew what she was doing, as she had fifteen years before. Her steps in the direction of the house were slow, but not unsteady; she seemed to be taking her time to reach this long-awaited destination. She walked as if this, the first visit she'd made to her old home since the night before her mother's memorial service, was more difficult than the last.

"How about you?" Taylor murmured into Bailey's ear. "Are you all right?"

She let her hand on his forearm serve as reply.

"This is the part I'm not supposed to share." Her aunt sounded hurt. Wounded, almost.

"Tell me."

"Your mother would. . . ."

"She'll never know."

There was a terrible moment of silence when Bailey feared that Bits, seeing the precipice before her, would back away and not return. Then, slowly, the words came. "The service . . . it was supposed to take place the next morning. But there was a visitation at the funeral home that night. Though what people had to visit, I don't know. There wasn't a body to look at. Only an urn of ashes. It's not the same, somehow. When I pass. . . ." Her words trailed off and her grip on Bailey's hand grew tighter. *"You girls were asleep. Tuckered out. Your mother—I told her I didn't want Bubble to have any part in it, but she wanted us both to be there. We waited until after that man had driven off. He would have skipped the funeral home and even the service if he could, you know. But there were important people due to come. The Mayor. A few of the town councilmen. Some businessmen. Mother had friends, I'll say that much for her. He probably thought if he put on a good act, he could get them to invest in one of his schemes."*

"And?"

"Well." Bits took another long pause to compose herself. *"Polly made Bubble stand by the drive, in the shadows, to*

*keep a watch on the road. I stood by the side door, in case
something happened. We were both scared. So scared."*

"It's okay," said Bailey, when Bits gulped down a sobbing
noise.

*"It wasn't then. Polly had a pair of Bubble's gardening
gloves, and made us wear something over our hands, too, in
case of fingerprints. I had a pair of proper kid gloves Mother
had given me for my seventeenth birthday, long before. I
think Bubble had to wear oven mitts. It turned out not to
matter. Neither of us went in that night."*

Standing in profile, he mother surveyed the house
with an expression impossible to read. It was neither
sad, nor angry, nor full of hatred. But her eyes were
alive. They were fierce. They were knowing. Her jaw
worked with some unknown emotion that made Bailey
clutch all the more tightly to Taylor. He, in return, held
her close.

Her mother knew exactly what she'd come for. She so
quickly leaned over that Jeanne, who had been walking
around from the back of the house, let out a worried yelp
and began hastening to her side. But their mother knew
what she was doing—she had wanted to pry from the
rich, clay-red mud a jagged stone.

*"She . . . she'd found a brick, earlier. Half a brick. I think it
was from the side of the road. And she stuffed it into a sock.
And when she swung it . . . it crashed through the back door
window with a terrible, terrible sound. I had to put my hands
over my ears. I was convinced that someone would have heard
it and that the police would be coming for us at any second,
and I begged her not to do it. But your mother knew what she
wanted. I thought she might slap me, if I didn't shut up, so I
quieted down in the end. Then she stuck her hand through the
hole and unlatched the door from the inside."*

"Mom?" Bailey had asked. "Mom broke into a house?"

"Which is why she didn't want you to know any of this!"
Bits had exclaimed. "She doesn't want you to think of her as a
thief. Or maybe she worried you'd think it was silly and make
fun of it. That would be worse, to her."

"What happened next?"

Bits had sighed, long and hard, as if trying to empty herself of guilt along with breath. "She went in by herself with only a flashlight, leaving us out there in the dark. Then the noises started. They weren't as loud as when she'd broken the glass, but they were just as terrible. I didn't know what to make of it. I never told Bubble this part, not that we've talked about it much since. Breaking in was bad. The noises your mother made were far, far more frightening."

"Like what?"

"Yelling. Screaming. It sounded as if she was fighting someone. There were several moments when I thought I should rush in and help, but I knew no one else was in there with her." No one, save ghosts, Bailey had thought to herself. No one, save ghosts. "It went on and on for what felt like forever. Things crashing. Enormous thumps. Oh. I shouldn't be. . . ."

"Go on," Bailey had said.

When her mother straightened up, able to balance herself without any assistance, both Bubble and Bits turned, suddenly aware that their elder sister was approaching. Bubble motioned for Polly to join them.

"Finally she came out. We honestly didn't want anything valuable, you see." Bits had seemed to be pleading for forgiveness—but who was Bailey to offer more than an ear? "None of us cared about the old-fashioned jewelry. We only wanted something small, to remember her by. That's all Polly brought out. Three very insignificant things that no one would ever notice were missing, one for each of us. She said she had to make it look like a real robbery, though, so that no one would ever suspect."

"Mom did this?" Bailey had asked, yet again. "Mom?"

"She hadn't unpacked. And of course, we'd hidden the car around the back of our house earlier, so we could say that the three of you had left after the argument earlier that afternoon. If it came up. All we had to do was get you girls from your bed and put you into the car. I don't think you woke up even when we carried you out, you were so tired. Your mother left *immediately, driving all the way back to Virginia overnight. I can't imagine what time you got home."*

She remembered. The puzzle pieces were falling into place. "It was morning," Bailey said with sudden certainty. "Very early morning. Because when I woke up, the moon was over the horizon. Big and fat, like a floured pie plate." She recollected that confused journey, now. "But why did we move? I don't understand."

"Well, Bubble and I had to go on to the funeral home after that and pretend that nothing had happened. It was the hardest thing I've ever had to do in my life with that man staring at us from across the room all evening. Then we went home and went to bed. But we weren't there for long. The sheriff came in the middle of the night, banging at the door like to raise the dead. I had to put on an act. 'What's the matter, officer?' I asked him, pretending to be sleepy, though Lord knows I hadn't caught a wink. He said there'd been an incident at my mother's house, and could we please come along, so it meant we had to get dressed again and pretend we didn't know what was happening."

"Did they suspect Mom?"

"I don't know. I don't think they did. That man hadn't made a lot of friends, and there'd been rumors around town that he kept Mother's money hidden under a mattress and that kind of nonsense. But Bailey." Bits's voice began to fail her a little. "That was the last time either of us went inside the house. The sight of it, when we walked in! There were books everywhere, and furniture on its end. She'd pulled out entire drawers in the kitchen and upstairs bedrooms and emptied them on the floor, and broken vases and glass and ruined half of the good china."

"The parlor . . . ?" Bailey breathed, remembering the stuffy room and how constrained it had always made her feel.

"Oh, the parlor got the worst of it! If Mother hadn't died of a stroke, she would have had a coronary, looking at the state of it! There was piano music everywhere, and figurines shattered, and she'd thrown the family Bible onto the floor. There *were photographs everywhere, like a thief had been looking in the backs of the frames for folded money. I didn't have to pretend to be shocked. I was shocked! But they didn't keep us for very long. I told them we'd been at the funeral home all evening and hadn't heard a thing, and Bubble said the same, so they let us go. Your mother, though."*

"What?"

"She was so frightened of being found out and getting us in trouble. She telephoned us the next day and told us she intended to put as much distance between herself and Carverton as possible. She had a fool notion that if the police ever got it into their heads that she had ruined Francisco's house, they might track her down to Virginia, but that going all the way North would be too much for them. We tried to calm her down, but she wouldn't have any of it. I think she wanted to punish herself."

"For what? For ruining Grandmother Whigfield's house?" Bailey had felt outraged at the thought. "She was striking out at everything that had held her back for all her life!"

"She was also trying to ruin everything your grandmother had owned so that man couldn't have any enjoyment of it," Bits had said, agreeing. *"And I don't think she could take the guilt. So I sold my house, and we bought yours, and you moved North before the spring."*

"She put herself in exile," Bailey had said, understanding. "For you two."

"Not just for us." Bits had sat back in her chair, tired. *"For you two as well."*

What was it like, giving up everything you had grown up knowing and loving, and replacing it with a single keepsake of the past? Bailey wanted to ask her mother that question, but she couldn't—not without betraying the secret that Bits had told her. It would have to be enough to know and to try to understand.

Her mother had long known what she wanted here in Carverton. For a moment, she regarded the stone lying in the flat of her hand. Then, once Jeanne had reached her side, she hauled back, swung, and let it fly in an arc across the morning sky. The stone landed with a sharp rap on a low pane of glass on the second story—very possibly the window through which her stepfather had argued with her, the last day she spent here. A hairline crack threaded its way across the glass.

"Good one, dear," said Bubble, applauding lightly.

"What's going on?" asked Jeanne. She seemed incredulous that her mother would be doing such a thing.

Bailey knew what she had to do. "Can you open up the back of your truck?" she asked Taylor. He, too, seemed a little confused, but without question he unlocked the gate and lifted up the tonneau. Bailey reached in, grabbed what she needed, and ran as quickly as she could to the Whigfield sisters' side. Slightly out of breath, she opened the top of the Charles Chips tin, revealing their contents. "Would these help?" she asked.

Her mother smiled. Without a word she reached in, selected a stone, and threw it at the house—this time much harder. She was rewarded with a tinkle of glass, this time, as one of the panes exploded and disappeared, leaving behind a jagged tooth. The next rebounded off the wood between the squares of glass, but the fourth connected and obliterated yet another pane. Bailey's heart swelled with pride. Her mom had worked hard to get so far.

"Your aim's not bad," said Bits, covering her mouth. "Try for the upstairs again."

"I wouldn't mind a go myself." Bubble helped herself to a rock. "Take that, Francisco!" she cried, letting it go. It landed into a blank garden bed with a thud. "I was aiming for his bedroom," she giggled.

In the meantime, her mother had let loose two more stones, each of which connected with their target. With every missing pane of glass, Grandmother Whigfield's house looked more and more tattered and beaten, less like a shell, and more like a ruin. "Good one!" said Bits, looking around in the dirt for something bigger to throw.

"You all have gone stark raving mad!" Jeanne marveled.

"It's a glorious lunacy." Taylor stood behind them, now, admiring their handiwork. "Let them have their fun."

"Here," said Bailey. She was reaching into the bin now and selecting rocks for her mother to throw, choosing those with the most heft that fit smoothly into the curve of the hand. With every new choice, her mother's smile grew more and more broad.

"I got one!" Bubble exulted, after her fourth or fifth throw.

"Fine, then. I want to try, too." Jeanne plunged her hand into the bin and withdrew a round of white quartz.

Amidst the chaos of glass tinkling and shattering, and the laughter of the other women, Bailey was surprised to find her mother refusing a stone she'd selected. Instead, she turned Bailey's hand upside-down and let the rock fall into her palm, then closed her daughter's fingers around it. "Now you," she said, looking into Bailey's eyes.

There was pride there, and the same fierceness Bailey had seen earlier. But now, in every line of her mother's face, in every fold of her flesh, in the very trembling she felt in her mother's limb, she could read thanks. "Me?" she asked.

"You," said her mother.

"Thanks." Her voice was uncertain. She looked over the stone as if not at all sure what to do with it.

"Thank you." Her mother closed her fingers over the rock's smooth surface. "Now, throw."

Was that the acknowledgment she'd craved all along? Odd, how unnecessary it seemed now, glad as she was to have it. There was only one way to respond. With a grin, Bailey turned and faced her grandmother's house, then let the rock fly. It thudded off a shutter, a few feet shy of its mark. "I'm not a great shot," she admitted, sorry that she hadn't contributed to the demolition.

Her mother laughed. It was a beautiful sound, accom-

panied by percussive strikes and the sounds of splinter-
ing glass. Warm inside, Bailey smiled and wondered, if
after they'd left and the bulldozers had done their
work, whether anyone would realize what had gone on
that morning. Very likely not. It would have to remain
one of the better memories of all their lives, that beautiful cacophony they'd all made on that drizzly morning
on a neglected Georgia mountainside.

Chapter Twenty-three

"You know what I think your first mistake was?" From the kitchen doorway, Sidney stuck the tip of her pinkie in the corner of her mouth and regarded Bailey with a critical eye. "When you agreed to let your aunt do your hair. You know?"

"And hello to you, too." Carefully, Bailey peered up in the direction of the kitchen ceiling. Somewhere above her head, her hair had been whipped, blended, sprayed, and teased into a towering confection large enough to house several families of birds as well as a colony of bees. Had it been colored pink or blue, children might have mistaken it for cotton candy. "Don't say that," she begged. "I couldn't look at it in the mirror. I had to fake it. I said my thank-you very sweetly and crawled away. Oh man, is it awful?" She lifted a hand to her head, then thought the better of touching anything. "No, don't tell me. I have to wear it all day."

"Why are you doing that . . . that thing?"

"What thing?" In response to the question, Sidney's neck shrank by about three inches as her shoulders rose. "I'm afraid to move!" Bailey explained. "I feel like I'm balancing the tower of Pisa on the top of my skull!"

"Hmmm. You're not wrong." Rising from where she had been waiting at the kitchen table took some doing, but Bailey's philosophy of the day was that if Las Vegas showgirls could make a living of prancing around with five-foot headdresses, she could live for the afternoon with an extra few inches of hair. "You're part of the sisterhood now, aren't you?" Sidney told her, watching her grope on the table for her purse. "The Sisterhood of Big Hair. Meetings every Tuesday night at the Elks Ladies Lodge. Bring your own Jell-O mold."

"If you're done?" It wasn't really a question. "Anyway, I know something you'll get more of a kick out of."

"What?"

Bailey couldn't help but smirk. This was going to be good. "Chandra!" she called up the stairs. Above, she heard the patter of little feet across the upstairs floor as her assistant made her way to the staircase. A moment later, a pair of ivory shoes with kitten heels appeared, followed by one of Chandra's pretty little print dresses, and then . . . well.

Bailey had to bite her lip at the sight of her friend's expression, which at first consisted of shock, then quickly developed into that barely concealed expression of glee that appears on the faces of those experiencing a vicious case of *schadenfreude*. "Hello, Annette Funicello!"

It was an unfortunate comparison—unfortunate, because it was true. With her suddenly expansive hairdo, expertly flipped at the points, Chandra resembled the most famous Mousketeer. Bailey couldn't at all say she was upset at the girl's obvious misery. "You look so cute!" she exclaimed, not meaning a word of it.

"Like a little dress-up doll!" exclaimed Sidney, reaching out to touch.

Chandra slapped her hand away. "It's itchy," she complained.

"Run and tell the rest of my family to meet us outside," Bailey told her in a no-nonsense voice. "Sid's here with the limo."

"For which you should thank both Euan and myself," said Sidney, *sotto voce*, once Chandra had gone on her not-so-merry way to deliver the message. Once they'd left the kitchen and secured the door behind them, she spoke normally again. "With all the budget cuts I made with the Munford's salary, I thought it would be a nice surprise for your folks. Especially your Aunt Bubble. Besides, the pageant coaches getting out of their stretch limo for the sixty-fourth annual Miss Watercress—"

"Tidewater," Bailey automatically corrected, helping Sidney up off the last of the steps and onto the walk that ran around the house.

"The sixty-fourth annual Miss Tidewater Lima Bean. . . ."

"Butter Bean."

"*Whatever*," Sidney said with meaning, cutting off any further corrections.

"Wait a minute," said Bailey, stopping abruptly. Too abruptly, it seemed because her hair threatened to keep on walking when the rest of her shuffled to a halt. After she steadied herself, she completed her thought. "What are you talking about, salary savings? I thought you said everything was good on the Munford front."

"I did."

Sidney seemed to keep wanting to walk, but Bailey refused to budge an inch. If this stupid, stupid contract issue hadn't been resolved, she wanted to know right then. "I thought you said she signed the contract."

"She did."

There was something Sidney wasn't telling her. She could tell by the smug, satisfied look on her friend's face that she held something back. "She was demanding one of the highest per-hour salaries that we've ever given on-air talent. You were complaining about it not three weeks ago at our Thursday meetings."

"All very true. Smile!" From her pocket, Sidney withdrew her cell phone and pointed its camera lens at Bailey's head.

"Goddamn it, Sid, this is not the time to be playing with that—!"

Sidney's lips disappeared into a dissatisfied grimace. "Ugh," she said. "You've taken better."

From the outstretched phone screen, Bailey caught a quick glance of her own face, lips stretched into a yell. In any ordinary photo, her wide-open mouth would have been the primary feature, but today, everything was definitely dwarfed by her tower of hair. "I'm sick of that toy of yours!"

"You shouldn't be. It's what saved your ass." Bailey didn't remember making a sound, but apparently she did, because Sid mocked her with a *Whuh?* "You betcha. That was going to be my second surprise, but now you've ruined it."

"Hold up." Bailey was vaguely grateful that the previous day's cold front had lowered the temperatures into the upper seventies, because if it had been any warmer, she would have had a serious case of the neck sweats by now. From the hot flashes Sidney was causing, she might suffer from one anyway. "Explain."

Sidney began walking again; Bailey had no choice but to catch up. Far ahead, idling in the drive, sat an impressive black limousine. Sidney had to have hired it from one of the bigger cities. As far as Bailey knew, Crestonville in general considered anything with four-wheel drive to be a swank set of wheels. She'd never understood the romance of a stretch limo, and she knew Bits would fuss about the extravagance, but at least Bubble and Jeanne would enjoy the experience. "Chandra is useless. Worse than useless, especially for someone out to nab your job," Sidney began.

"Tell me something I don't know?" As they rounded the side of the house, Bailey watched Jeanne trip out the front door wearing a pretty batik-style summer dress that managed to compliment her figure without hiding her swelling belly. Her hair had been tied back into a simple ponytail. Inwardly, Bailey cursed both her soft heart and her inability to say no to Bubble's pleas.

"Well, practically the moment you left town, Chandra came to me for help. Apparently she'd given the talking-to-the-Munford thing the old college try, but made such a botch of it that the woman more or less requested that she pack up and leave the inn."

"No!"

"Oh yes. Can you imagine?" Bailey could, actually. If she were a name-brand celeb—albeit B-list at most— and a senator's wife to boot, she could no more have stood Chandra's constant, mousy presence than she would have dirty towels in the bathroom. "So there was one major chunk of change saved, right there. When she showed up at the hotel downtown practically in tears, I got in a good snarky comment about how we should go out and see if we could find a diner that served hefty slices of humble pie." Bailey winced at that one. She could absolutely see Sidney saying something like that to her assistant's face. "She didn't get it. She thought it was some Southern delicacy. Next thing I know, she and Euan and I are sitting around a table at a diner. . . ."

"Not the same one we ate at!"

"No, there's a better one at the other end of the street. Fabulous coffee. You should give it a try. Anyway, there we were, listening to all her woes. Oh, don't worry. I didn't buy much of it, though it did sound like she got kind of a raw deal with Munford."

Bailey narrowed her eyes. "You're softening on her."

"Maybe a little. She's not such a bad kid. A little . . ." Sidney searched for a word.

"Bitch?"

"Green, I was going to say. Raw around the edges. Like, if she was pork, she'd give you trichinosis, raw. Hey, isn't that your mom? She looks great."

"Yeah, she does." On the porch, Bailey's mother had joined Jeanne against the railing. She leaned backward and turned her face to the sky, letting the sun fall down on her closed eyes and the curved line of her lips. "But if you don't finish this story, I'm going put my hair in your face and asphyxiate you with the spray."

"Jeez, take a pill already." Now that they were closer to an audience, Sidney lowered her voice. "I'm getting there. So anyway, there we were, having this cherry pie and coffee, kind of like a scene out of *Twin Peaks* before it got all, you know, unwatchable, and listening to her gripe—don't worry, she didn't dare say a word against you." Since that had been her next question, Bailey kept her mouth shut. "And afterward we came out and were talking to one of the camera guys by the truck, and who should drive by but that Munford woman?"

"On her way back to the inn?"

"No. *From* the inn on the way *somewhere else*." Sidney paused for a moment to let that sink in. "And we were all like, huh? Where's she going in this godforsaken place? No offense."

"None taken."

"So naturally, we all got into the truck and followed her."

"Naturally."

The word must have come out a little wry, because Sidney acted as if Bailey had questioned her personal integrity. "We were curious! It was hot! And we were kind of bored and the one alternative was getting drunk and drawing moustaches on each other with Sharpies, and as you remember, that gets old after about twenty minutes." They reached the fork in the path. Bailey had been about to head over to the porch to join the rest of her family, but Sidney expertly steered her in the direction of the limousine as she continued talking. "So we stayed kind of far back, and I don't think that the Munford's driver knew where he was going, because we seemed to wander around for a while. Finally, though, we turned into . . . you'll never guess." Before Bailey had a chance to try, Sidney provided the answer. "The driveway of none other than Taylor Montgomery."

If Bailey had been warm before, that piece of information turned her blood ice cold. "You have got to be kidding me. Taylor's farm? Why?" Scarcely had she uttered the words than she knew. "Oh, shit. She wouldn't. He wouldn't!"

"Calm down, already. He was with you on your road trip, remember?" Sidney seemed to be deriving no end of amusement from Bailey's discomfort. And it was true, she felt absolutely horrified at the thought of the Munford—or of anybody else!—attempting to seduce Taylor Montgomery. When Sid slyly tried to raise up her camera phone and take another photo, Bailey bared her teeth. "Okay, okay. I wish you could see the little passion play on your face right now, though. You slept with him, didn'tcha? Don't bother to answer that. I can tell. Anyway, look at these."

She fiddled with the buttons on her phone before handing it over. Bailey was glad to have an excuse not to look in her friend's direction any longer. Her face had to be beet red. "I've seen these," she said, looking at the photograph Sid had taken of her at the restaurant, her last afternoon in Manhattan. Her eyes were squinted; she seemed to be in mid-chew.

"Keep going." Bailey pushed the button that scrolled to the next photo, one of Euan draped in what looked like a shower curtain. "That was when he was practicing his signature runway walk on *America's Next Top Model* night. Keep going."

What followed was a small, grainy photo of Sidney's hotel room, followed by another shot of Bailey and Euan together at that awful diner earlier in the week. She was squinting again. "How did you know?" she asked in an aside. "That I slept with him?"

"Good lord, Bail. You were never that great an actor to

begin with, let's be frank. Hey, don't be embarrassed," she added. "Compared with Steve . . ."

"Steve doesn't compare." Bailey's cheeks still flamed, feeling like she'd been roasting in front of a fire. Didn't anyone else find it hot out here? At least if Sid had guessed that she and Taylor were involved, the rest of what she'd have to tell her later might be a little easier. For now, she concentrated on the photos of Euan and Sidney in front of the Kiwanis signs, and then flipped to one she hadn't yet seen. It looked vaguely familiar. "What's this?"

"Well, first she knocked at his door. Of course, he wasn't there to answer. So she went around to this, like, big old glass thing behind your boyfriend's place."

"The greenhouse, yes."

"Hah!" Sidney pointed a finger. "I knew he was your boyfriend now! You didn't bother to deny it." Bailey grinned; it was true, she hadn't. Nor did she particularly mind this one secret being out, though all the attention Sidney gave it made her feel a little like an eighth-grader caught with a Valentine's day card in her locker. "Keep going." The next photo was a little blurry. In fact, Bailey didn't have a clue what she was looking at until Sidney said, "Skip that one. We knocked over some plants and the camera went off. I meant to delete that one."

Bailey pushed the button. Almost immediately the image of toppled dirt was replaced with something more familiar. "That's Jessica Munford!" What was she doing? All Bailey could really see of her was the woman's back. "Were you on the floor or something?"

Sidney grinned. "Keep going."

The next photo was a clear side profile of the Munford talking to someone—a slender boy with a shock of black hair. He looked vaguely familiar, and Bailey had to search for a moment before she could place a name with the face. "Matteo," she said at last. She turned to Sidney and pointed at the screen. "He works for Taylor."

"Keep going."

"What's so . . . ? *Ack!*" Bailey nearly dropped the phone after she flipped to the next image. Her hair wobbled alarmingly, threatening to make her lose her balance. "Oh my God oh my God oh my God!"

"Bailey Rhodes, I hope that's praying you're doing over there." Aunt Bits stepped from the porch, a shiny patent-leather white purse dangling from her arm. Both she and Bubble had dressed for the occasion in the dresses Euan had helped them pick out from Crestonville's one and only consignment shop.

If she hadn't been so shocked by what she had in the palm of her hand, Bailey would have given the outfits a nice compliment. All she could say, though, was, "She's *kissing* him!"

"It gets better."

The next photo showed what was clearly Jessica Munford pushing Matteo down onto a flat of seedlings while her hands appeared to be ripping open his shirt. It was taken from such a close distance that Bailey was not at all surprised when the shot after that turned out to be a red-faced, screaming senator's wife running toward the camera lens, while in the background, Matteo was plainly fleeing. "Holy fuck," said Bailey, quietly enough that Bits couldn't accuse her of blasphemy.

"I know, isn't it great?"

"Holy . . . !" In case there was more of the damning evidence, Bailey flipped ahead, to be confronted with the photograph of her that Sidney had taken a few minutes before.

"All right," said Chandra, her Funicello flip bouncing up and down as she navigated the porch steps. "Ladies, let's go."

Bailey had a few more seconds before the others would be by the limousine's side. "He's only *in high school!*" she mouthed.

Sidney's tone was virtuous. "Sixteen. A fact I made sure

to emphasize as I cut her salary demands by thirty percent and eliminated all contractual mention of the Expedition Network's responsibility for covering housing
costs above and beyond her *per diem*. She signed immediately, naturally." Virtue turned to smugness.

Bailey wanted to shriek with delight, but contented
herself with a gleeful, "You're wicked!"

"Dynamite, baby!" her friend agreed. "Anyway. After
the limo, that's only my second surprise for you today."

After the amazing blackmail story, Bailey couldn't in
her wildest imagination picture what could top it.
"There's more?"

"You'll see."

"Surprise?" asked Bubble, who had cooed her way to
the car's side. "It's lovely, dear! Oh, thank you! Isn't that
a nice uniform?" The limo driver had already stepped
out from the car to open the rear doors and help the
women inside.

"I hope you're licensed, young man," Bits grumbled
as she entered. Then, pausing, she scolded Sidney. "We
could have gone in Taylor's truck, you know."

Sid waited until Bits had entered the limo before reacting with a choked laugh and exaggerated fear in her
eyes. "I don't think she likes me."

"Bits is like a Manhattan yellow traffic light," Bailey
tried to explain, helping Jeanne assist her mom into
the car.

"You get a fine for running through her?"

"Maybe. But mostly she's always about to switch to
red, and no one pays a bit of attention to her." Bailey
caught her friend by the upper arm before she'd fully
ducked into the limo. "And Sid? Thank you."

Chandra actually looked cowed for the entire trip. All
morning she had been unusually silent and cooperative,
helping Bits collect packets of Polaroid film and the last
of the girls' props in the sunroom and perform innu-
merable tasks involving mundane fetching and carrying. While the aunts fussed over the amenities of the

limousine on the ride into town, Chandra slumped down in her seat and seemed to be trying to pretend she wasn't there at all.

Bailey could see why Sidney had softened on the girl. She'd been a devious little hussy, but what was wrong with having a reach that exceeded one's grasp? At least the girl was stretching and trying to exercise her options, rather than persuading herself she was content when, at heart, she really wasn't. She'd find her way. "You and I need to have a long talk when we get back to Manhattan," she said, causing Chandra's eyes to widen.

"Why?" asked the girl. "So you can fire me?" Behind her tough shell, there was a sad defensiveness in her eyes.

Tempting as it might have been to pretend to be pondering this particular question, Bailey had probably tested the limits of her sadism when on a whim she'd suggested that Chandra submit to Bubble's hairbrush and can of Aqua Net. "No," she said gently, reaching across the aisle in the limo's middle to pat Chandra's knee. "So we can talk about what's next in your career."

The girl's chin lifted in defiance, yet at the same time, Bailey could see that she was barely restraining her lower lip from trembling. "You're going to pawn me off on someone else?"

"I'm saying, you're going to be in the area of talent for a long time." As the limo sawed around a narrow corner on the rural back roads, Bailey paused to let that sink in. She then lowered her voice. Sidney had chosen a seat closer to the front, where she animatedly talked about Manhattan hot spots with her sister. Bailey didn't want her friend to overhear any of this. She was already too busy trying to figure out how to break her other news to Sid. "We need to get you up to speed so that when an opportunity comes," she said with meaning, "you can hit the ground running. Okay?"

Apparently Chandra had been expecting the worst. Whether or not she understood what Bailey was trying to tell her, she recognized that she'd dodged a bullet. Rapidly, she nodded her head up and down, her little blue eyes wide and grateful. At the very least, Bailey was happy to see that her assistant spent the rest of the ride into Crestonville looking more like her usual self, and less like she might burst into tears at any moment. That could be counted victory enough.

"All right!" barked a voice from outside, the moment the car slid to a stop. The door opened before the driver could shift into park. Euan poked his head in. "Holy crap. It's the cast from *Hairspray*. Hey, baby!" he grinned at Bailey.

"Hey, baby!" she said back, glad to see him.

Euan had stayed casual, wearing a white summer shirt and a pair of pressed jeans. He immediately dropped the familiarity and began barking orders, though. "Everyone out. Except you two." He pointed twin fingers at the aunts. "Fix your faces or whatever it is you have to do, because thanks to your niece, the nice cameramen are going to get a shot of the two pageant coaches exiting their limousine. This is going to make the local interest portion of the segment, ladies, so make it good on the first try!"

In the end, the limo had to drive around the block again while everyone else stood on the other side of the street from the picturesque colonial-style town hall, so the camera crew could get a seamless shot of the long, black vehicle gliding to a standstill, followed by the driver running around to the door and pulling it back. While they waited, Bailey craned her neck, looking for any sign of Taylor or his truck. The street was crowded, as more and more of the townspeople made their way to the covered tent in the park where the pageant was scheduled to take place.

"Now!" said Euan, still giving the girls their cues.

Bubble exited first, a Mona Lisa smile on her face. Bailey had expected her to explode from the car's interior like a spring-loaded snake from a fake can of peanuts, full of giggles and shyness, but somehow in that cocoon of steel and glass her aunt had transformed into one of the graceful ladies she'd always asked her contestants to emulate. Somehow, the extra inches she seemed to have gained with her increased dignity made her look younger. Then, while the cameraman murmured with encouragement, Bits stepped out—or rather, she unfolded from the inside in such a fashion that she managed to maintain her trademark posture without fumbling for footing. Bailey could have imagined Grace Kelly or some other movie star of the golden age stepping out of her car in such a fashion. The cameraman must have approved, because after the car door slid shut behind them, he looked up and nodded. "Good one."

"All right, girls," Euan said. "Last minute preparations in the tent. Meet you there. Did you tell her, yet?" he added in Sidney's direction.

"Tell her what?" Bailey asked, instantly suspicious. "I heard about your greenhouse escapade, if that's what you mean."

She recognized the look on Euan's face, right then; it was the same he'd give her when she asked him about a date that had gone particularly badly that he didn't want to talk about. "Oops," he told Sidney, who was shaking her head. "Later."

When Bailey tore her eyes away from the sight of Euan scampering off in the direction of the rear end of the enclosure, she found Jeanne still regarding the aunts as they talked to townsfolk curious about their splendid arrival. Jeanne looked positively ill. "I wish we'd gone to charm school." She turned to their mother, who was lightly holding onto her arm. "You should've sent us to charm school."

"So you're saying we grew up charmless?" Bailey asked. "Maybe *you*. . . ."

"I've got plenty of charm, thank you!"

"You charmed one guy, that's for sure." With a grin, Bailey nodded at her sister's belly. Thankfully, Jeanne took the gibe in the spirit it was intended, gasping and pretending outrage, but not meaning it.

With a squeeze to both their arms, their mother said softly, but firmly, "Both my daughters grew up charming. Let's go see the girls."

Bailey was glad for the suggestion, but her curiosity was still unsatisfied. "Have you seen Taylor?" she asked Jeanne. "I haven't. . . ."

"It's bigger than I thought it would be," Jeanne said, shaking her head. A hundred or more chairs sat out on the grass of the park, oriented in the direction of the open-faced tent covering the pageant stage. A few youths milled around, adjusting the lights and preparing the sound system, observed by a few audience members who'd arrived extra early to nab the prime seats. Mr. Rice, in a natty old suit, sat squarely front row center, his hands neatly crossed in his lap. How sweet of him to be there for Bubble!

Bailey wondered if she ought to lay down a few items next to the old man to save seats for herself and the family. "Funny," she said, still looking around. Cars were parked all up and down the main street, but she couldn't for the life of her pick Taylor's out of the shining mass. "It seemed smaller than I expected."

Their mother, though steady, wasn't walking swiftly yet; it took little effort at all for first Bubble and Bits to overtake them, in a hurry to reach their girls, and then for Sidney and the crew to catch up. "I want a lot of shots of those Butter Beans looking gorgeous," Sid was telling them. "A few of the coaches doing some final sorts of adjustments. Then a few interview shots in front of the tent with the coaches, so we can get some sound bites for the show. Got it?"

"Shouldn't we wait for the director?" Bailey heard the sound guy ask.

"That schlub? I think not! Meet me there." She dropped back to walk by Bailey's side. "Doing okay, Mrs. Rhodes?" she asked with a big smile, not waiting for the answer. "Okay, there's one more thing. Look around when you get inside, and you'll notice something. Something big."

They were approaching the back of the tent now, where on a flap of hanging plastic hung a laminated sign bearing the words *Pageant Contestants Only!* "I knew it," said Bailey, her heart sinking. "It's something awful, isn't it?" God. What was the absolutely worst thing that could happen right then?

She almost smelled the man before she saw him. His cologne wafted through the tent flap moments before he slipped through and blocked their way, sweeter and more feminine than anything Bailey had ever worn in her life, including the Tinker Bell cherry-scented perfume she'd gotten as a birthday present when she was seven. Talk about awful! "Well, well, well!" he exclaimed, clasping his hands together over his belly, over which was stretched a jacket that exactly matched his Kelly green pants and tie. "If it's not Bailey Rhodes!" With a smile of sincere delight, his eyes lingered on Bailey's hair. "I *love* the new look! It's so fresh! You've never looked better, and if anyone says otherwise, you send them to me. And look," he said, scarcely pausing for breath. "Your dear mother! Why, hello, Polly! I'm so glad to see you out and about and convalescing!"

Sidney had been listening to the man's monologue with her arms crossed and a weird smile on her lips. "Hi there, Shirl!" she said at last, cheerful to the end.

"Look at you two, mother and daughter! So . . . so . . . so . . . !" Shirley Jones had utterly ignored Sidney's greeting. In fact, so intent was he on pretending he hadn't heard Sid, that he became utterly unable to finish his sentence. His lips, already white from some unknown emotion, pursed and tried to work out verbiage. After a moment, he snatched a white handkerchief from his pocket, pushed up the brim of his green Trilby, and dabbed at his forehead. "I'm so . . . !"

How he could ignore Sidney's sweet smile of interest, so falsely rapt at every word he wasn't saying? Apparently he couldn't, any longer. He turned to her with his hands on his hips. The lips that had been working to force out saccharine words could suddenly only produce a single angry one: "Whore."

"Oh, mercy, mercy me!" Sidney exclaimed, dropping her jaw and patting her chest as she appealed to her friend. She rapidly fanned her face, pretending to be flustered. "Is this that gracious Southern hospitality you've been telling me all about?"

Although Sidney didn't seem the least surprised at the epithet that Shirley Jones had thrown her way, Bailey was utterly shocked. She tried to summon some kind of words of reconciliation, but her mouth wouldn't cooperate. Without warning, her mother broke away from her side and stepped forward. "Better a whore than a total pussy, Jones," she announced, her neck erect with dignity. Then, pulling her purse up to her elbow, she walked forward with the proper small steps of a gracious and cultured grown lady.

The tidal wave of cologne left in the little man's wake had them all coughing—or at least, they pretended to cough while the three of them calmed their mutual laughter. "You go, Mom!" said Jeanne.

Bailey wheezed into the back of her wrist. "You know, I don't approve of the P-word, but in this case, I'm making an exception."

"I'm giving her two weeks until she's calling me on the phone and giving lectures about what fast-food restaurants contribute to which political party," said Sidney. "Two weeks. Tops. Wait and see."

God, Bailey surely hoped so. "What was he so mad at you about?" she wanted to know, but Sidney had already darted through the tent's opening after Bailey's mother. Jeanne followed.

Oh, so that's where Taylor had been, was Bailey's first thought on entering the crowded tent. Euan must have seen him and put him to work. The enclosure still smelled of Shirley Jones's cologne, but the smells of hairspray and of panic overwhelmed even that. Toward the back, holding out a professional makeup tray roughly the size of a toolbox, Taylor stood with a look of sheer dread on his face while Ellie obviously dilly-dallied over what shades she should apply to her face. She asked him a question; he shrugged, flummoxed. When his eyes met Bailey's, he mouthed two words: *Help me!*

The camera crew was already hard at work in the confines of the small space in which the girls had to dress. Over their heads, as they knelt on the floor to capture some usual angles that would properly convey the chaos of the scene on the small screen, Bailey recognized several of the faces that had become familiar over the course of the last two weeks. Pretty CeeCee, adjusting the Japanese-style headdress she would be wearing during the talent portion, nervously making certain she had her lyrics committed to memory. Tiny little Austyn, her hair teased not into one of her aunt's fluffy confections, but cut in a darling short bob and parted down the middle of a forehead to make her look more of a pixie than ever. Long-haired Norelle, who mercifully no longer looked like a Marvelette, walked by with a beautiful smile on her face as she balanced her batons in her hands. In fact, none of the girls sported the retro dos she'd expected; Euan had either herded them *en masse* to a real salon or had hired a hairdresser to start work on them early that morning. They all looked beautiful. Even Larkin, who sat by herself in the far corner of the area, combing her hair as if she hoped it would keep people away, looked beautiful, if a little sad and lonely and . . .

Wait a moment.

Aware that Sidney was at her side again, Bailey

scanned the room. One, two, three, five, eight, ten girls fought for mirror space around the periphery of the room, while the camera crews caught snippets of their preparation. Ten girls, all beautiful, all beauty queens in their own right. "What . . . ?" she exclaimed in wonder. Of India and Sapphire there was no sign, nor of their clones. "What happened to . . . ?"

"Hey, Euan!" Sidney called a distance of several feet. "Thirty whole seconds. You win. I guessed a minute and a half before you noticed."

"Oh my God. Where are they?" Was there a separate dressing room?

If Sidney looked smug one more time that day, Bailey knew her face was going to freeze that way. Her voice was low and deadly, like the evil queen shortly before she offered Snow White a poisoned apple. "Shirley Jones should *never* have called me fat. I told you I'd make him pay."

Agog, Bailey's head seemed to spin when Euan whizzed by carrying a scarf covered with spangles and somebody's flute. "She tracked down the guy who kept all the contestant names and addresses," he explained in passing.

"And then Euan batted his eyelashes at him and got a copy," Sidney interjected. "He liked that part."

Euan walked the other way still carrying the flute, but now with a bathing suit on a hanger instead of the scarf. "Then, while you were gone, one by one . . ."

"We tracked down the addresses and found they were fake. Those Fembots hadn't lived in the county for the four months the contest requires. Not a one of them. Well, except Larkin. So when Euan revealed that fact to his new little friend . . ."

"Oh, *stop!*" said Euan. Apparently he couldn't find the flute's owner. "I'd go out with him. Once. But we're not picking out patterns together."

Taylor was making his way to her, now, trying to of-fload the makeup case onto someone else. "Was this your other surprise?" Bailey asked. She wanted to howl with laughter, but she was so overwhelmed with a sudden realization that she stopped mid-gasp. "So there's only one way Shirley Jones can win this year!"

Sidney spread out her hands around her face. "Surprise! We had to give you something as a going-away present."

Bailey froze in a posture of guilt and shock. "What?" she said, half-afraid that her friends might actually answer.

Sid shook her head. "Sweetie. You didn't seriously think that I wouldn't hear you called Larry Gilbert last night to ask about a possible transfer to the D.C. branch? The Expedition Network is lousy with vicious gossips!"

"And she's the worst of them," Euan added. "She called me right away. We know it's just a matter of time. Right?"

This had been the one scene she'd been dreading more than any other. "I love you guys so much," she said, her eyes prickling. "But . . ."

"Yeah, trust me, I know how it goes." Euan rolled his eyes. "You love him more. See it on the soap all the time." But he gave her a hug.

Sidney joined in on the group display of affection. "Anyway, the people from the D.C. office are up in New York all the time. We'll still see each other lots."

Bailey felt overwhelmed by too much kindness. It was as if Taylor had laid the foundation, brick by brick, and today everyone else seemed determined to build upon it. "I can't believe everything you've done for me!"

"You Southerners are too polite. You needed a little New York City street smarts to win this game." Euan lowered his voice. "Even if that Larkin creature pulls it off today, your aunts can still grab the credit. From what I gather, most of the locals aren't all that happy with Mr. Jones after they heard that the sweet country farm girls they thought have been winning for the last fifteen

years turned out to be recruited from places like Balti-
more. And judging by the tongue-lashing our Mr. Jones
just gave little Larkin, I'm gathering she's not all that
anxious to bring her winning game this afternoon."

Would Larkin's winning game guarantee her the
tiara? Bailey couldn't help but wonder, when she looked
around the room. These weren't the same girls that
she'd left a few days ago. They seemed poised. Elegant.
Maybe none of them would be America's Next Top
Model, but they were all at their most beautiful today.
After the pageant's completion, after the bouquet and
the crown had been bestowed upon one lucky recipient,
they'd all scatter and go on to live the lives they carved
out for themselves—and they'd always have the memory of one day when they truly were at their prettiest.

A giant smile on her face, Bailey turned to her mother.
She was regarding the room with more than a trace of
tears in her eyes, looking at all the pretty girls as they
rushed around, putting the final touches on themselves.
"I heard a rumor that this was you, once," Bailey said.

Her mother's lips compressed as she bit back the
emotion overwhelming her. "Once," she said, clearing
her throat. "Was enough." But she reached out and
squeezed Bailey's hand, so hard that it was as if she
never intended to let go.

"Hi. Seriously. Help me." Taylor had pushed his way
across the room, but still carried the trays of colors he
hadn't been able to pawn off on anyone else. He spoke
his words in the rapid succession of the terrified. "They
keep asking me questions. I don't know what any of
this stuff is. I'm a man. Some of it has glitter. Please?"

Bailey grinned, then leaned up with her chin extended. A most grateful Taylor planted a kiss on her lips.
"They know," she told him, nodding to Euan and Sidney.

"I know they know! They gave me a talking-to! Plus
how do you think I got roped into this?" he asked, miserable. "Please? Help?"

Bailey laughed and allowed him to hand off his burden. "You're not going anywhere, mind you."

His mood had improved a hundredfold after releasing the cosmetics. "No," he grinned. "I'm not going anywhere."

Euan, in the meantime, was busily looking around the enclosure, trying to find someone. "Where is—? There you are." He reached out and snatched the wrist of a passing young woman taller than the others, a slender wisp of a girl dressed in a sheath of ivory covered with sparkling beads. Her hair had been gently curled to frame her lean face. Euan handed over the flute. "Put this somewhere safe," he ordered. "One of the camera crew nearly sat on it."

"Sorry, guy," said the girl with a voice so familiar that Bailey was forced to take a second look. "Hi," the girl said to her, a little shyly, as if she would rather have avoided Bailey altogether.

"Fawn?" Bailey spoke the word almost in a whisper, giving it a reverence the beautiful young woman absolutely deserved. She didn't know the girl played flute! "Is that you?"

Euan, fussing over Fawn's hair, murmured, "Amazing what you find under a four-inch growth of leg and armpit hair, isn't it?"

"Shut up," she retorted, slapping him on the stomach. With a bit of diffidence, as if she feared Bailey might spout out a told-you-so, she tossed her hair back over her shoulders and said, "There's nothing wrong with the way I look."

"Fawn has really buckled down the last couple of days," Euan said, kneeling down to adjust her dress.

Bailey wanted to shake the girl for totally fooling her. "I thought you quit!"

Euan looked up from the floor. "When did you quit?"

"I didn't," Fawn said. The set of her jaw defied anyone to contradict her. "I don't quit." She stared at Bailey in challenge, finally realizing, when Bailey nodded and smiled, that she wasn't going to meet with anything other than approval.

"You look pretty," said Taylor. "Even better than when you didn't have clothes. Ouch! Well, she does!" he said, when Bailey did a little stomach slapping of her own.

"More than pretty," Bailey agreed. The girl was beautiful, both inside and out, as she'd always been, no matter what clothes she was—or wasn't—wearing.

Once again, Fawn was reduced to a sweet and mercifully silent shyness. "Thanks," was the single word she could say. "There's nothing wrong with being pretty for one day, right?"

"Right," Bailey said, looking around the room. Because pretty girls grew older and hopefully a little wiser, just like everybody else.

Chapter Twenty-four

"Come on. Put it on," Taylor said from their bed, when she returned from brushing her teeth in the bathroom.

"You," she announced, not for the first time, "are a sex-crazed maniac."

"Put it on," he pleaded, sitting up so that the quilt fell from around his shoulders and exposed his naked torso. He stretched lazily, yawning, knowing that the display would weaken her resolve. "And come to bed."

Bailey's lips twitched. "It's two in the morning and we've been up all night talking. And you still want to fool around?" He waggled his eyebrows. She couldn't help but laugh—she wanted to, too. "Where is it, anyway?"

He pointed to the right half of the dresser, which he'd cleared out for her the week before. She'd filled the drawers with some of her own things earlier that afternoon; the other suitcases full of clothing from her old apartment, still waiting to be unpacked, lay on the floor beyond. "I tucked it in the top drawer," he said. "For handy access."

Surely enough, there it was, a circlet of filigree that sparkled with cheap shiny stones, right inside the top drawer. She pulled it out, remembering the day six weeks before when Fawn had passed it on to her. Apparently beauty queen tiaras weren't even a badge of ironic credibility within her circles. "Maybe *you* should wear it this time," she suggested, mischievous gleams dancing in her eyes.

"Nuh-uh!" he protested, but it was too late. She had already lunged at him and sat on his midsection, pinning him down while they mock-wrestled over the already-messy bed. At last she triumphed, and managed to pin both ends of the tiara over his temples.

"You look purty," she teased.

"Do I, Bailey Rhodes? Do I look an absolute sight? I do, and don't let anyone tell you different!"

They giggled, and kissed, and turned out the lights. When the tiara fell off a few minutes into their lovemaking, neither of them noticed.

Afterward, when the autumn breeze brought the smells of leaves and of sweetly decaying flowers into the bedroom, he sleepily murmured into her ear, "So what were the three things?"

"What?" she asked, unwilling to move. She too much enjoyed the feel of his strong arms grasping her from behind, and of how his chin seemed to fit exactly into the curve of her neck. "What three things?"

"The three things your mother took from your grandmother's house," he explained, referring back to the story she'd been sharing with him a little earlier that evening. "The three things she went to so much trouble to get."

She felt too secure to worry much about the secret she'd shared. "You won't tell anyone, will you?"

"Never."

"Okay. Mom picked out three things they loved, but that no one would ever miss. Ordinary things no real burglar would ever steal."

"Like?"

"The first was a recipe box, for Bubble." An old white box illustrated with a rooster, grimy from the years but stuffed with hundreds of clippings and cards Bailey's grandmother had collected for decades, through which Bubble's fingers could dance without effort. "And then for Bits, a framed picture." A postwar glamour shot of a young woman looking at a spot somewhere above and beyond the camera—the only photograph of their grandmother in the aunts' house.

There was a long pause before Taylor, his voice suffused with sleep, spoke again. "And then for herself?"

Bailey sighed into the darkness. "She picked something she'd loved since she was a kid. But she didn't keep it."

"She gave it away?"

"She gave it to one of her daughters, so she wouldn't forget where she came from. She gave it to me." Bailey shifted slightly, settling her naked body under the coverings. "A quilt. A quilt in the design of an apple tree that was battered and worn. It lay at the bottom of my grandmother's linen closet." An old quilt, pieced together by her great-grandmother—evidence of her mother's great folly that had lain on her own bed year after year.

His words were mere vibrations of air and teeth, now. "The one we're sleeping under?"

"Yes." The quilt that settled over their bodies to warm them both. Of all her possessions, now the most prized. "That's the one." She didn't miss at all the sounds of the city, nor its lights, nor its twenty-four-hour craziness. Here was where she wanted to be. In the dark, not at all lonely or alone, surrounded by warm blankets and warmer arms, and looking forward to what the next day, and the day after that, and all the coming months and years might bring.

Outside their window, the moon was round and fat and the countryside bathed in its white light. When Taylor spoke next, his words were the softest she had ever heard, and the sweetest. "Welcome home . . . Bailey Rhodes."

I WENT TO VASSAR FOR THIS?

NAOMI NEALE

How exactly did a microwave mishap blast a hip and sassy modern-day Manhattanite back to 1959? Cathy Voorhees has no idea. But even without her trusty Palm Pilot, she's going to sort everything out:

Well, these clothes give me a **killer** *figure...but the granny panties have to go! And I can change history...if only I knew any. Back here, I don't have to work for a short-sighted fuddy-duddy...but my boss thinks* goosing *is appropriate office behavior. Mmm, I wish our dreamy landlord would goose me...I can wow him with predictions of the future...and he'll have me committed...but padded walls could be fun....*

JENNIFER ASHLEY✲LISA CACH✲NAOMI NEALE

Christmas
Cards from the
Edge

HOLIDAY MADNESS:

One wannabe dominatrix. A sexy Scotsman. Twenty-seven relatives. An ex-convict uncle on the lam. A sheriff hot on his heels. A Christmas pageant decorated like a department store white sale. A Tony Award–winning actor better known for his Heat-n-Eat Meat Pie ads. A town conspiring on Christmas Eve to keep Manhattan refugees from escaping back to the city.

What are three nice girls to do?

Play naughty.

NAOMI NEALE

CALENDAR GIRL

Name: Nan Cloutier

Address: Follow the gang graffiti until you reach the decrepit bakery. See the rooms above that even a squatter wouldn't claim? That's my little Manhattan paradise.

Education: (Totally useless) Liberal Arts degree from an Ivy League university.

Employment History: Cheer Facilitator for Seasonal Staffers Inc. Responsible for spreading merriment and not throttling fellow employees or shoppers, as appropriate.

Career Goal: Is there a career track that will maybe, just maybe, help me attract the attention of the department store heir of my dreams?

No way. That's a full-time job in itself!

GHOULS JUST WANT TO HAVE FUN

KATHLEEN BACUS

This autumn, Tressa Jayne Turner isn't enjoying the frivolity of the season. After being stalked by a psycho dunk-tank clown, all she wants is a slower pace, some candy corn and toffee apples—and a serious story she can sniff out on her own.

She's in luck! Reclusive bestselling writer Elizabeth Courtney Howard is coming to town. So, what's stopping Tressa from getting the dope—besides a blackmailing high school homecoming queen candidate, a rival reporter, and the park ranger who's kept Tressa's knickers in a knot since the fourth grade? Only the fact that the skeletons to uncover are all in a closet in a house only Norman Bates could love.

SPYING IN HIGH HEELS

Gemma Halliday

L.A. shoe designer Maddie Springer lives her life by three rules: Fashion. Fashion. Fashion. But when she stumbles upon the work of a brutal killer, her life takes an unexpected turn from Manolos to murder. And things only get worse when her boyfriend disappears—along with $20 million in embezzled funds—and her every move is suddenly under scrutiny by LAPD's sexiest cop. With the help of her post-menopausal bridezilla of a mother, a 300-pound psychic and one seriously oversexed best friend, Maddie finds herself stepping out of her stilettos and onto the trail of a murderer. But can she catch a killer before the killer catches up to her?

Talk Gertie To Me

LOIS WINSTON

Nori Stedworth is living the good life. That is, until the dot-com company she works for goes bust, she finds her fiancé cavorting in the Jacuzzi with her best friend, and her mom flies in for a surprise visit....

Now suddenly, from out of nowhere, Nori's alter ego from adolescence, Gertie, is throwing her two cents in about everything in Nori's life. Like, Nori's new job at a radio station might finally be her niche. Like, Nori's droolworthy boss, Mac, just might be the man of her dreams. Like, it's time Nori stopped hiding in the shadows. Move over, Gertie—Nori's stepping up to the mic.

ATTENTION
BOOK LOVERS!

Can't get enough of your favorite **ROMANCE**?

Call **1-800-481-9191** to:

✳ order books,

✳ receive a **FREE** catalog,

✳ join our book clubs to **SAVE 30%!**

Open Mon.-Fri. 10 AM-9 PM EST

Visit **www.dorchesterpub.com**
for special offers and inside
information on the authors you love.

We accept Visa, MasterCard or Discover®.

LEISURE BOOKS ♥ LOVE SPELL